RUTTING SEASON

A novel by

ROY NESS

ISBN-10: 1467966517
EAN-13: 9781467966511

To Penelope

THANKS TO

RCMP 'M' Division in Whitehorse for info about search and rescue.

Jim Hajash for info on RCMP chain of command.

Trans North Helicopters for logistical info.

Rob Florkiewicz, YTG biologist, for reference text and info on moose biology.

Jerry Haigh, author and professor of veterinary medicine, for insights into the inner life of moose.

Jon Breen, for guidance in Jewish cuisine.

Michele Genest, Author of *The Boreal Gourmet* and *Fasting Girl*, for honest critique and sincere enthusiasm for an early draft of *Rutting Season*.

The Yukon Territorial Government's Advanced Artist Program.

Claire Ness, daughter, clown, and wolf whisperer, for putting up with rain, rapids and Roy on a canoe trip down the Macmillan River.

The Sage Hill Writing Experience.

Steven Galloway, author of *Finnie Walsh, The Cellist of Sarajevo* and *Ascension*, for his experienced, concise, positive advice.

Penelope, for her support in so many ways.

All the great wild rivers of the Yukon.

SEPT. 13

They were at it again, muffled grunts and rustling nylon fabric. Maybe they thought the wind and rain beating on the tent covered the sound of their lovemaking. Hannah rolled onto her side to face away from Andrea and Martin, pulled her sleeping bag over her head and let out a long breath. There was a whispered exchange then silence, held breaths, waiting, inches from her back. She hadn't intended an audible sigh…or had she?

She faked a soft snore and the rustling and groaning resumed. There was just enough light to see streaks of rainwater through the fly. A single drop grew and began to slide, gathering drops in its path, gaining speed, leaving a wavering trail down the yellow fabric. Sleep was impossible. They had been in their sleeping bags for twelve hours, waiting out the storm.

Was she feeling resentful? Or just envious? She didn't want to be prudish. This was a wilderness expedition. The usual rules of etiquette didn't apply here. They didn't hide to undress or pee. But what about sex? In all the planning and preparation it had never entered her mind. Grizzly Watch had put her sex life into hibernation.

Grizzly Watch: two years of work and planning were finally about to pay off. She had conceived the idea with Paul Williams, managing director of ARN, *Animal Rights Now*. The film she planned to shoot would expose the killing of grizzly bears for sport by wealthy hunters and indict the whole big game outfitting industry. She wanted confrontation, had thought about it, dreamed about it. Worried about it. The Hannah Weinberg of TV and radio was good at confrontation. Her public expected it. The Hannah Weinberg lying in her tent in a storm on a mountain in the Yukon was scared.

But at last she was doing something instead of just writing letters and attending conferences—preaching to the converted. Some journalists had called her an eco-warrior. She liked that. About a year ago an interviewer had introduced her as *The Grizzly Woman* and the nickname had stuck. She liked that, too. She was in the news, on TV and radio. ARN's website was getting millions of hits. Even late night talk show hosts were satirizing her. She liked all of it, but now it was crunch time. Time to deliver the goods. Everything was finally in place...except for the weather.

A knee bumped her on the calf then again, and again, pushing rhythmically, in time with the sound of barely stifled breaths. Intense. *In tents.* She smiled to herself. Maybe she could use it later.

Andrea's throttled gasps sounded like soft little piglet grunts. Martin's breathing had changed to strangled moans. Another bump against the small of her back. She wanted to sit up and shout, *Come already,* but that wouldn't do. They were the best—Andrea with the camera and Martin the experienced mountaineer with the strength of a mule. Hannah wouldn't jeopardize Grizzly Watch over a little sex, or even a lot of sex. Andrea gulped back a small cry while Martin buried his face in the down. She would wait a bit after it was all over then go outside for a look around. A gust of wind set the tent shaking and popping. The rain beat with renewed force. If only she didn't have to pee so badly.

A day and a night in this patch of willows, listening to raindrops on leaves. Water trickled down, off his antlers, past his ears and around his eyes. He waited, chewing his cud, occasionally tearing off a mouthful of leaves, shaking the rain from his face. The change was coming. The smell was in the leaves, the air, the ground. It always started when the nights got darker. He had felt it many times before in his long life.

The old bull moose shifted his hind legs back to urinate. A stiff knot of scar tissue at the back of his thigh, the old wound from wolves many seasons ago. Always when it rained. The warm scent of his urine rose around him. He backed and sniffed at the spot. A new aroma to it, growing stronger by the day—a sharp bite like the smell of freshly broken spruce. It made him restless.

"Wuh. Wuh." His short breathy call was swallowed by the sound of the rain. No answering grunt. He brushed his antlers against the bushes. It felt good.

Move.

As he walked downhill the hollow scrape of his antlers pushing through willow branches sent a vibration into his skull, down his spine, out into his muscles. Strong. Lifting his nose, spreading his big square nostrils, he sifted the air moving up from the valley bottom—sweet fruity poplar, dense sedge meadow turf, sulphur scent of bog, sickly pungent high-bush cranberry, resinous mature spruce, soft rich swirl of river water. Mixed in his memory of sixteen years was that other scent—females.

"Fuck, man, this fuckin' sucks." Artie James dropped the dry bag on the small flat grassy spot at the top of the riverbank and scanned the surrounding valley. "Can't even see the fuckin' mountains. You're goin' down this river in the rain by your fuckin' self?"

Dan McKay looked up from the bottom of the bank where his canoe was tied. "I'm not by myself. Raz is with me."

"Sure, man, he'll be a big help if you lose your fuckin' canoe in the rapids."

"Where is he?"

"Over there. Got a fuckin' squirrel up a tree. You're fucked up, man."

Dan laughed. "Of course I'm fucked up. You've always known that."

Artie had been his closest friend since they were kids. Growing up as the son of the school principal in the small First Nation community of Ross River had been hard enough. It would have been hell without Artie. Even the toughest bullies wouldn't mess with him. Artie was the nearest Dan had to a brother. Still, there were some things his friend would never understand. Like this—setting off alone to paddle 500 kilometers down the South Macmillan River to get a moose when he could get one closer to Ross. But there was more to this trip than shooting a moose for winter meat. How could he explain it without sounding like some kind of mystic loony? Artie was right. He was fucked up. He reached up the steep bank and wedged his foot on a tuft of grass and small willow shoots, ready to take the weight of the big, yellow, dry bag.

"Pass it down, buddy."

Artie lowered the bag to Dan. "Come back to Ross with me. Wait for the fuckin' rain to stop. We might get a moose on the way. Then you wouldn't have to go down the fuckin' river. I got a coupla days off comin'."

Dan let the bag down into the bottom of the canoe, unclipped the carry straps, looped them around a thwart then re-clipped them. He stood and looked up, squinting into the raindrops. "*I got a coupla days off coming.* Very good, Artie. Do you realize what you just did?"

"Fucked if I know."

"You just made a whole sentence without the word *fuck* in it."

"Fuck you. Your dad was my fuckin' teacher, not you."

"Sorry for offending your delicate sensibilities."

Artie's laugh was a startled dog's bark, high and exuberant, incongruous in such a big man. "Shit, dude, you even fuckin' sound like him."

"I'm nothing like him. Pass me the paddles."

Artie handed down the paddles and Dan leaned one on the canoe seat and wedged the spare in beside his dry bag. "I guess that's it. I can go."

"Aren't you forgetting something?"

Dan checked over his gear in the canoe. "I don't think so."

"You gonna leave your fuckin' gun behind?"

"Oh. Right. Where is it?"

"Leaning on this bush here. Fuck, man, you shouldn't be goin' alone." He passed the gun case to Dan. "Dude, don't go yet. You got time to smoke a doobie with your fuckin' bro'." Artie pulled a rolled joint from inside his jacket, sheltering it from the rain as he lit it.

Dan stashed the rifle in his canoe and climbed up the bank. "I guess so." He took the joint from his friend and inhaled a long puff. "Thanks, man."

"Don't have to thank me. It's just some weed."

"I mean thanks for everything…the ride up here."

"Thank Lyle Kessler. Holy fuck, dude, if Lyle ever found out I used his truck to bring you up here he'd fuckin' shit his pants. Anybody else and he wouldn't care." His shrill laugh echoed back from the trees across the river.

Dan passed back the joint. "Lyle's a prick."

"Yeah, but he gives me a job and a fuckin' paycheck."

"Artie, how come all the white people who live in Ross are assholes?"

"Man, that's fucked up. What the fuck are you…Oh. Right. Dude, your dad was not an asshole."

"What was he?"

"He was…"

"He was nuts." Dan gave three short, sharp whistles and a black and white dog came bounding out of the willows. "There you are Raz. Good boy." He ruffled the fur behind the dog's ears. "Now you stick around, mister. We gotta go soon."

They passed the joint back and forth in silence while looking out over the water. The canoe rested tight against the bank below them in a narrow channel on the outside of the bend. A gravel bar with a few hardy willows separated it from a wider, shallower channel on the other side.

Artie finally spoke. "So what was the real reason Kessler fired you?"

Dan knew what the rumour mill in Ross River could do. He searched Artie's face for any hint of what his friend might already know. "One of the clients shot an undersized ram. Lyle wanted me to go up the mountain and bury it. I refused."

"Yeah, I heard that." Artie had a playful smile on his face.

"What else did you hear?"

The smile turned to a wide grin. "I heard you fuckin' couldn't keep your dick in your pants with one o' the hunter's wives."

Dan sighed. "Don't believe everything you hear."

"So?"

"So what?"

"Did you nail her?"

"I didn't touch her, and that's the truth. Okay, she came into my tent one night, but I told her she had to leave. That's it. I guess the husband found out and complained to Kessler. Or maybe she did. Anyway, he was looking for an excuse to fire me. He knew I'd refuse to bury the ram."

Artie picked up a stick and tossed it out over the river. "I fuckin' don't know how you do it. You got a gift, dude." The stick clattered onto the gravel bar.

"For what, being fired from every job I get?"

"No, for women. They take one look at you and yank off their fuckin' panties."

"That's bullshit."

"Dude, it's true. It's the only reason I hang out with you, a chance at some fuckin' leftovers."

They both laughed. Dan put a hand on the big man's shoulder. "You're a piece of work, Artie."

"Fuck, you sound just like him."

"Who?"

"Who the fuck do you think?" Artie laughed.

Dan held out the stub of the joint. "You wanna keep this roach?"

"You keep it. You got enough for the trip? 'Cause I got a whole fuckin' bag in the truck."

"No. Thanks anyway. I brought a little, but I'm gonna run out."

"So let me give you some."

Dan was tempted. "Thanks, Artie, but it's time I slow down on this shit." He put the roach in his pocket.

"Whatever." Artie extended his hand. "I gotta go. Gotta be at the Twin Creek airstrip to pick up some meat and horns."

Dan shook his hand. "Take care, buddy."

"You're the one who should take care, you stupid fucker. You know, Stan Jackson would hire you quicker than fuck. He told me he's had clients asking for you. You could be making money instead of...fuck, you're so fuckin' stubborn."

"Go get in the canoe, Raz." The dog skipped down the bank . "In the front." Raz swerved and hopped into the space behind the front seat. Dan turned to Artie, put a hand on his back and started walking him to the white truck with the big *Mac Pass Outfitters* logo. "I'm not sure I wanna do it anymore. The whole head hunting thing. It's...I'm getting tired of it."

"What the fuck are you gonna do? It's a job. And you get big fuckin' tips from the hunters." They were at the truck. Artie opened the door and climbed in. As he was about to close it, he hesitated and started to laugh his high yipping bark.

Dan stood in the rain. "What's so funny?"

"Fuck me. I forgot to tell you. You're gonna love this. You know that animal rights bitch – what's her fuckin' name, Hannah..."

"Weinberg. Hannah Weinberg. Who hasn't heard of her?" Grizzly Watch—the news had been full of Hannah Weinberg for weeks. She was the biggest story in the Yukon. It was all over the Canadian papers, and some foreign news services had picked it up. He had read a piece in *McLean's* about her popularity in Germany and Britain. He had heard her radio interview after she arrived in Whitehorse when she announced she would pick one outfitter to follow and film. Which one she would choose was the biggest topic of conversation.

Artie nodded. "Yeah, Weinberg. Well, she's on Mount Riddell right now, only Lyle doesn't fuckin' know it. He went up there yesterday with some clients."

"Are you sure?" Dan looked southwest toward Mount Riddell. Everything was buried in cloud.

"Am I sure? Oh yeah. She knew he was goin' up there. She had inside information."

"Somebody in Ross? Somebody who works for Lyle? Who?"

"I can't tell you. I'd lose my fuckin' job."

"Who am I gonna tell? I'll be on the river."

Artie hesitated only a second. "Sharon."

"Sharon. Figures. Serves him right, the way he treated her." He imagined Lyle Kessler harassed by the animal rights people. A smile spread across his face. "Sweet. I think I like this Hannah Weinberg."

The dead caribou smelled delicious. He shook the rain from his face, lifted his nose and swung his head from side to side. The smells were thick in the wet air. There was a peculiar animal scent, a confused mix of smoky, sweet and salty. Vaguely familiar. Once, many seasons ago when he was a cub, his mother sounded a startled *woof* and ran, stopping nervously at the edge of a steep aspen-choked gully to let him catch up. If his mother had been afraid, it must be a dangerous animal. Then two years ago, after the long sleep, he had found a peculiar den made of tree trunks where the scent hung heavy. The flimsy opening was easy to push down. He had gorged on some white sweet powder, had nosed through cubbyholes to find strange delicacies encased in crinkly skin. Some round hard tubes leaked tasty sweet liquid when he pierced them with his teeth while others leaked a brightly colored, foul tasting stuff that made his nose itch. The walls of the den had been hung with incomprehensible things, which he scattered on the ground. A length of tree, flattened, hung along one wall, filled with a row of flat, square bundles of thin leaves that smelled of salty wood. The whole thing came down with a crash. He bit through some of the stacks of leaves before losing interest.

But he had never encountered the weird animals themselves. Could they be a danger? No, not to a full-grown male grizzly in his prime—large muscled forelegs and shoulders crowned with a saddle of dense brown fur tipped blonde. Even the other big males backed off when he claimed their food.

But the odd smell made him cautious. He moved out of the small patch of thick alpine firs and looked toward the caribou carcass. An eagle perched on top, its white head stained brownish red. At his approach, the eagle spread its wings, lifted up and glided downhill to gain speed then swooped up to land on a dead fir snag. The aroma of the caribou filled his nose— blood, meat, fat. There was no sign of other animals, nothing to drive off. He lowered his head and sniffed the ground. There was that strange smell again. It made him uneasy, but the sweet scent of fat drew him on.

Most of the caribou was there—the viscera, most of the flesh and bones, and best of all, the fat. There was no head and only bits of skin. It was a recent kill. The strange smelling animal might still be near, resting after gorging on…what, the skin and head? What kind of animal ate those first? A steady gentle breeze drifted up the mountain. He stood on his hind legs and stretched out his neck to test it, swinging his head back and forth as he sniffed. Nothing downhill. No movement uphill. No sounds but the steady patter of rain.

He let himself down over the carcass. Again, the rich sweet smell of belly fat filled his nose, spread into his mouth and curled down his throat. He lowered his muzzle and opened his jaws.

Something slammed into his abdomen then a clap of thunder so loud his ears went numb. The air was punched from his lungs. He staggered sideways. A sound came down the hill. Like birds calling.

"I hit him! I got him!"

"Good shot, Mike. He's still up. Hit him again."

It sounded like the gulls who screamed and dove at him when he found their nests. Two figures appeared over the ridge top, tall, standing up on their hind legs. One of them crouched. The ground exploded in front of him with another thunderclap. Bits of dirt and rock sprayed into his face, stinging his nose. The tall animals were coming towards him. He bounded down the hill over rocks and hummocks towards the thick firs.

The gull sounds again. "Oh fuck. He's heading for the trees."

The fir ahead of him splintered with a smack then boom, the awful thunder. He dove into the trees and ran.

The western peak of Mount Riddell was completely obscured. The ridge to the east faded into gray mist within twenty meters. Their fire from the night before was a small, miserable black stain. The aluminum pot in which she had made soup sat beside it, an inch of cold scummy water covering the bottom. Hannah surveyed the surrounding gray murk. "Shit."

Andrea spoke from inside the tent. "How is it out there?"

"Not as bad as it sounds from in there, but…" They would find out soon enough, if they bothered to get out of bed at all.

The zipper went up and the fly opened. Andrea's head poked out. "God, this sucks. What are we going to do?"

"You mean, what are we not going to do. We can't do anything much until it clears. Why don't you stay in there and keep dry. I'll go down the hill for some water and we'll cook in the tent."

Andrea crawled outside and stood. "I have to pee." She scurried a short distance from the tent and squatted.

"Right. Of course. What about Martin? He hasn't been out since last night."

"He already peed."

"Where?"

"In his water bottle."

"That's revolting."

Martin's voice came from the tent. "I heard that. It's a completely acceptable mountaineering practice. You're just envious because you can't do it."

Hannah snorted. "You think I can't hit the spout? How much do you wanna bet?"

"I would never bet against a woman of your immense talents." His hand, holding his water bottle, appeared from the open fly, filled to the brim with slightly foamy yellow liquid, "Could you empty this for me?"

"Get that out of my sight or I'll pour it all over you."

"Hmmm. Promise?"

"Where's my bear spray when I need it?"

Martin laughed and Andrea came back to stand beside Hannah, looking about and shivering. "This is awful. How long do you think it's going to last?"

"God knows…a few more hours, a few more days."

"What about Kessler and the hunters? How are we going to find them in this?"

"Well, I can only assume they'll be holed up in their camp just like us. I suppose we could go over there, but it would take us all day and we'd just get soaked. Anyway, I don't want to tip our hand. I don't think they realize we're here."

"Would we even be able to find their camp?"

"Yeah. We watched them go around the east peak yesterday. There are only so many places they could be. And they'll have bells on their horses." She put an arm around Andrea and gave her a friendly squeeze. "You're cold and you're not wearing your raingear. Get back in the tent for now."

"If I loved you…time and again I would try to say…all I'd want you to know." Dan sang the song out loud. He wasn't hunting yet. He'd be quiet further downriver, past the portages, the rapids and the boulder gardens, past the mouth of the Riddell River. "If I loved you…words wouldn't come in an easy way…" He liked floating a river alone. He could sing what he pleased, out loud, the old Broadway musicals his dad used to play. "Round in circles I'd go…Longing to tell you, but afraid and shy…" If Artie was here he'd tell Dan to *shut the fuck up*. Artie was an Iron Maiden guy. "I'd let my golden chances pass me…"

He stopped. The dog's head was up, ears cocked. "Whattaya see, mister?"

He reached inside his rain jacket for his binoculars. There it was, a bull moose standing head up, ears forward, ragged tatters of velvet hanging from a massive set of antlers. "That's a big boy, Raz. Too big, even if we were a week downstream." That was the reason almost nobody hunted the South Macmillan from the upper end down. You needed a boat small enough to portage and run the rapids in the upper stretches, and big enough to carry a moose to Pelly Crossing. His seventeen foot Hellman was just right—light and strong, but able to carry meat. Still, he would be looking for a small bull two or three years old, not a big bruiser like the one he was drifting by now.

The moose stared at him, unafraid. Dan resumed singing, more softly. "Soon you'd leave me…Off you would go in the mist of day…never, never to know…how I loved you…if I loved you." The canoe passed the moose twenty meters away. "Raz, I think he likes Rogers and Hammerstein. Then again, maybe we're just a weird noisy log floating by."

The dog stood up on the dry bag and sniffed, extending his nose out over the gunwale. "Raz, lie down." The dog sank to his belly. "If you think you're gonna chase that fella, you're crazier than I am."

Her feet were damp, and she could feel a trickle of water beginning to inch down her back. Hannah put up the hood on her rain jacket. What had happened to the beautiful sunny weather they had when they climbed up here three days ago? She should probably go back to the tent; nothing much to accomplish in this weather. Visibility was no more than a few meters.

She took off her pack and hunkered down in the lee of a big jagged rock, scant protection from the wind that blew cold clouds over the ridge. In fine weather this spot would give her a commanding view of the wide flat saddle between the east and west peaks of Mount Riddell. It might even let her spy on Kessler's camp.

But now all she saw was scudding clouds and black, slippery rock. "Not a living thing in sight," she said to the rocks and the rain. No, that wasn't quite true. Beside her left knee, pasted to the rock was a patch of bright orange lichen growing outwards in an irregular circle. She stared at it for awhile, gaining a small degree of comfort from this little bit of life at its most tenacious. That patch of orange had probably been clinging to this wind blasted rock, surviving the winter cold and the summer heat since before she was born.

A movement caught her eye, so small she would have missed it if she had not been focused so intently on the lichen. A tiny spider crawled out of a crack, its forelegs testing the rock like a blind person using a pair of canes. "How the hell did you get way up here? Is there anything for you to eat? Can I call you Spidey? Yes? Good. My name is Hannah and I'm talking to a spider. Would you like to join me for lunch? I'm afraid all I have is banana chips, but they're organic. I'd offer you an energy bar, but I have to ration them." The spider scurried back into the crack. "That's okay, I can handle rejection." She opened her pack and pulled out a bag of banana chips. As she munched she considered her options: go back to the tent and kill time with Martin and Andrea, or walk down onto the flats and get wetter. She had never been good at killing time, and carrying on down the ridge offered the only chance, however slight, of accomplishing anything for Grizzly Watch. Maybe there would be a break in the clouds.

As she closed her pack and stood up she felt a slight soreness in her nipples, the first sign of her impending period. "Oh, that's all I need now." It wasn't unexpected. She had a supply of tampons in her pack, even though she wouldn't need them for a day, maybe two. She headed down the ridge.

"Here she is." David Hellman stopped in front of box stall #22 and turned to the girl following him down the long center aisle of the barn. God, she was beautiful—tall, long legs, dark silky hair, almond eyes the color of honey, perfect teeth. "What do you think, Melanie?"

She looked into the stall. "Nice. Very nice." She read the tag on the gate. "*Hannah's Dream. Sire: Handyman. Dam: Dream Girl. Owned by David Hellman*' So you were telling the truth. You *do* own a racehorse."

"Of course I was telling the truth."

"I thought it might be just a pick-up line."

"What you see is what you get."

The horse stuck its nose through the bars and Melanie blew softly into its nostril. Her lips played gently over the mare's muzzle. David wished he could trade places with the horse for a moment. Well, if he played his cards right…He moved closer. "You seem to have a way with horses."

She raised a dark eyebrow. "I rode a lot when I was a kid. Had my own horse. But it's been ages."

"Can't be all that long ago." He guessed she was in her mid-twenties. He had met her the night before at a birthday party for the manager of one of his restaurants.

"Can I go into the stall?" she said.

"I'm afraid not. I'm breaking about six rules just bringing you into the barn. These race people are so paranoid. Her trainer won't even let me in the stall. If I want to get near a horse, I have to go to a public stable and rent a plug."

"So you do ride?"

"Actually, I've only been on a horse once in my life. They told me it was old and gentle, the one the handicapped kids rode. I climbed up onto its back and it went nuts, threw me on my ass." She tossed back her head and laughed. That was a good sign. He pressed on. "Yeah, while it was still tied to the fence. Horses don't like me."

"So why do you own a racehorse?"

"It's an investment." That was a stretch. More like a bad investment. *Hannah's Dream* had never won a race, never even placed or shown. She had cost him twenty three thousand, plus ridiculous amounts in training fees, vet and farrier bills and stable costs. But he liked the idea of owning a racehorse. With a little luck, and a touch of charm, his investment might pay off. "And it's a hobby."

"A hobby horse."

He smiled and gazed into her eyes. "Listen, I gotta go pay the trainer. After that, what do you say we get some dinner?"

"Sure."

They walked down the center of the aisle. David liked the smell of horses and leather, the sound their footsteps made on the clean concrete floor, the atmosphere of money. They stepped out of the barn, squinting into the sunlight of another wondrous late summer Vancouver day.

The office was attached to the jockeys' lounge. A few of them were talking and drinking. A TV was on in the corner. When they walked in, David saw the looks of admiration for Melanie. "Where's Fred?"

A jockey jerked a thumb. "In the office."

David turned and headed to the open door, but was stopped by another voice. "Hey David, someone you know is on TV."

They were all smiling, looking at him and Melanie. One muttered something behind his hand to another who laughed.

David looked at the TV. There was an image of his wife, Hannah, rappelling down a cliff, file footage a year old. Someone turned up the volume. The image changed to the reporter's face with a photo of a grizzly bear behind him. "...*will remain a secret for now, so as Grizzly Watch enters its final critical stage, the animal rights community and the hunters wait with bated breath. Will Hannah Weinberg...*"

David quickly steered Melanie into the trainer's office, but Melanie's interest was piqued. "Do you know Hannah Weinberg?"

"No." He closed the door.

"They seemed to think so."

"Oh...uh...they meant the reporter. He's a friend of mine. Hey Fred, how's the training going?"

He lay in a patch of labrador tea and dwarf birch. Here and there a few spiky stunted spruce stuck out of the boggy ground. The dull ache in his gut made it uncomfortable to lie down, but he needed to rest. He reached his head around to lick the dark brown fluid oozing from the hole in his side. It tasted of blood and berries, but bitter and unpleasant. He stood up and the ache eased a bit. He was thirsty. He lapped some water from a dark boggy seep then stood still and focused his attention up the mountain. He couldn't hear the weird gull sounds anymore. He had left them far behind, but he felt an urgent need to put more distance between himself and the animals with their terrible thunder. He headed down. The breeze blowing uphill brought the scent of big spruce and aspen and valley bottom. He could smell the river.

"Get in, Raz."

He hesitated. He loved going hunting with his Dan, but this part scared him. The big, noisy, churning, strong-smelling water when the canoe bucked and teetered. He had stayed close as his Dan had worked the boat over the ledge with the ropes.

"Come on, bozo, get in." His Dan sounded impatient, holding the canoe in the calmer water swirling below the ledge. He jumped in and stood in the bottom, spreading his paws wide for balance while trying to dig his claws into the hard hull.

"Get up to the bow." He knew it meant go forward, away from his Dan, when all he wanted was to push close against him. He moved gingerly ahead, further into the narrow part and jammed his haunches against the small pack. He shivered, and not from the cold.

"Okay. Geronimo." That sound meant scary. He'd heard his Dan make that sound before, once when the man had held him on the seat of a noisy smelly speeding machine with snow flying everywhere. His Dan gave a mighty shove and was in the canoe, quickly grabbing the stick with the flat end. A rock went by very close then the boat lurched. He started to pant. His Dan pulled hard on the stick and they were out in the middle of the river, rocking and swaying, rocking and swaying, all the while the water making its threatening roar. He looked ahead. The river bent out of sight.

He heard his Dan again. "Good. Lookin' good. Everything's fine, Raz, just fine." His Dan was frightened. The boat settled down a bit. His Dan moved the stick to the other side and the boat angled across the current. Now he could see around the bend. The water was not grey quiet. No. It was white angry.

"Holy fuck."

That meant danger. He braced himself. A scraping sound came from below his feet as the canoe began to pitch sideways. He scrambled upwards, his front paws gripped over the gunwale. Water poured into the boat on the low side then suddenly it levelled out and he was standing up to his hocks in water.

"Stay Raz. Don't move. Stay, stay, stay."

That meant stay. They were out of the angry water now, just some little waves lapping at the sides, some of them spilling in. His Dan, now kneeling up to his thighs in water, moved the unstable canoe carefully to the riverbank.

"Okay, boy, out you get."

Raz jumped out and turned around to watch his Dan get out of the canoe. He wagged his tail in relief, happy when his Dan stroked his neck and rubbed his side.

"Sorry, mister. I didn't see that rock. Went over it sideways, didn't we? Guess I shouldn't take chances like that. Could have been worse. Let's find a place to camp. It's getting dark."

Mister, that was him, same as *Raz.* The rest was love sounds. His Dan started to empty the water from the canoe. He hoped they would stop soon and put up the crinkly den. It was getting dark.

It was getting dark. The ridge seemed a lot steeper than she remembered. That was normal. It always seemed steeper when you went up. She got back into her breathing rhythm – one step on the breath in, one on the breath out, a pace she could keep up almost indefinitely, yet her body was tiring. She kept expecting to see the rock where she had stopped before, the one with the lichen patch and the spider, but she might easily have missed it. Maybe the camp was just over this next rise. Yes, it must be. She was hungry, looking forward to some warm food. She didn't care if it was freeze dried slop. Right now she would eat hamster bedding.

"That was a great meal, David. I've never had chateaubriand. Or truffles. Only the chocolate kind." She laughed.

"Melanie, I know this is going to sound cheesy, but you have the most delightful laugh."

They were strolling down the dock at the yacht club. The lights were on, but a thin glow still lingered. A soft breeze created a gentle tinkling of ropes and snaps against the masts.

Melanie admired the boat they were approaching. "That's a nice one. But where's this little boat of yours?"

"You're looking at it."

"What? This? You said little."

"By some standards it is. It's forty-two feet, but only thirty six on the water line."

She read the name printed in red across the hull. *"Hannah's Dream.* There's that name again."

"I…named her after my horse."

"You sure love that horse."

"I sure do. Would you like a drink?"

Melanie regarded him awhile. He wondered what she was considering—his age, his bald spot? She shrugged and smiled. "Permission to come aboard, sir?"

He beamed. "Permission granted."

Hannah looked up, not that she could see much of anything in the gathering dark and thick blowing clouds. What she saw was very disturbing. An almost perpendicular wall of rock rose where the ridge she had been climbing came to an end. It was plain now—she had taken the wrong ridge. She let out a sigh and slumped her shoulders. "Fuck. What now?" What about going back down? No, that would be foolish. What if she slipped and fell in the dark? What about Martin and Andrea? They would be worried sick, but there was nothing to be done about that. There was only one thing to do—find a sheltered spot and hunker down for the night. But where on this black wet windswept rock slide was shelter? The ridge fell off steeply on both sides. The lee side would be best.

She clambered down a short distance to a piano sized rock that stuck out from the jumble, took off her pack and crouched as far beneath the rock as she could. If she jammed her heels in under her she could just keep from slipping downhill. She opened her pack and dug inside for an energy bar then clutched her pack to her chest. The only sound was the wind and the rain. "Fuck me." Things would surely look better in the morning.

SEPT. 14

The light was stronger now, but the rain had not let up. She looked at her watch but it was fogged up, dead. That was the least of her worries. Her feet were soaked and her legs were cramped, tingling from lack of circulation. She was wet inside her raingear and shivering.

It had been the worst night of her life. Her brief periods of sleep had been fitful. With difficulty she stood up, gripping the wet rock to steady herself. She had to move, to walk, anything to generate some warmth. She started to climb the short distance back onto the ridge, but had to stop halfway. Even those few steps were exhausting and her balance was out of kilter. She guessed this was what being 90 years old must feel like. When she made it to the spine of the ridge, she stretched her aching legs and took a deep breath. In the dim light she began to slowly, painfully work her way down.

"I'd like to, David, but I have to go to work"

David Hellman put a hand on Melanie's stomach. "I own your workplace. I'll give you the day off."

"Can't." She got out of bed and went to the galley of the sailboat. "I work for Michael."

"I'll fire Michael and give you the day off."

"He's counting on me."

"I'd like to count on you. I'd like to count every pore on your magnificent…"

"You're nuts."

"My nuts? Go ahead and count them. Please."

"I'm not a bimbo, David. Don't patronize me."

"I'm just trying to be cute."

"You are cute. But I gotta go."

He watched her put on her shirt through the open door. He groaned when she bent over to put on her panties. She pulled on her trousers and slipped her shoes on. "Bye."

"How about later? Can I give you a call?"

"What have you got in mind?"

The only thing in his mind was sex with that beautiful body. "Umm…I don't know. What do you like to do?"

She thought for a moment. "The Canucks are playing an exhibition game tonight."

"Hockey? I never would have pegged you as a hockey fan."

"How about you? You like hockey?"

He lied. "Love it. You might not believe this, but I almost named this boat *The Great One.*"

"You're right. I don't believe it. So can you get tickets?"

"Is the Pope…uh, wait, you're not Catholic, are you?"

"Only in my tastes."

"Witty, too. Yes, I'll get tickets."

"Call me later." She climbed up to the deck.

David lay back with his hands behind his head. Things were good. No, things were great. He picked up his watch from the tiny shelf above the bed. "Oh crap." Today he had meetings with Aaron and Tina about the franchise deal and a conference call with the lawyers from Seattle.

"Hello, Gramma."

"Starla, darling, It's so nice to hear your voice."

"Is it too early to call?"

"Of course not. You can call me anytime."

"How are things in Ross?"

"The same. The band council is in turmoil as usual. Getting ready for elections."

"Are you running for chief again, Gramma?"

"Yes. One more term and that's it."

"You'll win again."

"Looks like it. I have to keep that Victor from getting his hands on the band's money. But you didn't call to talk about band politics, did you?"

"Has Dad left yet?"

"Yes. He left yesterday."

"Good. Where's he staying? Leonard's place?"

"What? No. He's on the South Macmillan River. Moose hunting."

Starla couldn't speak. Didn't Dad know how important this day was to her? Wasn't it just as important to him?

"Starla, is there something wrong?"

"He was supposed to be in Whitehorse today...for court."

"Oh dear. Dan never said anything about that. Starla, I...Maybe he forgot."

"How could he forget? If he doesn't show up, Mom is gonna get sole custody." Starla felt her throat begin to tighten and her eyes begin to sting. She fought against it, but couldn't keep her voice from quavering. "Doesn't he care?"

"Of course he cares. He loves you very much and he'd do anything to..."

"So why isn't he here?"

"Well, I don't know. I'm sure there's a reason."

"He promised it wouldn't happen again. Why does he do it, Gramma?"

"I know how difficult all this is for you. You shouldn't have to be put through...but you know, his father was the same. He resented the world. No. It was more like he resented needing the world. He finally grew out of it just after you came along, just before he died."

It always felt weird hearing her grandmother talk about John Mackay like this. Grandfathers were supposed to be wise, like in the movies. But whenever Dad and Gramma talked about him, even the funny stories, it was all about his flaws. "I don't get it."

"Dear, I'm sure they won't decide anything if he isn't there to speak for himself."

"I don't know. This is the second time."

"I'm sorry, darling. I wish there was something I could do."

"I guess there's nothing you can do." She kicked her backpack.

"How are things in Whitehorse?"

"Stupid. Mom's got a new boyfriend."

"Yes, I heard."

"She wants me to be nice to him. Next she's gonna want me to call him *Dad*. I'd rather shoot him in the head."

"That's a bit strong."

"I hate him."

"He hasn't…mistreated you, has he?"

"No. He tries to be all nice. He gives me the creeps."

"Well, dear, nobody's perfect. Give it time."

"Yeah, I know. It's just…I was hoping I could come and live with you and Dad in Ross."

"I was too, dear."

"I guess I'd better go. Don't wanna be late for school."

"Okay, and don't worry. Things have a way of working out."

"Thanks, Gramma. Bye."

"Good-bye dear."

Starla hung up the phone and stared out the window. The mountains were socked in. Someone on a quad drove by, shoulders hunched, hat pulled down against the rain. She didn't want to go to school. She wanted to be on the South Macmillan hunting moose with her dad.

Tara's voice came from the bathroom. "Starls, honey. You'd better get going. Don't wanna be late for school again."

"I'm going, Mom." She didn't like it when her mom called her Starls. She grabbed her backpack and her rain jacket.

"Don't forget my note for your teacher. You'll need it to get out early."

"I've got it."

"I'll pick you up at two, outside the front doors. Hey Gary. Get out of bed, sleepyhead."

Gary's voice came from the bedroom. "Yeah, yeah. I'm up."

Starla quickly left the house. She didn't want to be there when Gary came out.

The river parted around a jagged hump of black slate and disappeared over a ledge into the canyon. An occasional toss of white spray bounced into view beyond the smooth calm of the approach. Dan pulled the canoe up to the left shore and stepped out. This was the long, hard portage. He wouldn't make the same mistake he had last year when he missed the trail back down to the canyon. A one kilometer portage became a grueling three.

He sidled the canoe up to the left bank, got out and began unloading. This was the day he was supposed to be in court—the latest instalment of his ex-wife Tara's battle to get sole custody of Starla. All those bastards—the judges, the lawyers, the child advocates, even the clerks—all the sanctimonious assholes who thought they had the right to tell him how to live, how to care for his own daughter. They didn't give a shit about her. They only cared about winning, looking good to the judge, furthering their careers, playing the game until they retired to their pensions and their winter homes in some sunny climate.

He hoisted the canoe onto his shoulders and set off. Tara—why couldn't she sit down with him and work it out without the fucking court. He had tried everything to convince her—reason, logic, pleas, flattery—but it always ended up in a big fight. She had to win, had to have it all, and she seemed to relish tearing him down in public. He should never have married her. Meeting her family should have clued him in. All they did was fight. The whole useless bunch of them thrived on conflict.

Then again, if he hadn't married her, Starla wouldn't exist. Starla. The one who suffered most through this whole shitfest. He hoped she could forgive him for not showing up today. He hated himself for it, but he'd make it up to her. Nobody, not Tara, the courts, the police, nobody was going to tell him he couldn't see his own daughter. And nobody could tell him when he could go moose hunting. He suspected Tara had made sure the court date was set for rutting season.

The trail levelled off but his shoulders were beginning to ache from the canoe yoke. Up ahead was a big pine with a thick branch sticking straight out at head height. He rested the front end on it, let the back end down to the ground and stepped from beneath the hull. Raz came back along the trail and looked up expectantly.

"Shit, Raz, you'd think they could make a better yoke. State of the art materials, perfect hull design and they cheap out on the yoke. What's your view on the subject?" The dog wagged his tail. "Yeah, I know. Nobody expected I'd have to carry this thing so friggin' far. Come on. Let's have a look at the canyon."

Dan walked out to the edge and peered over. Upstream to the right the river boiled around a small island of black rock, cascading over a drop of about two meters. Where the two channels met the currents combined to produce a series of big standing waves. A tongue of rock on the north side created a nasty looking hole. He had heard that some people ran the whole canyon rather than portage the risky part. It wasn't his cup of tea, especially since he was alone. "The water's a lot higher than last year, Raz. Must be all this rain."

Downstream from the ledge was not so threatening—a couple of outcrops to avoid, a few moderate standing waves. The opposite side of the canyon was an impressive wall of black slate about ten meters high, its layers standing perpendicular—sheets of rock in the process of peeling off like pages torn from a book. "Beautiful." Dan sat and put an arm around the dog. "Mister, once upon a time that was the bottom of the Pacific Ocean. Imagine it, the kind of force it would take to push that up, not to mention all these mountains. Incredible. I know one thing for sure, mister. I couldn't do it." He looked into the dog's eyes. "What do you think? Could I do it?" Raz licked him on the nose. "I could? That's nice. You're a good dog."

Dan looked further down the canyon. "What the hell is that?" Something red stuck out of the water where the river ran around a big rock. He put up his binoculars. It was a canoe jammed against the rock along with some logs. A chunk missing from the bow looked like a shark bite. The force of the water on both ends had broken its spine and made ragged tears down its sides. It moved with surges in the current as if it was struggling to dislodge itself. "Ouch. I wonder what the story is behind that?"

He thought about his close call yesterday. He had taken a stupid risk. What would Starla think of him if he died like a fool trying to prove something? Still watching through the binoculars he said to Raz, "Mister, we were very lucky yesterday. We should have portaged. It's all your fault. I shouldn't have listened to you. You were so impatient to find a campsite. Oh yeah, I blame you." He looked down at Raz, who was busy licking his privates. "Okay, I guess anyone who can do that deserves forgiveness. Lucky bastard."

He put up the binoculars again. He couldn't remember seeing the red canoe last year. He would try for a closer look when he passed it, but he had to make sure he was in good position for the end of the canyon.

Even with the binoculars he couldn't get a clear view of the canyon's end, but he remembered seeing it from below last year. Another island blocked the middle and there was some nasty water on both sides. From this vantage point it looked as if he could pull over on the right for a look once he got down there. Maybe.

This was the last of the major rapids. The rest of the day would be a lot of boulder dodging, but nothing really serious. Still, it didn't mean he could afford to be cavalier. He was traveling alone and that red canoe wrapped around the rock was a pointed reminder of how high the stakes were.

He took one more look at it. "Raz, I think we should consider the long portage."

Susan Field walked into the Yukon Justice building, past the indoor fishpond, and headed for the staircase up to the courts. A familiar voice called her name.

"Suzy. Hey Suzy, wait up." It was Owen Orser, her former law partner. His friends called him 'double O.' He came puffing toward her, his rumpled suit jacket open, exposing an expanse of gut. "I'm sorry. It's Susan now. Right?"

"Right. Suzy Giller has ceased to exist. I'm Susan Field again."

"Good for you. So, how are you doing?"

"I'm fine." She didn't want to get into another discussion about how she was handling her break-up with Jim. She changed the subject. "How's life as a government lawyer?"

"Boring. Lots of bullshit. I'll tell you, though, I sure don't miss the monthly billing deadlines." Owen was a very clever lawyer, but careless when it came to collecting the money. "You here for court?"

"Yeah, another custody battle."

"There's no money in that."

"It's on the taxpayers' tab. Legal aid. I'm supposed to be meeting my client right now."

"I won't keep you then. But I'd like to talk to you. What are you doing for dinner?"

"Nothing planned."

"How would you like to join me at Giorgio's?"

What did Owen want? He'd always had a thing for her. She hoped he wasn't going to try to start anything, because she didn't want to have to turn him down. He was a nice guy. Good sense of humor. What harm could it do to have dinner with him? "Sure. What time?"

Owen beamed. "How about 7:30?"

"Okay."

"Great. I'll make the reservation. Good luck in court." He shuffled off to the elevators.

Susan continued up the stairs. She spotted her client sitting on the bench and sighed. She'd told Tara McKay to dress conservatively for court, but there she was in a tight black skirt and a silver leather jacket, her long hair teased into a glowing halo. Her ears were hung with multiple earrings and her hands glittered silver and gold. At least she wasn't wearing rings on her thumbs. Susan guessed this was conservative for Tara.

Tara hadn't seen her yet. She was fussing over her ten-year-old daughter, Starla. Susan felt sorry for the kid. She couldn't shake the feeling that if one parent had to win, it should be the child's father, Dan McKay. Oh well, Susan had her job to do and it didn't require that she like her client.

Starla saw Susan first and smiled. God, what a beautiful child. She had her father's eyes and mouth. Tara followed Starla's gaze. She left the child sitting on the bench and rushed over, a look of glee on her face.

"Susan, I've got great news. Guess."

"I don't know."

"He's not coming. He won't be contesting."

Susan felt a pang of disappointment. "Are you sure?"

"Positive. Starla phoned his mother in Ross this morning. He's moose hunting on the South Macmillan."

"His lawyer will be here, though."

"He still doesn't have one. That jerk-off can't get it together to wipe his own ass."

"Oh?" Susan looked concerned.

Tara patted Susan's arm. "That was so smart, what you did."

"What I did?"

"Scheduling the court date during rutting season."

"I didn't schedule it. The court did."

"Anyways, I heard something else. Dan lost his driver's license. Isn't that great?"

Susan hid her distaste of Tara's joy in her ex-husband's problems. "What for, drunk driving?"

"No such luck. No, just driving without insurance. Anyways, it all adds up against him." She laughed. "Man, we're gonna nail Dan's ass. Oh, and Gary's coming to sit in on it."

"Gary?"

"Gary Haines. My boyfriend. He said he knows you, sort of."

Indeed she did know Gary Haines, sort of. He had been a client of Owen's several years back, charged with trafficking in cocaine and assault against his girlfriend of the time, a young woman who refused to testify against him. Owen had got the trafficking charge reduced to possession and Gary had spent a couple of months in jail.

Tara was still bubbling with enthusiasm. "I thought it would be good to have him here. You know, like, it shows I have a stable relationship and Starla has a father figure."

"Tara, I don't think..."

Tara wasn't paying attention. She was looking down the stairs. "But he's not here yet. He said he'd be here."

Maybe Gary had the sense not to show up. "Why didn't you tell me about Gary?"

"I don't know. I didn't think it mattered."

"He was once a client of my firm. I might have a conflict."

"With Gary? No, he's a sweet guy. You'll like him."

"No, I mean a conflict of interest. The Law Society has rules about it. I might not be able to represent you."

"I'll have to get another lawyer? But we were just getting to know each other. Oh, that is so unfair. I want you. It's my right to have the lawyer I want. Fuck."

"It's almost time. Let's go in." Tara started for the courtroom, an angry petulant look on her face.

Susan stopped her. "What about Starla?"

"Oh, right." She turned back to her daughter. "Starla, come on. What are you doing? You're so dozy."

Jessica Giller turned off the Alaska Highway onto the Carcross Road and accelerated up to seventy then let her speed edge back down to sixty. This was a favorite spot for the cops to hang out, and she couldn't afford another speeding ticket. Aside from the fine, if she got any more points on her license her insurance would go through the roof.

Up the hill and around the bend the speed limit rose to ninety. As the little car accelerated, she relaxed back into the seat. Reaching down, she picked up a small cloth bag, loosened the drawstring and pulled out her pipe. She jammed her left knee against the steering wheel, took out a bag of marijuana and placed a piece of bud into the pipe.

Maybe she shouldn't smoke now. If Helga was at her Dad's place it would be too weird stoned.

"To hell with Helga." She lit her pipe, took a deep lungful, and held it in as her hand went back to the steering wheel.

Home.

The house she grew up in was no longer home. It was Dad's place now…and Helga's. She held her lighter to the pipe, sucked in another lungful of smoke and put the pipe away in its bag. Why did Mom and Dad have to split up. They were in their fifties, for Christ's sake. What did her Dad see in that bitch, anyway? Rich and beautiful and 35. That's what. What bothered her most was that her father was shallow enough to give up twenty-five years of marriage. Her parents had built a house together, raised her and her brother together, and Dad had thrown it away. It seemed so unfair. Dad had his exciting new girlfriend while Mom suffered. It must feel so humiliating to be cast aside.

Oh well, some of her friends' parents had split up. Mom would get over it. After all, she was independent, her law practice was doing well, and she'd bought a house downtown, something she'd wanted for a long time after so many years commuting from the Annie Lake Road.

Passing the sign for Raven's Edge she looked out over the valley to the mountains on the other side. The clouds were lifting. The Watson River valley curved down out of the mountains from the west. She remembered the horseback trips they had taken to Rose Lake—idyllic summer days spent riding, fishing, swimming, camping, and playing with her brother Charlie. Her father was a hero then. There wasn't anything he couldn't do. Now he was acting like some pathetic bozo. She'd heard of older men who tried to recapture their youth—mid-life crisis it was called—but she always thought her Dad was above that. He had let her mother down. He had let everyone down including her, especially her.

She came to the straight stretch before the Annie Lake Road and clicked on the right turn signal. Just a few more minutes. The weed had kicked in. Past the Community Center, past the golf course, she saw the familiar sign on the big pine: Giller.

Her Dad's truck was parked in front of the house. Helga's car wasn't there. Good. She opened her door and was met by Butcher, their big shepherd-cross dog. Not their dog anymore but Dad's. Dad's and Helga's. One more thing taken from her.

"Where's Jim, Butch? Where is he?"

The dog was wagging his whole body. His front paws went into her lap as he tried to lick her face.

"Go on, get down." She pushed him back and he ran towards the corral. Her father was there working with a dapple gray she hadn't seen before. The other horses stood lazing in the pines away from the action. The gray had its head and tail up, prancing around her dad at the end of a lead shank. It stopped and jerked its head toward the other horses, wanting to be in the comfort of the herd. Jim turned to face it, extending his left hand, the one holding the rope, out to his side while shaking his right index finger at the horse. The gray arched its neck, shook its head and trotted around to the left. After a quarter circle he said, "Whoa," and gave the rope a shake. The horse stopped. Jim pointed at the horse's rear.

"Move your butt." He shook the lead rope gently and the horse swung around to face him. "Back." He walked toward the horse. When the lead went slack it tried to turn away, so he gave the rope another shake and it backed up. He let it stand for a while, looking directly at its face then let his gaze fall and turned partially away. A gentle tug on the rope brought the horse in to stand with its nose at his waist. He stroked it over its eye and the horse responded by rubbing the side of its face on his arm.

"Is that halter itchy? Lemme scratch you. That feels good, doesn't it? Nothing to be afraid of. Hey, look what I've got for you." He reached into his pocket and held a handful of pale brown cubes under the horse's muzzle. "Crunchies. Your favorite."

Jessica was watching from the gate. "Monty Roberts says to never use treats."

Jim spun around. The horse lifted its head and backed away from him, startled. When Jim saw Jessica he smiled. "Jess. Hey, how's it goin'?"

"Nice horse. Yours?"

"Helga's. She bought it down south. Six-year-old gelding. Arab, with papers."

"Oooh. Fancy. I thought you said you'd never get a horse with papers."

"I didn't say never. I said I wouldn't pay all that money for papers when I can get an outfitter's horse for 800 bucks. Anyway, Helga wanted an Arab."

Jessica sang, "Whatever Helga wants, Helga gets."

"Don't start, Jess."

"A horse. She's really moving in."

"Jessica…"

"How much did she pay for it?"

"Five thousand, plus three grand to have it brought up here."

"Jesus."

"I told her she was nuts."

"I guess she can afford it. All that old German money. Or is it stolen Nazi gold?"

Jim gave her a brief look to say, *That's enough*, then turned his attention to the horse. "He's got great action. Very athletic."

"He's a beauty. Have you ridden him?"

"A few times. He doesn't know much, but that's okay. He'll learn. The problem is, he doesn't trust people."

A car pulled up to the house. It was Helga. Jessica wished she hadn't come to the corral first, should have gone right into the house and got the things from her room. Her ex-room. Damn. "Oh look, it's Ilsa, Queen of the…"

"Jess. Enough."

Helga got out of the car, looked toward them and waved. She opened the hatchback, took out a bag, waved again and went into the house.

Jessica waved in mock cheerfulness. "I don't have to like her."

"But you can try to give her a chance." They stood looking at each other for a moment. "How's Suzy?"

"Mom's okay. But it's not Suzy anymore, it's Susan."

"Oh yeah. I heard. More professional."

"Why don't you ask her yourself?"

"Yeah, I guess I should. But it always ends with…well, you know. So, what is it you need to get from the house?"

"I don't know. Just some clothes and pictures and stuff. And my old diary. I don't want her snooping around reading it."

"You go ahead. I'll be a few minutes more with this guy."

"I don't know."

"Just talk to her. You can try out your German."

"She's your German."

"Jess…"

"Haven't you been trying her out?"

"Oh, for Christ's sake."

"It's okay, Dad, I'm just kidding. Don't worry. I'll be civil." She started for the house. "Maybe I'll even call her Mommy."

The dim gray light gave a fuzzy impression of the passage of time. It was hard to tell if the clouds were thickening or it was getting late in the day. The fog and rain made everything look the same, each stony gully followed by the same boulder-studded slope of caribou moss, dwarf birch, and stunted willows, like the old cartoons that used a repeating background.

Hannah had decided to travel around the mountain, reasoning she would have to cross the horse trail. She focused on keeping a constant altitude. There were rock slides and thickets to climb around or descend below, but they pretty much equalled out. She was soaked to the skin, but not cold anymore. Movement produced warmth. She could keep it up a long time, but not forever, and not after nightfall.

Where were the landmarks from the trip up? They had followed the outfitter's horse trail until they were out of the trees and then veered off up towards the west peak. But where? Which rock slide or outcrop or gravel bank? A creek. They had followed a creek, had crossed it several times stepping from stone to stone until it had become a single narrow rivulet. It had finally disappeared where it sprang from under a mound of rock.

She came to a steep bank of grass and half-walked, half-slid down to a flat area of thick willows higher than her head. Small pools of still water dotted the bog, but above the sound of rain came the unmistakable rush of flowing water. Could this be the creek? If it was, by her reckoning, the horse trail should be on the other side. She plunged into the willows. It didn't matter that water came up to her shins or that the wet leaves rained down water as she pushed through, she was already soaked through. The creek was an easy jump, but ahead the willows ended at another steep bank, a mirror image of the one she had come down.

Hope vanished. Here was another bank to climb and another endless mountain shoulder to trudge across. Despair began to overtake her, an urge to give up, to sit down in the wet ground and cry. Instead, she marshalled her resolve and walked through the last of the thick brush.

There, between the willows and the bank, was a well-used trail beaten into the turf—animal tracks, lots of them, most filled with water. It must be the horse trail. Surely some of those were horse tracks. Maybe with a closer look her own tracks would show. But maybe not. The outfitter's horses plus the rain would have obliterated them. She flopped down onto a tuft of grass at the edge of the bank, relieved. A raven swooped low and landed on a large boulder at the top of the bank. She took off her pack and pulled out an energy bar—two left after this one.

What now? Her first instinct was to go uphill to her camp, to Martin and Andrea, but that would be a hard climb and she was not certain where to leave the horse trail. If she got onto the wrong ridge again it would be a repeat of last night, which was unthinkable. Time was a huge factor. Back down was farther, but it would be faster on a good trail, possible to follow even in failing light, maybe even in the dark. It would take her to the North Canol road right across from the Twin Creek airstrip. The three of them had flown there from Whitehorse four days ago in secret so as not to alert Lyle Kessler. Across the road from the airstrip sat an old school bus, up on blocks, fitted out as a cabin with a wood stove, beds and stores of dry food—flour, pasta, and soup mix. If she could make it there tonight she could get warm and dry, get a meal in her stomach and have a decent sleep. Then, as soon as the weather cleared, she would go back up the mountain.

She looked up at the lead-gray sky. "God, I don't know if you're up there, but thank you." With renewed vigor she hoisted her pack and set off down the trail to the old school bus.

"Hello, Jess. It's good to see you. Would you like something to drink?"

Why had she called her Jess? Only her friends and family did that. "No thanks. I'll just get my things."

"I can make some tea. Or there's pop, or beer if you like."

"No thanks." Couldn't Helga just leave her alone? Trying to be nice made it worse. It wasn't like they could ever be friends.

"Will you stay for supper? I've got some king crab. Jim says it's your favorite."

"I can't. I'm meeting Kyle."

"How was your trip down south?"

"It was okay, I guess. Good to be back, though."

"Did you find a school you like?"

"Yeah, a couple, but I've decided to stay for another year."

"Really? That's great. I thought you were dead against it. You know, get out of Whitehorse and hit the big city."

"Yeah, well, there's time for that. I might try to get some courses at Yukon College." She wasn't going to tell Helga the real reason, that although Mom had urged her to go to university, Jessica felt she needed her to be there for awhile.

"Suzy must be happy about it. Have you told your Dad yet?"

"Not yet." The bitch. She had no right to mention Mom, or call her Suzy.

"Of course he wants you to get your education, but you know how much he loves your company."

"Yeah."

"But you know, you shouldn't leave your schooling too long. You're a very bright girl."

How dare she give her advice as if she was her parent. Jessica was finding it hard not to blast Helga. "Thank you."

Helga was looking out the window toward the corral. Jim was still working the horse, getting it to move sideways and stroking its flank when it did. "Your father is so good with the horses. Dogs, too. I've never seen animals respond like that to anyone. I used to go out with an animal trainer in Germany. He was such a brute. With him it was submit or feel the whip. Asshole. But Jim, he just says, *Go there, do this*, and they do it willingly, no force, no intimidation. It's as if they read his mind. He's amazing." She turned to Jessica, smiling.

"Yeah, he's a regular Saint Francis of Asuzy."

"You mean Assisi."

"Asuzy."

"Oh…yes, I see…see." Helga smiled. There was an awkward silence.

"I'd better get my things." Jessica headed for her room before she said something nasty. She closed the door behind her and looked around at her life as it used to be. One whole wall of snowboarding pictures cut from magazines, pictures of her friends laughing, Kyle mooning the camera at a bush party. Her gaze fell on the enlargement of the family at Rose Lake, she and Charlie putting on goofy faces, and Mom and Dad with their arms around each other. She stared at it for a while and felt her eyes begin to burn, a lump rise in her throat. She flopped down on her old futon and gave in to the tears.

He was tired. His legs ached from continuous walking. He wanted to lie down, let his head rest in the soft wet moss, breathe in the rich mouldy aroma and drift off to sleep, but he knew if he did, the ache in his stomach would grow again. Instead he found the crotch of an upturned root and rested his chin on it. Each pulse of his heart sent a dull throb of pain into his head. He let his hind end down onto his haunches, accepting some slight relief from fatigue.

The danger from the thundermakers was gone. They were not following him. They would be eating the rest of the caribou now. They were welcome to it. The ache in his stomach left him with no desire for food. His only desire was a short rest before plodding on. He must get to the river.

Susan Field stood at the entrance to the restaurant and searched the crowd for Owen. She spotted his balding head over in the corner.

The maître d' came over. "Do you have a reservation?"

"Yes. No. Well, I'm meeting a friend. Right over there." She came up behind Owen and looked over his shoulder at the novel he was reading: *The Time Game.* "What are you reading, Owen?"

He quickly closed the book and put it face down on the table. "Oh, this? It's nothing. I'm a sucker for trashy sci-fi."

She sat down opposite him. "No need to justify it. I like the occasional space adventure myself."

"That surprises me. I'd have judged you a Margaret Atwood or Carol Shields girl."

"I like them, too."

"Trouble with sci-fi is, you have to wade through a lot of junk to find a good one."

"Just like life." Two menus lay on the table beside him. He handed her one.

"Ain't it the truth? How was your day in court?"

"Terrible. My client is pissed off at me."

"Why?"

"For not getting into a fight with the judge."

"Who's your client?"

"Tara McKay. Do you know her?"

"No."

She set her menu aside. "She's an airhead. Coarse, foul-mouthed little… Oh, maybe I shouldn't be too hard on her."

"As you know, I've had my share of those clients. Now that I'm a government lawyer my clients are bureaucrats and deputy ministers. Christ, it makes me nostalgic for the old days."

Susan laughed. "It does not. You can't fool me, Owen. You love it—the secure paycheck, the holiday time, the pension plan."

"Hey, don't forget the dental."

"And great secretaries. We train them and the government lures them away with salaries we can't possibly match. You took Rita with you when you went, you bastard."

"That's not true. She just happened to be hired at the same time I was. But let's not talk about me. It's really too depressing."

The waitress came to ask if they wanted drinks. Susan ordered a gin and tonic and Owen ordered a beer. When the waitress walked away, Susan saw Owen steal a glance at her retreating behind. "Try not to drool, Owen."

"What? Oh, I was just admiring the fit of her trousers. What material would you say that is?"

"I think it's called young firm flesh."

"Okay, you caught me, but I'm not a lecher. At my age, it's more like appreciating the conformation of a fine racehorse. It doesn't mean I want her in my stable."

"No, it means you want to mount her."

"You're wicked." There was a pause as they both looked at the menu. "Actually, I'm not really interested in young women. I'm much more interested in mature, experienced women." He glanced briefly into Susan's eyes.

She laughed. Was Owen trying to suggest something in his not-so-obtuse way? Better to ignore it. "Owen, I have a problem. I might not be able to represent Tara McKay. I might have a conflict."

"Good. Dump her and her custody battle. You said you don't like her, and you're making diddly-squat on it. Thank your lucky stars."

"It's not quite so simple. I'm worried about the kid. Starla."

"Starla. Wow. They always pick names like that—Starla, Skybird, Twilight. The kids are born and the parents are full of childish hope and romance. Then in a year or so the government has to take the kid away 'cause it's neglected or abused."

"She's not abused. Tara's no Mother Theresa, but she wouldn't harm Starla. No, I'm worried because Tara has a new boyfriend. You know him. Gary Haines."

"Haines. Jesus, no."

"What kind of a stepfather do you think he'd make?"

"A rabid dog would be better. That guy's a friggin…" he stopped when the waitress came with their drinks. She asked if they were ready to order. Owen looked at Susan.

She shook her head. "Give us a few more minutes, please." The waitress left. "You should see this child, Owen. She's so sweet, so innocent. And I'm sure she's about ten times as smart as her mother. It breaks my heart to think..." She trailed off, looked out the window and sipped her drink.

"Susan, you can't take on the troubles of the world. You're a lawyer. You have a responsibility to your client, not her kid."

"I can't help it."

"What about the father? Where's he in all this, on a bender?"

Susan leaned forward, her arms on the table. "That's just it. I can't understand him. Not that I know him all that well, but I've seen him in court. He seems articulate and intelligent. I'm sure he's not a drinker. And I know Starla adores him."

"So don't fret. He'll get shared custody. The kid'll be fine." He took a long swig from his beer.

"He didn't show up today. This is the second time it's happened. I'm afraid he's going to blow it."

"Who's his lawyer?"

"No lawyer."

"Terrific. What happened in court today?"

"The judge adjourned it. He was going to proceed until he found out the father was moose hunting. Starla was the one who brought it up. She stood up in court and interrupted the judge. She said her father always hunts moose this time of year and he needs the meat for himself and his mother. She even pointed out that her grandmother was Frances McKay, elder and chief of the Ross River Dene. The judge thanked her and said First Nations people should be allowed to pursue their way of life without interference from the court."

"Judge Cameron?"

"Yeah."

"You're right. She is a smart kid."

"But it's only going to delay the inevitable. What should I do?"

"Well, you can't act against your client. That would be unethical, and you could be disbarred."

She looked at Owen. "I know. Too bad." How would he take it, as a joke, or would he get the hint? She wasn't even sure what she was hinting at. He was the only lawyer she would ever trust with such a suggestion, however oblique.

He returned her gaze for a long moment. "Tell you what. I'll talk to Doug Innis. You know him?"

She nodded. Chief Superintendent Innis was the RCMP division commander for the Yukon. Owen continued. "He's on the curling club board with me. I'll see if Gary Haines has had any run-ins with the law, or popped up in any of their investigations. Innis should know what he's been up to. In the meantime you should talk to your client. Tell her what you know about Haines. Maybe she'll dump him."

"Thanks, Owen. You're a good friend."

"That's a start."

The waitress came over. "You folks ready yet?"

"Yeah, I'm starved. Suzy?"

She looked at the waitress, apology in her eyes. "I haven't even looked at the menu. Sorry. Owen, why don't you just order for me?"

"My pleasure." He studied the menu with relish. "Get your taste buds ready. You are going to love what they do with octopus here."

At the inside edge of a bend in the river, the stand of mature spruce had been spared by the forest fire. Even after days of steady rain the big trees were dry at their bases, the lower branches, still tinder that would burn at the touch of a flame. Dan rested under his lean to, drinking tea and staring into the fire as he stroked the dog's head. The sun had gone down hours ago, but he could still just make out the skeletons of burned trees on the opposite bank.

Was it lingering twilight? No, it must be the moon trying to shine through the cloud layer. That was a good sign. Maybe the clouds were thinning. Maybe this was the start of the weather he hoped for—clear, bright, September weather of cold frosty nights and warm, still days—the kind of weather that brought on the rut. Was it wishful thinking, or did the noise of the rain on the tarp seem less? He got out from under the tarp and looked up in time to see a single star appear briefly through a small break in the clouds.

"Good news, Raz. Looks like it might be clearing."

He had ambled all day down the small creek heading south into the valley, stopping now and then to eat, and sniff, and listen. Now the old bull moose stood in a small sedge meadow just above a slope down into the thicker forest of the main valley. He could smell the change in the weather. The rain had dwindled to an occasional spit. The air was colder in his nostrils, the smells sharper, more defined. The knot of scar tissue at the back of his thigh no longer ached. The sounds of the mountains were crisper, un-muted by the falling rain and the thick fog. It was no longer a vague restlessness that drove him. It was a sure steady build in his vigor, and a pressure in his loins.

He pawed at the ground several times, excavating a shallow pit then positioned himself above it and urinated. His rutting scent was powerful now, rising around him in a cloud of mist from the warm effluent. He turned and breathed it in, tasting the sharp tang deep in his sinuses.

"Wuh." It was a grunt of defiance, pride, a declaration of his strength. No answering grunt came. He lowered his muzzle and dug the brow palms of his antlers into the muddy depression, twisting his head back and forth to coat them in his smell. Then he moved to the edge of the small patch of sedge where a long-dead black spruce stood. He rubbed his antlers up and down the trunk, slowly at first then becoming more forceful until, with a quick powerful swipe he struck the tree, sending a loud hollow ring out over the valley.

"Wuh, wuh, wuh."

It was becoming difficult to stay on the trail in the dark. Several times she had had to search right and left before finding it again. The detours had cost her valuable time and effort, but if she could keep to the trail eventually she would come to the old school bus. Her situation was becoming desperate. Lack of sleep and many hours of sustained exertion were great weights strapped to her body. It was becoming difficult to focus on one thought for any length of time, even to stay on the trail. Worse, a sense of despair had begun to gnaw at the back of her mind. She forced herself to think of the positives. The rain had stopped. That was good, but she was still getting wet each time she disturbed a branch overhanging the trail. Stars could be seen above the trees. Maybe tomorrow the sun would come out to dry off the bush. But tomorrow was a long way off, and the air was getting much colder.

Could she afford a rest stop? Maybe a short one. A fire? Could she get one started in this wet bush? She took off her pack and gripped the zipper tab to open it. Her fingers slipped off, numb, weak, shaking. With all her concentration she held on and pulled the zipper back a short way then poked her two index fingers into the opening, pulled the pack open, reached in and rummaged in the bottom until she found the waterproof container of matches.

It took all her strength to unscrew the top with stiff, unresponsive fingers. Again, the full force of her concentration was needed to pull a single match from the container, grip it and strike it against the rough side of the tube. As the match sputtered to life a sudden spasm of shivering overcame her and the flame was shaken out. What the hell was the matter with her? Even if the match had stayed lit, what would she have set fire to?

A few steps away was a spruce tree. In the darkness she felt around its base for small dry twigs, broke some off and squeezed them into a bundle. Once again it seemed to take forever to fish out a match. It broke when she tried to strike it. By the third match she was sobbing with frustration at her unresponsive fingers and the drops of water falling onto her tiny bundle of twigs. She used up half the matches before giving up.

What now? Stay put and wait until morning? Without movement her body could not generate enough heat. Sleep would be impossible. No. However slow the progress might be, she must keep moving down the trail to the road.

She set off again, slowly and carefully so as not to lose the trail. "Focus, focus." she told herself, her mind fixed on the dim line of trail visible for only a few feet ahead at any one time.

She was unaware she had left her pack behind.

SEPT. 15

The glow to the east was stronger. Before long the sun would touch the top of the fir trees, glint icy yellow, blue and red until the frost melted and dried. The frosty night was welcome—a sure sign of clear days to come. She reached her long black beak down to her breast and tucked in a feather, the one that always slipped out of place to interrupt the smooth shiny black expanse over her flight muscles. After a lifetime of tucking in that same feather, it had become a habit as deeply ingrained as tilting her wings to catch an updraft. When she was happy, nervous, angry, tired, hungry or full, her beak always went down to the spot on her chest.

The thick boughs of the old squat fir had been a comfortable roost for the night, but now the light was strong enough to fly. Hungry. Time to move. Find the bobblehead she had followed off and on all the previous day. It might die soon, might already be dead. She hoped so. The longer it walked the less fat. Mmmm. Fat. She'd never eaten bobblehead, never seen a carcass. Even her mate, who had hatched at the big smoke where bobbleheads roosted in great numbers, had never tasted their flesh. Maybe they never died.

But always worth following for a meal, especially the ones who rode on the big warm grass eaters. Those ones killed big animals—moose, caribou, fat bears. They were good. They left lots of it behind—guts, flesh, fat, bone. They mostly ate the heads. Maybe that's what gave them their big funny wobbly heads that rolled around on their skinny necks. Good food where they ground roosted, too—dense, sweet food. Salty. If their flesh tasted like that…She wasn't about to give up on this one.

"Me." Her short raucous call bounced back from the hill behind. She launched out of the fir and soared over the valley, following the gully down in the direction the bobblehead had taken. They were easy to spot. Their colors were usually out of place, their movement was clumsy and erratic.

She pumped a few strokes to gain altitude—not much breeze up the slope this early. The mountain tops were etched in pink but a blanket of fog lay over the bottom of the valley. Long easy arcs back and forth brought her down to where a finger of mist crawled up the gully. The doomed creature had gotten farther than she expected. She would have to wait until the sun reached into the valley bottom to melt the fog.

Something caught her eye—blue. She banked sharply, descending in tight circles to alight on a dead aspen snag. It was the blue thing the bobblehead had been carrying. Those things often held treasures encased in thin, sparkly skins. But no carcass.

She let out a short caw and a gurgle – an announcement to any other ravens who might be near. "Me. Find."

Carefully she scanned the surrounding bush. It would be foolish to glide down among the trees before making sure there were no other animals nearby. Down there her avenues of escape would be limited. And she would need time to get the thing open. She spotted something moving through the bush, a round, black, slowly-rolling ball of fur.

"Shitbear," she called angrily at the young black bear as it moved toward the blue thing. She left her perch and flapped down to a lower branch. If she was with a group of ravens they might be able to distract it long enough to grab a few morsels, but alone she could only hope for what it missed. Knowing shitbears, that wouldn't be much. She could only watch helplessly as it nosed the blue thing a few times then picked it up and walked off into the fog-shrouded forest.

She voiced her frustration. "Bad shitbear. Black shit. Hate. Die."

"Let me ask you something." Melanie sat at the table in David's kitchen. The remains of breakfast, a plate with an empty egg shell in a cup surrounded by a few toast crumbs, sat before her. She poured herself another glass of orange juice.

Something in her tone gave David a sense of foreboding. He tried to sound cheerful. "Ask away. I am an open book."

She arched an eyebrow. "David, do you think I'm stupid?"

"Of course not. You're one of the most..."

"Why didn't you tell me you were married?" She took a sip of orange juice and eased back in her chair, fixing him with a look from those incredible amber eyes, a look that told him there was no point denying it.

"Um...I don't know. It didn't come up." He searched her face for any hint of her mood. She seemed impassive. "Does it matter to you?"

"What matters is your dishonesty."

"I never told you I wasn't married."

"No, but you went to great lengths to hide it. Did you think I wouldn't find out?"

"I don't know. I guess I thought...I thought it wasn't important."

"Oh yeah?"

"Yeah." He felt as if he had just put his foot into a trap. He feigned nonchalance by pouring himself a coffee from the carafe. "More coffee?"

"If you had told me at the start, if you'd been open about it, I might not mind, but..."

"Somebody at work told you, didn't they? It was that asshole Michael, wasn't it?"

"Nobody told me."

"Oh." He stared across the table at her, sitting there looking so beautiful in his blue dressing gown open down to her navel.

She pulled the dressing gown closer around her shoulders. "Your boat and your horse, both named *Hannah's Dream*. The jockeys snickering in the track lounge. Those were my first hints. And that might not have bothered me. No, what bothers me is how you tried to erase Hannah's presence in this house. That's why you resisted bringing me here."

"I never..."

"Where are the photos you took off the wall?"

"What photos?"

She leaned forward, put her elbows on the table and laced her fingers together. "David, give up the innocent act. There are empty picture hangers on the wall in the den and a whole empty closet in the bedroom. Where did you stash her clothes?"

"I did it for you. I didn't want you to feel self-conscious."

She put her cutlery on her plate, picked it up and rose from her chair. "It makes this whole thing so sordid."

"That's where you're wrong. Let me tell you something about Han… about my wife and me. We have a…"

"You can say her name, David. It's Hannah. Hannah Weinberg. And don't waste your breath trying to tell me you two have an open marriage, whatever that means. I've heard it before." She went to the sink, dropped the plate on the counter and headed for the stairs, but stopped at the doorway and turned back. "I'm gonna get dressed. Could you please call me a taxi?" She was about to leave again but turned back once more. "Oh, and by the way, a little piece of advice for the next time you bring some young bimbo here: the bottom drawer in the bathroom is where Hannah keeps her tampons."

Black and green. Black dead trees, still wet and slippery, leaning at crazy angles, many lying uprooted, interlocked tangles studded with half-burned, claw-like branches. Green willows, bright green thickets blocking her path. What path? What direction? She forced her mind to bear on it. Down. She must go downhill to the road. She had lost the trail sometime in the night, but if she kept on downhill…it was her only choice.

Hot. The sun beat hot on her face. Her skin was burning. She stripped off her raingear and felt a brief wash of cool air over her body. A willow thicket grew through a jumble of fallen trees. When she tried to step over her feet sank into a pool of black water. Dead branches clawed at her, caught on her shirt, tore at her skin. She stepped onto a fallen trunk to get a higher vantage point. The mountains on the far side of the valley—bathed in gold and red against an azure sky—stared down in serene, uncaring repose.

Somewhere between here and those mountains was the road and an end to this nightmare of sucking bog, blackflies, willow thickets, and fallen trees.

"...Melanie Walker is not at home. Leave a message and I'll get back to you...." Her voice sent a wave of longing into David's stomach. He had blown it with Melanie. How could he have been so stupid? Agreeing to take her to his place was moronic enough, but what the hell was he thinking trying to remove all traces of Hannah? The recorded voice was coming to an end. Maybe he could still salvage this thing. It was worth a try. He pictured her standing naked in the bedroom doorway last night, backlit. Oh yes, it was worth a try.

He had rehearsed what he was about to say. The beep sounded. "Hi... uh...it's me...uh...I'd like to talk to you if I...I mean if we..." His pulse beat in his brain, his skin tingled. He tried to take a deep breath to clear his head but his lungs were already full. His planned message had fled his mind. "I'm sorry. I'm really, really sorry I...I mean I'm sorry for the misunderstanding you...It's all my fault. I thought it was for the best but I guess I was wrong. I'd just like to explain and maybe...I don't know, I don't want it to end on a bad...uh, that is...I don't want it to end. I need to talk. We need to talk and...maybe you could give me a call. I'll be at the office all day. Please call. Please. So...uh...take care and...uh...hope to hear from you soon...I...okay...take care...please call. Bye."

Poker chips. Sliding down a huge pile of poker chips, the sound of them clicking and rustling loud in her ears. It was nice. It was cool. She opened her eyes. Black. Cool, so beautifully cool, soft, black poker chips, round and smooth, flowing around her body. Sensuous. And blue overhead, impossible sparkling dancing blue. Rest. Rest here on this pile of poker chips and wait for David. David would be here soon to take her home. That would be nice, snuggling with David in cool swirling poker chips.

The uphill breeze was stronger now, strong enough to use without much effort. The south side of the valley was a series of benches stepping down to a flat area of gravel eskers studded with pothole lakes which sparkled silver when the sun bounced off them. The river ran straight here where the valley was narrow and the mountains close.

She skimmed along the rim of a ridge, using the updraft to gain speed for a climb and a better view. A sudden flash of purple and there it was—the carcass. It lay at the bottom of a steep bank of small, smooth, black stones. Now she would eat. Good that it died out in the open so she could see other animals that might come along to claim it. She banked, descending in a long turn to land on a boulder which stuck out of the bank beside the dead creature.

Happy now. She tucked in her errant breast feather and let out a long, loud series of calls. "Me. Me. Find food. Food. Food."

She was hungry and eager to dig into the carcass, but she must still be cautious. Bobbleheads were unpredictable, treacherous. She had never seen one with its changeable-dead-skin this close before. The dull, blue skin over the hind legs looked tough, but over the upper part it was fuzzy, almost furry. It looked easy to rip with a few sharp tugs from her beak. Where to start? The bobblehead lay on its belly so the innards were out of reach. But the face was uncovered and turned to the side, masked only by a few hanks of the long fur which sometimes covered their big, round, crazy skulls. The eyes were closed but under those lids would be two tasty morsels. That's where she would start.

She called again. "Me. Food. Food. Me." She was about to hop onto the big, furry, round head when the creature shuddered and its eyes opened. Startled, she leaped into the air and hovered for an instant before coming back down onto the boulder. Was she too close? What if it made a quick grab at her with its long bony paws? She kept her wings open, ready to beat upwards out of reach. She let out two short, harsh warning calls. "Look out. Look out."

A bout of shivering and a voice singing some odd tuneless song roused her from her half-sleep. She lay for awhile relishing the cool softness of the bed. But the feeling didn't last long. Heat. Her skin felt as if she was too close to a raging fire. And thirst. Her throat felt like sandpaper. Who had been singing? She opened her eyes. "David?"

Black against a deep blue background. Someone in a black cloak stood over her. She could hear the fabric rustling and saw it rise gracefully up to hover over her head. It turned and circled away. Brilliant light shimmered off the luxuriant cloak, spinning out gold and silver, green and purple and blue—a constantly changing swirling halo of color. David? No. An angel? She rolled onto her back and smiled, reaching up to touch the flowing iridescent robe. "Who are you?"

The thing was still alive. She circled away when it reached its paw toward her and let out its feeble call—near death, but still strange and terrifying. And those eyes—scary, piercing, grabbing. Bobbleheads had fearsome powers. Their boomsticks could kill at a great distance. They could zoom across the land on their big, noisy, dead insects. They could even fly at great speed and height. Was it worth the risk? Not much fat on it. The thought of a meal brought back her hunger. She wanted to taste what was inside that crazy, round head.

A stand of large pines covered the flat below the bank where the bobblehead lay. She glided to a landing at the top of one, folded her wings and tucked in the breast feather. The river was below the next bench. Her soft gurgled call ended on a bell-like note. "Alive. Alive. Dead soon. Eat soon."

Another round of shivering rippled through her, driving away the sense of comfort. Her head ached, her limbs were sore and her skin tingled hot and cold. She pushed herself up to a sitting position and looked for the angel. It was gone. Had she been dreaming? It had seemed so real, so incredibly beautiful. And the song…what language was it with its gurgles and clicks and trills?

It had soared away, out over the trees. Was it showing her the way? The way to where? As hard as she tried, she couldn't remember. The only image in her mind was the angel in its shimmering cloak. She must follow it.

She stood and walked down the pile of poker chips into the trees. The ground was flat with a thin covering of bristly whitish moss—easy walking like a park. The angel sang again, loud and clear, its voice ringing through the trees. It sounded so beautiful, this time above and ahead of her. She called, "I'm coming. I'm coming. Wait for me. Wait."

"Shit. Stupid food walking. Me. Hungry. Shit." The bobblehead was up again, heading for the river. If it died in the river it might sink, as so many luscious soft salmon carcasses did. She saw it in her mind, hooked on a tangle of limbs at the outside of a bend where the trees fall into the river, imagined it waving in the current down under that cold smothering water, fat tender flesh just out of reach, slowly going white then gray then brown.

It walked beneath her tree, muttering its crazy oowaaee calls with the hissing and spitting all mixed in, as if it was strangling on its own tongue. Now it was struggling through deep moss. Only a matter of time before it succumbed. She could do nothing but watch as it stumbled toward the river. She rose from her perch and flew ahead, out over the steep gravel bank, out over the river. If the thing fell down the bank into the deep water it would be lost to her. "Go back. Now fall. Now die."

The angel voice sounded urgent. There was an opening through the trees ahead but it was difficult to walk. With each step her feet sank deep into a thick orange sponge. A dull ache throbbed through her hips and thighs every time she lifted her feet high out of the soft damp stuff. Her eyes were clouded by a film of mucous. She blinked and wiped them with a hand but it did no good. She pushed on in the direction of the light where the trees ended, in the direction she had last heard the beautiful black angel's voice.

At the edge of the trees she collapsed into the soft sponge with an overpowering urge to close her eyes and sleep, but before long the burning sensation in her skin returned. She pushed herself up to a sitting position. The sight which met her eyes made her weep with happiness.

She sat looking out over a valley, her feet dangling over the edge of a two meter drop down to a sloping bank of gravel and sand. Below, a highway curved in toward the bottom of the bank. A steady, muted swishing was the only sound—traffic. But she could see no cars passing. She wiped at her eyes again.

Where was she? Was this the Sea to Sky highway? It looked like it. That would put her somewhere between Squamish and Whistler. She tried to remember how she got here but could only think of David. Was she supposed to meet David on the highway? If so, she must get down there or she might miss him.

Off to her right and above came the angel voice again, this time abrupt and high pitched. What was it saying to her? The meaning seemed just beyond her reach. Did it say *Go*? Yes. That was it. Go. It wanted her to go down to the road. David would be there, waiting for her. Yes. She looked down over the edge of the drop.

She stood, swaying slightly, and felt her clothes rub against her skin – hot, itchy, painful, as if she were wearing steel wool.

Two ravens approached down the valley, just above the tops of the tallest spruce that lined the river. One gave out a short call. "Me."

She recognized the voice of her mate. She hadn't seen him since the salmon run, before the leaves began to color, when a bunch of them combed the banks and bars for carcasses. Competing with bears, wolves and the big shit whiteheads required teamwork.

She returned his call. "Me."

He pumped his wings, rising to reach the height of her perch high up the bank. His strength pleased her. When he landed to sit on a black spruce trunk that leaned out over the bank he called again. "Me. Me. Me."

There was happiness in his voice. She was happy to see him, too. The other raven, a young female, landed on a dead aspen that stuck out of the gravel partway down the bank. It struggled for balance, wings spread, bobbing and swaying until the branch quit bouncing. It folded its wings and called. "Me."

She called to her mate. "Who she?"

He gurgled back. "She with."

"She ugly shit."

The young female eyed the bobblehead that stood at the top of the bank. "Food?"

She tucked in her breast feather and barked at the young newcomer. "Me food. Me bobblehead. You shit. You ugly."

He drifted with the current, paddling only enough to keep the canoe pointed downstream. The sun on his bare arms felt good after three days bundled in rain gear. The mountains stood resplendent in gold and red against an azure sky. The leaves of willow and alder, still verdant along the shore, reflected rich dark greens with flashes of silver. The whole valley seemed to languish in relief at the change in weather. Dan reached into the pocket of his jacket, which lay over the thwart in front of him, and pulled out his pipe and the plastic bag of marijuana.

"Not much left, Raz."

The dog wagged his tail, but didn't raise his head from the pack it rested on.

He put a tiny piece of bud into the pipe bowl and lit it, took the smoke into his lungs, held his breath and leaned back, feeling the bite in his throat and fighting the urge to cough it all back out.

The rapids and boulder gardens were behind him. Now he could shoot a moose. There was still a lot of river to run, so he could afford to be choosy. A yearling bull would be just right, but he knew if he was too picky he could run the whole river and not get a chance at the perfect moose. If he shot a bigger one he could bone it out, but he'd rather not. Large pieces of meat were easier to handle and less waste. He could leave the skin behind— most hunters did—but his mother would be disappointed. She was one of the remaining few who tanned skins the old way.

He took another long draw on the pipe. A raven was making a commotion somewhere near the top of the gravel bank above the next bend. Two more ravens flew over him from behind, making a beeline for the top of the bank. They landed, one on a spruce whose roots had been undermined by the slowly collapsing gravel, causing it to lean out over the edge like a snaggled-tooth, the other halfway down on a dead aspen.

He liked watching ravens. To most people they were garbage eaters, raiding grocery bags left in the truck box, stealing the dog food from its dish. *Familiarity breeds contempt*, as his father used to say. Yet even in the darkest, coldest days of winter, when there were no other living things around, you could always count on seeing a raven, black in a white world. Strangely comforting. He loved to watch them play on the air currents of a cliff face, whole gangs of them—wheeling, diving, rising, banking, wrestling in mid-air. Once when he was a kid he had tried to get a raven to take food from his hand, like a whiskey jack. For days he tempted it with chunks of rendered moose fat, to the mild disapproval of his mother who wondered why he had to waste the fat she used for her tanning soap. The raven would come close, but never close enough to pluck a morsel from his hand. It didn't like being stared at. Eye contact always made it fly off.

Now the river carried him away from the high bank. He put up the binoculars to focus on the raven perched on the dead aspen. It stretched its neck and a second later its call reached him. It was answered by one at the top of the slope. He scanned up to get a look at it, twisting in his seat with the changing angle. As the binoculars' field of view passed the crest of the slide he saw something move with a flash of beige. Moose antlers? As the canoe turned he twisted more, but it was impossible to keep the image steady. He picked up his paddle and took a single stroke on the right, but when he put the glasses up again, tall spruce had drifted between him and the gravel bank. He took up the paddle again and pulled hard on the left to bring the canoe around, whispered to the dog. "Might be a moose around this bend, fella."

Raz looked up at him then rose on his front paws.

"Stay down. Raz lowered himself slowly into the bottom of the canoe. "Good dog."

Dan paddled, glancing back periodically for the moment the gravel bank came back into view. Ahead, the river bent around a long sandbar before curving left and back into the slope. It was no place to kill a moose—little chance of a clear shot unless it was right on the edge, and if so it would fall into the river at its deepest, swiftest part. But if he stopped on the bar at a point with a clear view, he might be able to call it down onto the flat of the gravel bar. He eased the canoe toward the shallow water at the inside of the bend, slipped on his hip waders and swung one leg over the gunwale, ready to step down and stop the canoe. The stones were small cobbles, closely packed. Just before the high bank came into view, he stopped and pulled the canoe up until he was sure it couldn't float away.

He pulled his rifle from its case on top of the big yellow drybag. Raz stood up and looked over the side into the water. "Stay, Raz."

Out here at the farthest point of the bar he was conspicuous, so he walked slowly around the wide curve of sand which sloped to a ring of tall thin willows fringing the dark green wall of mature spruce that covered the lobe of the river bend. A few more steps and he could look straight down the river opening at the crest of the bank. He walked carefully, went down on one knee, set his rifle down and tried to look like a tree stump stuck on the bar. He put up the binoculars, sweeping them quickly across the top of the bank. Nothing. He swept back more slowly. There would be a game trail just back from that overhang.

A thick mat of mottled green and orange moss hung over the lip. Here and there along the edge, spindly black spruce leaned out. Their long shallow roots arced out and down like dripping tendrils. Big hunks of moss clung to the roots, making the whole thing look like icing melting off the edge of a birthday cake, its candles slumping. He muttered to himself. "Christ, I shouldn't have smoked that pot."

He scanned further. There was the raven and there, standing on a big moss mat at the lip of the overhang, was a naked woman.

Much better. No clothes. Cooler. No more painful scratching on her skin. She strained her eyes. Where were the cars? She could hear them, a faraway rush in her ears, but she couldn't see them. The voices. Confusing. Angel voices? No. Someone shouting. More than one. Movement. Down there on the road. David? Was he here to take her home? She tried to raise her arms but couldn't get them higher than her waist. She shouted. "David."

He put up his binoculars again. Yes, it was a naked woman. Where the hell had she come from? Did this explain the wrecked canoe in the canyon? She called to him but he couldn't make out what she said. Was it a foreign language? Was it a name?

He waved to her. "Hello. Are you all right?"

She spread her arms out to the side, stepped off the overhang and fell the couple of meters to the steep, loose gravel, landing on her feet in a slide and setting off a cascade of smooth stones down the bank. They clattered down the slope, pelting the water in a shower of droplets. She took long, jerky, robot strides down the bank, several times almost losing her balance. The falling gravel multiplied with each step.

He yelled. "Hey. Be careful. The water's deep."

She hadn't heard him, but he was relieved to see her come to a stop on the narrow ledge of larger stones at the water's edge. He called again. "Stay there. Don't move. I'm coming." He grabbed his rifle and ran back to his canoe. Just before he rounded the curve out of her sight he looked back in time to see her step into the water and disappear.

"Shit." He got to his canoe, threw his rifle in and launched into the current. In a moment he could see the bottom of the bank. No sign of the woman. He paddled hard, scanning downstream and caught a glimpse of light skin and dark hair break the surface where the river undercut a grove of spruce. Big trunks, still clinging by a tangle of roots, angled downstream, their tops an interwoven mat of branches. A couple of big sweepers leaned out over the water. He hoped she didn't get into that mess. Her head popped up again. It looked like she would miss the undercut and he heard her take a sputtering breath. Her arms made weak spastic attempts to swim.

Ahead, the river widened and curved gently left. A long crescent gravel bar on the inside of the bend sheltered a back eddy of still water, grass covered mud and willows. Shallow water. Maybe she could get her feet under her. He pulled on the paddle as hard as he could, gaining on the spot he had last seen her. The water was churned up, murky after three days of rain. Would she come up again? Was she drowning down there? He squinted into the water, hoping for at least a faint blurry skin glow.

From the other side of the canoe came the sound of a gasping breath ending in a gurgle. He shifted over in time to see an arm disappear into the murk. He drove his hand down below the water and felt his fingers touch hair. With his weight all on one side, the gunwale was dangerously close to the surface. Grabbing a handful of hair he pulled her up beside the canoe. She took another gasping breath.

"I've got you. It's okay." The dog stood up to look over the side, making the canoe tip further and spilling some water over the gunwale. "Jesus Christ, Raz, lie down." The dog crouched back into the bottom of the canoe.

Dan got his hands under her armpits, jamming her against the side, trying to keep her head above water while he looked downstream. He couldn't hold her and paddle at the same time, but he needed to move left across the current to avoid being swept into the deeper channel. If he could hold her with one hand, and paddle with the other he might get close enough. He grabbed her by the hair again "Sorry, but I . . ."

"David?" Her voice was weak.

"Hold onto the canoe. Can you hold onto the canoe?"

"Yes, of course."

"Are you okay?" Stupid question. He paddled hard.

"Yes. I'm warm now." She sounded calm—a bad sign.

He spoke louder. "Hold onto the canoe."

"Okay."

She made no attempt to hold on. He put all he had into his one-handed stroke, across the current toward the left shore. Her body lurched. She was touching bottom. One final push and he jumped over the side. The water came up to his chest before his feet landed on stones. The cold hit him like a hammer, taking his breath away. He got behind her, put both hands under her armpits and braced his feet against the bottom. Now the canoe drifted away. Just in time he grabbed onto the gunwale and hooked the stern rope over his arm. He backed toward the bar, dragging her and the canoe with him.

"Are you okay?"

No answer.

As the water got shallower it was more difficult to drag her limp body. She couldn't keep her feet under her, so he half-slid, half-pulled her onto the bar to a patch of sedge grass then pulled the canoe up.

He rushed back to her. "Hello. Can you hear me?"

Her mouth moved and she muttered. "Mmm. I'm fine, David."

"What's your name?" Dan tried to recall what he'd learned in the first aid course he took when he worked for the Yukon Highways Department, something called the 'recovery position.' He rolled her onto her side. She was obviously in the latter stages of hypothermia. She needed to be warmed up as quickly as possible.

"Oh, fuck." He ran to the canoe and pulled out his dry bag then yanked out his sleeping bag as he ran back. He opened the bag, laid it out on the grass and rolled her on top, folded the other side over her and zipped it up. She groaned: that was good, but she still showed no sign of being aware what was going on. The sleeping bag alone wasn't enough. She needed heat. He stripped off his wet clothes and unzipped the bag.

"C'mere, Raz. Better two warm bodies than one." He wondered what his friend Artie would say if he saw him now, three days down the South

Macmillan, in the middle of nowhere, climbing into his sleeping bag with a nude woman.

David paced in front of the windows in his office. The glare off breeze-ruffled water reminded him of the boat, which reminded him of Melanie. Everything reminded him of Melanie. It was hard to concentrate on the franchise deal, and he couldn't afford to be distracted. It was a turning point for *Chives Restaurants*, the biggest deal of his life. People would be paying him to use the company name. If he could pull it off, the real money would start rolling in.

Tina Lewis, his assistant, walked in. He had lucked out finding her. She was smart, competent, loyal, and had beautiful breasts.

She put her open laptop on her end of the desk, the only part that wasn't cluttered. "Aaron's on his way." She watched him pace. "Anything wrong?"

Tina had a talent for reading people's faces and now she was regarding his.

"No. Why?"

"You look worried. That's all."

"Why shouldn't I be?"

"Oh, you have every reason to be. I've got several files open here, any one of which would give a shark an ulcer. I just wondered..." She turned to the computer screen, a slight smile on her face.

What was she thinking? Had she seen him leave the party with Melanie the other night?

Aaron Stevens, the company solicitor strolled through the door, immaculate in his expensive suit and shoes, every hair perfectly in place. David had always said, when picking a solicitor or a surgeon, always choose the best dressed ones.

Tina turned to Aaron. "How are things, Aaron?"

Aaron put a hand on Tina's shoulder. "Great. Better still if you'd have dinner with me tonight."

She smiled sweetly. "I'm meeting your wife and kids for dinner tonight. But I'm sure they'd love it if you join us. Want me to phone her and confirm?"

Aaron threw back his head and laughed. *A little too hard,* David thought. It was a running gag between them, although he sensed Tina was getting a bit tired of it. Aaron made it all seem harmless and playful, but David knew if Aaron thought he had a chance he'd go for it.

Tina went back to her computer. "Well, fellas, what would you like to start with: insurance, licenses and permits, American health regulations, the trade shows?"

Aaron joined David at the window. "I've already dealt with the insurance people. I'd rather talk about sailing. Look out there, David. Wouldn't it be nice to spend a lazy day at the helm, maybe head out across the strait and pick up a stronger breeze?"

David followed Aaron's gaze. "Um…yeah, nice."

"I saw you out on the dock a couple of nights ago."

"Huh?"

"I was in the dining room."

David turned away from Aaron, feeling heat rise up his neck to his cheeks. "Yeah, I was showing the boat to…uh…a person."

Aaron's feigned look of surprise belied his teasing tone. "Are you thinking of selling *Hannah's Dream*? If so, I know a few people who might…"

"No. Maybe. I don't know."

What the hell was Aaron up to? David stalked to his chair behind the desk and motioned Aaron to sit opposite. "Let's get right to the trade shows. That's our priority."

Aaron lingered by the window. "That was a smart move, David, showing off the boat on a beautiful evening, a three-quarter moon rising over the mountains, throwing silver reflections onto…"

"Aaron, I'm not selling the boat. Now shut up about it and sit down."

Aaron sidled up to the desk. "Next you'll be selling your racehorse."

Why was Aaron needling him? Was he so thick he couldn't catch the mood or was he jealous? He saw Tina smile again and shake her head as she fussed with the laptop. "What is it, Tina?"

"What is…what?"

"You shook your head."

"It was nothing."

"You shook your head at something."

"It was nothing! A little shake of the head, a moment of existential angst. Now can we talk about the trade shows?"

"Yes. Okay. Good." He thumped the desk with his fingers, composed himself and addressed Aaron, who now sat in the chair opposite. "What's the latest on the Seattle thing?"

"The meeting's all set with the American lawyers. We go down there the day after…"

The phone rang. David gave Tina a look of exasperation. "I thought you would have turned the thing off."

"I'll get it." She picked up the phone. "Hello, Chives Restaurants, Tina here."

She listened for a while. "Just a moment. I'll see if he's in." She covered the mouthpiece. "David, it's Paul Williams."

David made a face. "That asshole. Tell him I'm out. Tell him I'm sick. Tell him I'm dead."

Tina spoke into the phone. "Mr. Hellman can't come to the phone, but I can…" She paused, listened then covered the mouthpiece again. "He says it's urgent. He sounds upset. It's something about Hannah."

David looked at her a moment, confused then grabbed the phone. "What is it, Paul?"

"I had to call to tell you not to worry."

"Not to worry? What the hell do you mean calling me and telling me not to worry? What's…"

"I wanted you to hear it from me."

"Just tell me. Is Hannah all right?" A sudden feeling of dread swept over him.

"Hannah is missing."

"Missing." He saw Tina and Aaron exchange worried glances. "Since when?"

"Three days ago."

David rose from his chair. "Three days ago. And you're just calling me now? Paul, what the fuck?"

"David, I only found out a few hours ago. It took a while for Andrea and Martin to…"

"Those two morons. Too busy fucking their brains out to call."

"They started the search. They contacted the RCMP. They even got the outfitter and his clients to help."

David walked slowly around his desk to the window as Paul talked about rain, cloud cover, aircraft on hold, searchers delayed. He had feared this, almost to the point of expecting it. But Paul and Hannah hadn't listened. She had laughed, even teased him for being obsessed with that documentary, the one about a climb on a remote South American peak gone terribly wrong. And now it had come true. Now in his mind's eye was Hannah, two broken legs, crawling through the snow.

Paul was still talking. "The press is going to be contacting you. I can't stress enough how important it is that you say nothing until…"

"Paul, I told you this was going to happen. Goddamned publicity stunt." His pulse pounded. "What the hell do you propose to do?"

"Well, CBC wants an interview. It's going to air on the national news and I was hoping you could be here at the office at 5:30."

David was at the window now, looking out over sunlight on glittering water. Traffic buzzed on the street below. The paths along the shore were crowded with walkers and joggers enjoying the sun, talking, eating, laughing, people going about their lives. He turned back to stare at Tina and Aaron. His decision was sudden.

Paul's voice sounded tinny. "David? Are you still there?"

"Yes. Goodbye, Paul." As he clicked the phone off he heard Paul trying to stop him.

Aaron spoke up. "Hannah's missing?"

He walked back to the desk and put the phone down. "I'm going up there."

Aaron said, "Where…to the Yukon?"

"No, to the roof to jump off. Of course to the Yukon."

There was a look of disbelief on Aaron's face. "But surely they'll have searchers out looking."

"Yeah."

"Then there's nothing you can do. They're professionals. You're a restauranteur, not Davy Crocket."

"Tina, book me on the next flight to Yellowknife."

"You mean Whitehorse?"

"Whatever. Just get me there."

Aaron stood up, put his hands on the desk and leaned in. "David, this is crazy."

"I know."

"You can't leave now. We have the meeting with the Americans, the trade shows, the…"

"It's Hannah out there. Tina, you go to Seattle. You know as much as I do."

Tina looked panicked. "David, Aaron's right. You can't go. You're the key to this whole deal. The Seattle lawyers want to see you, not me."

"Book the flight, Tina."

"But who's going to look after the office?"

"I dunno. Find somebody."

"David, you're making a mistake."

"Maybe. What the hell do you take to the Yukon…toilet paper?"

She watched from the bare top of a dead spruce as the other bobblehead, the floater with the littlewolf, made its nest from a framework of straight dead sticks covered by the crackly blue skin the creatures often used. Good stuff. Torn up it went all stringy. Good for making nests.

She called. "Shit." She would be feasting if not for the floater bobblehead. Maybe they were a mated pair. Her mate had left with the young female. She tucked in her breast feather and leapt off the branch gathering air under her wings, pushing upward in strong thrusts to gain altitude, making a long curving turn toward the hillside to catch an updraft. Her chance to taste bobblehead was gone for now, but this pair would bear watching. The floater with the littlewolf had a boomstick. It was hunting moose. There might be a big gut pile to feed on. Maybe the dying one might still die.

The smell of smoke and the crackle of a fire. Was this part of the dream she'd been having? Not a dream really—just jumbled, confused images: dark shapes reaching out to grasp, gnarled clawed fingers ripping her clothes, piercing her skin, dark pools like malignant mouths sucking at her feet, holding her, pulling her down, insects flying into her eyes and mouth, itching behind her ears and in her hair. A vague memory tickled the back of her mind—an angel wearing a shimmering black cloak. Then water—cool, cool water, soothing at first, relieving the itch, but then closing over her mouth and nose. Struggling, her arms and legs refusing to move.

The itching started again. She scratched behind her ear and felt the pain of raw flesh under her fingernails. She opened her eyes. Dull ripples of firelight reflected off a blue plastic tarp held up by a framework of poles. The tarp sloped away from the fire. A pair of jeans and a t-shirt hung on a rope stretched near the flames.

A fire. How did she get here? There was a vague recollection of her husband David, but it might have been a dream. The warmth felt so good on her face. A black pot sat bubbling on a small wire rack. The sound of a stick breaking came to her then the dull thwack of an axe, and another, and another, footsteps crunching on sand, coming closer. A black and white dog lay curled under the tripod of poles at one end of the shelter. The dog's eyes looked up as the feet approached—black rubbers over moccasins. The rubbers reminded her of the overshoes her father wore to the office when she was a kid, except these were higher with rounded toes. The dog's tail thumped the ground. A pile of sticks landed near the fire.

The man went down on his knees, squinting as the smoke swirled into his face. He wore a blue windbreaker over a dirty brown sweater with a ragged hole just below the neck, blue jeans. A purple ball cap with a 'Yukon Brewing' logo covered his short-cropped black hair. She noticed his large dark eyes, full lips, wide face, brown skin. He picked up a spoon near the fire and stirred the pot. Then he looked over the fire at her and did a double-take.

"Oh, you're awake. How are you feeling?"

"Okay, I guess…No. Actually, I feel lousy. I'm so thirsty."

"Here, I've got some tea made. I'll get you a cup."

"Thanks."

He poured a cup of tea and moved around the fire to squat beside her. She pushed herself up on one hand and the sleeping bag fell off her shoulders. She suddenly realized she was naked. She pulled the bag up around her and shifted to a sitting position, looking at him with alarm.

"I found your clothes on the top of the bank where you went in. They're right there under the…Hey, Raz, Get off those clothes. Go lie down somewhere else." The dog slinked away behind the tarp. "I found your boots, socks, panties, pants, t-shirt and fleece. No jacket or coat. I washed the mud out of your boots." He pointed to the fire where her hiking boots were propped to dry. "They're still soaked." He held the clothes out to her. "I can go away for awhile if you wanna put these on."

"I think I'll wait a bit. Do you have any Tylenol? My head is killing me."

"Sorry, no."

She sipped her tea. "This is good."

"You hungry?"

"Yes. Very."

Dan stood up and moved to the other side of the fire, put on a glove and picked up the pot. "I made soup."

"What kind is it?"

"Chicken noodle. It's just packaged soup, but…"

"I'm a vegetarian."

"Huh? Oh…Look, I think you should have it. You gotta eat something."

"I don't know."

"There's hardly any chicken in it."

"Okay. Thanks. I'll have it."

"Good." He poured some soup into a mug, came back around the fire and handed it to her. "Careful, it's hot." She blew over the mug, sipped then gulped hungrily without taking her face away from the mug as the steam billowed out with every breath. He said, "So, how did you lose your canoe?"

"I didn't have a canoe."

"You had to have a canoe—or some kinda boat."

"No. I was on foot."

"That's impossible. You can't get here on foot."

"Where's here?"

"The South Macmillan River, about eighty, ninety kilometers from the North Canol Road. Maybe more. Where did you come from?"

"We were on Mount Riddell. I got separated from the others so I headed back to our camp. It was foggy and raining. I guess I went the wrong way."

"You walked here from Mount Riddel? Holy shit. That's hard country. How did you get through the burn? It must be like pick-up-sticks in there."

"I don't remember much about it. I guess I was kind of out of it."

"Wait a minute. What's your name?"

"Hannah Weinberg."

"Right. Grizzly Watch. I heard you on the radio and saw your picture in the paper. You look different."

She looked out to the river then back and forth to the mountains on either side. Her attention was caught by the green canoe, sitting on the muddy flat shore of the backwater. Just under the gunwale was the name 'Hellman' in large white letters. "David?"

"Pardon?"

"Why is my husband's name on that canoe? Is David here?"

"No. It's the brand name." When she didn't answer he continued. "Hellman Canoes. Does your husband own Hellman Canoes?"

She put her hand to her forehead. "No, he owns restaurants. Sorry, I'm kinda..."

"They'll be looking for you."

"Looking for me? David will be looking for me?"

"Was your husband with you up on Riddell?"

"No. He was supposed to pick me up on the Sea to...or maybe not. It's hard to remember."

"They'll have every helicopter and plane and search dog in the territory out. You're big news. Everybody was talking about you when I left Ross."

"Ross?"

"Ross River. I stay there."

"Oh. Are they still looking?"

He reached to the pile of sticks and put some on the fire. "Sure. They'll still be looking." He thought for a moment. "The only problem is..."

"What?"

"Well, they're not gonna be looking here. I mean, no one would think you could get this far."

"What day is it?"

"The fifteenth."

"The fifteenth? That's...three days. They probably think I'm dead."

"You almost were."

"Oh, yeah. I'm sorry, I don't even know who you are."

"Dan McKay."

"Thanks. Thanks for...everything. I guess I'm lucky you came along when you did. What are you doing here?"

"Moose hunting."

"Oh my god. No." She put down her empty cup.

"What do you mean?"

"Grizzly Watch. I'm here to protest the killing of grizzly bears and I get rescued by a hunter. Shit."

"I'm not hunting grizzlies."

"It's the same thing."

"No."

"Are you a First Nations hunter?"

He laughed. "Oh, I see. If I'm an Indian it's okay. We're kinda like wildlife. Well, you're halfway there, but sorry to disappoint you. My father was white."

"I can't help thinking what the media will do with this."

"Don't worry. As soon as they see my truck they'll know I'm an Indian. It's an old beater. If you want, I can hang a bunch of feathers from the mirror."

She watched him as he laughed then the realization of her predicament struck her. "How long before we get to...I mean you...where are you going?"

"Pelly Crossing. About nine, ten days. Maybe more."

"Ten days. That'll make it the 25th. Oh, no. Oh, my head hurts."

"I'll make you something for that headache."

"I thought you didn't have any Tylenol."

"I'll brew up some willow tea. You can put on your clothes while I cut some bark."

"You've already seen me without my clothes."

"Seen you? I was in the sack with you."

"What?" She pulled the sleeping bag tight around her neck.

"There was no other way to warm you up."

"Oh. Yeah. I guess...well...thanks."

"Don't worry. I was a perfect gentleman. Besides, you were a cold fish."

Raz trotted along behind His Dan to the gravel bar. When the man stopped and began cutting the bushes, he trotted out onto the curve of the bar and headed downstream, happy to explore the smells, maybe surprise an animal crossing the river. Moose hunting with His Dan was the best, out here where the smells were potent and exciting. The warm earthy smell of sedge meadow where the voles scurried, the greasy bear smell, the tasty fish smell where a creek met the river. The air was charged, alive, brittle. Anticipation hung sharp in the air—the rutting smell.

But His Dan was not hunting now. He was intent on the stranger. Maybe she was his new mate. Maybe he was adding to the pack at last. Maybe there would be little dans. That would be good for the pack. He missed Starla, the little dan from the old pack who liked to wrestle and play games of tag, but he didn't miss being tied in the yard at the old pack's home. The new home was better—freedom, more time with His Dan. There were some big, rough, dangerous dogs there, but he was safe with His Dan.

He sniffed the spot where His Dan had got into the bed bag with the new mate. He sifted the odors, concentrating, separating, divining. His Dan's smell was strongest, but spruce, smoke, and his own smell stood out clearly. He circled, testing the flattened grass where they had bedded. Her smell was there: female, near the end of her cycle, soon to have the big female scent. He nosed the ground again. She wasn't a meat eater. His Dan had never mated with a herbivore. He sniffed again—they hadn't mated.

He heard a splash in the river. He almost ran out onto the sandbar, but stopped. First he must urinate on this spot.

SEPT. 16

Hannah had laid awake thinking since before the sun came up. The bitter tea Dan made for her had taken the edge off her headache and she had slept soundly, but she had awoken early, worrying about her predicament, the embarrassment of getting lost, the worry she was causing. How could she have been so stupid, breaking the first rule of wilderness survival? If you're lost, stay put. She had given seminars on the subject. This would be the end of Grizzly Watch, the whole animal rights movement would be humiliated and she would be a laughingstock. It couldn't be worse. No, it could be worse. She could be dead.

Dan had given her his sleeping bag, laid down a thick bed of spruce boughs and put on an extra sweater, covering himself with a stained canvas tarp and changing his ball cap for a wool toque. He must have been cold. The morning had been frigid, with frost covering the tarp shelter and the surrounding sedge grass. But the sun had soon turned it to a fine sheen of tiny water droplets. Now they sat comfortably in their shirtsleeves eating oatmeal.

"Aren't there any towns closer than Pelly Crossing?"

"Nope."

"No roads?"

He spooned up the last of his oatmeal "Nope."

"Mining camps, air strips?"

He put his empty bowl down, picked up a stick and slid it under the wire handle on the pot boiling on the fire. "Lyle Kessler has a fly-in camp about a day and a half downriver. There might be somebody there." He held out the pot. "More coffee?"

"Thanks." She held out her cup as he poured. "I can't accept help from him."

"Oh…right."

She took the canned milk he offered her. "Shit…Are you sure its ten days to Pelly Crossing? I mean, is there any way to get there sooner?"

Dan poured himself coffee. "Maybe we can shave off one day but…"

"Could we travel at night?"

He laughed. "We have to be able to see the gravel bars and the sweepers."

"What about going back upstream? You said you've been on the river for three days. If I could get back to the North Canol Road I could rejoin Grizzly Watch where I left off."

"Sure. We can be there by Halloween." He sipped his coffee and turned to her with a smile.

"What do you mean?"

"We'd be paddling against the current. And there're rapids upstream. We'd have to pole and line and drag the canoe. And then there's the canyon. No, there's no other way. We have to go downstream. And if I get a moose, it'll add at least a day."

"You're still going to hunt a moose?"

"Yeah."

"You can't."

Dan looked at her then went back to his coffee.

"I'll pay you. I'll pay you to get me out of here."

Dan smiled. "How much?"

"Well, what's a moose worth?"

"Huh?"

"How much does it cost to buy a moose?"

"You can't buy moose meat. It's illegal."

"I know, but you could buy the equivalent in beef or pork or chicken, anything you want."

"I want moose meat."

"Well then, what is it worth to you?"

He smiled. "How about ten thousand?"

She glared at him. "You're enjoying this, aren't you? Only a sicko takes pleasure in another person's pain."

"Sicko is my middle name."

She thought for awhile. ARN would never agree to it. She and David could afford it, though. "All right. It's a deal. Ten thousand."

He looked up sharply. She could see he was surprised, examining her expression to see if she was serious. "I'll think about it...but it's not really about money."

"What is it about then?"

"It's...you wouldn't understand."

"What makes you think that?"

"Let me put it this way. My mother is an old native elder. She suffers from arthritis. She can't get out hunting anymore. I hunt all the meat she needs. She takes the skin and tans it. It's her way of life. She needs me to get a moose. Now, do you want me to let down my poor, sainted mother?"

Hannah knew he was making a joke of it, but she could hear the edge of irritation in his voice.

"Can't you take me to Pelly Crossing and then go out again and catch one?"

"Get or shoot."

"Pardon?"

"You don't catch a moose. You get one, or you shoot one."

"Whatever. Could you?"

"I could, but the rut will be over by the time we get to Pelly. The bulls will all be gone."

"What do you mean?"

"They don't eat much during the rut, and with all the thrashing about and fighting and mating they get worn out. They have to go up into the mountains to build up fat for the winter."

"So go up in the mountains and catch...shoot one."

"And how do I get a moose down out of the mountains? A big bull can weigh...Nevermind."

She could see he was finished considering it. "Oh."

"See, right now it's early in the rut. They've got lots of fat, they're in good shape and they're eager. They're not hooked up with any cows yet, so they come to a call. Plus you're on the river. You just have to pack the meat to the…"

Hannah wasn't listening. As he talked she held her head in her hands and thought about her limited options. She had to go down the river with this guy on his hunting trip. The press would eat it up. Grizzly Watch would become a joke. How could it be any worse? She felt the twinge of a menstrual cramp. She muttered to herself. "Oh shit." She remembered the package of tampons in her pack. She lifted her head and looked up at the hillside.

Dan was still talking. "…and it's always better to have the meat in bigger pieces 'cause…"

She interrupted him. "You didn't happen to find my pack up there with my clothes, did you?"

"No."

She stared out over the water, feeling tears beginning to well. She squeezed her eyes shut. "Shit, shit, shit, shit."

"Hey, it's not that bad. Have some more oatmeal and quit worrying. Look, it's a beautiful day, the sun is shining, and you're on the most gorgeous river on Earth. Enjoy it."

Hannah stood up abruptly, walked toward the river and looked upstream. "I know what I'll do. I'll walk back."

"Don't be stupid."

"I walked here. I can walk back."

"No tent, no matches, no food. You don't even have a jacket."

"I was assuming you would lend me enough supplies to…"

"I won't."

"What? You'd let me go with nothing?"

"No, I won't do that either."

"So you think you can stop me?"

"If I have to."

Hannah glared. Dan stared back impassively then smiled. "But I don't think I'll have to."

"Oh yeah?"

"I think you're too smart for that." He began to gather up the dishes and pots. "If you want to worry about something, worry about food."

"Why?"

"Take a wild guess."

"There's not enough?"

"It's gonna be tight. Really tight. And you being a vegetarian doesn't help."

"Sure, blame the victim."

"Victim." He laughed. "The only vegetarian food I have is oatmeal and flour, noodles and a bit of rice. Not much of that. Not enough for two. Even the couple of cans of beans have bacon. I've got some carrots and a couple of apples, but they won't go far. I brought my fishing rod, though. Do you eat fish?"

"No."

"Great."

"What about berries and wild plants, roots and things?"

He began to stuff the sleeping bag into its sack. "Not many good berries down in the bottom of the valley, mostly highbush cranberry and a few mossberries. The really good berries are up high. Lots of rosehips, though, and we might find a few wild onions on the sandbars, and there should be lots of good mushrooms after all the rain. But that won't work. It'd take hours to pick enough to feed you, which would cut into our traveling time."

"Catch-22."

"Yup. But that's the Yukon for you. Not vegetarian friendly. The real food has legs or fins. Here, finish this oatmeal."

She took the pot from him. "What about you?"

"I've had enough."

"I don't believe you."

"I'm on a diet."

"You're not."

"I'm a better hunter if I have that edge of hunger." He laughed. "My Dad used to say that. Of course he was joking. He was hopeless in the bush. He loved going out hunting, but he never could bring himself to kill a moose. My mom would shoot it and tell people he did." Dan laughed again.

Hannah watched him laugh—expressive brown eyes, white straight teeth, generous mouth...good looking...very.

"You're not from Whitehorse, are you?"

"No." David didn't want to talk to the large, loud man sitting beside him on the plane.

"What did you say your name was?"

"David Hellman."

"David Hellman. I'm sure I've seen you somewhere before. What takes you to Whitehorse?"

"My wife is…" Why should he tell this cretin his wife was lost in the wilderness, possibly dead. Dead. He didn't want to think about that. "Uh, business."

"What business are you in?"

Wasn't this idiot going to leave him alone? "The restaurant business."

"Really? That's great. Which restaurant?"

"Chives."

"Hey, that's where I've seen you. On TV. That CBC show, *Venture*. Something about franchising. That was a good show. Hey, you gonna open a Chives in Whitehorse?"

Fat chance. David imagined a typical Whitehorse restaurant meal— overcooked pork chops, frozen french fries, watery vegetables out of a can, elegantly served on a plastic table cloth covered with cigarette burns. He lied. "Possibly."

"Let me give you my card. I'm a building contractor." The man fished his wallet out of his hip pocket. As he did he squeezed over. David was pressed against the window and a whiff of body odor reached him. Did everybody in Whitehorse smell like this? "If you need something built, you call me. I do renovations, too."

David took the card and read it. 'Caribou Contracting, big or small we do it all'. How original. 'Ron Hewitt,' followed by an address. The flight attendant was coming down the aisle handing out newspapers. David chose a *Globe and Mail*. He turned to the cryptic crossword and folded the paper. Maybe it would distract him from worrying about Hannah. Ron got *The Whitehorse Star*. It was a miracle this moron could read. Maybe the man would shut up now and leave him alone.

The headline on *The Whitehorse Star* caught David's eye as Ron sat looking at the front page: "Hannah Weinberg Still Missing: third day of search turns up nothing."

Ron Hewitt snorted derisively and pointed to the headline. "Have you heard about this wingnut?"

David couldn't take his eyes off the front page. There was a picture of a helicopter lifting off, mountains in the background, a pile of equipment on the ground. He couldn't make out the caption. "Uh, no, I...a little. Do you mind if I read that?"

"No problem. Be my guest." They exchanged papers as Ron continued. "I said this was going to happen. I told my wife the stupid broad would get lost or killed or something. What a bunch of dummies. They go out there to stop the hunters from shooting bears. Those guys are armed. Nobody else around. You don't have to be Einstein to figure out that one."

David fought back the urge to tell this jerk to shut his mouth. He was relieved when Ron turned his attention to David's crossword. Feeling panic welling inside, he turned to page two and read:

Grizzly Watch on Hold as Search Enters Day Three.

The outlook has not improved for Hannah Weinberg, animal rights activist and leader of Grizzly Watch. Searchers have been combing the Mount Riddell area in the remote mountains north of Ross River. Spokesman for The RCMP search and rescue team, Sergeant Steve Godwin, says early attempts were hampered by clouds and rain, but now that good weather has returned, no effort will be spared to find the missing woman.

"We've sent our team into the area and enlisted the help of the local outfitter, whose camp is situated nearby. We have dogs working the hills, helicopters and fixed wing aircraft. If she's out there we'll find her."

Asked what he thought her chances of survival are, he stated, "If she stays put, her chances are good. If not, well, it's anybody's guess. She's experienced in the bush and she was carrying a pack with some supplies, food and matches, etc., so we're hopeful."

Paul Williams, head of Animal Rights Now, the group sponsoring Grizzly Watch, was unavailable for comment. His office in Vancouver said he is on his way to the Yukon to join in the search and co-ordinate his group's activities.

Martin Montgomery and Andrea Felinii, Ms. Weinberg's colleagues at their base camp on the North Canol Road, refused comment.

The article went on to describe the rugged terrain, quoted the outfitter and a couple of American hunters, and compared Hannah's situation to other search and rescue efforts, some successful, some not. This did not look good. At the bottom he read, "See page six for related stories." He turned to page six. It was letters to the editor. He read the first one:

Is anybody surprised when these animal rights Nazis come to the Yukon and get themselves into trouble? These city people have no place telling us how we should live our lives and manage our resources. Yukon grizzly bears are not threatened. It's down south where urban sprawl and highways and shopping centers have driven them out of their natural habitat. Why don't these bleeding hearts stay home? It's her fault she got lost out there, and Yukon taxpayers should not have to foot the bill for her rescue. I for one hope she learns her lesson. Wouldn't it be sweet if she got mauled by a grizzly? Dave Jenson, Faro.

David was appalled at the venom directed at his wife in the letters, all but one a variation on the theme of the first. The last was the only one sympathetic to Hannah:

Hannah Weinberg is a brave woman who is simply following her beliefs. Whether you agree with her or not, at least she has the courage to stand up for her cause. How many of us would leave the comfort of our homes and risk life and limb to protect defenseless animals from people who feel the need to prove their manhood by killing something? I am sickened by the reaction to her plight from some of the so-called 'civilized' people in this territory. I can only hope she will be found alive and well and we can put this unfortunate episode behind us. It reflects badly on all Yukoners.

Sarah Harrison, Whitehorse

At least one Yukoner wasn't howling for Hannah's blood. David stared out the plane's window. What would he do once he got to Whitehorse? He hadn't really thought much about that. It wasn't like him to have no plan of action. He supposed he'd have to go to this, what was the name, Mount Riddell? Where was it? How would he get there and what would he do when he arrived? He turned to Ron Hewitt, who sat puzzling over David's cryptic crossword.

"Excuse me. Mr...." The man ignored him. What was the matter with this ape? "Excuse me."

"Huh? Oh, sorry. Once I start doing one of these, the plane could fall out of the sky and I wouldn't notice."

David looked down at the crossword. It was almost finished. It usually took him hours. "I'm sorry, I've forgotten your name."

"Ron Hewitt. I'm havin' a little trouble with 14 across. 'Two companies joining on a silk product.' Six letters, starts with C."

"Ron, I was wondering. Where is this place my...uh, that woman went missing?"

"Cocoon."

"I beg your pardon?"

"Cocoon. Two companies – 'co', 'co', joining 'on'. Cocoon. It's a silk product." He smiled, shook his head and printed it in. "I love these cryptic crosswords. My wife and I do them in bed together. At our age, there ain't much else happenin' in the sack, if you know what I mean." He laughed and gave David a nudge.

"Yeah I guess. So do you know where Mount Riddell is?"

"Sure, it's up the North Canol. About three, four hours from Ross. Ross River, or Lost Liver as it's affectionately known. I built the community hall there. Been up the North Canol fishing a few times. Beautiful country."

"The North Canol. Is that how you get to Ross River?"

"Sorta. You take the Mayo Road to Carmacks then take the Robert Campbell to Ross."

"The Robert Campbell? What's that, a train?"

"No, it's a highway. You gonna open a Chives restaurant in Ross?"

"No, I..."

"I'm kidding. But if you're interested, I could find you a ride to Ross. A buddy of mine's doing a job there. He's back and forth to Whitehorse all the time."

"No, I appreciate the offer, but I'll probably rent a car. I can rent a car in Whitehorse, can I?"

"You can get anything you want in Whitehorse, except privacy."

"Oh." David forced a laugh, sighed and looked out the window again while Ron went back to the crossword. Looking down, David saw mountains, lakes, and rivers stretching to the horizon, not a road or a building in sight, an immense uninhabited wilderness. Then he turned back. He pointed at the headline. "So, what do you think this Hannah Weinberg's chances are?"

"Certain death."

"Really? But..."

"Certain death. Seven down. 'Juggle and eat thrice for a sure end'. It's an anagram of 'and eat thrice'. Jesus, I shoulda got that long ago." He printed it in. "Sorry, what'd you say?"

"I was just wondering about Hannah. Hannah Weinberg. You think she's alive?"

"Who knows. I hear the weather got better. The first two days were pure shit, though. I wouldn't want to be out there in the rain with no tent. Friggin' cold up in those mountains this time of year. If she got down into the trees where she could make a fire and just hunkered down, that'd be her best bet."

"So, she could be fine?"

"Yeah, sure."

"And even if she had a fire, they might not see it at first, right?"

"That's true. There's a lot of ground to cover. Even with aircraft. I know. I've flown over that country."

David felt much better. There was a chance. A good one. Hannah was mentally tough, and she was fit. She would be all right. She had to be. "Thanks, Ron."

"What for?"

"For the paper." Smiling, he handed the newspaper to Ron.

"Hey, no sweat. Here's yours. I finished the cryptic. Hope you don't mind."

"Oh, no. That's fine. I don't need it anymore."

Ron looked at the front page and thought for a while. "The thing that'll kill you out there is hypothermia. You get cold and wet and you shiver uncontrollably. If it's raining it's hard to start a fire, impossible sometimes. If you don't get warm soon, your brain starts to shut down. You can't think straight. And when the clouds close in, you can't see a foot in front of you. You can walk off a cliff without even knowing it was there. Last year they found a sheep hunter at the bottom of a slide. The ravens had picked him clean. I hear they start with the eyeballs. Then there's the bears. You surprise a sow with her cubs and you're dead meat, or one with a kill. Hell, sometimes they attack for no reason at all. Not just grizzlies either. There was a black bear a couple years ago killed two people and maimed another. He was actually hunting humans—to eat them. There're lots of bears out there. Especially in the Mount Riddell area."

"Would you like a drink, sir?" The flight attendant broke into Ron's tirade.

David nodded. "A scotch, please...a double."

"Take it easy. Don't wear yourself out." Dan couldn't believe how hard she was paddling, considering what she'd been through. They had stopped for a break a couple of hours ago. She ate two pieces of bannock like a starving dog. He had a pepperoni, just one in case she changed her mind about eating meat. "Let the river do the work for awhile."

"The more I paddle the sooner we'll get there."

"Suit yourself, but I'm a little worried you're gonna get sick or something. You haven't had time to recover."

"I never get sick."

She paddled harder. Dan was tempted to tell her the real reason he wanted her to ease up. They were traveling through good moose country—lot's of back channels, meadows and sloughs just off the river. A few times, Raz had raised his head and sniffed the air. Then there was her weight in the canoe. It would displace 120 pounds of moose meat. He thought about the ten thousand dollars, meant as a joke, a wild exaggeration, but she had agreed to it. That much money could go a long way. Maybe he could hire a lawyer. The thought depressed him. He pushed it from his mind.

Up ahead was a sandbar. Behind the screen of willows there appeared to be an opening. It could be a meadow, a good place for moose. He jiggled the canoe to get Hannah's attention. She continued paddling, so he said in a whisper, "Stop paddling."

"What? What do you want?"

"Sh. Keep it down."

"Why?"

"Sh. We'll stop up ahead."

"Why are you whispering?"

"There might be moose. Don't wanna spook them."

"Oh no. I thought you weren't going to..."

Dan gave her an angry look. "Be quiet."

Hannah glared at him then put her paddle down. It clunked in the bottom of the canoe.

"For Christ's sake." He edged the canoe up to shore and stepped out, whispering, "Stay, Raz." He picked up his rifle and went to the bow to get the rope. He searched the shore for something to tie the boat to, but the willows were too far. He bent towards Hannah. "Just keep the canoe here."

"How long is this going to take?"

At least now she was keeping her voice down. "Not long."

He went slowly toward the willows, checking the sand for tracks as he went. A grizzly had walked across the bar. He worked his way carefully through the willows, stopping every few meters to listen. The meadow was large. It curved back out of sight behind big spruce trees. He reached to his chest for his binoculars, put them to his eyes and scanned the edge of the meadow. This time of day the moose were likely lying down so there was little chance of seeing one. Still, you never knew, especially during the rut. He moved along the edge of the willows for a better look at the back of the meadow. Nothing. He headed back to the boat. Just before he reached the sand bar he found a spot where the sedge grass had been crushed flat. A moose had lain there. Nearby he saw a clump of willows splintered and broken and smelled the familiar odor of a bull moose in rut.

Dan emerged from the willows and walked across the sand bar to the canoe. Hannah still sat in the bow. As he approached she stuck her paddle into the sand and tried to push the boat out to float it. He put his hand on the gunwale beside her and held the canoe. "Wait. I wanna show you something."

"I just want to get going."

"Come on, you'll be interested. It won't take long."

"There's no time. I've been thinking. If I get off this river by the 22nd, Grizzly Watch can still go ahead."

"I don't wanna go yet. And you should stretch your legs. Come on. It'll only take a few minutes."

"All right." She got out of the boat and Dan pulled the bow up onto the sand. "Come on Raz." The dog leaped eagerly onto the bar and began sniffing the ground. "Heel."

"He's certainly well behaved."

"Yeah. I never used to take a dog hunting with me. They scare away the animals. But Raz is different. Smartest dog I've ever known. He seems to know exactly when to be quiet and when something's up." They started across the bar, the dog walking between them. "My dad always said you shouldn't own a dog that's smarter than you are." Halfway to the willows Dan stopped and pointed down. "There." The dog sniffed at the grizzly tracks briefly then lost interest.

Hannah looked down at the track. "Grizzly bear. It almost looks human."

"Yeah. Look at those claw prints." Five deep narrow impressions formed an arc about two inches away from the toe pads. Dan spread the fingers of one hand above the print. They barely stretched across. "Probably a big male."

"Do you think he's still around?"

"No. These are old...maybe a month. He was probably down here when the salmon were spawning."

"I'd love to see one."

"Yeah, from the boat. Come on, I'll show you something else."

He led Hannah into the willows, stopped and pointed to the smashed branches. "Bull moose."

"Why did he do that?"

"It announces him to any other moose around, cows and bulls. Maybe he just needs to fight with something. I don't know." He pointed down to a muddy depression in the middle of the clearing. "That's his rutting pit."

They walked over to stand above it. Hannah sniffed and curled her nose. "What's that smell?"

"That's him. He dug out this hole then he peed in it. During the rut their pee stinks to high heaven. There's no other smell like it. Then he rolled in it to get the scent all over him. It means he's ready for love."

"Charming."

"Yeah, well, it might smell bad to you, but to a cow moose it's pure aphrodisiac. A love sonnet sent out on the breeze."

"And you want to eat something that smells that bad?"

"It's all on the outside. It doesn't affect the meat as long as you're careful when you cut him up."

Hannah made a face. "So, are we going now?"

"I don't know. It might be a good idea to camp somewhere nearby. This guy might still be around. Even if he's not, this could bring in others. It's a good spot. Let's go back to the boat, have a snack and figure it out."

Hannah was first to get to the boat. She turned to Dan as he came up behind her. "Why can't we just stay on the river? That must be a good way to see one."

"Low percentage. And I don't like shooting from the boat. Better to call them."

"So call as we go."

"But then he comes and we're already around the next bend. Tonight's going to be perfect. Clear and still. You can hear them answer. Even if they don't come right away, they could be here in the morning. They can hear a call for miles."

"But surely there are places just as good farther down."

"Maybe."

"The one that was here…who knows, he might have gone downstream."

"Yeah."

"And you said they come for miles if you call. You must be quite good at it."

He looked up and down the river. "Sure."

"So, does it really matter where you call from?"

"Well,…" He looked up and down the bar, across the river then pointed upstream. "That's the place to camp, at the head of the bar in those big spruce trees."

He reached for the bow rope in Hannah's hand. She snatched it away. "No, you said we were going on."

"I didn't." He took the rope from her. "Listen, we don't have much traveling time anyway. An hour, maybe two. This is a great spot."

"But we could go another twenty miles at least." Dan ignored her and started pulling the boat upstream. Hannah stood where she was. "This is forcible confinement."

"So call a cop."

As the plane flew down the valley on its approach to Whitehorse David watched out the window. A few scattered houses dotted the valley bottom with the occasional road or trail snaking higher into the mountains. Ron Hewitt looked over his shoulder, crowding closer.

"I might be able to see my house soon. Yeah, there it is. Ha. Oh, it's gone. There's Jim and Suzy's place. I see his corral. I still can't believe they split up. Should be able to see Cowley Lake soon. No, It's gonna be right under us. Too bad, but if you look straight down you'll see the old White Pass rail line."

"Hmm. That's interesting." All David could think about was Hannah.

The flight attendant came by and politely reminded Ron to sit back down and fasten his seat belt. "Sorry, Tracy. I wanted to see my house from up here." He turned back to David and pointed out the large mountain glowing red and purple in the afternoon sun. "Beautiful, eh? That's Golden Horn Mountain, and there's the ski hill, Mount Sima, and the old Whitehorse Copper Mine. I worked there for a couple of years back in the seventies."

The plane began its final descent and David braced himself. He knew it would be useless in any kind of emergency, but that didn't matter. It was a habit he couldn't rationalize, one of those instinctive things. He sensed Ron was doing the same, because for once the man was silent. All the passengers were silent. The plane put down and taxied to the terminal building. There was an expectant murmur of conversation: locals happy to be home again, visitors embarking on a new adventure. He suddenly felt alone. Why had he dropped everything to come up here? The decision had come with no thought at all. No wonder Tina and Aaron were surprised. He had surprised himself. He and Hannah had drifted farther and farther apart in the past few years, she with Grizzly Watch and he with his business. They never went sailing together anymore. They could go for weeks with barely a, *Hi, how was your day?* But when he found out Hannah was missing in the wilderness, a huge dark hole seemed to open before him. He wanted nothing to do with this town yet. He was looking forward to getting into a hotel room where he didn't have to talk to anyone. He needed some time to think.

He was the last passenger off the plane, and when he entered the lobby of the terminal he held back from the busy crowd around the luggage carousel. He saw Ron Hewitt greeted by a woman and three teenage girls. He noticed the rental car booths and decided he might as well start the paper work while he waited for his bags. He had taken only a few steps when a commotion at the nearest entrance caught his eye. People were coming through the doors. Some of them held microphones and had electronic equipment slung over their shoulders, others carried notepads or cameras.

Bringing up the rear was a man with a large video camera, his assistant carrying a boom mike. David turned to a waiting passenger. "Must be somebody important on this plane." He continued toward the car rental booths.

A voice called out from the group. "There he is."

David looked up. They were coming his way. He looked around but there was nobody behind him. A familiar voice called his name. "David, David it's great to see you." Paul Williams separated from the approaching group. They surrounded him and microphones were shoved up to his face. Questions were fired at him and cameras flashed. A large fuzzy object swooped down from above—the boom mike.

"Mr. Hellman, how do you feel about your wife's disappearance?"

"Do you think your wife is still alive?"

"Are you going to join the search?"

"Do you hold Animal Rights Now responsible in any way?"

"What were your wife's last words to you?"

David turned to Paul who now stood beside him. "Paul, what the hell?"

Paul faced the reporters. "Of course, Mr. Hellman does not hold ARN responsible. He's been working closely with us on Grizzly Watch from its inception. And yes, he's worried about Hannah, as we all are, but he's confident she's all right and will be found soon."

David was aghast. "Paul, that's bullshit and you know it. Why did you bring them here? I didn't want this. I didn't want you to meet me at the airport. I didn't even know you were here yet. And I told you, if anything happens to Hannah, I'll slice off your fucking..." He stopped and looked around him.

The reporters were writing furiously and the camera continued to roll. Paul leaned close to David and whispered, "Jesus, David. We have to put the best light on this. I thought meeting you here would be a boost for the project."

David glared at him then turned to the reporters. "I,...I, uh,...don't have anything to say right now. Maybe later. Please, I just want some time and...and..."

Paul jumped in quickly. "That's right. Mr. Hellman is upset, as anyone would be in his circumstances. You have to respect his privacy as a grieving...as a concerned husband. That's all for now. It's all over. Please, will you all just back off? There'll be plenty of opportunity to ask him questions at the press conference tomorrow."

David's head snapped back to Paul. "Press conference?"

The bear stepped cautiously out of the willows onto the gravel and looked up and down the river. The sun was getting lower, but it still beat down with uncomfortable heat. His paws were hot and sore and he was panting. The ache in his stomach was constant.

He walked painfully across the gravel to the river. The cold water swirling around his legs felt good, promising relief from his raging thirst. He slurped water greedily for a long time then let his body down into the cool, healing liquid. He raised his head and closed his eyes.

The respite from pain was short lived. The cold water hit his stomach and sudden nausea overcame him. He retched, over and over again, barely able to take a breath between violent bouts of vomiting. Finally, his breath coming in short shallow gasps, his convulsions subsided. He stood, panting, pulse pounding in his head, watching the greenish red cloud swirl away downstream.

The big sedge meadow was a green gold expanse ringed by yellow willow leaves against the dark rich green of mature spruce. Here and there an aspen shouted orange in the last slanting rays of the sun. The flanks of the distant mountains were clothed in red dwarf birch and gray black of exposed rock. A couple of ravens were calling on the far side of the meadow, their range of sounds surprisingly complex. A marsh hawk glided low over the meadow then suddenly spun and pounced down into the grass. It rose a moment later with a small dark object in its talons.

Dan had been watching the hawk with his binoculars. "He got something."

"What do you think it was?"

"A vole. These meadows are full of them. If you look down through the grass you can see their trails. Voles are everywhere—down in the valleys and up high in the mountains. I think if you were to separate all the mammals in the North into their species and weigh them, the voles would win."

Hannah gazed out over the meadow. "This is really gorgeous."

"Yeah."

"So, do you just sit here and wait for a moose to walk out?"

"Yeah, mostly, in between calls. It's about that time now." Dan propped his rifle against a willow bush and put his hands up to his mouth, forming a funnel shape. His index fingers pressed in to close off his nostrils. He took a few breaths then sucked in a big lungful of air and let out a long loud nasal moan, starting up high and descending down the scale, followed by a slightly shorter moan, beginning and ending a little lower than the first. These continued, shorter and lower in pitch until he finished with a sharp deep grunt that seemed to come from way down in his abdomen.

Hannah laughed. "Sounds like a constipated elephant."

"Sh. Listen." Dan cupped his hands behind his ears and closed his eyes, intense concentration on his face.

Hannah watched him as he finally brought his hands down and stepped back into the willows beside her. "That's it?"

"No, We'll wait for awhile, and then I'll call again."

"How long are we going to be here?"

"Until it's too dark to shoot. You can go back to the camp anytime you want. If there's no action I might call some more after dark. Try to bring one in for the morning."

The sun was almost down. It surprised her how quickly it was getting cold. She was glad of the big jacket and toque Dan had given her. Her hiking boots were still damp, but that discomfort was nothing compared to the piece of Dan's dishtowel she had cut off and stuffed into her panties to catch her menstrual flow. It worked after a fashion but washing it out and putting it back still damp was unpleasant. She wondered if he had noticed the missing end of towel. She would need more pieces, so it was only a matter of time. "What are you saying to the moose?"

"That's the cow call. My Mom taught me, but I've heard cows do it plenty of times. Most hunters think it means the cow is horny, but there was this woman in the Gaspe who did research on moose and she said that's not true. I saw a film about her one time. She could call a moose up to within five feet. According to her, the call I just made means the cow is irritated by a young bull. She's telling him to go away and don't bother her."

"What do you think?"

"I think she might be right. I once watched a cow with a yearling calf. She'd give the call and then chase the calf away as if she was pissed off and wanted to be left alone. Maybe it's both. Maybe she only wants a bull who can do the job."

"Do the job? Can't any bull do the job?"

"Probably, but think of it from her point of view. A big mature bull has proven he's got the stuff to survive. A young bull hasn't yet. Sexual selection. Darwin's most original idea."

"She wants an older man."

"I don't know how much you can compare it to humans. After all, women don't get irritable at different times in their cycles. If they do, I've never noticed it." He was looking out at the meadow, but Hannah could see a slight smile of irony on his face.

"And men would never fall for a sexy come hither. They're much too sensible for that."

Dan laughed. "I think it could be a bit of both. Even if she's not ready to mate, when a bull hears that call he knows she will be soon."

"No means yes to moose and men?"

"Who knows? Cows make lots of different sounds. They talk to their calves all the time. Nobody really knows what it all means. The thing is, it works. When the bull hears it, he can't resist. He throws caution to the wind."

Hannah thought about her husband David. "Sounds familiar. Men are slaves to their libidos."

"Yeah. I guess so."

"The poor bull moose. He comes along thinking he's gonna get laid and you shoot him. It's not fair."

"Happens all the time. Fireflies. Each species has its own sequence of flashes to attract a mate. But there's one predatory kind. It mimics the flashes of the mating ones and then eats them when they arrive. Fascinating."

"I still think it's unfair to..."

He held a finger to his lips. "Not so loud. We shouldn't be talking at all. They've got radar hearing. We'll spook them."

"Good."

"If a moose comes out, you realize what I'm gonna do."

"Kill it."

"If all goes well."

"So?"

"So…are you gonna be able to handle it?"

"I told you, I support aboriginal subsistence hunting."

"Hmm." He scanned the edges of the meadow again with his binoculars then turned back to her. "What about white subsistence hunting."

"Are you joking?"

"No. I know white people who need a moose as much as I do, and some Indians who make six-figure salaries."

"But white people don't have aboriginal rights. That's been decided by the Supreme Court. It's not part of their heritage."

"Everybody's ancestors hunted animals, yours included. They didn't sit around in their caves roasting tofu dogs."

"That's not the point, and you know it."

"I'm half Indian. Do I get under the wire?"

"Yes."

"What about my daughter? She's a quarter."

"You have a daughter?"

"Yeah." He turned away and looked out over the grass, now muted gray and tan in the fading light. When he turned back his voice was back to a whisper. "Too much talking. I should do another call." He stepped out from the willows and repeated the long moaning call then stood and listened. He focused for a long time on the end of the meadow to their left. He looked back at Hannah, pointed down that way then listened again. When he came back to her, he whispered, "I thought I heard something 'way down there."

"What did you hear?"

"A grunt."

"A grunt?"

"Yeah, that's what the bulls do. I can't be sure, though. I should be ready just in case." He picked up his rifle and worked a cartridge into the chamber.

Hannah heard it—a deep low sound like a belch then branches breaking. She looked at Dan. He hadn't heard it. The noise of the willow bush rustling as he put his rifle back must have masked the sound of the moose. Dan fixed his attention on the end of the meadow where the sound had come from. Hannah held her breath, hoping the moose would be silent. She had to do something. She gave a cry and fell over into the willows, making as much noise as she could, thrashing about as if she was unable to get to her feet.

Dan reached down to help her up, urgently trying to quiet her. "Sh. Jesus, be quiet."

"It's these damn boots."

He put his finger to her lips. "Just stay there and shut up."

"I can't stay here, my ass is getting wet."

"Oh, for god's sake."

He pulled her to her feet and she looked over his shoulder. The antlers appeared first, gliding above the willows. They stopped and she saw them move back and forth, saw the top of a willow bush flail. The antlers began moving towards the open meadow. She let herself fall again, clutching at Dan, but he caught her, turning part of the way around. He was going to see the moose soon. Feigning surprise, she suddenly looked to the opposite end of the meadow. "There. I see one. A moose."

"Okay, be quiet. Stay here." He straightened up and scanned the area where she had pointed. He put his binoculars up to his eyes. "Are you sure?"

The moose emerged from the willows behind Dan, thirty meters away, ears turned toward them and head up, large squared-off nose sniffing the air. It was surprisingly dark—dull brown with lighter gray-brown on its legs. Dan was still glassing the far end of the meadow. She moved behind him, waving her arms and shouting. "There it is. There." She moved up beside him and pointed at nothing.

"Keep it down. Where? I don't see anything."

She looked back at the moose in time to see it turn and trot back toward the willows. Out of the corner of her eye she saw Dan take the binoculars from his eyes and turn to her.

"I don't see..." When he saw her looking behind him his head snapped around and his eyes went wide. "Holy fuck."

She was shoved over as he spun around to raise the rifle. She lost her balance and fell back into the brush. Before the gun reached his shoulder he stopped and put it back down. Through the branches she watched the moose disappear into the willows across the meadow. There was silence except for a hollow thump, thump, thump of retreating hoofs drumming the turf.

He stared for a long time at the spot where the moose had been then turned angry, blazing eyes on her. She tensed, wondering if he was going to hit her, but he said nothing.

"I...I didn't mean to..."

"Shut up." His eyes, full of venom, bored into hers. Then he began, low and ominous. "I let you come out here with me because you promised not to interfere. I told you a moose could walk out, and if it did, I would try to kill it. You said you could handle it."

"But it all happened so fast. I had no idea..."

He mocked her assertion of a few minutes ago. *"Oh, don't worry, I support aboriginal subsistence hunting.* Bullshit. When it comes down to the crunch, you fucking people retreat to your fantasy world of fuzzy bunnies playing in the moonlight with the friendly wolves. Stupid, hypocritical, self-righteous bitch." His voice was getting louder and more threatening with each word. She glanced with some concern at the rifle gripped in his hands. He noticed. "Oh. You think I'm gonna shoot you. Stupid asshole. Okay. That's it. From now on you stay by the camp and you don't make a sound." He stomped off toward their camp, muttering as he went. "Stupid, fucking, brainless..."

His voice faded with the sound of snapping twigs and swishing branches, leaving her crouched in the bushes, embarrassed and depressed and alone with a damp dishtowel stuffed into her panties. Silence, but for the two ravens still cackling and warbling to each other over the meadow. A small cold nudge at her hand startled her. It was Raz. She ran her hand over his head and scratched behind his ears. "What? You're not mad at me? Thanks, Raz. At least someone tries to understand." She took his head between her hands. "Now if you could only find me some tampons..."

"Stupid shit bobbleheads." Her mate was angry. His neck feathers bristled eloquently. "Boom? No. Fat? No. Guts? No."

She called back. "Crazy. Maybe mating season."

"Shitty. Fresh darkred? Me want."

"Me too."

"I go? Yes."

"Where?"

"Up mountain."

"Go. I stay." She shook out her feathers and swiped each side of her beak on her perch. "Bobbleheads make food."

"Bobbleheads stupid. Goodbye."

"Goodbye."

Her mate launched from his perch across the meadow. As he rose higher and broke into the sunlight his feathers glinted silver. He called back down to her. "Watch out. Sneaky littlewolf."

"Paul, I don't give a shit about Grizzly Watch. As far as I'm concerned, the damn bears can go extinct as long as I get Hannah back."

Paul Williams watched from the armchair as David paced about the hotel room. "David, David, calm yourself. Take a deep breath and blow it out slowly."

"You blow it out. Blow it out your ass."

"This is getting us nowhere."

"You know what's getting us nowhere, Paul? You. You and your media scrums and your press conferences. It's not doing a thing to get Hannah back. You're wasting precious time on damage control while she's out there dying of...Oh shit."

"David, you're overreacting."

"You wanna see overreacting? You just keep sitting around with your thumb in your ass and you'll see overreacting."

"I haven't been sitting around. I'm in discussion with a fellow who can supply us with aircraft. He has two ultralites he's willing to..."

"Ultralites." David laughed. "That is so like you, Paul. Ultralites. Why? Because they're more environmentally correct? Because you're so concerned with global warming? Go ahead, Paul. Get into your toy plane and fly off into the mountains. With any luck you'll crash and burn."

"David..."

"To hell with you. I'm gonna do something." He opened the drawer under the telephone and pulled out the phone book.

"Who are you calling?"

"Someone who can rent me a helicopter." He flipped to the yellow pages.

"Do you realize how much that will cost?"

"I don't care. Anyway, it's not your business. Get out." He took Paul by the arm and hauled him out of the chair.

Paul didn't resist as he was directed to the door. "Okay. I'll see you in the morning. The press conference is scheduled for ten, but you should be there by quarter to, so we can prepare."

"I won't be there."

"You have to be there. We must present a united front."

"Goodbye, Paul."

"David, listen…"

David pushed him out the door and slammed it shut. He went to the phone and punched the number for Trans North Helicopters. A recorded message told him office hours were eight to five weekdays and ten to two on weekends. He tried Capital Helicopters and got the same result then Heli-Dynamics. Ten minutes later he had exhausted all the local outfits, even one in a place called Fort Liard. An idea struck him. In his breast pocket was the business card with Ron Hewitt's home number.

"Hello?" It was a young girl's voice.

"May I speak to Ron Hewitt, please?" He could hear laughter in the background.

"Just a moment, please."

There was more laughter then Ron came on the line. "Hello."

"Hello Ron, This is David Hellman."

"David Hellman? Oh right." There was a slight pause, some fumbling with the phone then uproarious laughter in the background. "Hey you guys, cut it out. I'm on the phone. Sorry David. What can I do for you?"

"Well, uh, I guess I owe you an apology. I should have told you who I was when we were talking about Hannah."

"No, I understand. It must be really hard on you. Look, I'm sorry for some of the things I said about your wife. I can't really remember everything, but…"

"No. It was all my fault."

"That was quite a surprise at the airport, all the reporters…When I saw that, it all kinda fell into place."

"Yeah, well, it was a surprise to me, too. Anyway, the reason I called is I need your advice. I'm trying to contact a helicopter company, but of course it's after hours. I was wondering if you know anybody in the helicopter charter business. Maybe you could give me their home number."

"You thinking of mounting your own search?"

"Yes."

"Jeez, I don't know, David. They've got aircraft flying all over that place. They might not want you there. You know, safety considerations."

"Could they stop me?"

"I don't know. Even if they can't, do you know how much that'd cost you? I hope you've got a house to mortgage."

"The cost is not a consideration."

"You know what I'd do? I'd check with the RCMP search and rescue just to see if there's a problem with you flying around in your own chopper."

"Yeah, I guess so. But if they say no, I can't just stay in Whitehorse. I have to do something."

"I know how you must feel, but…Hey, I just thought of something. If the Mounties say you can't, I know a guy who takes horseback trips into the mountains. Jim Giller. He's all set up. He's the best. You'd be able to do a ground search and if you find her…I mean, when you find her, you can call in a chopper. I can give him a call right now."

"Uh, why don't I call the RCMP first, and if I need to, I'll call your friend. What's his number?" David wrote the name and number on Ron's business card. "Thanks Ron, I really appreciate your help."

"No problem. If you need anything else, let me know."

"I will. Thanks again. Bye."

"Good luck, buddy."

David's call to the RCMP confirmed Ron's guess. Flights in the search area were restricted to official aircraft for safety reasons. He punched the number for Ron's friend.

A man's voice answered after one ring. "Hello."

"Hello, is this Jim Giller?"

"Yes."

"My name is David Hellman. Your friend Ron Hewitt gave me your name."

"Yes Mr. Hellman, I was just talking to Ron. He told me you might call."

"So you know my situation?"

"I take it the search and rescue people weren't too keen on the chopper idea."

"Yeah, they were very polite, but advised against it. They said they have enough aircraft. But when I told them Ron's idea they were quite positive. So what do you think? Can you do it?"

"When do you want to leave?"

"Right away. Tomorrow if possible."

"Oh boy...Mister Hellman, I'm not sure I..."

David cut in before the man could decline. "Mr. Giller, I'm going to be frank with you. I'm desperate. I don't know if you can appreciate what I'm going through..." David took two deep breaths to control his emotions. "You're my best hope, maybe my only..." Another breath. His voice was beginning to crack. "I'm willing to pay anything. You can name your price."

"I'll charge you the going rate."

"So you'll do it?"

"Yes."

"Thank you. Thank you"

"How many people are going with you?"

"Just myself."

"Nobody else from Grizzly Watch?"

"They're idiots."

"Oh...Okay then, that simplifies things."

"Can we leave tomorrow?"

"Well, I guess so. I've got a lot to do. It won't be bright and early. I'll phone you tomorrow. Where are you staying?"

"The High Country Inn, room 218."

"Okay. See you tomorrow."

"I'll be waiting for your call. And thank you Jim. You don't know how much this means to me."

"I think I do. Don't worry too much. I'm sure your wife will turn up fine."

"Everybody's telling me that. I think they're just trying to spare me."

"Yeah, I know. I'll be there as soon as I can. Bye."

She felt like a bad kid coming home late, oversized jacket drooping at her shoulders. She muttered to the dog who followed. "Dressed the part, too, Raz."

She saw him through the trees. He must have heaped some wood on the fire. Big spruce trunks reflected orange, the closer ones bright, the further ones progressively duller, ranking back into black - an expectant audience in a hushed theater. She watched him for a while. The theater image persisted. *Lights up. Dan reclines half under the tarp. He lies on his side, legs crossed, staring into the fire, one arm slung over the rolled-up sleeping bag. Enter Hannah.*

She ducked under the last branches into the light and stood looking at him across the fire. He glanced up then back to the flames. She pulled the food box closer to the fire and perched on it. "I'm sorry."

"You're not." He said it matter-of-factly, without anger. He reached into his jacket and pulled out a plastic bag. From his other pocket he pulled a small pipe and began filling it from the bag. Until now he had been discreet about smoking pot. She had smelled it on his breath several times, after he went off to *check out a meadow*, or to *gather wood*. Whiffs of it drifted to her while paddling. He held up the pipe and looked at her. "Want some?"

"No thanks." She watched him light the pipe and take in a long lungful, hold it in then let out a slow thin stream that drifted toward the fire, leisurely at first then breaking as it raced to join the chaos of upward swirling sparks. "I'm sorry. Not that he got away, but that I interfered."

"It's okay."

"Obviously it's not okay. You were pretty mad."

"I was pretty mad." He drew again on the pipe then put it back into his pocket. He spoke while holding back the smoke. "I'm pretty when I'm mad." He exhaled and coughed.

She let out a surprised laugh. He didn't hold a grudge very long. "So, have you forgiven me already?"

"Forgiven? My mother sure wouldn't forgive you. If she'd been there she'd have decked you." He shrugged. "I'll get another chance. This valley, this weather, full moon, they're in the rut...and he was a little too big anyway. But next time you will...what?"

"Shut up and keep still."

"Very well. You are forgiven."

She nodded and looked into the fire. "You are forgiven, too."

"Me? For what?"

"For the things you said."

"Oh. The b-for-bitch word. I'm sorry. I was pretty mad. I get mad when I'm pretty."

"Not that. The fuzzy bunny thing. It was unfair."

He laughed. "I thought that was a good one, off the top of my head in the middle of a rant."

"I'm not a child. I know all about predator-prey relationships. I have a degree in ecology."

"Then you ought to realize I'm part of a predator-prey relationship. What you did had nothing to do with your degree. You said it yourself. It was a gut reaction, spur of the moment. Deep down, you believe killing anything is immoral. You wonder why Indian people don't trust the animal rights movement. That's why. They've been burned before."

"Burned? How can you say that?"

"Indians have been knocked down by everything—disease, discrimination, poverty, alcohol, residential schools..."

"Those are not the fault of the animal rights movement. Quite the contrary. I and all..."

"You and all your friends have the best intentions. I know. You support land claims and alcohol programs and education and preserving languages. But have you ever been to an anti-fur demonstration?"

"Yes. I've organized a few. But it's not about anti-fur. It's anti-cruelty. Nobody can dispute that catching an animal by its foot in a steel trap is cruel."

"I don't dispute it. But when trappers made the change to instant-kill traps, was anybody paying attention? Did anybody say, *Good on y*a? No. The discussion was over. Wearing fur is cruel. The bottom fell out of the market and one of the last ways to make a living out on the land was virtually gone. For Indians, the timing couldn't have been worse. Just when they're dragging themselves out of a hole, getting some pride and respect, you come along and tell them their way of life is immoral."

"I keep telling you, that is not my..."

"What about the seal hunt?"

"The seal hunt in Newfoundland? That has nothing to do with aboriginal people."

"Oh? After the protests died down, do you think any Inuit hunters could sell their sealskins? It didn't matter that they were from adult seals, not white coat babies. All seal hunting was bad."

"That's unfortunate, but the problem runs deeper. You know as well as I do, a fur coat is not clothing. It's not meant to keep you warm. It's worn as a status symbol, maybe twice a year to the opera. Animals who live in places like this die in order to fuel someone's vanity. Is that just? Is that right?"

He stared at her for a while. "No." After a few moments of silence, he hiked himself into a sitting position on the rolled up sleeping bag. "Let me tell you a story."

"Sure."

"Okay. My daughter's been…"

"What's her name? How old is she?"

He ignored the questions. "She's been raised on moose and caribou and fish and berries. She loves to go out in the bush with me. She's seen me kill a moose and helped field dress it. She's helped me cut and wrap the meat. She knows how to clean a fish. She loves to cut open the stomachs to see what they ate. In fact, it's her favorite way to gross out Tara."

"Tara's her mother?"

"Yeah. Anyway, one day about four years ago…Starla would have been…"

"Starla. That's an interesting name."

"I'm used to it now. I didn't like it at first. I wanted to call her Rose. We settled on Rose for her second name."

"You're right. Rose is better."

"Are you gonna let me tell you this?"

"Sorry, go ahead."

"She was six. I rented *Bambi* for us to watch. You've seen it, I'm sure."

"Of course."

"So you know how the hunters are portrayed—murderers, villains, blasting everything that moves. I was a little worried about how she'd take it, but I was most worried about the big moment. You know which one I mean?"

"Yes. When Bambi's mother gets killed. It was heartbreaking."

"Yeah. So there I am. Starla is sitting in my lap, and the shot goes off. Bambi stops, looks around and no mother. Starla looks up at me and says, *Is Bambi's mother dead?* I say, *Yes.* She thinks for awhile and asks, *Did the hunters shoot Bambi's mother?* By this time I'm squirming a bit. *Yes.* She looks back at the TV and Bambi is searching the bush calling, *Mother, mother,* as the snow falls. She looks up at me again with a puzzled expression. I'm bracing myself for the really tough question—something like, *Daddy, you're a hunter, so does that make you a Bambi mother killer?* But no. Instead she says, *Are we gonna see them cut up Bambi's mother?'* Dan laughed.

"That's not very funny."

Dan was still laughing. "But do you see my point?"

"Yes. You've brainwashed her."

"No. She knows where her food comes from. These days not many people do. You know the part where the kindly old owl sings to the little forest animals? She knew it was fantasy. She's seen the kindly old owl carrying Thumper the Rabbit in his claws."

"I've heard all those arguments, but Grizzly Watch isn't like that. The issue is environmental and ecological. Grizzlies have been wiped out over most of their range. Don't you think they should be protected in the little bit that's left? And they're killed for sport, not food. It's unconscionable, and yes, I believe it's immoral."

"It wouldn't bother me to see grizzly hunting end. I've never hunted them. Not many Yukoners do."

"Then why are they all so opposed to Grizzly Watch?"

"They take it personally, you know, *tarred with the same brush* as my Dad used to say. Then of course there's the money. Trophy hunters spend big bucks to get a bear. People earn their livings from it. I've guided grizzly hunts."

"Money. It always comes down to money."

"That's for sure. And money's at the heart of the real problem all over the world—loss of habitat."

"Yes, but the focus of Grizzly Watch is to draw attention to the one issue."

"Well then, you've succeeded. You've got folks' attention now."

Hannah threw a stick on the fire. "Hmm. I wonder. If they think I'm dead then all those people will be saying, *I told you so.*"

"But you're not dead, so what the hell."

Hannah stared into the fire. What the hell, indeed. She turned to him. "How old is your daughter?"

Dan looked quickly away into the fire. "Ten."

"I didn't think you were married."

"I'm not."

"So, is your daughter with her mother?"

"Yeah. I think I'll go out to the meadow and do another call. Come on, Raz." He stood up abruptly and left, the dog following a step behind.

Hannah watched him fade into the dark. She didn't want him to leave. He had been so talkative. She wondered why he seemed sensitive about his daughter. Oh well, it would give her a chance to cut another piece off the dishtowel.

SEPT 17

A slight tickling woke him. He could feel it move from his rump to his back then down to the open wound on his side. A sharp tug on the raw flesh made him lift his head. The whiskeyjack flew to a nearby alder branch, sending a small cloud of frost drifting down, glittering in the first rays of the sun.

The stab of pain caused by the bird was almost a relief, a momentary distraction from the incessant, gnawing agony in his gut. The thirst was constant now, but he dare not drink, because it would be followed by painful retching. He was exhausted after the night in the alder thicket. Even his short snatches of sleep were filled with dreams of pain.

The bear got slowly to his feet. When he stood, the discomfort eased a little. He walked, following the trail etched deep in the moss along the river. The smell of moose was strong and fresh, but it aroused no interest in him. The trail took him to an open sandbar. Easier walking. The river beckoned, cool and refreshing. At the water's edge he lapped at it, swallowed a little and moved on. At the downstream end of the bar was a back channel, once the main river course. Across a short stretch of dark, still water was a high, steep bank. Perhaps there was an easier way around. Groaning with each step, he waded into the back channel.

Hannah watched from the warmth of the sleeping bag as Dan set fire to a big bundle of dry spruce twigs. "You're shivering."

"Yeah. It was cold out there. No moose." The small flame took hold and soon grew into a bright, hot, crackling pillar. Dan broke some bigger branches over his knee and threw them on. "What do you want for breakfast—oatmeal with brown sugar, or would you prefer brown sugar with oatmeal?"

"Decisions, decisions."

Dan placed two bigger logs, one on each side of the fire then put a wire grate over them. He picked up a blackened cooking pot, turned it upside down and hit the bottom with the heel of his hand. A cylinder of ice fell out. "I'll go get some water." He headed for the river, out through the big spruce trees and hopped down the short bank onto the gravel.

Through the trees Hannah could see mist in gentle columns swirling slowly downstream. She had heard him get up early when the sky was beginning to show grayish light, heard his moose calls sounding eerie and plaintive in the stillness. He'd given her the sleeping bag again last night. He must have been very cold.

She got out of the bag and went to the fire. The kindling had burned down so she picked up some bigger sticks to put on, but the wire rack was in the way. She picked it off the fire, the hot metal seared her fingers and she snatched her hand away. The rack flew in an arc to land at Dan's feet as he returned with the pot of water. "Ow. Oh Jesus." She sucked her fingers.

"You shouldn't do that. You might burn yourself."

"Shit, I'm so stupid."

"Here. Stick your fingers in this water."

"But it's the cooking water."

"That's okay. Unless you've got Ebola."

The cold water instantly numbed her pain.

Dan took the lid off the plastic food box and pulled out a bag of rolled oats. "This isn't gonna last much longer—three, maybe four days. We'll cook enough for you."

"No, you have some, too. I'm eating all your food."

"I'll eat something else. You want tea or coffee?"

"Coffee…if there's enough." She knelt to put more sticks on the fire.

"It's one thing we've got plenty of."

"Let me cook breakfast."

"Do you know how to make oatmeal?"

"Of course. Two to one with a dash of salt."

"How about coffee?"

"Just show me where you keep the espresso machine."

"Here it is." He handed her the other pot.

"How elegant. Leave it to me."

Dan was looking at her. She met his eyes for a couple of beats. There was that gorgeous smile again. She looked away. "Well, I'd better get busy."

"Okay, I'll leave you to it. I have something to do. Come on, Raz." The dog followed and they disappeared into the trees upstream.

She replaced the rack, measured two cups of water into the empty pot and put both pots on to boil. She stuffed the sleeping bag into its sack and sat looking out of the lean to. The sun was beginning to break through the trees, etching the wood smoke into slanting rays as it drifted up and out over the river to join the slow march of mist. Every sound seemed amplified in the stillness: the bell-like call of a raven, the constant velvet gurgle of moving water. She sat, lost in the beauty and stillness, listening, breathing, in the moment for the first time in a long while.

A soft whoosh made her turn her head in time to see a whiskeyjack spread its wings to land on the edge of the open food box. Its claws made tiny scratching sounds on the hard surface. It tilted its black capped head and fixed one eye on her. Hannah sat still, not wanting to scare it away. "Hello. What is it you want?"

As if in answer, the bird hopped down into the box and began poking into the plastic bags of food.

"Hey, you'd better get out of there." She moved out of the shelter towards the box and the whiskeyjack flew to a low spruce branch an arm's length away.

"You want some food? I'll see what I can do." She rummaged down into the box and found a bag of pepperonis. She broke off a small piece and held it out. The whiskeyjack eyed the morsel intently then looked into her eye. Hannah stayed motionless, and after a long look at the chunk of meat, the bird hopped from the branch to her hand. It took the piece of meat and flew off into the trees.

"You're a soft touch." It was Dan returning carrying something in his upturned hat.

"Did you see that?" Hannah was beaming. "He landed right on my hand."

"He'll be back for more." Dan was looking at the bag of pepperonis in her hand.

"Oh. I'm sorry. It was the only thing I could think he might want."

"I guess he's not a vegetarian. Your limit is one pepperoni. We don't want to give him heartburn." He sat down to lean against a big spruce trunk and set his hat on his lap. "Just don't let Raz catch you giving away his dog food.' He pointed to the fire. "The water's boiling."

Hannah put the pepperonis back in the food box and took out the oatmeal. "I've never had a wild bird sit on my hand. What a feeling."

"You've got a way with animals. What do you think, Raz? Should we get her to call a moose out?" The dog lay with its head on the ground, tail wagging, looking at Dan. "Don't wag your tail." The dog's tail wagged harder. "Dan shook his finger. "I told you. Quit wagging that tail." Raz rolled onto his side. His tail thumped the ground furiously, raising clouds of dust. "If you don't stop wagging that tail, you're in trouble, Mister." Raz couldn't stand it any longer. He got up and went to Dan, his whole body wriggling. "Yeah, that's a good boy." Hannah was laughing. Dan stroked the dog's face and gave his chest a rub. "Now go lie down, or make yourself useful. Go change the batteries in my head lamp."

Hannah lifted the big pot off the fire to make coffee. "I think he could."

"Watch this. Hey, Raz. Where's my fishing rod?" The dog bounded toward the river and disappeared down the bank. "Hannah, could you hand me that cup?"

"Sure. What are you doing? What have you got in the hat?"

"Rose hips. For your oatmeal. You ever had them?"

"No."

"They're good. They taste kinda like apples. Very nutritious. Lots of vitamin C."

Hannah gave him the cup. "I've seen them on the rose bushes around Vancouver, but nobody eats them."

"You have to remove the nasty bits – the flower ends and the seeds. It's kinda tedious." He began pulling off the spiky sepals and opening each fruit to take out the cluster of seeds inside.

Raz returned up the bank with something in his mouth. It looked to Hannah like only the handle of a fishing rod with a reel attached. As he passed her she reached down to give him a pat. "Good boy, Raz. He's amazing."

"Yeah. He's a smart one." The dog marched proudly to Dan and dropped the rod at his side.

"That's kind of short for a fishing rod."

"Hey. Don't ever make fun of the length of a guy's rod. You gotta have faith." He picked it up and pulled on the end. It telescoped upward in sections until it was a meter and a half long.

Hannah laughed. "Oooh. Very impressive." Dan went back to preparing the rosehips and she stirred the oatmeal. She hadn't laughed like this for ages. Andrea was always so serious and Martin only wanted to talk about himself and all his expeditions to this peak and that glacier. Not with David, either, at least not in a long time. David. He had been on her mind often, his name on the side of the canoe a constant reminder. They used to laugh a lot, but David's affairs had put up a barrier. She'd thought of leaving. Why hadn't she? Too comfortable, too used to the life David provided—the house, the sailboat, the vacations, the security? The freedom? Freedom to pursue her interests, the things that mattered—her work for ARN. Being right on the front lines of Grizzly Watch was a chance to do something worthwhile, to actually save the lives of endangered animals. She enjoyed the interviews, the PR shoots, liked seeing herself in the paper and on TV. But was it freedom, or was she merely a dilettante? She wouldn't be here if it wasn't for David. Here. Where was here? The South Macmillan River, days from the nearest person, traveling and living with a strange man. A good-looking strange man. The irony made her chuckle.

Dan looked up. "What?"

"Nothing. I just thought of something funny." She stirred the bubbling oatmeal and moved it to the side, off the direct flames. She watched him as he worked on the rose hips. The dog watched him too, seeming to wait for the man's next move. "Why did you name him Raz?"

"Huh? Oh, it's short for Raskolnikov."

"Who?"

"The guy in Crime and Punishment."

"Crime and Punishment?"

"It's a book."

"I know it's a book, I just…"

"You just thought, *How could a Ross River bozo hunter read a book without pictures?*"

"No…Okay, yes. So, how did that happen?"

"My dad was the principal of the school in Ross. When I was a kid, our house was full of books. Dad had subscriptions to all kinds of magazines from *National Geographic* to *The Utne Reader.* He even got regular bulletins from the Communist Party of Canada. But I didn't read much. He was always going on about how I should read more than comic books. He also had a list of chores he wrote up every week: dishes, firewood, water, that kinda thing. There was no getting around it, no excuses except maybe a fever of a hundred and four. One day—I was nine—he said he'd come up with a new rule. If I read a book of his choice, he would match the time doing my chores himself."

"Seems like it worked."

"Not at first. I was stubborn. I didn't like my dad back then. I'd do my chores fast and out the door to be with my friends. Anyway, one week he put a new job on the list—sanding and varnishing the kitchen floor. I knew he thought it up just to make me give in, so I started sanding. It was so friggin' hard. I worked for an hour and got about a square foot done. I thought, *Okay, maybe it's giving in, but if I read then he's gonna have to do this.* I handed him the sandpaper and told him I'd read his stupid book. Guess what it was."

"I don't know, something depressing and heavy, *One Day in the Life of Ivan Denisovitch?*"

Another bundle of seeds hit the ground and another bit of fruit dropped into the pot. *"Tarzan of the Apes."*

"Oh. Your dad was a cagey one."

"Yeah. It kinda backfired on him, though. He had to sand and paint the whole floor by himself. But I was hooked. The next book was *The Lion, the Witch and the Wardrobe.* By the end of the year I'd read *Treasure Island, The Three Musketeers, The Hobbit, The Lord of the Rings* and *A Tale of Two Cities.* And Dad bought a power sander." He stood up and handed her the cup of pared rosehips. "Here you go."

She took the cup and tried one. "They're delicious."

"They've had a few frosts. It improves them. Put them in your oatmeal."

"You have to eat some, too."

"No. You need them. I've got some dried moose meat." He handed her a bag of brown sugar and a can of milk. "Put lots on. You need that, too."

Susan saw Jim's big blue diesel 4-wheel-drive with the stock trailer pull up in front of the house as she was getting ready for work. Seeing Jim was always difficult, always gave her a butterfly feeling in her stomach—fight or flight. Which would it be this time? Would she end up crying, or angry, or both? At least Helga wasn't with him. She hoped he'd pick up Jessica and be gone soon. She called downstairs. "Jess, Jim's here."

"What? Shit, I'm not ready, yet."

"You've been sitting there reading the paper for half an hour." She heard Jessica get up from the table and go to her bedroom.

"There's a story about Hannah Weinberg and that other guy, Paul Williams."

"You could take it with you. There'll be lots of time to read on the way up there."

"Gotta know who I'm lookin' for."

Susan looked out the window again. Should she pretend to be dressing for work so she wouldn't have to face him? No. That would be cowardly.

Jim got out of the truck and checked the tires, the tarp over the gear in the back, the horses. He walked around the trailer. He glanced toward the house, and Susan pulled back into the room then realized he could see only reflections off the glass. He reached in through the open driver's door and popped the hood latch then went to the front of the truck, lifted the hood and pulled out the oil stick. Was he killing time to avoid facing her? No. That would be cowardly.

She got to the bottom of the stairs just as the doorbell rang. She opened the door and he stood looking in. "Hi, Suzy."

"Hello, Jim."

"She ready, yet?"

"Of course not, she's Jessica. Come in."

He stepped into the entranceway and looked around. "Nice place."

"Thanks."

"You've got a doorbell."

"Of course I've got a doorbell."

"It's kinda funny. You always bugged me to put in a doorbell at home, and I always said I would and never got around to it."

"Oh. Yeah. Funny."

"That chair looks good there." He pointed to the pine chair he had made for her last Christmas.

"Uh huh. Would you like some tea or are you drinking coffee again?" Oh, she shouldn't have said that. They had given up coffee together five years ago. He might think it was a jibe at his new relationship.

"Tea please. If you have time. If you don't, I'm fine."

Susan led the way into the kitchen, went to the cupboard, got a cup and lifted the teapot. "Jess must have finished it. I'll make more."

He perched on a chair, but didn't move his legs under the kitchen table. "Don't go to any trouble."

"It's no trouble." She fussed with filling the kettle and putting it on its stand.

"So...I see you got one of those kettles with the separate stand. Those are handy."

"Yes, they're very handy." She looked through several drawers for the tea. She finally took it out of the first one she had opened.

"Does it have one of those automatic switches?"

"Yes."

"So it turns itself off. That's really...handy."

"Yes."

"Saves energy. You know...electricity and, uh...well, electricity."

"Yes. The thing I like about it is it's quite fast."

There was a long pause. Jim looked out the window and back again. "So it boils faster?"

"Much faster." Susan stood with her back to him looking at the kettle. Where was Jessica? She'd much rather deal with her daughter's sarcasm than this. Oh, to hell with it. She turned to face him and as soon as she looked in his eyes she could feel hers begin to sting. "Jim, why are we doing this?"

"What?"

"You know what...talking about the fucking kettle and the fucking doorbell and the fucking chair."

"I'm sorry...I don't know what to say." He looked so helpless sitting there, dumb, staring at the floor.

The kettle finally boiled and gave off a small click. She turned back to the counter and made the tea. "How long is this going to take?"

"I don't know. We need time to get over the anger, I guess."

"I mean this trip with Hannah Weinberg's husband."

"Oh, yeah." Relief was on his face. "As long as it takes. I don't think it'll go over a week. Our chances of finding her are pretty slim, maybe non-existent. I hope to hell we don't find her body."

She poured a cup of tea and set it on the table in front of him. "Take care of Jessica."

"I will. More like she'll be taking care of me."

"Don't let her smoke too much dope."

"I'll try."

Jessica came down the hall and they both turned to meet her as she entered the kitchen.

Jim stood. "At last. Hey, what have you got in the bag? I said you only need your personal gear."

"Dad, we're gonna have three pack horses."

"Okay, let's get going. We've got a long day ahead of us. We have to stop to buy some food. And we have to get to Ross before the ferry shuts down."

"Where's Hellman?"

"We're picking him up at the hotel."

Jessica pointed at the paper on the table. "Did you read this?"

"Yeah."

"She's been out there five days now."

"Yeah. It's a long time, but we have to think positive. Back in the sixties two people survived fifty days after their plane crashed. And it was the middle of winter. Maybe you could find the right moment to drop that into the conversation on the way up, you know, for David."

"What's he like?"

"I don't know. I've only talked to him on the phone. Let's go find out. He's waiting for us."

Susan followed them to the truck.

Jessica threw her bag in the back then went to the trailer "Hi Jasper. Hi Spider, you're a good girl." She reached through the grate and scratched each of the six horses then climbed into the passenger seat. Susan moved around to Jessica's side and stood looking in the open window. "You be careful...both of you. Don't take any silly chances."

"Don't worry, Mom."

She looked at Jim. "Drive carefully."

"I will. See you in a week or so." He started the engine and pulled away.

Susan watched the truck receding. She wished she could go with them.

The pickings at the bobblehead firenest were small: a few flakes of the big tasty grass seeds they ate. What the littlewolf didn't lick up, the whiskeyjack got. Stupid little gray shitbird couldn't see danger in their eyes. She had watched it hide the piece of meat stuffed intestine it took from the bobblehead, impaling it on a twig in amongst a dense cluster of spruce branches. She had eaten the morsel when the stupid bird had gone back for more. Delicious. Salty and filling with a pleasant afterburn that made her want more.

"So how come you didn't bring Helga?"

"She has some kind of appointment she says she can't miss."

Jessica forgot she'd told herself to control the sarcasm. "Her dentist or her fashion consultant or what?"

"I don't know. She didn't say. Besides, someone has to look after the place, plus she's got her new horse she wants to work with."

"Busy girl."

Jim turned onto Fourth Avenue and got the finger from a motorist who had to slow down to let the big rig in. "Asshole."

"Jeez, Dad, lighten up."

"I meant the guy behind me, not you. No, I'm glad you're coming. I'd rather have you along, anyway. I need someone who knows her stuff in the bush, and you're the best."

"Gee, I guess Hailey was right. She said when her parents split up, all of a sudden they were really nice to her."

"Oh God. So young, yet so cynical."

"Sorry Dad. So how is Helga? She gonna look after the place while you're gone?" Jim didn't answer, just gave her a look that said he wasn't in the mood for more needling. "Dad, I promise, no more sarcasm."

"Yeah, she'll be fine. She knows how to tend the woodstove and there's only Captain to look after."

"Captain?"

"Her name for the new horse." He gave his head a small shake.

"You worried?"

"Somewhat. She's...headstrong. So is the horse."

Jessica shifted to face him, genuinely interested. "Yeah?"

"Yesterday we took him out for his first trail ride. He fussed a bit, but he was fine as long as he stayed behind Jasper. When we got to the quad trail on the way home she wanted to race. Before I could stop her she was pounding out of sight in a cloud of dust."

"She get him stopped okay?"

"She had to take his head away. I told her that's not how we want to teach him to stop. She promised to ride him only in the corral while I'm away. I'm not sure she's gonna keep that promise." He flicked on the left turn signal for the turn into the High Country Inn. "Shit. No room to park. I'll pull over here. He flicked on the right hand signal and eased to the curb. The driver behind gave him another finger and a blast from his horn as he passed.

Susan always felt a bit sheepish when she pulled into the Walmart parking lot. She had been opposed to the big box store when it was first planned for the vacant lot at the north end of town, and had joined the antis when they crowded city council meetings. Her letter published in the *Yukon News* predicted the death of small family owned businesses in Whitehorse. If someone had told her back then that Whitehorse would eventually have, not only Walmart, but a new Superstore and a Canadian Tire duking it out for the town's consumer dollar, she would have been appalled.

She drove past the area where the tourist motor homes were parked— just a few of them this time of year, but in the height of summer there would have been upwards of thirty parked for the night. The furor over Walmart allowing them free overnight parking had died down for the season, but it would start up again next year. She had signed a petition and adopted her own private boycott. But sometimes the lure of acres of shopping was too much to resist. To wander the aisles for hours, reading labels and lists of ingredients for products she wasn't even interested in, escaping into a pleasant daze, where shopping was recreation, shopping was therapy, shopping was a drug.

This was not one of those times, though. She had a list and just enough time before her pre-trial conference at one o'clock. The size of the place always amazed her, crammed with products that all seemed to be on sale at once. She met the eye of the bored-looking greeter, consulted her list and approached the young man, smiling, not really needing his help. "I wonder if you could help me?" He looked at her list and told her where she could find the items. "Thank you very much," she said.

"Have a nice day," he said.

She went to the freezer aisle and opened the door to the frozen juices. As she stood deciding, a small tug on the hem of her suit jacket made her turn. Starla was looking up at her. "Oh. Starla, hi. How are you?" Susan always felt the urge to take her in her arms. It made her long for the days when her kids were young.

"Okay. I got a new puppet. See?" Starla was wearing a hand puppet, a tiger brightly colored in orange, black and white.

Susan went down on one knee. She looked into the glass eyes of the tiger. "Hello, Mister Tiger. What's your name?"

"My name is Samantha."

"Pardon me. I'm sorry. You're Ms. Tiger. Tell me, what are you doing here? I thought tigers lived in the jungle."

"Not me. I'm a Siberian tiger."

Susan made a surprised expression, "Oh, I see. Siberian tigers live in stores."

Starla laughed. "No, we live in Siberia. I'm here to visit my friend."

"Let me guess who your friend is. Could her name be Starla?"

"Yes. I protect her because I'm a tiger. Rowwwr."

"Oh my, such a fierce roar."

"Yes. I'm fierce."

A deep voice came from down at the end of the aisle. "Starla. Come on. We have to get going."

Susan looked up to see Gary Haines approaching. She hadn't seen him in years. His beard had some gray in it now, and he'd developed a bit of a gut, but his craggy good looks were unchanged. She stood up to face him as Starla moved behind her and took the puppet off her hand.

Gary recognized Susan when he was halfway down the aisle. "Oh. It's you."

"Hello Gary. Starla wasn't bothering me. In fact, she was showing me her new puppet and telling me all about Siberian tigers."

Gary looked down at Starla. "What are you doing with that?"

"Mom said I could."

"No she didn't. I was there. She told you to put it back. We can't afford it. Now go do it." Starla didn't move, remaining partly behind Susan and glaring back at Gary. Before Starla could respond Susan broke in. "I'm sorry. This is a misunderstanding. It's all my fault. I told Starla I'd buy it for her. I didn't dream it would cause any trouble." Gary looked at Susan, suspicious, but she kept smiling. "Just a little gift between friends. Right, Starla?" She met the big man's eyes. "I hope you don't mind."

"No, I don't mind."

Susan saw Tara come around the end of the aisle pushing a cart loaded almost to the top. Tara looked at them and then away, distracted by something inside the freezer. She opened the door and Susan couldn't see her anymore. "How much is it, Starla?"

Starla looked up at Gary then back to Susan. "Twelve ninety nine."

Susan took fifteen dollars out of her bag. "There you are, Starla. Now you, Ms. Tiger, you take care of this girl. She's precious." She turned back to Gary. He looked away. She couldn't see Tara anymore.

Gary said, "We'd better go find your mom. Come on, Starla."

Susan felt Starla's hand go into hers.

Gary was walking away. He stopped and looked back. "Starla?"

Starla didn't move. Susan didn't know what to do. The child wouldn't let go of her hand. "What's the matter, Starla?"

Starla's dark eyes bored into hers, flicked towards Gary and back. Then her expression changed, the intensity gone. "Thank you for the puppet." She withdrew her hand and followed the man around the end of the aisle. Just before she disappeared out of sight she turned and looked back. Susan couldn't read her expression. Was it resignation? Was it fear?

Susan stood looking down the empty aisle. Had she made a mistake giving Starla the money for the puppet? Would it cause her problems with Gary and Tara? She felt Starla had been on the verge of telling her something.

"Excuse me, please." Another shopper wanted to get to the frozen juice.

"Oh. Yes. I'm sorry." She looked at her list then stuck it into her bag and left the store. As she headed for the exit Gary, Tara and Starla were going through the check out. She went outside and sat in her car, thinking. Through the rear view mirror she saw the three of them coming out the doors, heading for Tara's car. Starla went to the passenger door and waited. Susan couldn't make out what Gary and Tara were saying but it looked like they were arguing. She rolled down her window.

"Gary, if she wants to give her a present, it's okay with me. I don't know why you're getting so mad about it."

"She deliberately undercut me. How is the kid going to learn respect with that stupid bitch lawyer sticking her nose in? Get in the car, Starla."

Tara said, "How can she? The door's locked."

Gary yanked the keys from the hatchback and went to the passenger door. Starla went around to the driver's side. Gary unlocked the door. "What's the matter? I'm not gonna bite you. Jesus."

Tara had finished loading the groceries. "Gary, get rid of this cart and let's get the hell out of here." She took Starla back to the passenger door as Gary shoved the grocery cart out into the driving lane. Starla climbed into the back and Tara got into the front. Gary backed the car out, hitting the grocery cart and sending it spinning into a parked car. He gunned the engine and sped off. Susan could just make out Tara's raised voice.

"What the fuck? You're gonna wreck my…"

"This is the CBC Yukon news with Nora Kylie.

Animal rights activist Hannah Weinberg is still missing in the rugged mountains north of Ross River. The woman went missing five days ago while protesting the hunting of grizzly bears. Her group, Animal Rights Now, was attempting to film hunters on the slopes of Mount Riddell, north of Ross River. Spokesman for the RCMP coordinated search effort, Sergeant Steve Godwin, said this morning that a grid search by helicopter has turned up nothing, and the ground search has been widened.

In related news, it appears a rift has developed between ARN spokesman Paul Williams and the missing woman's husband, David Hellman, who arrived in Whitehorse yesterday. The two exchanged harsh words at the Whitehorse airport yesterday on Mr. Hellman's arrival. Mr. Hellman refused to attend the ARN news conference this morning. He is on his way to the Mount Riddell area to join the search and was unavailable for comment.

When asked about the disagreement, Paul Williams explained:

'David is understandably upset about Hannah, and people under stress can say things they don't mean. But I talked with him last night and I can tell you we are both in agreement that the prime objective is to find Hannah. David and I have a close working relationship and any inference of...'"

"Moron. *Close working relationship.* He means I was close to strangling him. Do you mind if I turn this off?" David sat in the passenger seat of Jim Giller's truck, a bag of food on his lap and a coffee cup in his hand. Jessica sat in the back seat surrounded by bags of gear.

Jim nodded. "Be my guest. It'll fade out in a few minutes anyway. The signal drops off out of Carmacks."

"They got it wrong. I didn't refuse to go to the press conference, I simply didn't show up." He looked into the bag of food. "What are these potato things?"

Jessica leaned forward. "Mojos."

"My God, they're hideous. Fried chicken and mojos and ketchup. Why did I buy this?"

"Comfort food."

"You can't tell a soul. If my staff found out I'd have a full scale revolt on my hands." He popped a mojo into his mouth. "Oh no. They're delicious."

Jessica laughed. "Your secret is safe with us."

The Robert Campbell Highway rose higher up the side of the valley. On the left were dry south facing slopes clothed in silver-green wormwood and tawny grass that had finished its growth for the season.

David looked down to the right at the big river flowing in wide lazy bends. "What river is that?"

Jim shifted down a gear and checked the trailer in the rearview mirror. "The Yukon River."

"Oh. I imagined it would be faster flowing."

"It's faster than it looks from up here. It's going about 10 or 12 K. You see that rock outcrop up ahead? It's called Eagle Rock. Back in the seventies the government wanted to build a dam across the valley right up there. Mega-projects. All the rage back then. It would have flooded a huge area. Thank God it never happened."

David said, "It would have produced a lot of hydro power."

"With no one to use it."

"But it would stimulate economic growth, promote industry. You know, *If you build it they will come.*"

"Well, I don't want it…the population, the pollution. Too much change."

"Progress means change."

Jim snorted. "Who says we want it to change?"

Jessica could see where this might be leading. Dad could really get hot about development. She'd heard it a million times—*Why do you think the Europeans come here? It's the most valuable thing we've got, way more valuable than minerals and fucking gold, and its getting more valuable by the decade. When its all gone we'll be sorry and some rich bastards down south will be*—Dad was on the verge of forgetting his cardinal rule: *never argue with the client.* She spoke up from the back seat. "Gee, David, I thought you'd be a raving conservationist like Hannah."

"Hannah and I have differing political views, although I've supported her all along, 'cause it means a lot to her. This Grizzly Watch thing was a different story, though. I tried to talk her out of it. I told her it was crazy to come up here and antagonize people…way out in the middle of nowhere, nobody else around. And they have guns. Who knows what they might do?"

"They wouldn't do anything to her. They might get pissed off, but they're not murderers."

"That's comforting."

Jessica caught the irony in his voice. Maybe she'd steered the subject in the wrong direction, but what the hell, the whole point of this trip was to search for Hannah. "They've been helping to look for her. Doesn't that say something?"

"Maybe, but what about the other dangers, like bears. Ron Hewitt was saying…"

"Bears are the least of her worries. Right, Dad?" She knew Jim could go on at length about bears. It was one of his pet peeves.

"That's for sure. Everyone's a bear expert up here. They've all got their stories, mostly second and third hand. The stories that make the news are the attacks. You never see a headline reading, *Grizzly Sees Hiker and Flees.*"

Jessica said, "Yeah, cause bears don't like hikers with fleas."

David laughed. "Oh, that is comforting. Where do I buy some fleas?"

"They sell them at the store in Ross River." Jessica was glad to hear David laughing. She sensed he was one of those people who loved to laugh.

Her father was determined to finish his thought. "The biggest danger in the Yukon is not the bears, it's the water. I know people who won't go camping, won't spend a night out in the bush, because they're afraid of bears, but they'll happily pack the whole family in a boat and head out across Kluane Lake in a strong wind."

"And they can't swim?"

"Christ, it doesn't matter. It's the cold that gets you. You can be Mark Spitz and you've still only got about fifteen minutes. If you're not rescued by then, you're in deep shit. So don't worry, 'cause there are no lakes up on Mount Riddell."

"That's good then. How long before we get there?"

Jessica parroted from the back, "Yeah, when are we gonna get there, Dad?"

"Three hours to Ross River. There'll be time before the ferry shuts down to get some eats if we're hungry then another two and a half, three hours to Twin Creek airstrip. We have to check in with the Mounties. They're calling all the shots, so we can't go up the mountain without their instructions. We'll stay somewhere near the trailhead for the night, find a good spot with lots of grass for the horses. How much riding have you done, David?"

"I'm a beginner."

"Who should we put him on, Jess?"

"I think he should ride Killer."

David turned in his seat to look back at her. "Killer. Great. You're trying to comfort me again."

"Don't worry. Killer's a sweetheart. One day in the saddle and you'll love him like a brother."

"Okay, a brother. But that's as intimate as I'm willing to get."

"You must have seen lots of bears." Hannah hadn't been paddling for some time, content to pat Raz and let the current and Dan's slow strokes move them along.

"Yeah, lots."

"Have you ever been charged by one?"

"Nope…Well, once. It was kinda funny, really."

"What happened?"

"I was staying at a cabin on the Pelly River. I was walking along the trail, not paying any attention, when suddenly all hell broke loose. Right beside the trail, about four feet away, this big black thing took off crashing through the bush. It was a bear. I guess he'd been feeding, not paying attention either. I startled him, he startled me. He ran about thirty feet then turned around and stood up. I thought, *Okay, he's already scared. I can just chase him away.* I had an axe so I banged it on a tree and yelled, agressively, *Go on, get. Get outta here. RRRRR.* Instead of running away, he charged, but only about ten feet. He stopped then started to huff and puff and tear up the moss, snapping his jaws, clacking his teeth together. Only time I've ever heard that. I guess he was trying to scare me away. This went on for a while, and I was beginning to think I might have to use the axe to defend myself. Trouble was, at that point it was looking less like an axe and more like a marshmallow on a stick. I don't know why, but I started to sing the first song that popped into my head."

"What did you sing?"

"*People Will Say We're in Love.* Do you know it?"

"Rogers and Hammerstein. It's from *Oklahoma.*"

"Yeah. It was one of my Dad's favorites. He used to sing it a lot. Had all the big Broadway shows on vinyl. So there I was, trying to muster up my sweetest voice: *Don't throw bouquets at me. Don't please my folks too much. Don't laugh at my jokes too much. People will say we're in love.* I'm no Gordon McRae, and I'm sure not Shirley Jones, even in a dress. But the change in the bear was instant. As soon as I started singing, he quit huffing and puffing and clacking his teeth and tearing the moss. He calmed right down. His ears came up and I'm sure he was listening. I kept singing and slowly walking on along the trail. I had to pass about ten feet from him, and he just stood there and watched me go by."

"Music hath charms to soothe the savage beast."

"Breast."

"Breast? Are you sure?"

"Yeah, unless my Dad had it wrong all those years. But it sure as hell soothed the savage beast that time."

"Your father sounds like an interesting guy."

"Interesting...that's one way to put it."

"What's another way to put it?"

"Insane."

"That's harsh. He was your father."

"He was the source of all my problems when I was young. Most of the town thought he was nuts. Can you imagine? I'm thirteen, fourteen-years-old, desperate to fit in, be cool, and there's my dad at the front of the classroom, singing Broadway show tunes."

"That's not so weird. Music class should include all the different..."

"We didn't have music class. He'd sing in math, english, gym. He'd sing at the drop of a hat."

"Okay, he was an odd duck. But maybe he saved your life."

"What do you mean?"

"If you hadn't known that song, the bear might have attacked you."

Dan laughed. "I could have sung another song. The Rolling Stones', *Under My Thumb*."

"The bear would have torn out your liver."

They went along in silence for some time. The river was faster now. Hannah watched the patterns of light play on the stones below the boat as they glided over them. The sun was high and warm. They passed close to a steep bank topped by a stand of birch, trunks shining white, leaves an impossible yellow. She felt the canoe jiggle from side to side and thought Dan was shifting his weight to change sides for paddling. It happened again and she remembered him telling her it meant to be quiet because something was up. She looked back at him. He had his binoculars up, pointed down the long straight stretch they had just entered. She looked ahead. The outside of the next bend was a high gravel bank, the inside a wide bar studded with clumps of willow. Then she saw movement. Several dark shapes were coming down the bank.

She kept her voice low. "What are they?"

"Caribou. Here." He leaned forward over the gear and handed her the binoculars. "One of them's a nice bull."

She put up the binoculars and saw them enter the water. There were six. They swam fast, their backs high out of the water. All but two had antlers, but one had a much bigger set than the rest. Two wide palms reached forward the length of his nose. The main shafts formed two graceful curves up and back, topped by palms studded with tines. "They're so beautiful."

"Yeah."

When she turned back to Dan to hand him the binoculars, he was pulling his rifle from its case. "You're not going to shoot them, are you?"

"Why not?"

"I thought you were hunting moose."

"Caribou's just as good. Better. Keep quiet and stay down. You too, Raz."

She hunched down as far as she could, gripped the dog's head and clutched it to her, wanting to bury her face in his fur to block out what was about to happen, but she couldn't take her eyes off the caribou. They were approaching shallower water. The feet of the first two cows began to touch gravel, their shoulders bouncing slightly higher with each step. She muttered under her breath. "Quick. Run. Get away." The boat slid closer. The two lead cows were now well ahead of the others, water boiling white at their shoulders, lean wet muscle glistening, moving faster and faster as they got further out of the water.

She turned to look at Dan, and saw him put the gun down. Had he changed his mind? He took his paddle and made one stroke, shifting the angle of the boat so it pointed directly at the two cows, who were trotting in high bouncing strides towards the gravel bar. One of the calves had reached the shallows and would be with them soon. She looked back again to see Dan pick up his rifle.

She looked ahead. Four of the caribou were on shore. They had seen the boat. She flinched at the jagged metal sound of a cartridge being worked into the chamber of Dan's gun. The caribou stood perfectly still, ears forward, feet spread wide in the river mud. The other calf was trotting to join them. Hannah's muscles tightened, expecting the boom of the rifle at any instant. Then what? She whispered to Raz. "You can't kill them." The bull was out of the river now, water streaming off his thick white neck hair. He was walking so slowly. She willed him to run, whispering through clenched teeth, "Move. Go."

The three cows and two calves stood together, curious, ears forward. The bull hadn't shown any sign of seeing the boat. He walked sedately through the shallows, stopped and shook himself, water drops flying, glistening gold in the sun, a brief rainbow above his neck ruff. She heard Dan take a deep breath. She looked back to see him raise the rifle to his shoulder.

"Go. Go. Go." Hannah repeated it under her breath, over and over, vision now swimming, the dog whimpering softly from her steadily tightening grip. The bull caribou was a blur of gray and white, antlers jagged against the sky. She couldn't breath, waiting for the boom, for the caribou to fall, heaving, kicking, groaning, screaming. She could only imagine. She glanced back at Dan. He had the rifle up, pointing at the bull. The cows were running, high bouncing steps of alarm, calves at their sides. Nine, ten strides then they stopped again in unison to stare back. Hannah was past the bull now. Dan would be just coming abreast of him. She finally tore her eyes away and hugged the dog harder, her face against his, holding her breath, bracing herself.

At last she looked up. The canoe was starting into faster water as it crowded to the outside of the bend, the high gravel bank getting closer. Dan was turned around watching the last three caribou disappear into the willows. His gun rested on top of the dry bag. The bull stopped and looked back then was gone. She watched the antlers receding, bobbing above the brush as the boat made its half circle around the bar. "What happened?"

"They ran away."

"What?" She let out her pent up breath in a barrage. "I thought...I was sure you...Oh God. Oh God."

"You win some, you lose some."

"Why didn't you...?"

"The cows ran. Made the bull go, too. Couldn't get a shot. I don't like shooting from a boat."

"Oh my God, they were amazing. Did you see how they moved? I've never...I don't think I'll ever...Oh my God. Oh my God. Can we stop? I have to pee."

"Starla, why didn't you go when we stopped at the cut-off?"

"I didn't have to."

"You're so out of it. You should know better. Christ Almighty, we'll never get to Little Atlin."

Tara turned forward to look ahead. "There's some trees. Pull over there, Gary."

Gary pulled the car over. "You stay here. I'll take her."

"She can go by herself. She's not afraid."

"I gotta go, too."

"You, too?" She got her cigarettes off the dash. "Fuck, like a travelling friggin' daycare."

Starla opened the door and ran down the bank into the thick alders near the small stream. Gary walked around the car and made his way carefully down, his cowboy boots slipping on the grass. "Starla. Where are you?"

She didn't answer. She squatted by the stream, hidden by the dense alders and tall grass near the water. She finished peeing and lifted her pants back up just as Gary came through the trees. He spotted her as she stood.

"There you are." He began to undo his fly. She turned to go back through the alders. Gary was facing away talking over his shoulder. "Don't go. Stay here."

"Why?"

"Why? Keep me company."

"You don't need company."

"I'm afraid."

"Of what?"

"Lions and tigers and bears." He smiled.

"There aren't any here."

"See? It works having you here. I'm not afraid anymore" He was turning around as he spoke. She looked down at his hands. He was holding his penis, wrinkled and funny looking. She looked up. He was staring into her eyes, the hint of a smile on his face. Then he pushed it back into his pants and zipped up his fly. "That's it. All done."

Starla turned and slipped quickly through the trees, bounded up the bank and got into the back. She slammed the door and buckled her seatbelt.

The bear walked slowly up the edge of the gravel bank, getting higher above the river. He came to a place where the trail had been undercut and had fallen away. Not many animals had passed by to thread a new path through the thick spruce. He wanted to lie down, but the ache in his gut would only get worse, so he stood, panting. The smell of hedysarum roots under thick moss triggered no hunger, no urge to dig, only agony in his stomach and weariness in his legs. He sat on his haunches for a moment, but the pressure on his gut forced him to his feet again. He pushed through the thick, prickly, dry branches of spruce, over a fallen trunk, back to the trail. The top of the ridge was near. Soon it would be downhill, easier.

"There's a creek coming in up ahead. Let's stop there."

Hannah stopped paddling. "Okay. Can you show me where we are on the map?"

"I haven't been following it too closely, but I've been watching the bends and the creeks so I think I know. The Riddell River isn't too far. Pull hard on the left."

Dan steered the canoe into the eddy where the creek had pushed cobbles out into the current in a small arc. He looked down into the deeper hole as they passed over it.

The canoe edged up to shore and Hannah hopped out, took the bow rope across the narrow stony beach to a willow bush and tied it. "What's for lunch?"

"We had lunch."

"I'm starved."

"I'd offer you a pepperoni, but…"

"I almost could."

"It's caribou."

"Really?"

"Yeah, a friend of mine made it. He's into sausage. He even makes bear salami."

"I'll pass."

He stood and stepped out of the canoe. "I think I should make it my goal for this trip."

"What?"

"To get you to eat a pepperoni."

"Now that I know, you can't possibly succeed."

"Fine. I probably won't. Something to strive for." He took his fishing rod out of the top of his pack, telescoped it to full length and began threading the line through the eyes. "I feel like a pepperoni right now. Would you like one?"

"You're a pepperoni."

"You could start a fire for tea. Or coffee if you like."

"Sure. Looks like you're going fishing."

"Don't watch."

"Fishing doesn't bother me so much. You might find this hard to believe, but I've caught fish before."

He began to tie a small spinner to the line. "At a fair with a magnet on a string."

"No. Bonefish in the Florida keys."

"You lie."

"It's true. I used to go out with my father when we went down there on vacation. He loved fishing. I did, too. It was our quality time together."

"You wanna try?" He held out the rod.

"No. I'll make tea. Come on Raz. You can help me."

Dan finished tying the spinner onto his line and walked out on the gravel fan. He sent the first cast out into the river, let it sink a few seconds then retrieved it slowly. Hannah was breaking dry spruce twigs to start the fire. She had been a different person today—not so driven, not so obsessed with moving on. And since the caribou she'd been buzzing as if she were high on something.

He knew why. It was always intense. Why didn't he shoot? He should have. Ten meters standing broadside. He'd seldom had a better chance. It was probably for the best. Even a large bull caribou had less meat than a small moose, and he wanted to go home with as much as he could carry. Still, caribou was his favorite.

He sent his second cast along the current line between creek water and river and tipped his rod toward the bank to bring the lure into the eddy. The turbulence tugged slightly then eased as the lure entered slack water. The line jerked briefly. He reeled in a short distance then let the lure sink. On the second hit he was ready, setting the hook with a sharp tug. The fish flashed silver with a hint of pink and blue. It struggled back and forth in the eddy, raising its high dorsal fin to catch the current then dashed for the faster water. He steered it back and brought it in close then lifted the rod up high. He wouldn't do that with any other fish but grayling. His mother had shown him it's the only fish that goes limp when it's lifted up on the end of a line. He walked to the stony beach with the twelve-inch fish dangling inert, but as soon as he put it on the stones it began to thrash and bounce. The hook popped out of its mouth. He caught the fish, held it tightly in his left hand, put his right index finger under its mouth, his thumb behind the top of its head and pried up. In an instant it was dead, blood streaming from its gills. He looked up and saw Hannah standing above him on the bank, eating rosehips. He said, "I told you not to watch."

"What kind of fish is it?"

"Grayling."

"It's beautiful."

Dan wiped the mud off the side of the fish to reveal the pearly irides-cence of its scales then fanned out the large dorsal fin, blue with pink and black spots. "Yes it is. Beautiful."

"The tea's almost ready. Are you going to cook that?"

"Yeah. You want to eat some?"

"Yes." She spit out a clump of seeds. "I'm getting a little tired of these."

"Good. I'll catch one more."

At the Twin Creek airstrip a bunch of cars and trucks were parked near the end of the runway. Nearby, a small plane sat next to a row of orange 45-gallon fuel drums. A knot of people stood together near the vehicles. A tall man in a cowboy hat was gesticulating and talking while two others seemed to be taking notes.

Jim set the brake and opened the door. "Whew. I'm glad that's over. And we made it before dark." He looked into the back seat. "You awake?"

"Yup."

David got out of the truck and stretched. "What happens now?"

Jim walked back to the trailer to check on the horses. "I wanna let these guys out as soon as possible. We can camp down by the creek over there. Good grass. But we'll have to check with the Mounties. It might be too near the airstrip. Why don't you guys go over and see if Steve Godwin is with that group. He's in charge. I have to give the horses some hay. I'll be along in a minute."

Jessica and David walked down the edge of the airstrip towards the group of people. The big man's voice became louder. She couldn't hear what he was saying, but the tone was angry. They walked around the big RCMP truck and stopped to listen.

"Do you know how much this is costing me, Godwin? I gotta move my whole operation. I've got clients sitting on their asses. Do you know what that does to my reputation?"

Two people furiously scribbled notes while another held a small recording device.

Jessica leaned close to David and whispered. "The big guy is Lyle Kessler, the outfitter, and the one in the ball cap is Sergeant Steve Godwin, RCMP."

Steve Godwin stared placidly back into the eyes of the man towering over him. "Lyle, I understand your frustration, but there's a missing person out there and it's my job to find her."

"Stupid bitch." Lyle Kessler turned to the reporters. "And you can quote me."

Godwin continued in a reasonable tone. "What would you have me do? Call off the search until your clients get their trophies?"

"It's too fuckin' late. With all the aircraft and the people traipsing over the mountain there's not an animal for a hundred miles. You should have stopped those bastards from going up there in the first place."

"You know we can't do that."

"Well if you can't then I will. If this ever happens again, I'll make sure the bastards are never found. Fuckers."

"Lyle. Calm down." Steve turned to see Jessica and David standing there. "Yes? Can I help you?" He looked past them to the horse trailer. "Oh, you're Jim's daughter."

"Yes. This is David Hellman."

Godwin walked over and held out his hand. "I'm Sergeant Steve Godwin. I'm afraid we don't have anything new to report about your wife."

That got Lyle's attention. "Wife? Wife?" He pointed at the mountain. "She's your wife?"

The reporters rushed over to David. A recorder was thrust up to his face. Lyle pushed his hat back and walked slowly, menacingly towards him.

Sergeant Godwin pointed his finger at the big man. "Lyle."

Lyle stopped. The reporters fired questions.

"Mr. Hellman, how confident are you your wife will be found?"

"I'm…confident. She's a very tough, resourceful person. If anyone can survive out there, she can."

Lyle snorted.

"Does Hannah have much wilderness experience?"

"Yes. Quite a bit, actually. We've camped at Long Beach on Vancouver Island. She's done a lot of sailing…"

Lyle guffawed. "Sailing."

"…and heli-skiing."

"Hah. I'll bet she makes a dynamite gin and tonic after a hard day's heli-skiing."

Steve turned to Lyle. "You shut up, Kessler."

David continued. "Not just skiing and sailing. She was a wilderness guide before we met and she's an expert whitewater canoeist."

Another reporter asked, "Mr. Hellman, can you comment on your disagreement with Paul Williams of ARN?"

"I'd rather not. Mr. Williams has his views and I have mine."

Jim arrived from the trailer, caught Lyle's eye and motioned him away from the group. "Hi Lyle. You're looking fit for an old guy. How's the trail up Riddell?"

"Well used. Christ, now everybody in the world knows where it is. The bastards have taken their four wheelers in there. It's like a friggin' highway for the first part. "You know the soft ground after the first crossing?"

"Yeah."

"They turned it into a mud hole. I had horses sinking up to their bellies."

"Shit. That's almost halfway up."

"Not quite. That side hill stopped the bastards, though. You know, with the big rocks."

"Yeah, nasty for them, but the horses have no trouble."

"Naw, the only hard part is up around the rock fall."

"Yeah, at the base of the bowl up there." He pointed at the mountain.

"It's not that bowl, Jim. It's that one." Lyle pointed.

Jim sighted down his arm. "Yeah that's where I meant."

"From there on it's a piece of cake, ride anywhere."

"Do you still have to go through the thick shit to get to the east side?"

"What thick shit? The only thick shit is the first part and they've hacked it all out."

"Oh, I must be thinking of Mount Mye. Jeez, gettin' old, Lyle. Lots of grass this year?"

"Oh yeah. Always is. You know that. Anyhow, it's all yours. I'm pulling out. Game's all been chased off the mountain. Four days wasted looking for that goddamn woman. Clients are crying the blues, demanding refunds. These guys've only got a week left and they want one of everything. I'm gonna try up near the NWT border."

"There's big caribou up there. Your guys'll be happy."

"Well, if they're not, I'm suing somebody." Lyle looked over at David. "That's her husband, eh? He got any money?"

"No. Owns a little restaurant in Van. Cashed in his RRSP's to get up here."

"Shit. Just my luck. Hey, we're camped down by the creek about a quarter mile from the trail. Come on over for a drink later."

"Thanks, maybe I will."

"Bring him." He jerked his thumb at David. "My hunters' aims are gettin' rusty from lack of practice. Well, I'm outta here." Lyle walked off to his truck.

Jessica stepped closer to Jim. "That's good news." They watched him start his truck and drive away. "Dad, I didn't think you've been up this trail before."

"I haven't. I don't even know where it starts."

"Oh, crafty. And that was pretty slick about the poor little restaurant owner. You're quite the con man."

Jim put on an ominous voice. "They call me The Chameleon."

She plucked the last of the fish fins from the moss, gulped it down and tucked in her wayward breast feather. Poor pickings again. These bobbleheads were a hungry pair. Maybe she should go back up mountain where she had begun, before she started following the dying one. Her mate would be there now. The bobbleheads who sat on the big warm grass eaters were a sure source of meat, fresh and fat, opened up, skinned. Those bobbleheads left more than the guts. They ate the heads and were full.

She walked a few steps through the trampled grass of the bobblehead firenest. Hungry. Shitty littlewolf ate all the bones. Littlewolves, all shapes and sizes and colors. All hateful. All sneaky. Taste not too bad. A bit stringy. Bobbleheads and littlewolves. Strange.

A couple of rolling hops as she opened her wings sent her off the short bank and over the fan of stones. She gathered the air in great wingfuls and came to a flapping, grasping, teetering landing on a tree leaning out over the water. The few fins sat lonely in her gullet. At least she was flying light.

She should go back up the mountain. Tomorrow, after the mist, after the sun warmed the valley floor and the air became a flowing current upstream. She would catch it along the ridges of the big mountain where it stuck out into the valley. But lots of hard pumping in between.

What if she stayed in the valley? Nice weather for it. Lotsa moose. Lotsa wolves. Easy to spot a carcass. River going down. Maybe something washes up—an old salmon carcass, a dead beaver. Big bobblehead nest downstream, where they come in their big flying dead beetles for the rutting season. Good food place. Big juicy gutpiles on open bars. Lotsa food at their lognest. Sweet bobblehead food. No littlewolves.

And what about this pair with the littlewolf? Scratch around their groundroosts to get a few bony fins? She let out a rasping trill. "Shittyshittyshitty."

Rest here. Watch the river go by. The pair were hunting. Maybe fat and guts and flesh tomorrow. She'd hear the boom. It was the rutting season. Anything could happen. She might even get her first taste of bobblehead.

"Here's the road. You see the orange tape?" Tara pointed ahead.

Gary slowed the car. "Yeah."

"Right there. Slow down. Jeezus."

"I'm driving, Tara."

"You're gonna miss it."

"I'm not. I see the fuckin' tape." He turned into the drive and the car headed down through the trees.

Tara craned her neck to look ahead. "I see the cabin first. Beat you Starla."

Starla sat in the back seat looking at the tiger puppet on her hand. The car went down the dark lane edged with tall spruce, a thick layer of damp green sphagnum moss covering the ground beneath the trees. A few spindly willows stretched for the little light available. In places where a big tree had fallen, allowing light to penetrate, red currants and highbush cranberries hung in clusters. Brightness ahead showed a clearing and beyond that the blue sparkle of the lake.

They pulled up to the cabin. Starla got out quickly and headed for the lake. She made only a few steps before Tara stopped her. "Starla, don't go anywhere until we unload the car." She lifted the hatchback and held out two bags of groceries. "Come on, Gary."

Gary still sat in the car. "Okay, okay." He got out slowly and stretched. "This is nice. How's the fishing here, Starla?"

Starla was at the door, waiting for it to be unlocked. "It's good."

"Maybe you could take me out there later, show me some good spots."

Starla didn't answer.

Tara reached the door with an armload of bags. "There won't be time for anything if we don't get the door open. The sun's gonna be down soon. Hurry up."

Gary walked to the door and unlocked it. Starla was about to go in, but he stepped in front of her. "I'll take those bags in. Why don't you go have fun. I'll get the rest of the stuff." Starla handed him the bags and ran down to the lake.

Starla sat on the old swing with the puppet on her hand. It climbed up the rope and looked around. "What do you see up there, Samantha?" Her voice went deeper. "I see the ocean. It's big. I want to sail across to the other side, far away."

"Why would you want to sail away from a great place like this?" Gary was behind her, the water bucket in his hand.

She shot a startled look at him. Then looked down and took the tiger off her hand. "I don't know."

He put the water pail down. "Great fishing, great company. Are there any moose around here?"

"No."

"Oh well. I brought my gun just in case. You never know. A bull can show up anywhere during the rutting season. And I brought my .22 for grouse. Do you want me to push you?" Before Starla could get off the swing he took hold of the ropes and pulled back then let go and she swung down and over the trench scuffed into the dirt. When she swung back again she felt his hands on her hips. He pushed and she swung higher. Several pushes and she was at the full height of the swing. Each time, his hands gave her hips a small squeeze

"I wanna get off."

"Not yet. I can get you higher."

"I don't wanna." His hands squeezed her hips again. She shifted her seat forward and as the swing began its upward arc she leapt off, sailed through the air and landed on her feet. She ran past the small overgrown garden fenced with chicken wire, around the sauna and turned onto the trail that followed the lakeshore.

Gary was back at the empty swing. "Nice jump. Hey don't go too far. We're gonna eat soon."

Tara called from the door. "Hey Gary, hurry up with the water."

"You didn't have to bring two bottles of wine, Owen." Susan was in the kitchen, checking the oven.

Owen sat at the counter that separated the kitchen from the dining room. "Yes I did. I didn't know if you were serving fish or meat." He lifted a bottle in each hand. "So one white and one red."

She closed the oven. "We're having Taku River salmon."

"Oh, heaven. Susan, if you're trying to break down my resistance so you can have your way with me, you're doing all the right things."

"Can I pour you a glass?"

"Red please."

"But we're having fish."

"How long will it be?"

"Fifteen minutes."

"Then we'll drink the red now and have the white with the salmon."

"You're impossible Owen."

"I disagree. I think I'm quite possible."

Susan poured two glasses of red wine. Owen was at it again—making his innuendos. Two bottles of wine. Did he think he was going to get her drunk? She could have invited another friend to join them, but she couldn't discuss Tara and Starla with anyone else. She shouldn't discuss them with Owen. She handed him his wine and held hers up. "Salut."

"To old law partners getting together to eat fish and drink wine and—" Owen reached down to the briefcase leaning against his stool and brought out two DVDs and a large brown envelope. "—watch a movie."

"What is it?"

"Gosford Park. Have you seen it?"

"Yes."

"I was hoping you'd say that, because I also brought *Hollywood, Bollywood.* Please say you haven't seen it."

"Haven't seen it."

"Great. You're gonna love it. But I warn you, I've been known to dance along. You might need a blindfold." He took a large swig of wine.

"What's in the envelope?"

"Another little present."

Susan pulled a stack of papers out of the envelope and looked at the top sheet. She saw the Yukon Territorial Government logo: Department of Health and Social Services. It was a photocopy of an affidavit by a social worker for a child welfare case. The name of the subject was at the top. "Amanda Morris. Who's she?"

"A kid. eighteen by now. Her mother is an ex- of Gary Haines."

"Owen, these are confidential. How did you get them?"

"I can't recall."

"You could lose your job."

"Fine. I'll get another one. Hey, I'll come back to the firm. Does this mean I have to give back my going away presents?"

"You could be disbarred."

"That's okay. I'm tired of the law anyway. I'll get liposuction and hair implants and become an international sex symbol."

"I could get disbarred, too."

"Great. We'll buy...no, wait...we'll steal a gypsy caravan and travel the world. You can tell fortunes and perform seductive dances and I'll be an acrobat. Or maybe I'll just drink." He took another gulp of wine and looked her in the eye, serious now. "Susan, you're the only person in the world I'd trust with this stuff, and it's not because I'm hopelessly attracted to you. It's because you have integrity and heart. I know you won't abuse this and you'll be very careful, very discreet."

"I don't know, Owen. I feel uncomfortable with this. I'm not sure what I can do with it."

"Well you can't do anything with it, but it might help you decide what needs to be done."

"Yeah. I'm really worried about Starla."

"I'm afraid those papers aren't going to make you worry any less. By the way, I talked to Innis of the RCMP. Haines isn't involved in any current investigations. He's been keeping a low profile, holding down a job."

"I saw them at the store today. I even talked to Gary. It gave me a really bad feeling. Starla's afraid of him."

"Have you talked to Tara yet?"

"No. I tried to call her this afternoon, but no answer, so I called her mother. She said the three of them went to Tara's cabin at Little Atlin Lake."

"How long will they be gone?"

"A week, maybe. She didn't know."

"I don't suppose they have a phone."

"No."

"So there's nothing you can do right now."

"Nothing."

"And 'a really bad feeling' isn't much to go on."

"No."

"Won't stand up in court."

"No."

"Then you should put it out of your mind, drink some wine, eat a fabulous meal, watch a brilliant movie, and enjoy the scintillating company of a devastatingly handsome chap."

Susan wasn't listening. "Unless…"

"These fish are delicious." Hannah was eating with gusto.

Dan watched her eat. She was finally getting a good meal. She needed it. She had eaten one grayling at the creek where they stopped for tea, so before they moved on he caught four more for supper. "It's my special secret ingredient."

"What is it?"

"Hunger."

"I've never been so ravenous."

"I feel as if I'm leading you astray, down into the evil world of the carnivore."

"Don't worry. I've been there. I didn't grow up a vegetarian, you know. Jewish cooking is very fleshy. My father made his own corned beef from his grandmother's recipe. And if you promise not to tell, I confess I occasionally eat fish." She finished off the last of her grayling.

"No kidding." Dan pointed at the three backbones, picked clean, lying neatly intact on her plate, eighteen fins in a small pile beside them. "You know your way around a fish carcass."

She looked down at his plate. "That's not fair. You only got one. You tricked me. You don't have to be so noble."

"I'm not. I'm gonna get my share. In fact, I'm gonna get the best part. "He reached back to a plate behind him and picked up a dripping mass of pink, white and gray. He put the frying pan on the fire and dropped the slippery handful in. "The guts."

"Lovely. Oh, that is revolting."

"Indian calamari. My mom loves it. You should try some. The stomach and intestines have been washed out. You just gotta get over the fact it's the guts."

"I don't think so. I'm having one of those Bambi moments."

"If you're still hungry, there's pepperoni."

She chuckled. "Up yours. You can't get me to eat one of those." She scraped the bones and fins to the edge of her plate and tilted it toward the fire.

Dan stopped her. "Hey don't burn them. He took the plate from her, reached it as far as he could away from the fire and put it on the ground. "Raz." The dog trotted up to the plate and ate, lifting his gums and shearing the skeletons into pieces with his back teeth so they disappeared, crunching bit by bit into the side of his mouth.

Hannah looked up to the sky. "Dear Miss Manners. Help." She leaned back under the tarp against the rolled up sleeping bag. "I'm warm now."

"It's getting cold, though. There'll be frost again tonight."

She watched him stir the pan then lean the spoon against a rock by the fire. "Why didn't you shoot the caribou?"

"I told you. He ran. I couldn't get a shot."

"But he was so close. Standing right there. I've never been that close to a wild animal—not one that big—never mind six of them."

"Yeah but the boat was moving, too. And the light was in my eyes. And my hair was out of place and my nails were a mess. They still are. See? What do you want from me?"

She sat forward, closer, laughing. "A complete list of excuses, typed and bound."

"Then send me a stamped, self addressed envelope."

They both laughed. Hannah put her hand on his shoulder. For a moment it rested there, a small unconscious act suddenly intimate and significant. He didn't move, wondering if she felt awkward, if she was resisting the urge to snatch it away. Instead she gave his shoulder a brotherly pat, removed her hand and looked away into the fire.

Dan looked into the fire, too. It was as if her hand was still on his shoulder, the warmth. It probably meant nothing. Two people sharing a joke. How many times had he done the same with Artie? But this wasn't Artie. It was a woman. It had been awhile since a woman had touched him. Had her hand lingered that second longer? No. He stirred the frying pan.

Hannah broke the silence. "Was it because I was there?"

"What? The caribou?"

"Yes."

"No."

"If I hadn't been with you, would you have killed it?"

He stirred the frying pan. "If you weren't there, I wouldn't have seen those caribou. I'd have been somewhere else on the river."

"No, you know what I mean. Given all the same circumstances, except for me."

"Okay." He hesitated awhile. "Yeah, I probably would have killed it. You saved the life of a caribou. Are you happy?"

"Yes I am. But I don't want to interfere with your life."

"We've got a lot more river ahead, and I won't pass up a chance like that again. My mother will give me hell when she finds out."

"Why?"

"Indian people believe an opportunity like that is a gift from the creator. The animal is offering itself to you. It's disrespectful to refuse it."

"Do you believe it?"

"No. Maybe. I don't know. Sometimes it seems that way. The first sheep I ever shot was kinda like that. He was the biggest ram in a group of eight. They walked by me about thirty meters away, all in a line, the big one in the lead, like a shooting gallery...except I didn't shoot. When they saw me and took off up through the rocks, all I could see through the scope was moving backs and horns—no way I could take a shot. I was just watching them run and thinking, *Oh well, they're gone. I won't be getting another crack at him.* Then about eighty meters away he stopped, stepped out of the group, and looked at me." Dan stopped talking.

Hannah waited. "So..."

"So what?"

"So, you shot him?"

"Yeah. I didn't think you wanted to hear that part."

"So you believe he offered himself to you?"

"I don't know. I'm kinda caught in between my mother and my father. She never lost the old beliefs. For her the world is full of spirits. My father was a devout atheist."

"Hmm. What does it feel like to kill an animal?"

Dan stared at her then into the fire for a long moment. "Big question. If you mean do I enjoy the killing, the answer is no. I've known some who do. They're rare enough. I always feel...I don't know...of course I feel sorry for the animal. Remorse. But at the same time there's satisfaction—lots of good quality meat and a skin. There's a sense of accomplishment—you know, the provider thing—but the kill, the moment of it...I'd be lying if I said there's no excitement. You'd call it bloodlust or something, but it is definitely a charged moment. The adrenaline is pumping. Everything—the sounds, the wind, the water, the light—all come into sharp focus. Time goes away. I've killed lots of animals—moose, caribou, sheep—and I can remember every one of them in vivid detail. Intense. I think you felt it."

"I felt it, but I wanted them to run away."

"Maybe it's why they did. They read your mind."

"He stopped and looked back...the bull."

"Yeah, I saw it, but by then the boat was moving too fast. Not a good shot. Wouldn't want to wound him."

"What if you were to wound an animal and it ran away. How would you feel?"

"White bwana lady ask many questions." He picked the frying pan off the fire, held it under his nose and sniffed. "Aah. This is ready. Can I tempt you?"

"No thanks. Well? It must happen sometimes."

Dan picked up a piece of rubbery tissue, popped it in his mouth and chewed. "It happens. You've gotta be sure of your shot. I won't shoot if I'm not sure."

"You can't possibly be absolutely sure. Has it ever happened to you?"

Dan stared into the fire, eating mouthfuls of fish organs. He seemed to have ignored the question. She was about to repeat it when he looked her in the eye. "Yeah, eight years ago. It was a moose. The weather had been really bad, rain and snow. The moose don't answer calls when it's like that. They just clam up. I was on the Pelly River. I came around a bend and there was a moose. He took off as soon as he saw the canoe. I put the gun up fast and fired. I heard the bullet hit him. I'm pretty sure I hit him in the hind leg. I searched for a whole day, but there wasn't much blood. I never saw him again."

"How did you feel?"

"Horrible. I imagined the long lingering death, the suffering. I tried to tell myself he could heal, but I knew I was kidding myself. I almost gave up hunting. For three years I didn't go alone. I made sure I took along a buddy who was keen to do the shooting. One time I was with some friends calling moose and this huge bull walked right by me, no more than ten feet away. I didn't shoot. I thought maybe they could see the moose, you know, get a shot at him, but the trees were too thick. The bull finally got our scent and walked off. My friends were really pissed off at me. I made all kinds of good sounding excuses, but I didn't tell them the real reason." He looked her in the eye. "I've never even told my Mom that. You, of all people, are the only one."

"I won't tell a soul."

"Thanks."

They both stared into the fire.

She said, "If it happened to you, someone who seems to be very careful then it must happen a lot...wounded animals dying painfully. Can you understand my views on hunting?"

"I told you I understand, but giving it up is not the answer. Not for me. It's part of my way of life, my ancestors' way of life. It's part of my... religion, if you want. No, the answer is to become better, to be sure of the kill, don't be greedy, treat the animals with respect, before and after they're dead."

"I see."

Dan smiled and mocked her tone. "I see." He held up the pan. "Last chance. One piece left." She shook her head, so he scooped up the last of the entrails, ate them and licked his fingers. "Okay, my turn. What about you? You've killed things. Fish."

"Yes, I suppose it's the same thing."

"It is. Care to elaborate? Do you think buying a fish is any different from catching it yourself?"

"I know. It doesn't matter who kills it. If I buy it, I'm as guilty as the person who did. And there's the by-catch issue, and the longline issue, and the bottom trawling and the dolphins. But I only eat it on rare occasions."

"Fine. Do you swat mosquitoes?"

"That's self preservation."

"When you swat mosquitoes, do you ever get a little sadistic thrill?"

"No...Yes."

"Aha. Do you wear clothes and shoes?"

"Not from animal sources."

"No? How about synthetic fibers."

"Of course."

"Ever heard of the Exxon Valdez, the Torry Canyon? Ever seen the sea birds and mammals dying, covered with goo? Ever seen the effluent from a polypropylene factory?"

"What's your canoe made of? Did you make your rifle from organic fibers? Everything we do has an impact. I'm trying to reduce mine."

"Good. But so am I. If I take a moose from this river, I don't affect the ability of this valley to produce more. The habitat is intact. And I don't buy meat from the grocery store, which requires trucks and fuel and feed lots and fertilizers and pesticides and..."

"Okay. I've heard all that stuff before." She smiled. "Why do you feel so threatened by me?"

"Because you're a devil woman."

Hannah burst out laughing.

Dan called the dog. "Raz. Come here." The dog rose from where he was lying behind them and came up between the two people, wagging his tail. "Raz, she's a witch. Get her." Raz wagged his tail and tried to lick Hannah's face. She leaned back laughing. Dan held the dog's head toward her and lifted its lips to show the teeth. "Good boy. She's like one of those pod people who suck out your brains. I saw it in a movie, Raz. She's evil. She's gonna point at us and make a screechy sound and take away our souls." Raz was wagging his tail furiously. Dan took his hand away and the dog's lips dropped. "Keep them up, boy." He folded the dog's lips under so they showed the fangs. Raz tried to lick her again and they popped back down.

Hannah was laughing harder. "The poor dog. Leave him alone. He doesn't understand."

"He does. Good boy, Raz. Now go lie down." The dog tried to lick Hannah's face again. "No, Raz. Lie down." Raz lay down behind Dan, who leaned back to rest his head on the dog's flank. Raz put his head on his paws.

Hannah was leaning on one elbow. "I wonder if he knows it's a joke."

"I'm sure he does."

"Good boy, Raz." She rolled over and reached a hand back to pat the dog. Her other hand rested on Dan's arm.

Starla lay in her bed with the tiger puppet on her hand and watched the flickering orange light from the fire outside dance on the ceiling. She could hear Tara and Gary as they sat by the fire drinking and talking, but she couldn't make out what was said. Occasionally her mother's laugh rang out.

The tiger peeked above a fold in the blanket out into the darkness of the room. It turned back to Starla, put it's paw to its mouth and said, "Shhh. There's a bear out there somewhere. He's sneaking up on us."

Starla whispered, "I can't see."

"As soon as he moves, I'll see him. I have night eyes."

She knew what her friends would think if they found out she was playing with a hand puppet—knew she was too old for it—but it helped pass the time and ease the loneliness. Before Mom and Dad split up, it hadn't been lonely. She loved coming here with her parents—fishing, swimming, cards at night, treats, roasted marshmallows, reading, telling stories, eating, joking, laughing—except when Mom and Dad were arguing.

Now Mom spent most of her attention on Gary, and Starla was expected to go away and occupy herself. She was fine with that, welcomed the solitude if the alternative was him. She'd found him intimidating when Tara brought him home one night two months ago. He had ignored her for the most part, but sometimes she got the feeling she was being watched. A couple of times she had turned to find him staring at her. It was unnerving. Whenever he touched her it felt like more than a touch. Even in a casual hand on her shoulder she sensed a furtive hunger. She'd seen his temper a few times, when he and Tara argued. He'd shown it when they met Susan Field in Walmart. She could tell he was controlling it. He was capable of much more.

What was happening today when they stopped by the stream? It was confusing and scary. Had Gary deliberately shown her his penis? She'd seen them before, from baby boy cousins, Dad in the sauna, a drunken uncle relieving himself in the bushes, clumsy with the zipper, groggily turning around too soon. Is that what happened today with Gary? But he wasn't drunk, and the smile on his face was weird.

The tiger sniffed. "I can smell him. He's very close. Don't worry. I'll fight him."

She hoped someone would be at Brian and Ann's place on the north side of the point, the only other cabin on this part of the lake. Brian and Ann were an older couple like her grandparents, and their place was probably deserted this time of year, but someone might come on the weekend. Maybe it would be Natalie, their granddaughter. Natalie was cool, old enough for a driver's license and a boyfriend, but she and Starla had always hit it off. Starla was drawn by Natalie's love of life—confident, optimistic, funny, always the center of attention. Sometimes Natalie brought a bunch of friends. That would be so good, to hang out with them and watch them party.

She heard the cabin door open and someone come in. Tara's voice came from outside. "I'll be there in a minute, sugar. I'm gonna brush my teeth in the lake."

The door closed. Gary's footsteps moved to the sink and Starla heard him brushing his teeth. She didn't make a sound, barely breathed. She heard him spit into the sink and pour some water down the drain. His footsteps moved to the short hallway leading to the two bedrooms and stopped at her door. She held her breath, heard him breathing and shuffling slightly, perhaps hesitating, trying to decide something. *Go away,* she thought. There was a clump, clump on the porch, the cabin door opened and Tara, her voice loud and a bit slurred by alcohol said, "Gary, you should come down to the lake. The northern lights are so cool. Gary?"

Gary walked out of the hallway to the main room. "I wanna go to bed."

"Oh, there you are. What are you doin' in the hall. You tryin' to play hide and seek? I'm good at that game. I'll find you." Starla heard Tara move across the kitchen then some rustling. Tara said, "Mmmm. Gotcha. Hey, what's this? This game turn you on? It'll be easy to catch you now. I'll just grab you by this." She laughed. More rustling and shuffling, Gary laughing then her mother's voice. "I'm gonna pour myself another rum and coke. You want one?"

"No, I'm okay."

"Okay, Big Bear, I'll see you in a moment."

Starla heard them kissing again, Gary walking down the hall, the other bedroom door opening, Tara clinking a glass, making her way unsteadily down the hall, the bedroom door closing. She listened to the muffled sounds of their lovemaking. The thought of her mother and Gary doing it...yuck.

The tiger growled. "Rrrrr."

"They're magnificent. I've never seen them so bright. Look, over there. They're rippling. The edges are pink." Hannah gazed up, enthralled. A glowing, swirling river of light stretched in a wide band across the sky from horizon to horizon—the Aurora. She nudged Dan and pointed directly above them. "It looks like spreading wings."

"Yeah, it's beautiful. But you're cold. You're shivering. You should get into the sleeping bag."

"I'm not cold."

"Okay then, freeze your ass off, but I'm gonna go to bed."

"It's not fair that I get your sleeping bag and you have to sleep in your coat. I've been thinking about it. Why don't we open up the sleeping bag and both get under it."

"That's fine with me if you don't mind."

"I don't."

"Okay. I'll put the canvas tarp down over the spruce boughs. I'll go get it ready. You coming?"

"In a minute or two." She went back to looking up at the northern lights.

Dan walked over the sand bar to their camp in the trees. She saw a puff of sparks leap up as he put some wood on the fire. She walked across the gravel to the water's edge. She knew he couldn't see her, but she tossed a look over her shoulder, anyway. Undoing her jeans and reaching her hand inside, she pulled out the damp piece of dishtowel, washed it in the river then wrung it out as hard as she could. The shock of cold when she stuffed it back into her panties made her wince. There had to be a better way.

She returned to the fire and squatted near it, holding her hands out to warm them. "Thanks."

Dan turned to her. "For what?"

"For today. It was...amazing. I can't remember when I've had a better day."

"Good."

"Except..."

He was arranging the bed, unzipping and spreading out the sleeping bag. "Except what?"

She hesitated, wondering if she should tell him about her period. Was he one of those guys who couldn't handle it, like David? "I have my period."

"Oh. Is that a big problem?"

"Yes. It's very uncomfortable...messy. The maddening thing is, I had some tampons in my pack."

The dog jumped up from where he had been lying, went to Dan and nudged his hand with his nose. Dan patted his head. "So what have you been using?"

"I've been using...other methods."

He stared at her, puzzled then his eyes went wide. She could almost see the cartoon light bulb go on above his head. He laughed. "The amazing shrinking dishtowel."

"I'm hoping you might have a bush version of tampons."

The dog bounded over to Hannah, bounced off her with his forepaws, trotted away from the fire and turned around excitedly.

Hannah laughed. "What's gotten into him all of a sudden?"

"I dunno."

"It looks like he wants to go for a walk."

Dan stood. Raz was in the play position, forelegs on the ground, butt in the air, tail wagging. "Raz, we're trying to have a serious conversation about tampons. If you wanna go for a walk, go by yourself."

Raz bounded away to the river.

Dan shook his head. "Weird dog."

"Maybe he's gone to get some tampons."

Dan laughed. "Yeah, to the store in Ross River. Trouble is, he didn't wait for me to give him any cash."

"I guess he'll have to use his credit card."

"Yup. He should be back in time for your next period."

"Great. So in the meantime, what do I use?"

"Sphagnum moss. Been used for centuries. It's absorbent and disposable." He went into the trees and scooped up a handful of moss. "Here you go. Plenty more where that came from." He held it out to her. "My mother told me she's used it."

She took it from him. "It has twigs in it."

"I think you're supposed to pick those out."

"I don't know. I..." She held out her handful of moss and inspected it. "What if there are bugs?"

"I don't think there's anything large in the moss. Of course you wouldn't want to be surprised by a big honkin' spruce beetle crawling around your..."

"Please, Dan, stop trying to reassure me."

A banging sound came from the river. Dan turned to look, "Raz is in the boat. What the fuck?" He turned back to her. "Anyway, if you wanna use the dishtowel go ahead. Maybe we can get another one at Lyle's fly in camp downriver—some food, too. Hell, they might even have some tampons.

"I can't accept help from him."

Raz came running back to the fire with a small white plastic-wrapped package in his mouth. He went to Hannah and dropped it at her feet then sat back looking up expectantly. She picked up the package. "What the hell? Tampons. Raz, where did you get these?"

Dan came closer and looked into her hand. "Oh yeah. In my boat pack I forgot all about those. Whenever we went into the bush Tara always left her tampons behind, so I got into the habit of carrying them with my fishing gear. But Raz remembered."

She got down to the dog's level and hugged him. "I don't believe it. Thank you, Raz. You don't know how much this means to me."

"Dad was right. Never own a dog smarter than you."

"Excuse me. I'll be right back." She hurried to the river.

When she got back to the fire Dan had finished setting up the bed. "Ready." He took off his jacket. "You wear this."

"But you…"

"I insist." He reached into his dry bag and pulled out his toque. "This, too."

"Yes, mother." Hannah took the jacket and toque from him and put them on.

Dan took off his boots, lay down on the bed and pulled the sleeping bag over him. Hannah slipped in beside him, careful not to touch, keeping her hands folded over her chest. She lay still for a while, feeling the heat from his body a few centimeters away. She watched the fire's reflection dance on the roof of the lean to and listened to the sound of Dan's breathing.

She didn't feel sleepy. Her mind was running in high gear, sorting through the tumble of events since she'd left Vancouver two weeks ago. Two weeks—it seemed so long ago, so far away. Grizzly Watch had been her whole life for over a year—the work, meetings, fund-raisers, training, planning, all the media events, being filmed rock climbing in the Bugaboo Mountains. It had been exciting and different—what she'd been longing for—the impetus to break out of her comfortable rut, the chance to do something that mattered, to take a leading part in something larger than herself.

She remembered the big day leaving for the Yukon: cameras, interviews, farewell speeches, Andrea and Martin looking so young and committed. She remembered the CBC radio call-in show in Whitehorse and the feeling of satisfaction as she answered her critics with reasoned, impassioned arguments.

Everything was going so well until the weather turned bad. If not for that…but the weather was not to blame. Stupid, stupid, stupid. If it hadn't been for her first mistake things would have been so different. That first night out had been horrid, crouching under the rock, no sleep, cold water dripping down her back. The rest was a blur—days of despair, pain, and exhaustion, nights of fear and hopelessness, endless bog and thick forested hillsides, pools of black water, the huge burned forest where lifeless trees stood at crazy angles, the utter desolation of being alone in an uncaring wilderness, the strange vision of the black angel.

Lying here now, it all seemed so remote, as if her memories were those of another person, as if she had awakened to an alternate reality. And this man sleeping beside her…how did she feel about him? She would be dead now if he hadn't come along. He was funny, caring, gentle, well-read, handsome. And when he produced those tampons from his pack he was too good to be true. There must be something wrong with this guy. Yes, there was that one thing—he was a hunter. She wondered how a man like him could bring himself to kill.

He rolled onto his side, facing away from her and she felt a wisp of cold air come under the edge of the sleeping bag, soon replaced by a wave of heat pouring off his body. She looked at his back and felt a fleeting urge to touch him.

Susan lay in bed, staring into the dark. The affidavits, parenting assessments, home study reports and social workers' notes were a depressing read…a litany of neglect, abuse, and alcoholism. There wasn't anything in them that directly implicated Gary Haines, but the case histories, all young girls, all children of his ex-partners showed a disturbing trend. Psychological assessments on three of the girls noted a suspicion of *sexual interference by an individual in a position of trust*, although they stopped short of naming Haines.

Amanda Morris was the saddest case. She came to the attention of the Health and Social Services department when she was five years old, found outside her house in downtown Whitehorse at three a.m. wearing no winter clothing. The temperature was −20C. A neighbor took her in and after knocking on her mother's door with no success, called the police. When they finally got someone to answer the door they found six adults, all in extreme states of intoxication. Amanda was taken into care and her mother, Leslie Morris, went to detox.

Amanda spent the next five years in and out of foster homes. Whenever her mother dried out enough she went back home. When Amanda was eleven, Leslie took up with Gary Haines and applied for a permanent order to get her daughter back. For two years the department had little involvement in Amanda's life then shortly after she turned thirteen she was picked up in a police raid on a hotel room. Drunk and high on cocaine, she had been turning tricks with middle-aged men. The police investigation did not mention Haines. He had left Leslie Morris six months before. The psychologist who examined Amanda suspected a history of sexual interference.

Amanda was placed in a group home and her next few years were tightly controlled by social workers. She was a handful: rebellious, angry, verbally abusive to anyone in a position of authority. She ran away twice and both times was found at her boyfriend's place, drunk and high on drugs. She finally disappeared for good from the group home at the age of sixteen and the reports stopped there.

Susan switched on the bedside light and lifted the photo of a smiling six-year-old from the top of the pile of papers—such a sweet looking kid, innocent and happy. What happened to mess her up? Amanda had had a tough life, to be sure, but what could turn a thirteen-year-old girl, with all the support and safety nets society could muster, into a drug addicted hooker? Susan couldn't shake a disturbing feeling. What if Gary Haines had a hand in it?

A bright moon lit the cow moose feeding on willows at the shore. The young bull had swum across the small lake, drawn by her scent, but he dared not go near, for a different smell, much stronger, told him another bull was with her, probably back further in the trees. The young bull now stood chest deep in the water. He grunted once and was answered with a deep rumble and the sound of snapping branches as the other bull raked his antlers on the trees—big. The willows rustled to the sound of antlers pushing them aside. The old bull appeared on the shore. It grunted again and tipped its head toward him, showing a wide breadth of palms armed with long sharp tines.

The young bull turned and walked parallel to the shore, staying in deep water until he was a safe distance away. Another grunt as he walked up on shore. He would keep his distance, but he wouldn't leave. His need to stay near the cow was an ache he had never felt before.

"Chai tea?" Jessica took the pot of boiling water from the fire.

"Yes please. You are really quite remarkable. I can't believe you made pizza over an open fire." David sat in a folding chair with his feet stuck out toward the heat. Horse bells clanked in the darkness beyond the firelight. The northern lights danced above.

Jessica poured hot water over the tea and put a small pot of milk on the fire. "It's all in the timing."

"It's more than that. I know. I have to deal with spoiled chefs who complain if their hats aren't laundered daily. Young lady, you have a talent. Plus ,you can wrangle horses and drive a truck and God knows what else. If you ever want to move to Vancouver, I'll give you a job."

"Watch out. I might take you up on it."

"I'm serious. It's hard to find intelligent, resourceful people who can think for themselves. In any business the most important thing is being able to handle people. You have a talent for it."

"How could you possibly know that? You just met me."

"You think I didn't notice how you manage your father?"

She laughed. "Bullshit. I don't..."

"You do. You keep him on track, keep the conversation moving, steer him away from confrontation."

"That's easy to do. He's my Dad. I've had a lifetime of training." She took the milk off the fire and poured it into two cups then added the chai tea. She handed one to David and sat across the fire from him. "Have you ever thought of opening a Chives in Whitehorse?"

"No. It never occurred to me, but I'm sure it wouldn't work. The market's too small."

"You don't know Whitehorse. There's a big demand for restaurant food. It's a government town, lots of money floating around and people love to eat out. I think a Chives would be a big hit. They want something a few levels above fast food, something healthy and trendy so they can feel big city."

"Maybe you're right, but it's a moot point now. I won't be opening any new Chives."

"Why not?"

"I'm franchising it. Other people will be opening them."

"How does that work?"

"They buy the rights to the Chives name and reputation. We supply the menus and décor, and we control the distribution and advertising. That's pretty much it."

"Somebody in Whitehorse should do it. Dad would say it's a license to print money."

"Maybe you should do it."

"Me? I have no experience, and I certainly don't have enough money."

"Money? That's the easy part." David turned to look out from the fire. The road was a gray wash fading to black. "How long do you think he'll be? It's dark."

"Don't worry about Dad. He's got the night vision of a cat. Besides, the northern lights are bright and the moon's up. There's no way to tell when he'll be back. He'll be over there pumping Lyle and his guides for information about the trails and camping spots. And those American hunters are always generous with their whiskey. You don't have to wait for him. Your bed is all made up in the tent."

"I don't think I can sleep yet…too much to think about."

"I know. It must be hard."

"My damned imagination. Hannah torn to pieces by a bear, Hannah lying at the bottom of a cliff with broken legs, slowly dying of exposure."

The gentle sound of flowing water, the soft crackle from the dying fire, a full stomach and the warmth from Dan's body gave her a feeling of peace and well being. Hannah closed her eyes and drifted off to sleep.

SEPT. 18

Starla woke early. As she got dressed she could hear Gary snoring in the other room. She guessed those two would sleep for another couple of hours, which was fine with her. She walked down to the dock over the frost-covered ground and smelled the sweet balsam scent of autumn aspen trees. It was cold, but she knew the day would warm as soon as the sun topped the mountains behind her. The marsh grass on the far side of the lake shone yellow green through wispy columns of mist. If her Dad was here they'd be over there right now trying to call a moose, or out in the canoe fishing, or playing a game of hide and seek, or just hanging out together, talking and joking.

She looked down into the water and remembered the stories her Dad used to make up about the tiny people who lived on the lake bottom. One of them was named Starla, Queen of the lake people, and she was always the heroine. "Have you ever seen the little people, Dad?" He would get a serious look on his face and say "Only once. That was the time Queen Starla saved my life. I was drowning, almost dead, lying on the bottom. She got all the lake people to cut waterweeds and make them into ropes. Then she called seven great big trout from the deepest part of the lake and she tied the ropes to them and they pulled me to the shore just like a dog team pulling a sled with her driving." She wished he was here now. But he would never be here again, not unless he got back together with Tara, and there was no chance of that. It was so unfair. Now there was nothing to do. It was no fun here without him.

She heard the cabin door open, looked back and saw Gary come outside. He waved at her and went to the car. She hoped he'd go back inside but instead he came toward her, holding a long plastic-wrapped object in his hand. She looked back down into the water as Gary approached.

"Morning, Starla. Beautiful day, eh?"

She didn't look up. "Mm hmm." She heard the plastic rustling.

"I've got a present for you."

She looked at him as he held out the package. "What is it?"

"Open it and find out."

Starla took the package from him and tore off the plastic bag taped over the end to see a fishing reel. It was one of those kids' sets mounted on cardboard and covered by hard plastic: rod, reel, and line. "Uh, I don't really need it. I have a rod and reel."

"That old thing of Dan's? The bail doesn't work anymore. Besides it's too big for you. I thought you needed a new one."

Starla wasn't sure what to say. Could she tell Gary she didn't want a kid's rod, that she liked her old one because it used to be Dad's? But she didn't want to seem ungrateful and it was a nice gesture. "Thanks."

Gary started to sit down beside her on the dock. She shifted away.

"You don't have to move. There's lots of room." He settled himself and reached out to put a hand on her shoulder. She shifted further. "Starla, I know you're upset about your parents splitting up, and I know it's hard to get used to the new…arrangements, but I want to be your friend. I can't be Dan, 'cause I'm not. I'm different, so our relationship will be different. It could even be better." Starla looked sharply at him. "Okay, for now we'll just say different. I'm asking you to give me a chance, that's all." He patted her thigh then abruptly stood up. "I'm starved. I'll go and see if Tara's up yet. Why don't you try out the new rod?"

"Draw hard on the left. Hard."

Hannah could hear the urgency in Dan's voice over the roar of the water. They were almost through the rapids, but the canoe was heading straight for a big round boulder that looked like the back of a huge, half-submerged hippo. Water poured around each side of it in two slick flumes then met and broke into a tumbling white wave behind it. She leaned out over the gunwale, reached her paddle as far as she could and bracing her left leg, pulled back hard. Flipping the paddle out again she pulled once more, feeling the canoe gain speed down the slope of the big rock's bow wave.

As the canoe's bow cut into the standing wave behind the rock she looked up. Another one loomed ahead. Judging the momentum of the boat and the push of the current, she quickly shifted to the other side of the seat and reached out with her paddle a split second before Dan shouted. "Draw right." She pulled in hard in one powerful sweep. The canoe slipped by the rock with a comfortable margin, far enough to miss the chaotic downstream swirl behind the big boulder. They were through the worst of the rapids. Now there was only the leftover chop before the river settled into its former relaxed pace.

Dan's voice came from behind her. "That was a little too exciting for me."

Hannah turned in her seat and smiled. "Go on. Don't be a wuss. It was fun."

He looked back upstream. "I thought we were past all the rapids. I guess I forgot about that one." He turned back forward. "Hey, you're pretty good. You've done this before."

"Sure. I've been through much bigger water than that. Haven't you?"

"Not unless I have to."

"You never run the rapids for fun? Why not?"

"Two reasons: wet and cold. No sweat if there's a road next to the river, but out here we'd be in a fine mess if we busted the canoe and lost all our gear. I'm glad we didn't have a moose on board for that."

She turned back to him with an impish smile. "Good thing I chased away that moose."

Dan flipped the lid of the food box and reached in. "Pepperoni?"

"No thanks." Hannah turned around so she couldn't see Dan eating. The temptation was hard to resist. She leaned back against the pack behind her and looked up at the mountains to the north. It was probably cold up there but down here in the valley the sun beat warm on her face and bare arms.

She felt a small tap on her shoulder and turned her head to see Dan's paddle beside her with a piece of bannock, heavily smeared with jam, perched on the blade. "Oh, thanks. Where did this come from? I thought we ate it all for breakfast."

"I made an extra."

She bit into the bannock eagerly, savoring the sweet bland comfort of fried dough and jam. In Vancouver she would never touch anything like this, but right now it was the most delicious thing she could imagine. She turned onto her side and looked back at Dan, who was munching and scanning the shores ahead, paddling occasionally, just enough to keep the boat straight. "Tell me about your daughter."

Dan glanced down at her then back up to scan the river. "Not much to tell."

"There must be. What grade is she in?"

"Six."

There was a long pause. Hannah waited, watching him then turned away to look ahead. "Sorry. Everybody tells me I'm too nosey. I guess you don't want to talk about it." The canoe drifted lazily. She looked down into the water. The river was clearer and noticeably lower. She watched the gravel bottom go by, mesmerized by dancing webs of refracted light on colored stones.

After a long silence Dan's voice surprised her. "Looks like her mother's gonna get sole custody."

"Why?"

"Because she has a job and a home."

"And you don't?"

"I've been staying with my mother in Ross. I got...laid off from Highways about a year ago."

"Why?"

"Why, why. You are nosey. Okay, I got fired...caught smoking pot on the job."

"Oh. That'll do it."

"The bugger of it is I was supplying my crew boss with the stuff. Whenever I went for days off he'd ask me to bring some back for him. Anyway, without a job or a home my chances of getting custody of Starla are about nil."

"There's such a thing as shared custody, isn't there?"

"Yeah, but you wouldn't believe the shit Tara brings up in court, stuff I did when I was a teenager. From what I hear she was just as bad back then, but that never gets mentioned."

"Mention it then. Fight back."

"I'm not like that. Besides, it's too hard on Starla. I just want the whole thing to be over. Anyway, what have I got to offer her? I don't want her to live in Ross. She has school and friends in Whitehorse. And if I'm away working I don't wanna leave her with Mom. She says she'd love to look after Starla, but…"

"I'm sure there must be a way to work it out. You could move to Whitehorse and get a job."

"Easy to say. No, I think the best thing for Starla is to stay where she is…for now anyway."

Susan listened to the phone ringing on the other end of the line. She was nervous, unsure what she would say when it was answered. If she told the truth, she could open herself up to investigation by the law society and if it was discovered she was in possession of confidential papers it could be disastrous. If she lied it could lead to the same thing.

The phone was picked up at the other end. "Hello."

"Hello, may I speak to Leslie Morris, please?"

"That's me."

"Hi. My name is Susan Field. I'm trying to locate your daughter, Amanda. I wonder if you could help me."

"Who are you? Is this some kinda sick fuckin' joke?"

"No, I…uh…"

"Are you from the police or the government or what?"

"No, I'm a lawyer. I don't understand. Do you know where Amanda is?"

"Yeah. She's dead."

Susan wasn't ready for this. "Oh. I'm sorry. I had no idea…"

"Yeah, well I didn't put one of those ads in the paper."

"Do you mind me asking how she died?"

"Heroin overdose in Edmonton."

"Oh my God. I'm so sorry. When did it happen?"

"Last February. Why do you want to know about her?"

"I wanted to talk to her about…her life."

"Why? What kind of lawyer are you?"

"I'm doing some research for another case and I thought…"

"If you're defending one of her johns, you can fuck right off. She was a kid for God's sake and those assholes…"

"No, no, that's not it. I'm representing a woman who's living with Gary Haines." She was taking a big chance, but there it was. She'd said it. There was a long silence on the line.

Finally Leslie answered. "Gary. What's he charged with?"

"Nothing. He hasn't done anything."

"Huh. That's a laugh."

"What do you mean?"

"Before she went to Edmonton, Amanda told me what that bastard did to her. It started when she was eleven." Leslie started to cry. "I never knew. I wasn't a good mother, I know that, but I'd never let something like that happen if I'd known. She was my baby, for Christ sake. I made my mistakes with Amanda, but the worst one was shacking up with that asshole Gary."

Susan heard Leslie sniff, set the phone on the table, blow her nose then come back on the line.

"This woman, your client…she got any kids?"

"This is a lousy place to camp, especially in bad weather. Way too exposed, no firewood. Look at that." Jim pointed down at a small black stain in the tundra where a fire had been. "They must have hiked away down to those little willows to get enough wood for this."

Jessica looked around. In every direction mountains marched to the horizon. "Great view, though. That's probably why they picked it, so they could keep an eye on the hunters. The only part of the mountain you can't see from here is the east side."

"Wouldn't help at all if the clouds closed in, which they did."

"So what do we do now?" David sat on a rock with his shoes off, massaging his feet.

Jim looked down the slope to the south where the horses were grazing in a small hollow. "We should find a place to camp." He pointed down the north slope of the mountain. "Looks like a good spot down there where the hill flattens out. There's water and grass for the horses and some trees for firewood. Can you tell what kind they are from here, Jess?"

"Mostly fir, but there's a few spruce."

"Perfect. We'll lose the sun in the evening but we should get it early in the morning. Let's go get the horses." He heard David give a small groan as he started to put his socks back on. "You stay here, David. We'll bring them up."

"Thanks. I don't know what hurts most, my feet or my ass."

The bear stood panting over the water. His raging thirst almost matched the agony in his gut. He turned to lick the oozing wound on his side and was met with the fetid smell of his own infection. He took a few slurps of water and the nausea mounted. His legs were exhausted. He longed to lie down, but he knew the intolerable ache would return, so he stood and closed his eyes, his whole world now filled only with pain and thirst.

Starla walked up the path from the lake. After an hour or so of fooling around with her tiger puppet, sending it out on a board and letting the gentle breeze push it back, she was tired of the game.

Tara was engrossed in one of her mystery novels while Gary sat sunning himself, shirt off, a beer in his hand, dark glasses hiding his eyes.

Starla walked up beside her mother's chair. "Mom, can you help me push the boat into the water?"

"Sure honey." Her head didn't rise from the book. Once she got into a novel it was nearly impossible to pry her out.

"Can you come now? I'm going fishing."

"Okay. Just let me finish this bit."

Gary was staring at her now. "I'll help you launch the boat. Tara, you stay here. Read your book."

Tara's head came up. "Thanks Gary. You're a treasure."

Starla didn't want this. "It's okay. I can do it by myself." She turned to go, wondering if she could do it herself.

Tara stopped her. "Starla, don't be rude. Gary just offered to help."

Gary waved a hand. "It's okay. No offence."

"No. She has to learn. Starla, I think you should apologize."

Gary laughed. "It's not a big deal." He finished his beer and rose from his chair. "Hey, Starla, do mind if I go with you? I love fishing."

She was backed into a corner now. To refuse him would really bring Tara down on her. "Um…I…"

Gary said, "If you don't want me along, that's fine. Don't wanna cramp your style. You go out and get us a fish for supper. I'll push the boat in while you get your fishing gear. You can try out your new rod. Is there gas in the tank?"

"Yes." That was a relief. It was strange feeling grateful to Gary. "Thanks."

"But you know, Starla, I'm not sure it's a great idea to go out alone. Something might happen."

"I've been out alone lots of times."

"I knew a guy who drowned in Lake Lebarge. Out fishing and his boat capsized."

"I can swim."

Tara said, "Yeah, Starla's like a dolphin in the water."

Gary turned to Tara. "This guy was a good swimmer, too. He tried to make it to shore, but the cold water got him. His family watched it all from their dock. There was nothing they could do."

Starla saw her mother's expression change as it sunk in.

Tara closed her book. "Okay, that's it. We'll all go fishing."

Starla could see her mother's mind was made up. But it wasn't so bad. At least Tara would be with them.

Gary put a hand on Tara's shoulder before she had a chance to rise. "Naw, you wanna read."

Starla said, "You can read in the boat."

Gary shrugged. "Sure. But those hard boat seats…"

Tara smiled up at him. "You're right as usual. You two go and catch supper. Thanks Gary. You're a dream."

The young bull watched the cow feeding at the edge of the meadow. The strange ache returned. He took a few steps out of the willows into the grass, but as he did he heard the old bull rise with a huff from the place he'd been lying, saw the big antlers top the willows, heard him grunt, deep and powerful. "Wuh, wuh, wuh."

The young bull stopped, head up, ears forward. He answered with his own "Wuh, wuh, wuh." The old bull stepped out of the willows, wide flat antler palms pushing the branches ahead like a standing wave. He swung his head toward the young one, grunted again and took three stiff-legged steps forward. Then he turned broadside, showing the full size of his massive body, his swollen muscled neck with its bell of black furred skin swinging beneath, pulsing with every grunt.

The young bull walked a few steps away, stopped and turned to watch the old bull paw the ground. Divots of soft black earth flew behind him. He stretched over the hole he'd made and urinated then turned and rubbed his antlers in it. When he lifted his head, bits of muddy marsh grass and turf hung from his long curved brow tines and draped over his nose. The cow continued to browse, ignoring the commotion. Grunting again, the old bull went down on his knees and rolled onto his shoulder—rubbing, squirming, covering himself with his own smell—then heaved himself up to his feet with a groan and shook. Bits of mud and grass spattered onto the surrounding bushes. He moved away from his pit, closer to the cow. The young bull lowered his head and approached the muddy scrape, ready to spin and run. Sharp, musky, rutting-smell filled his nose, made his heart pound, made his desire grow. Bolder now, he lowered himself and rolled, coating his body in the old bull's scent.

He stood up and shook, feeling powerful and alive. Another scent even more delicious came from the cow, a new warm scent that seemed to swirl into his nose, flow down his spine and spill into his belly.

"Put yourself in her position."

Jim and Jessica sat on top of the west ridge of Mount Riddell. After setting up the camp and letting the horses out to graze, Jim had suggested they climb up to have a look around. David had declined and retired to his tent for a nap, which was fine with Jim, because now he and Jessica could talk freely, wouldn't have to skirt carefully around the subject of Hannah's fate.

Jim looked back along the ridge. "We know she and her friends were camped back up there in that little saddle, exposed, and the weather was crap, so they must have been pretty cold and miserable."

"Very." Jessica pulled her cloth bag from her pocket, took out a bag of marijuana and her pipe and began filling it.

"From what David says she's a woman who hates to be…what are you doing?"

"Smoking some pot."

"Jess, I don't know if that's such a…"

"Oh, come on, Dad. It's not like you never do it."

"I use discretion."

"You're a great one to talk about discretion."

"All right, let's not take that one any further."

Jessica laughed. "Anyway, it helps me think."

"Oh sure, that's a good one."

"You want some?"

"No…uh…yeah, what the hell. But don't tell Suzy."

Jessica lit the pipe, took a deep draw then passed it to her dad.

"Anyway, being tent-bound would drive her crazy. She's a woman who thrives on action. What if she got fed up and decided to go look for the hunters by herself? Where would she go?" He sucked on the pipe, but got nothing.

Jessica handed him the lighter. "She'd come up here. You can see most of the mountain from here…except it was socked in. She'd see nothing."

Jim handed the pipe and lighter back to her. "There could have been breaks in the cloud, we don't know. But maybe that didn't matter to her. Maybe she just had to get out of the tent. We all know that feeling. Let's go along the ridge a little further."

"You want some more of this, Dad?"

"No thanks."

Jessica put the pipe and bag back into her pocket and followed Jim along the ridge. The sun was getting low, but it was still warm on their backs, sending long shadows ahead as they made their way down. Rounding a large, jagged rock Jim suddenly stopped and reached down. When he turned he had a green and yellow plastic wrapper in his hand. "Look at this."

Jessica read the package. "Organic banana chips."

"Someone sat here for awhile. See the marks—boot heels—and the smoothed spot where someone brushed away the stones to sit? Probably used the rock for shelter in the wind. Great view down onto that flat, too."

"You think it was her? That's quite a leap in logic. It could have been anyone, even one of the hunters."

"Organic banana chips?" He looked at the wrapper again and read. "Fair trade organic banana chips?"

"Okay, suppose it was her. What next?"

"I don't know. What would you do?"

"I'd go back to the camp. I'd follow the ridge back to camp."

"If you were her, and not stoned out of your mind. Remember, she's a driven woman."

"Driven. Result oriented. Alpha personality. I'd be frustrated not being able to see anything. I'd go down the ridge to the east, down there, maybe get under the clouds to the flat on the chance of running into the hunters. Then I'd go back to camp around the south side of the ridge to cover more ground."

"Then, once you're on the flat and you can't see more than a few meters ahead, it would be easy to get turned around, go the wrong way, maybe get on the north side of the ridge instead of the south. Then it would be almost impossible to tell which direction the camp was."

"Yeah, you could walk and walk and never hit the camp."

"So now she's lost, wet, possibly hypothermic. Suppose she decides to go back down to the road." They both looked down and to the southeast. The road was a few, brief, squiggly lines visible through breaks in the terrain.

"She's sure she's on the south side, but really she's on the north. She heads down hill northwest instead of southeast."

They both looked down to the northwest at a tortured landscape of rockslides, bog, stunted spruce and pothole lakes. In the distance the black trunks of dead trees showed where a huge fire had raged three years before. In the bottom of the valley, here and there, they could see the South Macmillan River snaking its way west. On the other side of the valley the mountains formed a purple-red wall lit by the lowering sun. Beyond that a wilderness of mountain and valley stretched a thousand miles to the Beaufort Sea.

Jessica spoke first. "She's toast."

"A toast." Sitting in the back of the boat beside the idling outboard, Gary raised his beer can to Starla. "Hold up your pop can." Starla held up her can and Gary stretched to tap it with his. "To new beginnings." He settled back in his seat and scanned the lake. "I love this time of year. Makes me feel alive."

Starla looked across to the east side of the lake where the pike waited in the weeds. The marsh grass was rich green only a couple of weeks ago. In a couple more it would turn dull brown against a gray windy sky and dark, wave-tossed water.

"How's the new rod?"

"It's fine." Why did he have to talk all the time? The fishing rod wasn't fine. In fact it was a kid's rod, fluorescent green, short and flimsy, with a frail push button reel. The line was too light for a proper lake trout rig, so her lure was a small Gibbs-Stewart spoon. Gary was using her Dad's old rod. She had given him a weighted three-way swivel with a number four Len Thompson five of diamonds. She looked again at her new gear and was glad no one could see her. But…it was nice of him to buy it for her when it wasn't even her birthday. Why was he being so nice?

Gary let out more line. Starla wanted to tell him he had too much out already, but he was a grown up and she didn't feel right telling him how to fish. Still, he had let her rig up his line. He'd even complimented her on her expertise. *I can tell you know your fishing gear. I've never seen the three way swivel trick.*

Starla watched as Gary peeled off line. She could see what was about to happen. He turned the handle of the reel, expecting the bail to flip over and stop the line going out. When it didn't he fumbled with the reel. "Shit. I can't…" The weight had hit the bottom and the line went slack, causing a large tangle just above the reel.

"Flip it over with your hand." She moved back towards him and held out her rod. "Here, take mine and reel it in. Give that one to me."

"With pleasure." Gary took the rod, cut the motor, and began reeling.

The steady hum of the motor had been a small barrier between them. In the silence, Starla felt Gary's presence loom larger, and their isolation grow starker. She focused on the tangle in the line.

Gary reeled her line in then cast it out again. "Hey. This baby really casts."

"Mm hm."

"I might catch a trout while you're busy with that. Wouldn't that burn your ass?"

"I don't mind." She carefully pulled a loop of line out.

"On your own rod? While you're fixing my mess? It wouldn't bother you?"

"Nope."

"You're a very mature girl, I mean, young woman."

"Yup."

"And very beautiful."

Starla kept her head down, working with renewed concentration, but she felt her face getting hot.

Gary glanced towards her then back to his next cast. "You shouldn't be embarrassed. It's true. You have a lovely smile."

Starla looked up. Gary's eyes bored deep into hers. She looked away, back to the line in her hands. "There. I got it." Glad of the chance to change the subject, she started to reel in the line, slowing down as it came taut. If it was snagged on the bottom she didn't want to break the line. With a steady pull, the weight came free of the mud so she reeled in steadily.

"You could be a model if you wanted."

Why wouldn't he stop talking?

"I could help you. I know some people."

There was a sharp tug on the line. She stopped reeling for a moment then brought the rod up in a smooth motion. Nothing. She let it back down, seeing in her mind's eye the lure fluttering as it descended, the trout circling.

Gary was still talking, but she barely heard him.

"You can make big money if you do it right."

Starla brought the rod tip up again. When the tug came she gave a sharp pull to set the hook and felt the fish pull back. She backed off the tension, discovering Gary had it set to the maximum. The trout ran and she let it go, but kept some pressure on the line.

"I know about these things. You're going to develop into a..." The buzzing reel stopped him. "Hey. What's going on?"

"Got a fish." It took ten minutes to get her first look at the trout, about five pounds. It took three runs away from the boat, but finally tired and came in close.

Gary was clumping around in the stern "Shit, we forgot the landing net."

Starla reached down over the side of the boat. As the fish came close to the surface she grabbed it behind the gills. Her hand was barely big enough to stretch around the trout's back, but with her thumb on one side and her middle finger on the other, she squeezed hard, just as Dan had shown her. Feeling the trout's nerves tingle beneath her grip, she knew it was immobilized. She lifted it out of the water and over the gunwale.

Gary stared in disbelief at the fish. "Wow." He looked in her eyes, smiled and gave her thigh a pat. "Not just a pretty face."

"Dirty shit whitehead. Go. Die." She touched her breast feather with her beak and stared down angrily at the eagle perched on the crest of bones above the rib cage of the dead moose. It sat there, its gullet full, guarding the carcass.

The moose was a bobblehead kill, out on an open sand bar. Bobbleheads sometimes stripped off the meat, leaving plenty to pick from between the bones. She could see a white mass sunk in the river at the bottom of the eddy—guts and most of the skin, out of reach. Stupid bobbleheads. She screamed at the whitehead again. "Go. Die." The stupid bird, like all its hateful kind, couldn't understand the simplest calls.

The bobblehead pair with the littlewolf were well upstream. She would check on them tomorrow. Maybe they would kill something, leave a gut pile. For now she would wait until the stupid shit whitehead moved on and she could eat.

The water pot tilted precariously as the freshly lit fire burned away its supporting tangle of spruce branches. Hannah lifted the edge of the wire rack and stuffed some branches under it.

Dan came up the steep bank carrying the last backpack from the boat, dropped it beside her, picked up the axe and saw, and walked into the spruce. He hopped up onto a deadfall and walked to where a smaller tree had fallen over it. Stepping onto it, he took a moment to balance then walked down the trunk to the ground, found the right deadfall, and began sawing.

Hannah noticed his agility. He moved easily—economy of motion— evident in the small things like getting in and out of the boat, tying up a lean-to pole, cutting up firewood. Her father would have called Dan *a natural*. Her dad always called Joe Namath a natural, and never failed to add that Joe was also Jewish. She wondered what her dad would think of Dan. He sure wasn't Jewish.

She unrolled the tarp. It was still wet from the morning's frost, so she shook it out and laid it over a fallen tree to catch the last rays of the sun. Next came the sleeping bag. It wasn't damp but she spread it over the tree to air. Bubbles were starting to rise around the sides of the pot. Soon there'd be hot water, so she opened the food box and got out two tea bags and went back to the fire. Repositioning the rack again, she shoved a few more branches under it.

She knew this feeling, when a trip—backpacking, skiing, canoeing— reached a rhythm. When the weather and the land and the water and the wind combined to make a perfect rhythm. She had hoped that once Grizzly Watch got going, and the three of them were in the mountains, they would find that rhythm. It hadn't happened.

But now, after only two days with Dan, it was there. Everything—unloading the canoe, cooking, gathering enough firewood for the night and next morning, setting up the lean-to, cutting and arranging spruce boughs for the bed—all of it had a direct effect on their immediate lives. Every task, no matter how simple, took on a greater meaning. Perhaps the river was imposing its rhythm on them.

Dan came back, walking along a big deadfall with the axe and saw in one hand and three logs balanced on his opposite shoulder. He let the logs drop and jumped lightly down to the ground. "Lots of firewood here."

"You ever do any sports?"

"Hockey."

"Oh."

Dan exaggerated her Oh. "Oh. So what's wrong with hockey?"

She lifted the boiling pot off the fire and dropped in the tea bags. "Nothing. I just thought…"

"You just thought hockey was vulgar and violent, and how could such a refined gentleman like myself be a hockey fan? Look at these hands, so soft, so sensitive." He held out his palms to show the grime etched into the creases, black rimmed fingernails and some dirty, partially healed cuts. "Could these be the hands of a hockey player?"

For a fleeting moment Hannah wondered what those hands would feel like on her body. She caught herself and laughed. "You seem very athletic, that's all."

"So what sport would you pick for me?"

She smiled. "Dancing."

"You think I can't dance?" He did a turn, a few steps back and forth then moon-walked towards the steep riverbank, almost falling over the edge, but catching himself at the last moment. Sensing a game, Raz dashed up to him and bit at his ankle. "Raz, cut it out."

Hannah almost knocked over the tea laughing, but couldn't help noticing he really could dance. He was so different from David. What was she doing comparing him to David? David...he must be sick with worry.

"I'm worried about the horses." David called up to Jessica and Jim as they came down the hill towards the camp. "They went down the mountain. I think they went back to the road."

"The road's over the other side." Jim jerked his thumb over his shoulder. "They're fine, grazing just past the knoll below us. We could see them from up there."

"Did you see...anything else?"

"It's almost certain she was on the ridge up there. And we saw where she might have gone."

"What do you mean?"

"We know she's not on the mountain 'cause the searchers found no trace of her. If she went down the southeast side she would have been found, or she would have come out on the road. So if she went down the mountain it would likely have been to the northwest." Jim saw Jessica standing behind David, drawing her hand across her throat.

"And which way is northwest?"

"That way."

David looked downhill where Jim was pointing. "Oh my god."

Jessica quickly interjected. "It's not as bad as it looks. It would have been warmer down there. More shelter, lots of firewood. And she might have been picked up by someone going down the river."

David looked to Jim for confirmation. "Really?"

Jessica knew it was the slimmest of hopes. No one was on the river at this time of year. The tourists were all gone except for the odd German. Moose hunters were even more scarce. The upper section had too many rapids. But it was important to keep up David's hopes.

Jim nodded. "Sure. There's a...good chance."

Jessica lied again. "Oh yeah, there's hunters on the river...and tourists. We know several guides who take parties down the South Macmillan."

Jim took up Jessica's lie. "Yeah, there's Ralph Emmett of Klondike River Tours, and Joe Jackson from Ross. Heck, it's a steady stream of canoes down there."

Behind David's back Jessica rolled her eyes at her father. "The sun's almost down. Let's make a hot drink before supper. Tomorrow we'll see what we can find."

"Great. I could do with a strong coffee." David walked to the tarp set up over their kitchen area.

Jessica tapped Jim on the shoulder and whispered. "A steady stream of canoes? That's stretching it."

"Why not? He doesn't know. Anyway, it was your idea she could have been picked up on the river. Even if she made it that far, what are the chances?"

"Almost zero, but we should at least stay in Kansas."

"But we were gonna split up anyway. We couldn't live together so it doesn't matter, except..." Dan trailed off. He was stretched out on his side, absorbing heat from the fire, his elbow on a rolled-up dry bag, head resting on his shoulder. Raz was curled tight against his back.

"Except for your daughter." Hannah squatted beside the fire, one hand in a large work glove, holding a blackened pot, the other holding a stick. She tilted the pot carefully with the stick, trying to pour so that no leaves got into the cups. She had found labrador tea growing out of the thick moss in a stand of pines. She wondered when Dan would notice. Would he be surprised? Would he say something like *Hey, how do you know about this?* Why did she want to impress him?

What about him? He was interested in her. She had sensed him checking out her body, his eyes subtly lingering on her hip, her breasts. More than that, it was an attitude, an ambience. He always wanted to make sure she was comfortable, wanted to say the right thing. More even than that, it was a feeling in the air, an aura of sexual energy. More than once she had thought he was about to touch her then changed his mind.

What about her? Yes, she was attracted to him. What about sex? How weird would it be with this guy she barely knew, from a small Yukon town, a guy who intended to kill a moose at the first opportunity? She shook her head. This was ridiculous. Why was she even thinking this?

He was watching her, a hint of smile on his face—that gorgeous smile. "Why did you shake your head?"

"Oh, did I? No reason." She held out a cup of tea. "I guess I was thinking about you...about your ex, your daughter." That was it. Stay on the subject of his custody battle. Put thoughts of sex out of her mind. He took the cup from her and she felt his fingers brush hers.

He looked down into the steam. "I don't know. It all seems so pointless. With all the crap Tara brings up in court, I don't look like much of a father. She remembers every little detail: conversations that happened years ago, things I did, things I didn't do. Half the stuff is taken out of context. Most of it I don't even remember. For all I know she's making it up. I can't fight that hard."

"So, get somebody who can. A lawyer."

"Can't afford it. That really bugs me, you know. She gets a legal aid lawyer and I don't. She owns a property on Little Atlin that's worth a hundred and fifty thousand, and I live with my mother in Ross."

"How did she manage to get legal aid?"

"I told you, she's very persuasive and she doesn't let go. She hounded them 'til they gave in."

"Why don't you do what she did?"

"I can't. I'm not like that. With her it's all or nothing, take no prisoners. She wants sole custody of Starla, wants to prove I'm a bad influence, says I have no ambition." He took a sip of tea. "Sometimes I start to believe her."

"I'm sure that's not true. You have experience at all kinds of things. You've told me about the jobs you've done."

"It's all such a huge hassle, so destructive. The whole court thing... it's...depressing. After I lost the job with Highways, I went into a real slump, living in Whitehorse, telling myself I didn't want the job, didn't want to bulldoze trees, tear the living skin off the land. I told myself it was against my principles. Lyle Kessler was calling me all the time to go back guiding for him. I did for awhile, but...then I went back to Whitehorse for a time...a lot of partying, drinking, smoking dope, trying to get time with Starla, fighting with Tara. It all got out of hand. Too weird. I went back to Ross, picked mushrooms. My trouble is I can't play the game. I think I get it from my dad, some kind of mutant gene. He was the same. He didn't wanna play the game. Got out of it completely. He gave up a lot." He was silent for a while, thinking. "A lot of money. His parents were loaded. Old Toronto establishment. Rosedale. You want some pot?" He reached into his jacket.

The question took her off guard. Did she dare? She hadn't smoked it in years. It always made her neurotic. "I dunno."

He pulled out his small pipe then took an unburned twig from the edge of the fire. "It's the last of it." He flipped a small red coal onto the moss then maneuvered it into the pipe.

"Really? I don't wanna smoke the last of..."

"Don't worry." He puffed a few times then took in a long breath and held it. "I planned to run out." He exhaled a diffuse cloud. "I'll tell you what. If you smoke some, I won't call tonight or tomorrow morning."

"Call who?"

"Moose."

She smiled. "Smoke dope and save a moose." Maybe it wouldn't be so bad. The moon was an orange balloon hanging in the U of the valley upstream. Stars filled a black sky along with a few curtains of northern lights. The river swished by gently. "Deal." She took the pipe from him. It was made from a hard substance, polished by use, crazed by small black cracks running its length. The rim of the bowl and mouthpiece were stained with black residue. Carved around the bottom of the bowl was an eye. "What is this made of?"

"Quick. Puff it before it goes out."

She took in a few short gulps and held her breath, fighting the urge to cough. She held out the pipe and squeezed her eyes shut, fanning her hand in front of her face. If she coughed it would be painful. She felt his fingers on hers when he took the pipe. Did hers linger on his a bit too long? Did he think she was giving him some signal? Was the paranoia starting with one little puff?

He took another lungful and spoke through his held breath. "It's made outta the tip of a moose antler."

She blew out a thin blue cloud. "Did you make it?"

"Yeah."

"Is everything moose with you?"

"Yeah. I'm thinking of legally changing my name to Moose."

She looked more closely at the carving. "Beautiful. It must have taken a long time."

"Too long." He held out the pipe to her. "Time to put it into retirement. You want some more?"

She waved her hand. "That's enough for me. I'm not used to this stuff. So what happened?"

"What happened to what?"

"Your father. Did they disown him?"

"More like he disowned himself. He gave up more than money...much more."

"Did you ever meet them, your grandparents?"

"Yeah. When I was seven we went down there for Christmas. We got picked up at the airport in their limousine. The chauffeur wore a uniform. When we arrived at the house I thought it was a castle. The biggest building in Ross was the Rec Center. Their house was four times its size. I asked my dad if they were the king and queen of Toronto. The thing I remember most was the bowls of candy and fruit in every room. The TV room was full of stuffed animal heads. They had set up a big Christmas tree in there, and underneath was a pile of gifts, most of them with my name." He threw a few branches on the fire. "I never got to open them. Two days before Christmas there was a huge fight. I could hear them from my room. I don't know what it was all about. I remember them saying something about him being *able to do better.* Mostly I remember him yelling, saying all sorts of awful things. He called his mother a dried up old harridan. I had to look it up in the dictionary. The next morning, Christmas Eve, we left without saying goodbye. I was so mad at him."

Dan stared into the fire, lost in thought. Her instincts told her he wanted to talk and she didn't want him to stop. The fire cracked, a branch split and flared, tossing orange light across his face. A thin stream of mist curled upwards from the cup in his hand. She fussed with her teacup, took a sip. Should she say something, a gentle prompt?

He looked at his cup then sniffed it. "Hey...this tea, what is it?"

"Labrador tea."

"How do know about labrador tea?"

"Every Jewish princess knows about labrador tea. It's the first thing they teach us in Hebrew school." She wasn't going to let the subject slip away. "Did he ever speak to them again?'

"Never. Not a letter or a phone call. He never went back, not even for their funerals."

"What happened to their money?"

"He was an only child, so they put it into a foundation that went all over the world building hospitals. Still does."

"That's some consolation, I guess."

"Sure. It's great. Wonderful. Meanwhile, I'm broke, living with my mother, trying to scratch a few bucks together to get to Whitehorse to see my daughter."

His daughter. She wanted to know about her. Maybe now she had him talking he'd open up some more. "How's she doing in all this?"

"Starla's having a hard time of it. She wants it to go back to the way it was, but she knows it can't. It's tough on her."

"Do you talk to her much?"

"Yeah, she phones me all the time, says she wants to come and live with me in Ross. She doesn't like Tara's new boyfriend, some guy named Gary."

Starla leaned back against the sauna wall, closed her eyes and listened to the little tin stove roar, hot stones hissing, waiting for the steam to hit her. Tara and Gary couldn't stand it this hot, so she had waited until they went to cool off in the lake before taking a dipper of steaming water from the pail on the stove to throw on the rocks. She heard Tara's laugh and the slap of bare feet on the wet path.

The door jerked open. Tara entered, breathless. "Holy shit, Starla. I'm turning bright pink. Oh man, that feels incredible."

"Close the door, Mom, you're letting out the steam." She watched Tara, still giggling, close the door and turn beaming towards her. Her mother was always happy at Little Atlin, more relaxed, less intense. It was partly the drinks and pot, but Starla knew it went deeper. Tara was proud of the place. She had told her it was more than anyone in her family had ever owned.

"Isn't this place the best?" Tara plunked onto the upper bench beside her.

"Yeah, he sure did a great job on it."

"Wha..? Oh, the sauna. I meant the cabin, the property. Listen, young lady, I worked on this sauna, too."

Starla regretted mentioning Dan. She knew where this was going—deadbeat Dan, jerk Dan, loser Dan. "Where's Gary?"

"He went to get a drink. God, it's beautiful out there. You should see the moonlight." She put her arm around Starla. "Not as beautiful as you, honey. Look at you in that swimsuit. You're a knockout." Starla squirmed. "Sorry sweetie, I know you don't like me to do that. No more, I promise." She turned Starla's face toward hers. "I just want you to be happy. You're the reason for all this. I'm very proud of you, and I love you *so* much."

Starla put her arms around Tara's waist and snuggled against her. She liked it when her mother got mushy. It felt good and safe, engulfed in swirling hot moisture, their limbs shiny with sweat in the light of a struggling candle.

The door flew open. "Boo."

Tara reacted instantly, putting herself in front of Starla as Gary burst through the door, laughing. "Ha, ha. Gotcha."

Starla, pinned in her mother's grip, sat wide-eyed, startled as much by the power and speed of Tara's response as by Gary's prank. Her mother relaxed and turned laughing to face him. He stood halfway in the door, swaying slightly, a drink in his hand.

Tara climbed off the bench and gave him a playful swat on the chest. "Jesus Christ, Gary, are you trying to give me a heart attack?"

"Keeping you guys on your toes." He squeezed through the door and sat on the lower bench as Tara climbed back up beside Starla. "Jeez, it's hot. How do you stand it?"

"It's a sauna, stupid. It's supposed to be hot." Tara reached down and pulled the dipper out of the pail on the stove then tossed some water onto the stones. It hissed into the air and a wave of heat washed over them.

Gary turned, put his feet on the bench and leaned against the wall, facing them. "Oh yeah, so why are we wearing swimsuits? I hear if you want a real sauna you're supposed to be naked." He was laughing, smiling, joking, looking at Tara, but Starla saw his eyes flicker over her.

Tara pushed herself off the bench. "You've had too much to drink, buster. Well that's enough for me. One more dive in the lake and I'm going back to the cabin. Don't be too long, Starla, or you'll cook yourself."

When Tara left there was a long silence. Gary sat on the lower bench, back against the wall, facing Starla, eyes closed. She stared at the dull red glow of the stovepipe, wishing Tara hadn't left, not wanting to look at him, hoping he would ignore her.

His eyes opened, he took a sip from his glass then put it on the floor. "What's it like up there?" He was looking at her now. She tried to will him to stay where he was, but he climbed up to sit beside her. She felt small and helpless with his big body between her and the door. The sickly sweet odor of alcohol was on his breath. Her heart pounded in her ears.

Gary sighed. "Mmmm, this is nice. I could get used to this." He shifted so his leg was touching hers. She crowded into the wall away from him. He didn't seem to notice. "You know, Starla, you can take off your swimsuit if you want." His speech slurred on *swimsuit*. "It won't bother me... won't make any difference. You're safe with me. I'm your...friend. Your good friend. Heck, we're almost family, now." He smiled at her, his eyes unfocussed.

She looked away, heart beating wildly, wanting to escape, get out of there and run, but she couldn't move, couldn't speak, her muscles unable to respond to the rising panic in her brain. It was hard to breath. The steam that felt so good before was oppressive now. Finally, legs shaking, she mustered the courage to move. She stood to get down off the bench, still unable to meet his gaze, waiting, hoping he would shift out of the way and let her pass. "I...I gotta go."

"Where you goin'?"

"To the lake." She tried to push past him, but his hand came up to her shoulder.

"Don't go yet. This is nice."

She twisted away from him and jumped over his legs to the lower bench. One more step and she'd be at the door. She felt his hand grab at her. She pulled back and his hand slipped down her sweat-slick arm. For a moment she thought she was free, but when his hand reached her wrist it clamped harder.

"Starla, it's okay. There's nothing to..."

She saw the handle of the dipper sticking out of the steaming bucket on the stove. She grabbed it and splashed scalding water on his knees. He swore and let go of her. In an instant she was out the door and down the path to the dock. Cool, soothing air filled her lungs as she ran, her feet barely touching the cold frosted boards. Without slowing she dove off the end of the dock, feeling the water engulfing, invigorating her. She swam out under water, opening her eyes to the fuzzy silver glow of moonlight playing on the bottom. She heard a muffled whoosh—Gary diving in. She surfaced and brushed the wet hair from her eyes.

His head bobbed halfway between her and the shore. "Hey Starla. Why did you do that? What's going on?"

She filled her lungs, ducked under again and swam for the bottom. The water was starting to feel cold now. She swam for the shore, feeling water weeds slide across her arms and legs. Gary was above her now, treading water, a large indistinct white shape. She could hear him calling through the rush in her ears, felt the swirl of his flailing limbs as she passed beneath him. She needed to come up for air, but she kept going, fighting back panic, streamlining her body, ignoring the numbing ache in her forehead, stroke by stroke, the bottom rising as she approached the shallows. At last the dark shape of dock pilings loomed before her. She came up beneath the dock, hidden from him. Should she wait there until he left? No, she was already too cold. She swam to the other side of the dock, slipped quietly out of the water, and ran for the soft yellow light in the cabin window, to safety, to warmth, to her mother.

Hannah lay back against the dry bag and looked up. The surrounding spruce, needle straight, all pointed to a spot in the sky directly above, a patch of deep blue-black in a river of stars. "Why are there no stars?"

"What do you mean no stars? There's lots of stars." He lay back on the dry bag beside her.

"Yes, but up there where the trees are pointing. That patch of black."

"Oh that. Big cloud of gas and dust. Blocks the stars behind."

"Oh yeah. I think I remember it from university. It's called the Coalsack, isn't it?"

"You can't see the Coalsack from this latitude, but that patch up there is kind of an extension of the same thing. Dust and gas in the plane of the galaxy."

"Where's the Big Dipper?"

Dan sat up and looked to the northwest, moving his head from side to side while peering through the trees. He pointed. "Over there. We'd have to go out on the sandbar to see it clearly."

"Let's go."

"Okay. Put the jacket on. It's getting cold."

The moonlight was bright enough to illuminate the game trail along the bank downstream to where it angled down to a long bar separated from the shore by a channel small enough to jump. They walked out to the middle of the bar. Dan pointed up. "There—the Big Dipper. Can't miss it. Of course the official name is Ursa Major, the Great Bear. If you line up the two stars on the outside of the dipper they point to the north star, Polaris, right there."

"Where's the Little Dipper? Or is it Ursa Minor?"

"Both. Polaris is the end of the handle. It curves down to those four stars that make the cup. See it?"

"Yeah. How did you learn about astronomy?"

"Books. Just like everyone else." They stared up in silence for a while, both lost in the vastness of the night sky. The Milky Way arched up from the horizon in the southwest, stretching to the dark patch directly overhead. Hannah had never seen the sky so three dimensional, a feeling of being embedded in a sea of twinkling lights. Up and down began to have no meaning. "Wow. Dope has become more potent since the last time I smoked it."

"You know what's weird?" Dan stood looking up pensively. "All over the world, people have called those two constellations The Great Bear and The Little Bear—Greeks, Romans, Indian people, Tibetans, Inuit. A whole lot of different cultures independent of each other saw them as bears."

"What's so weird? The bear has always been a symbol of power since we lived in caves. And those are conspicuous constellations. It makes sense."

"Sure, but that's not what's weird. The weird thing is the long tail. A square of four stars for the body and a string of them for a tail. Bears have short stubby tails. There isn't a bear on Earth with a long tail. So how did all those people get it wrong?"

"It never occurred to me."

"I guess it didn't occur to them either. I think they made the bear fit the picture."

"Hmmm. It's a very human quality. We do it all the time, don't we? We make things fit into our own reality...like the sheep who gave himself to you." Oh god, what a thing to say. He would think she was making fun of his beliefs. "I mean...everybody does it. I do it."

They both gazed in silence at the sky for a time then Dan said, "So, what do you believe?"

"You mean am I religious?"

"Yeah."

She eyed him, while he stared up. "That's a big question. If you mean do I believe in God...I don't know. I'm undecided. I guess that makes me an agnostic."

"Agnostic. My father always said that's wimpy. He was an atheist. A fundamentalist atheist if there is such a thing. He never missed a chance to sound off about it. He used to say, *Man wasn't made in God's image. It was the other way around.* Got himself into trouble with the school board for talking about it to his classes. Funny thing was, he could quote more bible than a Jehovah's Witness."

"What about your mother?"

"Mom? She didn't talk about it much. I guess she started out as an Anglican, but after residential school..." He trailed off.

"Did she have a bad experience there?"

"I think so, but that was another thing she never talked about. I guess you'd call Mom an Animist. She believes everything has a spirit, not just living things, but the rocks and the earth and the water."

"What about you? Do you believe in God?"

He looked at her and smiled. "No. But I asked you first, and Agnostic doesn't count."

"I'm a Jew. I grew up in a Jewish family. Until my brother and I left home my mother kept Kosher...except when we went to Florida. Then all rules were suspended. The first thing my father would do was go to a restaurant and order a big plate of bacon."

"Are you telling me bacon led you to doubt the existence of God?"

"Plenty of things make me do that. Bacon is just one of them." She scanned the gravel bar, the river rippling silver in moonlight, the trees black against a star filled sky. "Out here it's hard not to believe in something."

"Yeah." He turned to her, about to say something more when Raz came running over the sand to a stop between Dan's legs. The sound of splashing came down the river. It sounded like a large animal taking great leaps through the water. At first she couldn't see it in the shade of the far shore trees, but when it rounded the bend its white neck ruff caught the moonlight. It plunged into deep water and she could see its antlers silhouetted against a dazzle of ripples on the surface.

She whispered to Dan. "A caribou. It's coming right down the middle of the river."

"Raz is freaked out. Weird." He reached down and stroked the dog's head. "Whatsamatter, Raz? You're shivering." He straightened and whispered to her. "Let's go back to the camp."

They walked across the bar and up the bank. As they moved along the trail at the top of the bank Hannah glimpsed a dark shape dash past in the opposite direction, rustling through the underbrush a few feet away. "What was that?"

Dan hadn't seen it. "What?"

"Something just ran by." She heard the bushes rustle again and another fleeting movement. "There's another."

"A caribou?"

"Smaller."

They reached the fire. Dan went to the lean-to, dug into the dry bag and came out with his head lamp, a small LED. He shone it into the bushes, back and forth until two bright green spots appeared a short distance from them then winked out. "Ah. There you are." He shut off the light.

"What are they?" As if in answer a long low howl came from the other side of the river. It was answered by two more on their side, just downstream.

"Wolves."

She looked out on the river. The caribou was passing, swimming for the sandbar. When it reached the shallows it stopped, up to its belly in water.

She could hear it breathing and see clouds of mist puffing out of its nostrils into the cold air. A black shape detached from the willows at the edge of the bar and slowly, head and tail level, walked towards the caribou. As it approached, the caribou turned and walked back upstream. The wolf entered the water and tried to swim but the current forced it back. It came out on the bar and shook then disappeared into the willows.

She heard another animal enter the water on the other side and saw its head drifting downstream towards the caribou, which lunged for the sandbar again but stayed in the water, running full tilt, surrounded by a spray of silver droplets. Rounding the curve of the bar, it plunged again into deep water and disappeared around the bend. Three wolves appeared out of the willows onto the bar. Four more came out of the bush along the opposite shore, keeping pace with the caribou.

Hannah watched them go in open-mouthed amazement. "Jesus."

Dan turned back to the fire and sat down. "Wow. You don't see that often. I've never seen it."

"Do you think they'll catch him?"

"Who knows? No wonder Raz was scared. Where is he?"

"I don't know. I was too busy watching them."

"Raz. C'mere Raz."

There was a rustle in the lean-to and the dog's head poked up from under the sleeping bag.

SEPT. 19

He was still on edge. He had been on edge all night—listening, sniffing, alert. Creeping out from under the lean-to, ears up, he edged around the dead fire to the trail. He carefully sniffed the trampled moss and twigs at the top of the bank. Against the tart resinous background the smells stood out: him, his Dan, the new mate, squirrel, vole, a rank, musky smell that was probably a mink. No wolves. Good. A shiver buzzed through his body. They were like him but more...big, strong, fast, smelling of flesh and bone and blood and fur. And something else—something unimaginably huge.

But they had gone downriver, where the moon now hung, its light glittering on the frosty sandbar. Down where the river bent out of sight, the spruce trees were a black-toothed jaw line. He wanted to go down the trail to the sandbar, to find their tracks and taste that wonderful, fearful scent again. But what if they returned?

He went back under the tarp to the new mate's side of the bed bag. He knew his Dan would push him away if he snuggled in close under the cover. He started near her feet, wriggled under the edge of the bag and worked gradually up along her side. She rolled towards him. Had he wakened her? Would she push him away? Her arm reached over him and she hugged him closer, drawing up her legs to let him nestle in against her belly. Nice. With the outside sounds muffled and his nose filled with the warm scents of the new mate, he finally drifted into sleep.

Their camp at the edge of a willow thicket overlooked a slope of hummocky grass. Thirty meters from their shelter, water seeped out of the mountainside in a wide band under the edge of the willows. It percolated down through a boggy area, collecting in pools here and there where the grass grew vivid green. The horses had grazed it as soon as they had been let loose earlier. Now, most of the pools had been churned to muddy brown.

Jessica picked her way higher to a small, undisturbed pool edged with ice, just big enough for the water pail. She carefully dipped into the pool, letting the edge of the pail down slowly to fill. Lifting it out she noticed some dark brown bits had got in. "Oh well. It's for coffee. No one will know." She stood and looked down the mountain. The sun had just struck the slope, but the warmth was immediate. Already the willow and dwarf birch leaves were shiny with melted frost. Soon they would be dry. Another clear, warm day lay ahead.

She reached into her jacket pocket and her hand closed around her pipe and bag of marijuana. Jim and David weren't up yet, the sun felt good, the mountains were in glorious color, etched with long shadows. No, maybe she should wait. She had a lot of work ahead this morning: cooking breakfast, packing up, saddling the horses. Maybe once they got going she would find a moment for a toke.

She scanned down, in the direction they would be going: easy, open hillsides of moss and lichen, patches of willow and grass where water seeped out. Further down, where the shoulder of the mountain flattened, the bright red of dwarf birch studded with dark green clumps of gnarled spruce told her it would be tough going, impossible to follow any signs left by a lone hiker. Beyond that the hill fell away out of her sight—no way to tell what the terrain held in store. It looked as if it got steep, likely thick, alpine fir growing over big boulders—nasty footing for the horses. She hoped they wouldn't have to go down there.

Her gaze followed around to the west, where a bright yellow band of willows cut though the flat red shoulder of the mountain. That would be the best way down. Although the footing would be wet and the willows high, there would be no thick, wiry, dwarf birch to struggle through, and fewer rocks. There would likely be moose trails.

A tiny dot, jet black, appeared at the top of the cut, where the willows began then moved uphill onto an open knoll. A black bear, probably following a well-used game trail up the gully, a natural corridor from the valley below to the open mountainside. If animals were funneled that way, why not a person? Why not Hannah?

Her eyes followed the gully down to the valley bottom, still in shadow. She imagined Hannah, struggling through deadfall, bog, thick, tangled willows, sinking halfway to her knees in moss through dark spruce forest, unable to see ahead, always expecting to come out onto the road, not realizing it would never appear. Further down the valley was an enormous burn. If by some miracle of endurance Hannah had made it that far—alone, confused, wet, cold, exhausted—she would surely have succumbed in that chaos of fallen trees. Seven days since Hannah went missing. There was no doubt in her mind now. If Hannah was down there, they were searching for her dead body.

Starla walked quickly along the trail, ducking low when she passed any opening in the trees where she could be seen from the cabin. She had got up and dressed and out the door as soon as she heard the others stir. She didn't want to see them, didn't want to have to talk to them, didn't want to think about what had happened the night before. But it wouldn't leave her thoughts.

Once she got around the point and out of sight, her pace slowed and her gait relaxed. The trail snaked through some low ground where yellow cinquefoil, labrador tea, and the occasional clump of wispy grass vied for space with moss. She liked to make a game of jumping from root to root over the hollows created by the passage of people and animals.

Her game was no distraction from the muddle of questions in her mind. Should she tell Tara she was frightened of Gary? Her mother would only say she was being paranoid, Gary was just joking, she didn't understand his sense of humor, he was just a bit drunk, to give him a chance. The usual.

Was Gary joking? She didn't think so. She could see the hunger in his eyes, hear it in his voice, feel it in his touch. What did he want from her? She knew about sex. She had giggled in the schoolyard with her friends at tales of parents seen in the act, things older brothers and cousins had told them, talk of condoms and periods and semen and orgasms. But it had always seemed like stories from another world, not something she had to think about. Sex was like some strange, revolting cartoon. Is that what

Gary really wanted—to put his penis inside her? Why? It was impossible. The thought was too appalling to imagine. Could she stop him if he tried? She didn't think so.

The trail took her through the trees a short way back from the shore. A breeze had begun to ruffle the surface of the lake. Ahead was the clearing where Brian and Anne's cabin nestled into the base of the hill. It would be so good if they were there—even better if Natalie was there. Then she'd have an excuse to spend the day away from Gary. Maybe they had arrived late last night. She crossed her fingers as she came out of the bush, through the fireweed edging the lawn.

The cabin stood deserted, dark staring windows, chairs propped against the railing of the deck that stretched across the front. Leaves from the tall aspens on the hill behind lay undisturbed on the steps. The only vehicle was the rusted pick-up truck they used to haul wood, a summer's growth of fireweed sprouting around its doors. She knew how to get into the cabin. Brian had shown her his secret way—crawl under the porch into the crawl-space to the trap door under the kitchen.

She walked up past the fire pit and bent low under the deck. As she squeezed between the supports she felt her pants catch on a nail head. There was a ripping sound and a stab of pain as the nail bit into her skin just above the knee. She winced and put her hand over the spot. When she took it away she saw blood soaking into the fabric of her jeans. She sat down in the molding leaves and felt her eyes begin to sting. She closed them tight and felt lonely, confused tears trickle down over her cheeks. Why couldn't someone come and take her away? Where were Brian and Anne? Where was Natalie? Where was her father?

"I was thinking about last night. Those wolves were only a few feet away from us."

"You don't see that every day."

"Do you think they'd ever attack us?"

"No."

"Why not. We'd have been easy prey."

"Wolves seem to have some kind of inhibition about people. Maybe it's fear. Maybe they just don't recognize us as prey. Maybe we taste bad." They paddled in silence for a while. The river curved back and forth in long sweeps across the valley, a repeating pattern of gravel bars on the insides of the bends and steep cut banks bristling with sweepers on the outsides. Some of the bars had huge piles of gray, weathered logs at their upstream ends.

Dan said, "A few years ago I was hunting on the Yukon River. Staying in a cabin. I'd shot a moose that morning and had the skin soaking near the shore to loosen the hair. I had a dog with me—Raz's mother—and I'd told her not to touch it. So late that night I went down to the river to get a bucket of water. No moon. Almost pitch dark. I got to the top of the bank and there was my dog, chewing on the corner of the skin. I jumped down onto the beach and yelled, *Bad dog, get away from that.* She scurried away along the beach, but the canoe was pulled up, blocking her path, so she turned back and ran by me. I was just about to give her a little bump in the ass with my foot when I remembered the dog was still back in the cabin."

"It was a wolf?"

"Yeah, and I almost kicked it in the butt. Maybe that's the thing about wolves. They know they're just dogs at heart."

"What about dogs? Why was Raz so frightened last night? I would have thought he'd want to…I don't know…join them in the chase."

Dan laughed. "That only happens in stories. The smart ones are scared shitless of wolves. The only way a dog joins a wolf pack is in their stomachs."

"What? Really?"

"Really."

"But that's cannibalism."

"Yeah. I guess it is. Strange. Cannibalism is such a human quality. He's not keeping you from paddling, is he?"

"Who, Raz? No."

"You can tell him to move back this way."

"He likes it here."

"How do you know?"

"I know."

"He likes you."

"How do you know?"

"I know. I'm only concerned he's cramping your style. Distracting you."

"Oh. I get it. You're pissed off that I'm not paddling."

"Heavens, no."

"Before, you wanted me to stop paddling. Now you complain."

"I'm not complaining. I'm kidding. No, this is the perfect speed. Save your strength. There'll be plenty of hard paddling after we get a moose."

"We?"

"I." They drifted past the head of an island where a tangle of bleached logs were jammed by the current. "Does the offer still stand?"

"The ten thousand?"

"Yeah."

She thought for a while. "Yes. It still stands."

"So you could write a check for that much?"

"Yes."

"Fuck. Must be nice."

"It has its good points." She had never had to worry about money. Her parents were wealthy by most standards. Her father had built a flourishing business and sold out just before the shoe industry moved to China. She had married David, who was even savvier when it came to money. She could easily afford the ten thousand, but was it what she wanted?

David braced his feet in the stirrups and leaned back as Jessica had shown him. He fought the urge to pull back on the reins as the line of horses started down a steep, brushy hillside. A moment of vertigo as his horse followed Jessica's over the lip then he got his balance. He was starting to enjoy this. It was a bit like skiing. He smiled at her when she turned in the saddle to look back at him. "How am I doing?"

"Great. Looking like a mountain man."

David did a Walter Brennan voice. "Just gimme my buffalo gun."

"How's your sore butt?"

"Just gimme a bullet to bite down on."

She laughed and turned further around toward him. How effortlessly she kept her balance, the way her hips moved with the horse. Her laugh was a delight. He knew he shouldn't be thinking these things. She was 22, her father was just up ahead in front of the packhorses, and they were here to search for Hannah, his wife. But who could blame him? Nevertheless, he must put any erotic thoughts of Jessica out of his mind. He smiled at her, trying to assume an avuncular tone, trying to avoid glances at her breasts under her loose fitting t-shirt.

"Jessica, you're a very good teacher."

"Thank you. You're a very good student."

"That thing you told me about keeping my weight on the balls of my feet in the stirrups is very helpful." This was better—friendly, neutral banter.

With a grin she said, "It's my advice to all my students: ride on your balls."

David guffawed. What a marvelous sense of humor she had. "Yes, *ride on my balls*. It makes perfect sense—completely takes my mind off my sore ass." He gripped the saddle horn as the horses hopped down the last bit of steep hill onto a grassy flat that formed a terrace around the mountainside.

Jessica moved her horse out of line and slowed to let David come up beside her. "You're a good rider, David. You trust the horse."

"It's only ignorance. I've never fallen off, so I trust him." He patted the horse's neck. "Killer, you're a good guy."

"No, it's more than that. Most beginners want to keep a tight rein all the time, but in the bush the horse needs to have it loose for balance. You reserve the right to hold him back, but mostly he's deciding where to walk, and how. It's called *giving him his head*."

"Giving him his head? I thought you told me I only had to love him like a brother." He watched her head go back, her hair catch the sun, imagined her stomach muscles rippling under her shirt as she laughed.

"I think you have to become a horse whisperer for that."

"Did you hear that, Killer? You're outta luck."

"Okay, I'm gonna show you another thing. You can direct him with your legs and your weight. Suppose you want to avoid a clump of branches ahead. You want him to move over. Watch my leg. I'm going to push him with this leg, open up with my opposite one, and lean a bit that way." Her horse sidled away from him. "Do you see how I'm pushing, even with my cheek?" She indicated with a hand on the side of her buttock.

"I see." She had his full attention.

"I'm gonna come back now." Her horse sidled back closer. "See how my leg is opened up on this side?"

"Oh yeah." He struggled to keep his thoughts neutral while his eyes moved from her knee, up her thigh to where it met her buttocks.

"You try."

David leaned away from Jessica, but he found it difficult to push with the other leg. Killer's only reaction was a switching tail. Jessica shook her finger at Killer's head. "Behave yourself, Killer. Try again, David. Imagine you're pointing to the left with your hips, just like John Travolta. Look and think where you want to go." This time it worked. The horse drifted sideways. "You got it."

Jim called from up ahead of the packhorses. "We'll stop for a bit here, let them eat, and we'll have a look at the map." He dismounted.

As soon as they stopped the horses began to rip mouthfuls of grass. David got down and turned to Jessica. "Should I tie him up?"

"No, just let his reins drag on the ground. Let's go talk to Dad."

They walked past the feeding pack horses. Jim was bent over inspecting the front leg of his horse. He straightened at their approach and pointed down. "Jasper's got a cut on his knee."

David saw a line of blood over the joint. He thought a moment, casting his eye up the leg. "Isn't that his wrist?"

Jim's look said *dumb question.* "No, it's his knee."

"But look at the leg—the way it bends. The joint above it corresponds to our elbow, so that must be the wrist."

"It's called his knee. Look in all the books—knee."

David was about to respond, but Jessica interrupted. "Doesn't matter what it's called, but for the record, Dad, David's right." Before Jim could reply she went on. "Anyway, it's just a scratch, nothing serious. Where are we gonna go?"

Jim reached into his saddlebag. "We'll have a snack, a look at the map, glass around and try to figure out where a person might go down there."

David got the impression Jessica's *where are we gonna go* wasn't a question at all. She was prompting her father, keeping him on track. And it worked. She definitely had people skills.

The river divided, the side channel on the left pouring into a maze of small islands, each covered in a dense growth of willow and small spruce growing under gray standing trunks of burned old growth. A giant spruce lay out from the shore, deposited by the spring flood. The river piled against its fan of roots and rushed around both sides. Thirty meters of trunk, stripped clean of bark and branches, trailed downstream.

Hannah felt Dan pull hard on the left to avoid the roots and the canoe angled into the main channel, a gradual curve to the right along a steep, heavily forested hillside.

Dan said, "Looks like the fire didn't jump the river."

"Huh? What's that?" The canoe was broadside to the current, the bow facing the right shore. Its momentum had carried it close to the narrow flat shelf between the hill and the water. She twisted around in her seat to look back at him but her eyes were drawn to the bank behind the drowned tree.

"I said the fire..." He stopped when he saw her expression and turned to look across the river.

A wolf, completely black except for a gray tinge to the fur along its spine and a sprinkling of gray around its muzzle, walked slowly along the bank.

Dan turned back to face her. She thought he was about to say something, but he remained mute, his mouth hanging open. She turned forward and found herself looking into a pair of orange eyes glowing from a jet black face, a long muzzle stretched towards her, nose twitching. As the canoe slid past, its changing angle made silver lines of reflected sun move slowly along the curved black whiskers. If she stretched forward on her knees, and reached out, she could just touch...but the eyes held her still.

Raz whined and crowded against her knees, shivering. The orange eyes flicked down at the dog then back to Hannah. One brief look over the canoe and the wolf slipped behind a clump of willows. Another one, gray with white and rust, rose from the brush and followed. A few glimpses of flowing fur and tails as they trotted away upstream and melted into the bush.

She turned and looked at Dan. "I don't know what to say."

"Duck."

"What?"

"Duck." He was bowing forward over the dry bag and looking downstream. "Sweeper."

She crouched down and felt spruce needles brush over her back. They passed under the tree sticking horizontally out over the water, its roots undermined but still fixed to the bank, its crown bending up to the vertical. They got the canoe heading downriver again and drifted.

Eventually Dan said, "They're the ones from last night."

She looked back upstream. "That was unbelievable. Those eyes. I feel like I've just had surgery."

"You could go down this river a million times and not see that again."

"God, I wish I had a camera. No. On second thought, I would have missed those eyes."

"Hey. Look. There's the caribou."

She looked downstream. Against the right shore a lump of gray brown stuck out of the water, and a bit further out, the end of a tan antler emerged from the surface. As they drifted closer she saw that the lump was the edge of the animal's rib cage. Dan paddled a few strokes to bring them closer. Half the caribou lay in the water, head and shoulders submerged, lifeless eyes open, long white hairs of neck ruff waving in the current. The rear half was gone except for a few bits of skin and one hoof sticking out from the trampled grass, muck, and protruding roots on the bank. Red tinged water swirled slowly in the open rib cage. The end of a pink lung bobbed..

Hannah pointed her paddle at a yellow brown blanket of fuzzy tissue draped over one side of the cavity. "What's that? It looks like velcro."

"The stomach. Inside out."

"Wow."

"Looks like they grabbed him on the shore. When he tried to jump back in they held on. The water's deep. He probably drowned. Then they just ate him as they dragged him out."

"The poor thing."

"Yeah. The poor thing."

"What's that supposed to mean?"

"Huh? I don't...."

"You mimicked the way I said *poor thing*. You think I'm being naive and sentimental."

"You said *poor thing* and I said *yeah*. I agreed with you."

Raz craned his neck over the gunwale to look past the new mate, back at the half eaten caribou. Why weren't they turning the canoe? If they didn't turn now, get to the bank...ooh. The edge of the rib, red, white, yellow. Receding upstream. He looked at his Dan. The paddle rested on his knees.

The new mate was facing forward, paddling downstream, not up.

"You were making fun of me."

"So?"

"So, it's not fair."

They were quarrelling the way humans did, not with growls and snarls, but with their hands and voices. Were they fighting over the meat? Meanwhile the current carried them away around the bend. His last sight of the caribou was an arch of ribs against a silver glare on the water. They were leaving it behind.

He had to squeeze himself into the narrow part when the new mate turned around on her haunch to face his Dan.

"I don't mind being called sentimental, but I resent being called naïve."

"I never said you were either. I agreed with you."

"Your tone did not."

"My tone?"

Their tones were angry. Faint whiffs of it were coming from both of them. What had gone wrong? He wanted to go back to the muddy, bloody, trampled bank, awash in a warm, wolfy, fleshy, swamp of aroma. To roll in it.

"Yes, your tone. I'm not an imbecile."

To urinate on it.

"I didn't call you an imbecile."

"I can feel sorry for the caribou without blaming the wolves. I'm not saying they're cruel. They have to kill to survive."

Ooh. To poop on an upturned root. To leave a part of himself in the wolf smell.

"But the same doesn't apply to people. I suppose people have a choice. We can eat oatmeal."

"Now you're being sarcastic."

"Very perceptive of you."

He lay down to try to get comfortable, jammed into the narrow part, wondering when the hunting was going to happen. Not now. This noise would scare away the animals. Yapping, snarling. Happened a lot with mates. Especially the old mate. Especially when the big female scent was on her breath.

"Oh my god, Starla. Look at your knee." Tara cleared the three steps from the porch to the ground and ran to her daughter.

"It's all right, Mom."

Tara knelt before her and put her hand to the wound. "It's not all right. It's bleeding. And you've been crying. We're gonna hafta get your pant leg up and have a look. Come on." Tara led her to the steps and sat her down. She tried to roll up the leg of Starla's jeans but had trouble getting it over the knee. "Stand up, honey, I'll have to take the pants down."

"No. I'm okay." She looked toward the cabin windows.

Her mother noticed. "Starls, don't worry about Gary seeing you. You have your undies on." She lowered Starla's jeans. "Oh that's a nasty scrape. I'll get the first aid kit. You wait here." Tara went into the cabin.

Gary's voice came through the open door. "What's up?"

"Starla's cut herself. I gotta get the first aid kit."

"It's in the cupboard in our room."

Gary walked onto the porch, yawning and stretching. When Starla saw him she quickly made an effort to cover herself, pulling up her jeans. He moved along the deck and leaned both elbows on the railing, looking away, out over the lake. "Is your leg sore?"

"A little." She sat and crunched forward, hugging her knees, staring at the ground.

"Yeah, so's mine. A little." He looked at her and smiled. "Jeez, I was pretty drunk last night. Maybe that was a good thing…dulled the pain of the boiling water."

She turned away and mumbled, "Sorry."

"Don't be. It's me who should be sorry. Listen, Starla, I hope I didn't scare you or anything. I think you might have misunderstood. I was just joking around." He searched her eyes.

Tara bustled through the door, opening a box of bandages as she went to Starla. "Here we go, honey. We'll have you right as rain in no time."

Gary sauntered back to the door. "I'll start breakfast. What does the injured soldier want?"

Starla didn't answer.

Tara looked up at her as she cleaned the scrape with disinfectant. "He means you, sweetie."

Starla made no reply.

"How about pancakes? That's your favorite."

Still no answer.

Tara looked to Gary. "Pancakes. Thanks Gary. You're a swell guy. Isn't he a charmer, Starla?"

"Whoa Jasper."

"Whoa Spider." Jessica's horse stopped behind Jasper. The trail down the gully was wet, tracks of moose and caribou standing out in sharp relief in the black soil. Tall willows made riding difficult, and Jessica was glad she was not in the lead, getting all the spider webs crossing the path. The packhorses behind, their loads protruding on each side, had had to break their way through the bush in several places.

Her father dismounted, let Jasper's reins fall to the ground and went ahead, bent low, looking down at the trail. "Come down here. Tie your horses."

Jessica squeezed past Jasper "What is it Dad?"

Jim waited until David reached them before pointing down. "There."

It was a boot print, so clear in the mud they could see each individual tread.

David peered at it. "Do you think it's hers?"

"I don't know, but we're pretty far down the mountain. And from what Sergeant Godwin said, none of the searchers even came over this way. Who else could it be?"

Jessica got down on one knee. "Is this about her size, David?"

"Yes."

"What brand of hiking boots did she wear?"

"Merrell. Only Merrell."

Jessica looked closer. "A circle with a crooked M."

David gazed down at the track. "So she was here. She stepped right here."

Jessica stood. "We don't know that for sure. It could have been a hunter." Jim gave her his *tell me another one* look. She shrugged. "A smallish hunter."

"You know as well as I do, Jess, nobody hunts down here in this thick shit."

"Maybe they had to. Maybe they were following a wounded animal."

"One set of human tracks? No horses? Come on."

David broke in. "So, she's headed down into the valley. She might be somewhere ahead of us."

Jessica could hear the hope in his voice. She didn't want to remind David that Hannah had made the track seven, possibly eight days ago. And it did head down the valley…down into dense, boggy hell. Time for some diplomacy. "Yeah, we should keep our eyes open for signs of smoke."

She pushed easily up the valley, following the river, just enough to make steady speed, eyes scanning the bars and logjams for anything interesting. She was in no hurry. Her gullet was not full, but not empty. She had managed to strip a few beakfuls from the bobblehead kill while the big shit whitehead was distracted by some other ravens.

She heard the pair before she saw them. Floating. Squabbling, judging by the tone. But maybe not. Bobbleheads made lots of sounds. Good mimics, too. She remembered the moose call one of them had made two nights ago. Decent.

She made a wide circle above them, her attention on the hard, straight-sided thing with the blue top. That was where their food would be.

She was about to continue upriver, but noticed them moving towards a sandbar that partly blocked a long crescent shaped backwater. They were stopping. She knew when bobbleheads stopped the food came out. She slowed and spun down to land on a big spruce. "Me." she called.

"So you believe people aren't part of nature." The canoe sidled up to the sandbar and Dan reached his paddle to hold it against the shore. Raz jumped out and immediately began sniffing some recent moose tracks.

"I don't believe that. You're twisting my words." Hannah got out of the canoe and held it for Dan. "I said it's not natural to kill an animal for sport, and I don't think every yahoo with a gun should be allowed to do it. How many times do I have to repeat that I don't include subsistence hunting if there is a real need for food? In most cases, there isn't."

He stepped out of the canoe. "Food has to come from somewhere. Look at this valley. Would you rather it be fields of oats and a factory making granola? I'd rather it stay like this, growing moose and fish and caribou and berries."

"Dan, I'm tired of this. And I'm starving. I don't want to argue anymore. If you want the last word, be my guest."

He regarded her a moment. "Last word, huh?" He smiled. "You're a bambi-thumper."

She couldn't hold back a laugh. "Good last word. Asshole." She pulled the bow onto the sand and tied the rope to a struggling willow. "Now, what do we have to eat?"

The bigger one went off up the bar to a pile of dead trees and started breaking pieces off. The littlewolf went, too. Good. They would be making their fire. Eating. The smaller one carried the straight-sided thing onto the bar and pulled off the blue top. It pulled something out and stood, turning its crazy round bobbly head on the end of its skinny neck, looking to its mate, which was out of its sight. It went back to the river and pulled down its dead lower skin to reach a bony paw between its legs. When the paw came out again it was holding a small red and white thing. Might be good to eat, but the stupid shit bobblehead threw it in the river.

The open box caught her attention. She tucked in her breast feather and launched from the top of her tree, dove and spread her wings to skim over the sand. She landed on the edge of the box and cocked her head to the side. Bright colored food in its crinkly skins. Easy to tear open. She kept an eye on the bobblehead. Its paw was between its legs again. She reached her beak down and poked through a skin—orange, grainy stuff, sweet, sweet, sweet. A hillside of berries in one taste. Where did the bobbleheads find this? She had to have it. The whole thing. She took the skin in her beak to lift it out.

It was coming back across the sand. Startled, she dropped the bag and flapped into the air. She would have flown away, out over the river, but the bobblehead stopped. It wasn't chasing her. She glided to an old dead tree lying half buried in sand. Close but far enough if the bobblehead made a sudden dash.

It walked slowly to the box, making soft, cooing, shushing noises, a glance every now and then with its penetrating eyes. It took another bag out of the box, reached its paw into the crinkly skin and brought out one of the long, brown-red sticks—the ones she had taken from the stupid little gray shitbird. Rich, salty, meaty, fatty, nice after burn. It walked toward her slowly. She crouched and cocked her wings, ready to leap up, but the bobblehead stopped, broke off a piece of the stick and placed it on the ground. It walked back to the box, making more cooing sounds.

The delicious burnstick lay between her and the bobblehead. Was it trying to trap her—tease her with the stick? It sat down on the ground by the box and looked away. No more eyes peering inside her. The red-brown burnstick lay on the sand. Bobbleheads were too weird to trust, but there was something about this one, something about the tone of the cooing, something in its body language. She hopped down off the log and walked across the sand, stopping a neck's reach from the morsel. The bobblehead looked her way and she hopped back a step. Soft low melodic sounds came from its throat.

"It's okay. I'm not gonna hurt you. Have the pepperoni."

Funny little popping sounds. It looked away, leaning relaxed, its foreleg on the box. She snaked her neck along the ground as if ducking the swipe of a paw, picked up the stick, jumped into the air and flew back to the log. She swallowed. A pleasant burn filled her crop as the bobblehead's eyes brushed all over her. She tucked in her breast feather and called. "Me."

It called back. "Me." A bit garbled, but not bad for a bobblehead.

She called again. "Me."

It repeated. "Me." Better.

She puffed out her neck feathers. "Food. Good."

The bobblehead repeated it. Close, but didn't get the trill at the end.

She called back. "Fat, meat, mine."

It's round head rolled forward on its scrawny neck. It said something like, *softhard.* It was trying. Its eyes were on her again.

"Come closer. There's more pepperoni."

Popping again. Funny. She tried a couple of pops but they came out as clicks. The bony paws moved. One flipped toward her. She flinched, her wings ready to spring open. Another piece of burnstick landed between them. She jumped and glided, landed beside the stick, picked it up and gulped it down. Nice burn. The bobblehead's bony paw was extended towards her now, holding a piece of burnstick. Could she? It was a bobblehead. Weird. Dangerous. Unpredictable. Boomsticks. Hairy heads rolling around on scrawny necks. Eyes. Scary eyes, as if their bony paws reached right inside you. But she had seen this one's eyes up close when it was dying. She had a feeling about this one.

It took its eyes off her. Better. She walked closer, wings cocked slightly at the elbows, ready to spring back and up. Another step and she stretched her neck. Her head tilted to the side, she opened her beak and gingerly nibbled the burnstick.

Dan walked around the jumble of dead, gray tree trunks with an armload of firewood. "Raz, my man, we're lucky with the weather. Nice dry wood." The dog wasn't paying any attention to him. He was stopped, ears up, looking out over the bar to where Hannah sat leaning against the food box, arm extended towards a raven, whose beak reached to touch her hand. In two strides the dog was in full flight, spurts of sand popping up behind him. "Raz!" It was too late. The surprised raven leapt back and up. Two powerful wing strokes and it was out over the water. Raz came to a sliding stop at the shore and watched the bird rise in a curve, up to a teetering balance at the top of a high spruce.

Dan walked over to Hannah and dropped the wood. "I've never been able to do that."

"What—get a bird to come to you?"

"Whiskeyjacks. The occasional magpie. Never a raven."

"She was going to take it from my hand."

"She?"

Hannah was watching the raven, eyes squinting, brow furrowed in concentration. "Oh. Did I say she? I don't know. I just thought she's...I dunno, just a feeling."

"Are you sure you weren't raised by wolves?" He began to break the smaller sticks into kindling. No reply. He looked up. She was still fixed on the raven, her head tilted up, her hair backlit by the sun, glowing around the edges. He liked her large eyes and lips. *Generous features*, his father would have said. His eyes wandered down her neck, over her shoulder and down her arm, her muscles visible under the skin. *Small but wiry*, his father would have said. After what she had been through she still looked healthy. A little thin, but...too bad her arm was blocking her breasts from view.

She suddenly took a deep breath and turned. "What?"

He was caught off guard. "Huh?"

"You had this funny look...like you're stoned."

He went back to breaking twigs. "Don't I wish?"

"You miss it? Marijuana?"

The air was still, the sun was shining and the river swirls dazzled silver. "No, not at all. If I don't have it, I don't miss it." He thought if he held his lighter to his pipe and sucked hard there was probably enough tarry deposit to give him a buzz.

"So what was the stoned look?"

He fussed with the fire. "Uh...it was a look of complete admiration. I was saying you have a way with animals. Hannah the Jungle Girl. All the creatures love her and do her bidding. No man can tame her wild spirit."

"You're mocking me again."

"Hannah the Jungle Girl, with a sixth sense for mockery, taught to her by the great harpy eagle."

"And who taught you social skills—the great warthog?"

She had beautiful laugh lines. He looked down to the bundle of sticks in his hand and held his lighter under it. "What are we gonna eat? We have some bannock, but we're getting low on jam." The twigs caught fire, he piled a few bigger ones carefully on top and leaned over to peer into the food box. He noticed the open bag of pepperonis. "You were feeding my pepperonis to the birds again?"

"Oh. Yeah." She looked at her hand. The piece of pepperoni was still there. "Only one. They seem to like it. There's still some left." She held it out to him.

"Uh...not right now. Why don't you have it?" He piled more sticks onto the fire.

She looked at the end of pepperoni. He could see she was tempted. He knew she was hungry by the way she had eaten her oatmeal that morning. The pepperoni sat in her hand, trembling slightly. It looked as if she would pop it into her mouth. Instead she reached for the bag to put it back.

"Hey, don't put it away. I'll have it." She gave it to him. He ate with exaggerated relish, closing his eyes and making appreciative sounds. "Mmmm. Aaaah...Salty. Meaty. Heavenly after burn." He opened an eye. She was looking up at the raven. He swallowed the pepperoni and went back to making the fire. "You're a tough nut to crack, Hannah Weinberg."

She seemed to be struggling with a thought. When she spoke it was more to herself than to him. "She looks so black from here. Up close she's silver and blue and green and purple. Like a…I dunno, a tropical fish or… that black silk cloak my mother used to wear or…and she's always poking at that breast feather."

Owen Orser's house sat on a quiet street of houses built during the war to house military families. Now most of the homes were in various stages of disrepair. Some were being renovated, some retrofitted, and one had recently been torn down and trucked away, its open concrete basement awaiting the dreams of its new owners. Next to it was Owen's place, set back in the shade of thick poplars, green peeling paint showing irregular patches of gray wood. Owen often said he'd planned it that way—the camo effect. People were always surprised when they found out a lawyer lived there.

Susan hurried across Owen's overgrown lawn and mounted the steps to his front door. She wanted to be rid of the envelope clutched tightly under her arm. It felt like drugs or porn, something illicit, which in fact it was. She knocked on the door and looked up and down the street.

After a long wait, she heard movement inside. The door opened to reveal Owen dressed in a striped bathrobe, hair mussed and a groggy expression. "Suzy. What a surprise."

"Owen, I'm sorry. Did I wake you?"

"Yeah, don't worry about it."

"Sorry. I thought it would be okay. It's past noon."

"I should get up now anyway. What's up?"

"I have to give you back these papers. Thanks for your help. You've been so great."

Owen took the envelope from her with a puzzled expression. "There's no rush for this stuff. It's all copies anyway. Burn them."

"Well, I'm going away for a few days and I thought it best."

"Where are you going?"

"Just…camping."

"Come on in. I'll make some coffee."

"I don't want to impose. I've disturbed you enough." As she turned she gripped the rail to go down the steps. There was a sound of cracking wood as the rail sagged outward. "Oh. I'm sorry, Owen, I…"

"Don't worry. It was already broken. I've gotta get it fixed. Come in." He held the door open. "You'll have to ignore the mess."

She stepped in the door and looked around at empty pizza boxes, clothes scattered on frayed furniture, papers strewn about.

Owen picked a pair of socks off a lampshade. "My brother was visiting. He's such a slob."

"I didn't know you have a brother."

"I don't." He made some room on the couch, picked up several dirty cups and glasses from the coffee table and went into the kitchen. "Where are you going camping?"

"Little Atlin Lake."

He called back. "Oh that's beautiful this time of…" He appeared in the doorway. "Suzy, you can't."

"Who says I can't? It's a public road last time I checked."

"And what do you propose to do? Swoop down like an avenging Valkyrie and take Starla away to Nirvana?"

"I think that's Valhalla."

"I just woke up. Gimme a break."

"I don't know what I'm going to do, Owen, but I have to do something."

"Based on your terrible gut feeling again?"

"No. Yes. I don't know. Look, all I want is to check in with her, make sure she's okay. I'm probably worried for nothing. She's probably perfectly safe. After all, Tara wouldn't let anything happen. Maybe Gary's changed."

"Hmmm."

"What?"

"Nothing." Owen brought two cups of coffee on a tray with sugar and milk. "Oops, forgot the spoons. I'll be right back. When he returned Susan was looking out the window. "You didn't sleep much last night."

"Does it show?"

He sat in the chair opposite her. "I'm going with you."

"No. You've done enough already. I don't want to drag you any further into this. Getting those documents for me was too much as it is. You're too good a friend."

"I won't be going as your friend. I'll be going as your lawyer."

Moose rutting smell. Big sharp and big heavy at the same time. The slightest trace of it cut into his nose. Even when he shifted to rest his head in the new mate's lap and the big female scent surrounded him, the rutting smell cut in.

It was getting stronger now, closer. He lifted his chin off the new mate's lap and straightened to peer over the bow. The smell began to sting his nose. He shivered in anticipation. Next his Dan would growl the whattaya thing that goes up at the end.

"Whattaya see, Mister? Moose?"

"I think he smells something."

The new mate should be quiet. Now for the big eyes that hung around his Dan's neck.

His Dan put them up and whispered, "I don't see anything."

The dog rose slowly, ears up, eyes searching for movement. The sound of breaking brush echoed around the river bend. An undercut bank on the left, full of big dead trees. Can't go there. His Dan would move the canoe closer to the bar on the other side.

"Let's get closer to the bar on the right."

His Dan and the new mate took several hard strokes and they both looked across the curve of the bar. His Dan stood up then quickly down again.

"It's a moose."

His Dan had seen a moose. Now it would get exciting. He almost whined in anticipation. But no sound must come from him. Now his Dan would slide the boom stick from its sheath. They would quietly drift around the bar and edge into the slack water below. He glanced back. The boom stick was still in its sheath.

"He's crossing to the bar."

"Are you going to shoot him?"

"Too big. Stay quiet, we'll drift by."

He could see the moose now, stepping onto the gravel. They would have him for sure this time. Meat, fur, bone, gristly, slippery-chewy bits. But not yet. The moose belly heaved and three deep grunts came rolling over the water, bouncing off the cut bank behind. His Dan would keep the boat pointed at the moose.

"Keep the canoe pointed at him."

"My god, he's immense."

The new mate should not make sounds. His Dan would tell her to be silent.

His Dan whispered, "Try calling. Do a grunt like his."

The moose saw them. His big square nose tasted the air in large gulps. His big ears were trained on them. The antlers spread great curving palms out and up to a forest of tines. Raz knew he must remain perfectly still, for now his Dan would be pointing the boom stick. He waited for the boom. For the smack. For the big dead moose. For the flesh and the guts and the... he snatched a look back. The boom stick hadn't moved.

"Wuh, wuh, wuh."

What was happening? They had drifted past the moose. No boom. And now the new mate was trying to call. Crazy. The moose would run. His Dan would be furious. The new mate would be in trouble. No meat. No chewy bits. They would fight again only worse with big growls and squeals. But when his Dan answered it wasn't with anger.

"Good. Watch. He's coming."

The moose extended his head level with the ground, his massive neck merging with the hump over his shoulder, his bell swinging below his neck side to side with each step as he walked towards them along the water's edge.

He answered the new mate's call. "Wuh, wuh, wuh." His Dan still made no move to pick up the boom stick.

Again the new mate broke the rule of silence. "Wow. It worked."

The canoe drifted into slack water, a slow swirl below the bar where a stagnant back channel languished, curving out of sight away from the river. He saw his Dan's intent now—to call the moose closer and boom it from the calm water of the eddy. Surely now the boom stick would come out.

"He's stopped. Give him another call." His Dan wasn't whispering anymore. Now even he was breaking the rule.

The new mate called. "Wuh, wuh, wuh, wuh."

The moose broke into a trot and covered the last of the distance around the bar. For a nervous moment, Raz thought the huge animal would charge straight into the water at them, but it stopped at the edge, feet buried in soft sand. The head went up again and he heard it take in a long taste of air, filling its cavernous chest in a low rumble. The slight breeze was blowing to it. It smelled them now.

"He smells us now. He'll turn his butt to us in a moment."

It was clear his Dan would not boom this one. Raz watched the moose turn slowly around. The lighter gray of its hind legs merged with the dark rump, the stump of its small tail clamped over its rear. The wide antlers turned as the head swiveled to glare back at them.

"Amazing. What a magnificent animal."

"Yeah. He's in his prime."

"How old do you think he is?"

"Hard to tell. Seven or eight. As old as ten, maybe."

All this noise would break the spell. There would be no dead moose this time. The moose walked off to the fringe of thick willows and with one brief look back melted into the branches. Raz stared at the spot for a while and settled back down onto the small pack wedged into the front of the canoe. Had his Dan lost his mind?

His Dan made some sounds. "Raz must think I've lost my mind."

This was a good place, the best food they had found in several days. The hedysarum roots were sweet and thick. Engrossed in the digging, her nose filled with the odor of torn up moss, she hadn't noticed the approach of the big male bear. It was one of her cubs who spotted him first, alerting her with three tiny sharp huffs. Her head shot up. Ambling slowly along the trail by the river was the biggest bear she had ever seen. A male—the greatest danger her cubs could face. Given the chance, he would kill them. Without her cubs she would soon come into estrous. Then he would mate with her. She huffed a warning and the two cubs gathered under her. Run or fight? She could outrun him, but could the cubs? If she must, she would fight, but he was so big. She stood to her full height and barked a warning. The big male showed no sign of hearing, or seeing, or scenting them. He kept plodding, head down. She could hear his breaths, short, shallow, agonized.

She ran a short distance away and stood again, waiting for her cubs to catch up. His coat rippled with each step, glistening thick over fat and muscle. Healthy. Strong. But he moved stiff and old and sick. She saw him catch her scent, his snout rising as if by great effort, weakly sweeping the air and down again, still plodding, barely noticing or caring. Now she caught a whiff of his scent, powerful and foul. Sickness. Pain. Fear.

She quietly urged the cubs ahead, hurried them through the moss. They had to scramble over a big fallen tree. They followed her up the steep hillside to the safety of the ridge. From there she watched and listened. The cubs, frightened and nervous, crowded close. She could still hear the breathing.

She gathered her cubs in her arms and they curled up together, the three of them a furry ball in the moss. The breathing faded away. The big male was gone downriver. She wanted to go back to the hedysarum roots. But she would wait. Sleep a bit. The smell still lingered down there.

"Lyle's camp is on the left." Dan put up his binoculars. "There's the boat. The motor's on it. Smoke coming from the chimney. Somebody there." He put the binoculars down.

"I don't want to stop."

"I know, but we could score some food. You can stay in the canoe."

"I can't accept help from him."

"You can't, but I can…unless Lyle's there himself."

"What does that mean? You don't get along with Lyle?"

"It's a long story. But he's not likely to be there. He's with that bunch of hunters on Mount Riddell. No, it'll be Lawrence or Neil with a client or two. They fly in to a pothole lake just back off the river." He paddled hard on the right.

"But I don't want them to know where I am. They'll recognize me."

"Maybe, but if it's Neil he might not know what you look like. He's been out in the bush with a client from Toledo for two weeks, and before that he was game spotting by plane and doing some work on the camps."

"How do you know all this?"

"I was working for Lyle until I…stopped."

"He fired you?"

"It's a long story."

Hannah was silent for a while as the current carried them closer to the blue haze of wood smoke hanging over the river. "Why can't we just paddle by?"

"We can. But you're gonna feel awful sorry when we have to eat Raz."

"Don't be silly." She patted the dog's head, which rested in her lap. "Don't listen to him, Raz."

They drifted closer. The cabin was visible now, set back from the bank, low, the color of the forest. A figure appeared at the top of the bank between two big spruce trees. Dan put up his binoculars. So did the person on the bank.

A voice floated over the water. "Hey, Dan. Is that you?"

Dan called back. "Hi, Neil. How's it goin'?"

The man waved. "Hey, stranger, come on in here, man."

Dan paddled and the canoe angled across the current towards the left shore. "Gotta stop now."

As they beached the canoe Neil stood smiling at the top of the bank. "Dan, for chrissake, what the hell are you doin' here?"

Dan climbed to the top of the bank and stretched. He looked up into the smiling face of the tall lanky man and took the proffered hand in his. "Good to see you, Neil." He glanced down at Hannah, still sitting in the canoe. He wondered how he would explain her. They hadn't had time to concoct a story. Neil was scrutinizing her, a smile beginning to crease his face. Dan knew what the next question would be. He walked away from the river towards the cabin. "The place is lookin' good. You here with a client?"

"Yup. A dentist from Toledo, Ohio."

Dan noticed a freshly skinned moose skull leaning against the sawhorse near the door. It was big, a wide expanse of antlers, huge flat palms like extended wings, brow palms each sprouting two long sharp tines forward over the nose. "Big moose. Your dentist must be happy."

"Yeah, we got him yesterday. Just down river." Neil jerked a thumb at the river. "So who's the hot number?"

"Hot number? Christ, Neil, when was the last time you went to town, 1946?"

The door of the cabin opened and a voice boomed out. "Who the heck is there, Neil?" The man came out the door, squinting in the sun through a pair of thick glasses. He was almost as tall as Neil and wore a pair of camouflage bib overalls and a checked shirt.

Neil moved up beside Dan. "This is a friend of mine, Dan MacKay. Dan, this is Mike Farnell."

Mike spoke just below a shout. "Pleased to meet you. Where the hell did you come from?"

"Upriver. North Canol Road."

Mike turned to Neil and boomed, "Shit, Neil, I thought we were in the middle of nowhere. You didn't tell me we'd see people. I haven't had a chance to do my hair." His laugh was twice as loud as his speech. Its echo bounced back and forth across the river.

Neil looked back at the river. Dan spoke before he could. "Nice moose you got there, Mike." He guessed Mike would talk at length about it.

"You bet. I'm proud of that fella. Sixty two inches. Gonna look mighty good in my den." The man proceeded to describe in minute detail and stentorian tone the whole episode—Neil's calls from the edge of the gravel bar, the sounds of the bull thrashing trees, grunting, emerging from the willows, saliva dripping from his mouth down over his bell, the shot, the moose crashing to the sand.

When Mike finished, Dan asked, "What kinda rifle you use, Mike?" He knew hunters loved to talk about their guns.

Neil interjected. Why don't you come in and have a coffee. It's on. Ask your friend, too."

"Sure." boomed Mike. "Come on in...Dan, is it? I can show you my gun."

"Uh...sure." He resisted the urge to glance back at the river. The three of them stepped into the gloom of the cabin, one large kitchen, a table in the middle, a woodstove near the wall, a sink under the window, bunk beds at the back. The heat was uncomfortable.

Mike said, "You want something to eat? We got lotsa leftover moose stew. I'm sure not gonna eat it."

"Why not?"

"Chewy, very chewy. You folks up here must have strong jaw muscles." His eyes twinkled as he turned to Neil.

Neil was at the stove pouring three cups of coffee from a large black pot. Dan noticed a pained look cross his face. The stew was a sore point. "It just needs a little more cooking."

"And more trimming." Mike turned back to Dan with a smile. "As a dentist I can tell you, sand ain't the best thing for your teeth."

Neil put three cups of coffee on the table and said with a strained smile, "So, I missed a spot. I never claimed to be Martha fuckin' Stewart."

Mike's laugh filled the room. Dan felt sorry for Neil. He knew all about spending a couple of weeks with a client who irritates you. But Neil would never jeopardize his tip by letting it show.

Dan said, "The meat will be fine if it hangs awhile."

Mike laughed. "It can hang 'til it fossilizes for all I care. You want it? You can have it."

Neil quickly interjected. "Dan, aren't you gonna invite your friend in?"

"Uh...I think she wants to stay in the canoe. Tired. We gotta get goin' if we're gonna find a good spot to camp."

"You can stay here the night. Got an extra bunk." Neil had that little mocking smile again.

"Thanks, Neil, but..."

"So who is she?"

Dan's mind scrambled for some likely sounding story. "Uh...she's..."

"Sarah Hoffmann. I'm from Switzerland." The three men turned in unison to see Hannah standing confidently in the open doorway. "This is a beautiful spot. What a sweet little cabin."

Dan had to suppress a smile. Hannah's German accent was perfect. He stood. "Oh. There you are, uh...Sarah. This is Neil and Mike."

Hannah stuck out a hand. "How do you do, Neil? Mike?" She shook hands with both men and sat in the chair next to Dan's.

"Coffee, Sarah?" Neil held out a full cup to her and she took it.

"Thank you."

Neil went back to the stove to pour a cup for himself. "What brings you here, Sarah?"

"Moose. I am with Dan as he hunts the moose."

"Really?"

"Yes. Since I am a little girl it is my dream. The river, the mountains, the wolves and bears. Magnificent."

Mike had a puzzled look. "You gonna shoot a moose?"

"Oh no, not me. I just come along. I wish to film for Swiss television."

Neil's deep voice was a soft counterpoint to Mike's. "Where's the camera gear. By the looks of your canoe you're traveling light."

"Not this year I film. Maybe next year. This time I only look."

"Location scouting?"

"Yah, yah. Location…scouting? This is how you say it?"

Neil turned to Dan. "Is this for Lyle?"

Dan shook his head. He decided not to elaborate. He wanted to find out how much Neil knew about Hannah and Grizzly Watch. "How long have you guys been here?"

"Three or four days."

Mike spoke up. "Three. Before we came here we were 'way down the valley in the mountains south of the river for almost two weeks. What was the name of that mountain, Neil? Camel or something?"

Dan said, "Dromedary Mountain?"

"Yup. That's it."

Dan looked into Neil's eyes. "That's not in Lyle's area."

Mike turned a puzzled look to Neil. "Huh? What's that?"

Dan, still looking into Neil's eyes, explained. "Each outfitter has a designated hunting area. Lyle's boundary is Russell Creek, about a day downstream."

Mike was concerned. "I wanna do things by the book, Neil. I don't wanna chance a fine, or worse, have my trophies confiscated."

Neil looked uncomfortable. He gave Dan a knowing glance. "No Dan. You're forgetting. Maybe you haven't heard. Lyle had his area extended."

"I didn't know that. What did the folks at Pelly have to say about it?"

Neil's discomfort was all over his face. "I dunno."

Mike broke in. "Got a nice big bull caribou up there. Almost got a grizzly. Big sucker, huh Neil?"

"Yeah." Color rose up Neil's neck. He turned to Hannah. "Sarah, would you like something to eat?"

Before she could reply Mike continued at high decibels. "I hit him with the first shot but he got away. Ran like stink down the mountain. I'd sure like to get another crack at that bastard. Oh well, maybe we'll see another one on the river. I've got a few days left."

Dan checked on Hannah. She was glaring at Mike, looking as if she was about to explode. He thought he should change the subject but didn't get the chance.

Hannah stood abruptly. Her chair tipped back to smack the floorboards. "You stupid fucking asshole. You shot a grizzly bear, wounded it, and now you want to do it again. Then you call the bear a bastard because he ran away. What kind of psychopathic moron are you? I suppose you think you have the right to come here and kill and maim, inflict pain and suffering on innocent animals? For what? To satisfy your juvenile male urges with your big fucking gun? To pretend you have balls? You're pathetic."

Mike was leaning back in his chair as if pushed by a strong wind. "What the...Jeez." He let out a nervous laugh and looked to Neil. "She thinks animals feel pain."

Dan thought Hannah was going to strike the man. Instead she stormed out the door and headed for the riverbank.

The three men exchanged awkward looks. Dan wondered if they noticed her accent had disappeared. His plan to ask Neil for some flour and oatmeal and a few cans of vegetables was gone. He shrugged. "Well gents, I guess we'll be going."

The old bull lay in his muddy pit while the sun beat warm onto the sedge meadow. The cow was bedded down nearby. A sound of branches sliding over a large body came from the thick willows—the young bull. He turned an ear in that direction. There was no need to drive him away, no need to even rise from his bed and the comfort of his own rutting smell. He knew the young bull was no rival for his cow. He could ignore him.

He heard the young one step out of the willows. With a half open eye, he saw him approach with tentative steps, nose almost touching the trampled grass, soft smacking sounds coming from his mouth. He recognized the submissive gestures and remained indifferent as the young one came a step closer, extending his nose, sniffing carefully.

The old bull extended his nose as well and they tasted each other's breath. The young one smelled of fresh willow leaves and nervous energy. The old bull made no effort to rise, staying immobile while the other, bolder now, moved slowly closer to sniff the tips of his antlers.

"I can't get through here." Jim faced a thick tangle where a big fallen tree blocked the trail. "Can you guys back up?"

Jessica turned around to David. "Give him a bump with the reins and sit back. Go on, Killer, go." The horse stepped back carefully over a root.

Her father's voice came from ahead. "We'll get around this and stop. I see a meadow." His horse backed away from the fallen tree and plunged through the thick brush to his right. "Take it easy, Jasper."

The packhorses followed, breaking branches as they went. They rode through forest now, where horse packs bumped against tree trunks, sometimes blocking the animal's passage. It was difficult to see the terrain ahead. The trail was petering out, branching into side trails.

They rode to the edge of a small boggy meadow. Jessica was relieved to be in the open. They dismounted and the horses immediately began to crop the thin yellow grass.

Jessica looked at David, at the dirt and leaf dust stuck to the sweat on his face. It seemed to etch the lines of worry deeper. "How ya doin'?"

"I've been better."

Jim dropped his reins and walked back to them. "We have a decision to make."

Jessica reached into her saddlebag and pulled out a bag of snacks—nuts, granola bars, dried apricots, chocolate. She took a granola bar and handed the bag to David. She knew what was coming. She hoped her Dad would be tactful.

David looked like he had already guessed. "You mean, how much farther can we go?"

"Yeah."

There was a long silence while David looked all around the meadow and back into the bush, as if he was willing Hannah to appear, to walk out of the trees and wave. Finally he sighed and said, almost to himself, "When do we call off the search?"

Jim said, "I guess that's the question. Our problem is, we're just crashing around in the rhubarb down here. We don't know if she stayed on this trail. We haven't seen any more footprints, and the bush is getting thick. Eventually, we're gonna hit that burn. If you think the going's hard now…" He trailed off.

"I understand. What do you think, Jessica?"

"I don't know. I'm just the wrangler/cook/ water carrier."

"I value your opinion."

"I think we have two options—unpack the horses and ride ahead, or leave the horses here and walk, leaving enough time to get back here tonight.

Problem is, either way, we don't have enough time left today. I think we should camp here. I know it's early, but everybody's tired, including the horses."

Jim nodded. "You're right. It won't be so bad without the horse packs."

David said, "So if we don't find any sign of her, that's it? After tomorrow we give up."

Jessica could see the resignation on his face. "Well…yes, but…" She couldn't think what else to say. She wasn't about to tell him what she was thinking, that they had to be realistic. It had been eight days. What were the odds they would find her? What were the odds she was still alive?

David searched Jessica's face. "All right then, we'll camp."

"That's gross."

"It must be the one Mike shot. It's not the best way to butcher a moose. The eagle seems to like it, though. Look at him. Perched on those bones as if he owns them."

"It's wasteful, isn't it? Leaving the bones behind?"

"Yeah. And it exposes a lot more meat to the air. More spoilage. You can't hang it properly. More trimming later. Neil's just trying to save on weight. They have to fly it out."

"But the bones are good. Bones add flavor. What's a roast without a bone?"

"Jeez, a vegetarian composing a haiku to meat."

"Yeah. I can't believe I'm salivating over a pile of bones lying on a sandbar, covered with eagle shit. Christ, I'm so fucking hungry, I could eat the east end of a westbound skunk."

She could hear them over the sound of air rushing past her wings. Bobbleheads never seemed to stop the chatter. She was glad of it now. Their noise worked in her favor. The big stupid shit whitehead had its attention fixed on them. It still sat on the crest of backbones where it had been that morning, and the day before. Stupid shit. Now its back was to her. She tucked in her breast feather and pulled her elbows in so she rode only on the outer third of her wings. She descended, aiming her body at the whitehead, picking up speed until the rush of air became a whistling roar in her head. This was going to be fun.

"Hey, look at that raven. Coming down behind the eagle. I think he's gonna nail him."

Good. Keep chattering, bobbleheads. She knew the risk she took doing this. If she hit the whitehead too hard she could injure herself. If the big stupid bird saw her in time, she could be slashed by its heavy, hooked, yellow beak, and at any speed that could kill her. But even if she had to pull up, it would be worth it just to startle the big dumb shit. She pushed her wings wider to slow a bit and make some last fine adjustments.

She kept her eyes on the whitehead, ready for the moment it sensed her. It was coming up fast. Suddenly its head turned and it saw her. It flinched, ducking low. Ha. As she passed over she drove her beak down into neck feathers, feeling it bump against bone. She spread her wings and her speed took her up, turning as she went, to see the whitehead off balance, flapping its giant wings, hanging on to the bone with its horrible curved talons. She circled above and watched it clumsily regain its perch. She called. "Ha. Ha. Ha."

The burnstick bobblehead, the one at the front of the floater, called back. "Ha. Ha. Ha." Did she think it was funny, too?

She? Why did she think of this bobblehead as a she?

The sun was down. It was time to go back. Her mother would be worrying. Starla was bored and lonely, anyway. But boredom and loneliness were preferable to Gary. Why couldn't he ignore her like Tara's other boyfriends had?

She crawled down through the trap door in the kitchen of Brian and Anne's cabin, under the house and the deck to the overgrown patch of grass in front. Fireweed and horsetails encroached, lines of sprouts from underground stems re-invading the turf. The sky was still light. The lake was a dark green mirror reflecting pink mountaintops. It would be another cold night.

This was her favorite time of year—warm days, cold nights, clear air, crisp sounds, bright colors, the feeling of big things about to happen—the rutting season. If only her dad could have taken her moose hunting. That would have been perfect. He knew how much she loved moose hunting. She was missing school now, anyway. Lots of kids were off school during the rut.

What if he didn't care anymore? What if he didn't like her anymore? What if it was her fault? She didn't like thinking about it. Her dad probably had a good reason for not taking her moose hunting and not showing up for court. He would explain it all when he got back and she could go visit him in Ross—him and Gramma and Raz.

She felt a little better as she made her way along the lake trail. She noticed a glow behind the mountains to the east. The full moon. Being here was not all bad. If she had to avoid Gary for a few more days she could, but it would be easier if she wasn't so alone.

"I blew it. They'll figure out who I am, now."

"Maybe not...at least not until they get back to Ross. They said they were staying at the cabin another few days."

They sat with their legs dangling over the edge of the two-meter high bank. The canoe rested in the slack current below them. A steep forested hill plunged down to the water on the other side. On their side the land was low, a narrow swath of mature spruce edging the river, a large willow flat behind. A small gravel bar lay downstream where the bank dropped lower, fringed by tall, thickly-growing willow. In the backwater below the bar a few stones poked above the surface and marked a shallow shelf near the shore. The sun was down, but the long, northern twilight still lit the sky deep blue. The moon was an inflated orange ball rising upstream.

Hannah picked up a twig and tossed it into the water. "Fuck."

"Don't let it get you down. Eventually people are going to find out you're alive."

"I don't want Lyle Kessler to break the news. He'll make me look like some kind of idiot, getting lost and almost dying."

"You're too hard on yourself. It can happen to anyone."

"Sure, if you're an idiot."

"Hey, listen. If Lyle ever mentions the subject of getting lost in the bush, you just ask him about the Prevost River two years ago." Dan chuckled.

"What happened?"

"Lyle has a trap line up there. It was late November, snowing, and he went out on his snowmobile to set some trail. He got up into a valley and his machine broke down, so he started walking back, but he decided to take a short cut to his cabin. He got down into some thick trees where he couldn't see very far ahead, and the clouds were low so he couldn't see the mountains. He walked for a long time. It was just getting dark when he came across human footprints in the snow. He wondered who the hell could be out there that time of year. He followed the tracks for about an hour and then all of a sudden there were two sets of tracks."

"He was following his own tracks. He'd walked in a circle."

"Yeah, just like that Winnie the Pooh story. You know it?"

"Yes. Oh, that's rich. I hope I get a chance to use it."

"Wait. It gets better. His wife Sharon—his ex-wife now—"

"Sharon. She's the one who tipped us off about Mount Riddell."

"Yeah, Artie told me. Anyway, she was back at the cabin waiting for him. When it got dark, and there was no sign of Lyle, she went looking for him. By the time she found him he had fallen through the ice crossing a creek and he was huddled under a tree crying like a baby. He'd be dead now if it wasn't for her, which was really lucky, 'cause it was one of the rare occasions she went with him on the trap line." Dan laughed.

Hannah rose. "Thanks. That makes me feel a lot better." She walked back into the small clearing amongst the spruce. "People have camped here before. There's a fire pit."

"Yeah. I remember this spot. I stopped here for a break last year. There's a big willow flat back there. A long stretch of sedge meadows. Great place for moose. I would've camped here, but it was early in the day and I already had a moose. Christ, I should shut up." He changed to a hoarse whisper while he unpacked the dry bag. "I should shut up..." He pulled out the roll of canvas tarp. "...button my mouth..." He pulled out the bag of pots and cooking gear and set it close to the fire. "I should not rattle the cutlery..." He pulled out the sleeping bag. "...I should close my yap..." He pulled out the clothes bag. "...zip it..." He pulled his headlamp out of the bag and put it on under his ball cap. "...let no word pass my lips..." He reached to pick up the axe. "I should stop this inane chatter and go cut some...Oh my god, I broke a nail."

Hannah whispered, "Dan of the Forest: Mighty Hunter." She broke some small dry spruce twigs onto the small pile of cold black coals enclosed by a few river stones.

Three limbed poles leaned against a large spruce near the fire pit. "Good. Won't have to cut new poles for the lean-to." He lifted them down. "Don't make the fire too big. Just enough to cook then we'll put it out."

"Are you serious? On top of having to whisper?"

"Sure. Hearing and smell. That's moose for you."

"What's that? I can't hear you."

"You're lying. Dan of The Forest knows a liar when he hears one."

"Well, I don't think I can break sticks more quietly."

"Breaking sticks is okay. Break away."

"Can't they smell us without the fire?"

"Yeah." He tied the end of a pole to the tree.

Hannah opened the food box and rummaged in the bottom for a lighter. "It's too dark to shoot a moose now."

"Yeah. But tomorrow morning…This is a great spot." He finished tying the ridgepole to the cross poles. "I'll get some spruce boughs." He walked away from the fire pit. Raz trotted ahead, sniffing, nosing at something beside the trail. Dan shone his light on it. "Whatcha got, man?" Dan picked up a small square metal box with designs of fish and fly rods on the lid. He brought it back to the fire and showed Hannah, whispering, "Look what Raz found. He got me a tackle box. Looks like fish flies. Good boy, Raz." He rubbed the dog behind the ear.

Hannah took the box and opened it. Inside was a plastic bag with something greenish showing through. Jammed in beside it was a pipe with a small metal bowl.

Dan lifted out the bag and held it in the light of his headlamp for a moment. "Holy shit. I don't believe it. There must be a half ou—" He clamped his hand over his mouth as *half ou—* echoed back from the hill across the river.

"Hannah patted his arm, leaned closer and whispered, "Try to keep the noise down."

Dan was beaming. "Damn. No sooner do I run out of the stuff…" he rubbed the dog behind its ears. "Good boy, Raz. This is a sign from the gods."

"I thought you didn't believe in the gods."

"I just changed my mind."

SEPT. 20

The bear eased his body into the river, feeling some slight relief as the water accepted the terrible gnawing weight in his belly. Gone for now was the smell of putrid ooze from the hole in his side, but the taste of it still filled his mouth. He half-closed his eyes as he paddled across to the opposite shore, a dark green blur moving slowly across his line of vision. As he approached the high undercut mud bank he saw it was too steep to climb. A spruce trunk, ancient, long dead, skinned smooth by water and ice, angled down into the water. He held onto it and let the current flow softly over him. If he could stay here, like this, maybe the pain could be borne. But no, he must keep moving, keep searching. He let go of the log and drifted downstream, paddling only enough to keep his head above water. His whole life had been a search—for a shoreline where the pea vines grew, for a wide shallow riffle where the red salmon spawned, for a clump of willows with strong roots on a south-facing slope where he could dig his den for the long sleep of winter, for a sunny springtime mountainside where the first wildflowers tasted sweet. Now he searched for a different kind of place, a place he didn't know how to find—a place where his agony would end.

The young bull stood on top of the high bank, tense, ready to spin and run to join the old bull and the cow, who were far upstream by now. He had barely moved since he heard the bear clatter out of the trees on the other side. Only his ears, the slow swing of his head, and a slight tremble in his thighs could give away his presence. He had heard it enter the water, listened to its breaths as it swam the river, coming downstream towards him, closer and closer until it stopped below him to hold onto a dead spruce trunk. He should run, wanted to run, but something told him this bear was not a danger. He watched it float lazily awhile then let go of the log and turn downstream. A slow swirl of air brought its scent to him, musky-bear-smell and another odor—a strange, frightening presence of pain, disease, decay.

He turned upstream and trotted fast, ears back, stepping high over a fallen tree. He brushed past a low hanging bough and caught the scent of the other two moose—the warm rich smell of the cow, the pine sharp smell of the old bull. He felt the familiar ache in his loins again, the need he could not ignore.

The trail turned away from the river into dense undergrowth. A raven called from somewhere far upriver. The sound told him there was a wide, grassy opening ahead. As he moved through a thick stand of alder, his small antlers brushed over the branches. The strange new ache became stronger. Now he could see the opening, a large meadow, yellow, bright. A stab of light through the trees told him the first rays of morning sun shone into the valley.

He paused before walking out into the meadow, a habit taught to him by his mother. Opening his wide nostrils he tested the air, the sweet tang of red barked willow, the deep robust bitterness of felt leaf willow, the damp black moldy smell of marsh soil.

"Wuh. Wuh." From far at the meadow's end. The old bull.

He answered, "Wuh. Wuh." He turned to scrape his antlers on an alder. The sound of snapping branches felt good, his neck and shoulder muscles felt strong. He stepped out into the meadow grass and trotted around the edge to join the others, his steps making a powerful, satisfying thump, thump, thump in the matted roots beneath his feet.

"…naaaaaaaaaaaah…naaaaaaah…naaaaah…naaah…nyuh, nyuh." Dan waited for the last echo of his call to die out then cupped his hands behind his ears and listened. It was a perfect morning—clear, frosty and still—hard sunlight tinted the tops of a line of willows at the far end of the big meadow, and mist spilled off the river into the near end. Beyond the line he could see another opening further down the valley. The map showed a long chain of meadows stretching far downstream on his side of the river. No answer. Not yet.

He whispered to the dog sitting beside him. "Hey Raz, if I don't get an answer here, I've lost my sex appeal." The dog looked up at him and wagged his tail. Dan scratched him behind the ear and smiled. "Good boy."

Thinking about sex appeal made him think about Hannah—her small firm breasts, the way her nipples angled out slightly when they pushed against her shirt, the bulge where her waist met her hips, the way her buttocks swelled at the top of her thighs, the taut—no. Stupid. He shouldn't be thinking about it. He should put it out of his mind. Had she noticed his interest? Most women noticed. So what did she think about it? He thought he'd seen…something, but maybe he was wrong. They were too different. She was married, had a life in Vancouver. He was an unemployed guy from Ross River: a hunter. Still, there had been times he was sure from the look in her eyes she was attracted, too.

Last night they had smoked some pot, talked and laughed under the sleeping bag for a long time, a rambling succession of stories about their lives, growing up, school days, love affairs. When they had finally said goodnight, their eyes had met. He could still see it in his mind— the firelight dancing across her face. She had touched his arm—no words. Had it been an invitation? Had he blown it? Maybe he would never know.

He sighed and Raz raised his head. He sat down beside the dog and put his arm around him. "Raz, old buddy, count your lucky stars you've been neutered. Sex only gets you into trouble."

A sound came to him, far away, a faint *knock, knock, knock,* as if someone were softly clicking a tongue in his ear. The dog raised his head and looked down the valley. There it was again, from far beyond the line of willows. He stood and put his hands behind his ears. He felt the familiar spurt of adrenaline in his gut, felt his pulse pound harder, could hear it in his ears.

"Might have some action, boy." He would wait ten minutes, and call again.

Hannah dreamed she was driving down a big hill, the ocean glittering in the distance. David was driving. Martin, Andrea, and some other woman she didn't know were in the back seat. There was urgency in the air, a feeling she must get to the ocean now, no delays. A pond came into view on the left: a farm pond in a field, a house standing high on a hill above it. David turned the car and stopped at the edge of the pond. She told him he must not stop, must keep going, but he turned to her and his face went fuzzy so it didn't look like him anymore. He began to cry. "Naaaaaaaaaah. Naaaaaaah."

She opened her eyes but the sound continued, farther away. She felt a moment of confusion then realized where she was. She lay wondering about the dream as Dan's call ended in eerie echoes off the hill on the other side of the river.

She thought about last night, the northern lights swirling overhead, the fire out, talking long into the night, and then getting into bed. Had she lost her mind? She had tried to stop herself from touching him, but before she knew it, there it was, her hand resting on his arm, feeling the warmth of his skin, the muscles of his shoulder. After a long pause he had said, *Well, goodnight. Tomorrow's a long day.* She told herself it meant nothing, but did it? Had she wanted to feel him close, feel his warmth surround her, feel his breath on her body, make love to him?

The air was cold on her nose. She hunkered down into the sleeping bag. Why did sex have to be so complicated? It certainly wasn't for David. He seemed to be able to have a fling without a second thought. Of course it was different for men, wasn't it? But what about Dan? She could tell he wanted her, but he seemed to be suffering, too.

All three moose stood erect, ears forward, nostrils flared, staring intently up the valley. As the distant cow's call faded away, the old bull lowered his head and let out a series of deep, guttural grunts, his breath blowing great puffs of fog in the cold morning air. He stepped into the willows and raked his antlers over their branches then began walking toward the call. He stopped and looked back at the cow to see if she was following.

The young bull made a tentative step to her. It brought the old bull striding back out of the bushes, turning to show his antlers. He stepped beside the cow and raised his head to rest it over her buttocks. She moved away into the willows, in the direction of the other cow. The old bull, chin out, followed closely. When she stopped he began to lick her vulva. She urinated and he lapped at the cloudy yellow stream. When she was finished she walked off again. The old bull followed, leaving the young one standing confused in the meadow.

The young bull stood for a while listening to their departing sounds then moved in line after them.

There it was again—four deep grunts and the sound of breaking sticks. Dan picked up his rifle and worked a cartridge into the chamber. He checked the scope for condensation then took some deep breaths to compose himself. His heart raced. His knees trembled. His hands shook. How many times had he been in this situation—a moose coming to his call?

"You'd think I'd be used to this by now, Raz." he whispered. The dog stood and wagged his tail. "Down. Stay." Raz went down and put his chin on his paws. "Good boy." Dan brought his binoculars up and scanned the line of willows. He heard it again—five grunts in quick succession. The bull was coming. Where would he step out?

Hannah lifted herself onto one elbow. That sound—short deep grunts, faint but clear, was the same sound she had heard four days ago. The crackle of breaking branches came from far downriver. She wondered if she should get up and go out to the meadow with Dan. No. If he shot a moose, she didn't want to see it. She pulled the sleeping bag over her head.

Dan watched the meadow's edge, now bathed in the full light of the sun. It seemed a long time since the last grunts and smashing willows. Why was this one so slow? Maybe he was with a cow and didn't want to leave her. Should he call again? If the bull was close by, he might be spooked. Patience. Another grunt, just one this time, still far away. He raised his hands to his mouth and made a funnel of them, closed off his nostrils with his index fingers.

"Naaaaaaaaaah. Naaaaaaaah. Naaaah. Nyuh, nyuh, nyuh." The long moaning call sent a wave of desire down through the young bull's belly. This new cow hadn't moved since she first called. Echoes from the trees, the grass, the water, the hill across the river. She was at the end of the next meadow, beyond a line of willows, the edge of the dark spruce trees at the bend in the river. The old bull was trying to coax his cow forward. She was feeding.

This new cow could be his. He grunted once and trotted to the river, down the short bank into the shallow water and ran upstream in a shower of spray, feet splayed wide in the muddy bottom.

Hannah heard Dan's call and pushed the sleeping bag back. She couldn't lie there any longer. She got to her feet and pulled the sleeping bag around her, looking back through the trees where Dan's calls had come from. She heard splashing in the river, something running upstream towards her. She moved to the edge of the bank and saw it: a moose trotting, big square nose stretched straight out, water exploding spray at each stride. Without slowing it turned and leaped up the bank. For a moment Hannah thought it would charge straight along the bank, over her and through the camp. She almost jumped out of the way, but it suddenly stopped as if hit by an invisible barrier. The moose was so close she could see individual hairs bristling along the top of the back, hear each breath, see its chest move. She remained motionless. It hadn't seen her. It was looking through the thick screen of tall willows between the bank and the meadow, head up, ears turned forward, alert.

He saw the cow first. She walked out of the willows and looked in his direction, ears spread wide, nose up. Slowly he put up the binoculars, trying to blend into the outline of the stump of fallen tree. The bull would not be far behind. About 150 meters away. He might come closer. A clear shot with a big solid spruce stump to rest his gun. He put the binoculars up again, searching the willows behind the cow. There it was. Movement in the branches. The rusty tan of antlers parting the bushes. The bull stepped into the meadow. "The size of him," Dan muttered to himself. The bull stopped and lowered his head. A puff of steamy breath and an instant later the sound of the grunt. The bull turned its head to look in Dan's direction. Big. Too big. The neck alone would weigh more than a hundred pounds. He turned to Raz behind him and said, "Too big, Raz. I'd never get that in the canoe."

What was that soft hissing-popping sound? Just beyond the tall thick willows it seemed to slink like a wolf, waiting in the dark spruce. But the new cow was there. It must be safe. He stepped into the willows. The branches brushed his antlers. Hollow scraping made them sound big. Feel big.

The moose slid out of view into the trees. The sound was like a wooden paddle dragged over a hedge. Before its hind leg slipped out of sight it paused as if held in a pose for her inspection—the hollow where the big tendon joined the muscles of the upper leg, over the heel to a cowlick of dense hair down the back of the long leg bone. Where the lower leg swelled into the joint above the foot, two dew claws then two long hard black, shining wet toes. A drop of water glistened on the end of one. Then it was gone.

Hannah stared at the spot where the moose had disappeared, still seeing the foot, there in her mind like a photograph.

Raz was staring intently across the corner of the meadow to the tall willows edging the river. Dan followed his gaze and saw a dark shape emerge from the trees fifteen meters away. It was a young bull, its small antler palms barely wider than its ears. Those ears were trained on him.

He watched the moose take a tentative step forward into the meadow and lift its nose, nervous, suspicious. Damn. If it caught his scent it would be gone in an instant, but the slight breeze, blowing upstream, was in Dan's favor.

Slowly he reached for the rifle propped against the broken spruce, trying not to let his shaking hand betray him. He could only trust Raz to stay still, could not risk voicing even the smallest *Stay* or *Down*. It seemed to take forever…the slow reach, his fingers closing on the stock, inch by agonizing inch turning his body into position, trying to steady his breathing. The moose was facing him head on. If he could put the bullet into the V at the base of the neck it would strike through the heart, a clean, sure kill. He wished he had been more alert, not so focused on the big bull across the meadow. He might have seen or heard this one coming. The moose's ears swiveled back and his weight began a slight shift to his hind legs. Getting ready to run. The sound of breaking branches came from behind. Hannah was coming through the trees from the camp.

The young bull was confused, nervous. The soft hissing he had heard was not cow sound. Something watched him from the edge of the dark spruce. He could feel its eyes on him, feel it trying to probe into him, into his chest. He shifted his weight back over his hind legs, ready to spin and run.

Then the sound of twigs breaking in the thick spruce. The cow? A large dark shape moving towards the meadow.

Hannah tried to move as quietly as she could, but the sleeping bag kept getting caught on dead branches. The light of the open meadow was ahead. She skirted a large spruce and again the bag caught on the thick dead branches at its base. She groaned. "Oh, no." She pulled and a branch snapped sharply in the still air.

A groan. Appreciation. The way it warbled and whined. For him. She was coming to him. He turned and rose stiff legged to show her the fullness of his size, the strength of his ardor. He tipped his antlers toward her.

When the moose turned broadside, Dan lifted the gun to his shoulder and put his eye to the scope. It was so close all he could see was hair at first, but he found the spot just behind the front leg, low on the chest. His mother's words came to him. *See his heart.* He took one long breath as his finger reached to find the trigger.

A sound of thunder hit the young bull and came echoing back off the hill across the river. Something kicked him in the ribs behind the front leg, pushing a snort of breath from his lungs. He ran three steps and stood dazed in the meadow. He looked back to the cow in the dark spruce trees. Should he run to her? Should he run away? He wanted to run, but a great weight pressed down on him. It was hard to breath. Something squeezed deep in his chest.

His legs buckled. He saw the marsh grass coming up to meet him, felt his nose crash into the ground, smelled the rich earth, heard a raven call above the soft gurgle of the river. A yellow willow leaf drifted slowly past his eye and came to rest on his nose.

Dan looked back into the trees. Hannah was trying to untangle the sleeping bag from the branches of a large spruce.

"Dan, where are you?"

"Over here."

She left the bag and pushed through the thick brush to the edge of the meadow.

"You scared the shit out of me." She looked across the expanse of marsh grass and saw the cow and bull trotting away along the line of willows. "You missed?"

"Nope." He pointed to the moose lying in the grass. He watched her eyes go wide as she took in the scene: a dark lifeless mass, one antler sticking up above the yellow sedge, a thin stream of mist from its nose caught in the sunlight. Raz approached it warily, sniffing, ready to retreat at the slightest movement.

He waited for her to speak, for her tears, her anger. She stared at the dead moose for a long time then looked at him. He held her gaze for a while then looked to the moose. He knew he shouldn't feel any guilt. He was on the river to hunt moose, not taxi her back to town. It was his food, winter meat for him and his mother. It was his way of life. His ancestors had hunted for centuries. He didn't have to stand there while some pampered city woman stared accusingly. Why should he care? Why did he care?

He turned back to her, ready for an argument. "Look, I told you. You knew I was going to kill a moose if I could. You can't…"

"That's the one I saw at the river." Her voice was barely audible, far away, as if she was talking to herself.

It wasn't what he had expected. "Oh."

She started walking toward the moose. "Yeah. I thought he was going to run right into our camp."

Dan was unsure what to say. He followed her into the meadow. "Don't get too close yet. We have to make sure he's dead." He put his hand on her shoulder and stepped between her and the moose with his gun ready.

"You're going to shoot him again?"

"Not unless he's still alive." He walked closer, and gave the hind leg a shove with his foot. "It's okay. He's dead." He popped the cartridge out and put it back in the magazine as Hannah approached the moose. When he looked back at her she was crouched by its head, her hand stroking the stiff fur along the top of its neck. She ran her hand over the big square nose and picked up a willow leaf that had landed there.

"It's so beautiful." When she looked up he saw tears in her eyes. Did she mean the leaf or the moose? She stood and gazed down at the body. "It's huge."

She didn't seem angry. She seemed to be in a daze. When was she going to say *poor thing* and look at him with those accusing eyes.

"About half the size of that other one." He knew he must sound idiotic.

"Yeah...Will it fit in the boat?"

He wondered why she was thinking about that. It didn't jibe with the tears streaming down her face. "Yeah. He's perfect—small, young, tender, the meat will..." He caught himself before going too far with the thought. He sensed it was a delicate moment. "Yeah, we'll...I'll...get it all in."

"So...What's next?"

Next was to skin it, gut it, and cut it into manageable pieces—a big messy job. He would need to get his hip waders from the boat. "I have to field dress him." That didn't sound too bad.

"What's field dressing?" Her voice still had a weird, dreamy quality. She was staring at the small yellow leaf in her hand.

"Um...skinning, gutting, cutting."

"I think I'll go back and start a fire."

"Good idea. I'll be with you in a minute. Gotta get my axe and saw... some rope."

"Okay."

She walked away through the grass into the trees. Dan was relieved. He wanted to be alone with the moose for what he was about to do. He sat down, put both hands on its head and closed his eyes. Remembering the moose as it looked, standing in the meadow before it died, he addressed it quietly, thanking it for giving its life and its strength to him and promising he would use it well. It was a brief personal ritual he performed with every animal he killed—as close as he ever came to religion or spirituality. His father would have scoffed but his mother would approve. She had her own ritual.

The thought of his mother made him smile. She would be pleased with this moose —barely old enough to rut, young tender meat. The skin would be easier to tan than the thick, heavy hide of a big bull. She would be happy. There was another ritual they would perform when he got back home. At the sound of his truck pulling up to the house she would be at the door. *Well? Did you get a moose?* He would look down at the ground, dejected. *No. No luck this year. Sorry Mom. Come and help me unload the truck.* Her eyes would twinkle as she walked out to the truck. Then he would pull back the tarp and she'd punch his arm, laugh and give him a hug, tell him he was a bad boy for fooling his old mother.

The air was warm now. He looked out across the sunlit meadow, sparkling with drops of water from the melted frost. Three ravens flew lazily overhead and landed in the tall trees near the camp, their clicking, warbling calls ringing in the still air, anticipating their feast. A marsh hawk zig-zagged over the sedge grass, its day of hunting begun. The sound of the river was a soft hush behind the screen of willows. He felt good. This was where his gods lived—in the river, the mountains, the grass, the trees, the ravens, the hawk, the moose, in him.

Could Hannah ever understand? Could he even attempt to put it into words? How the moose hunt meant more than killing an animal, more than a full freezer, a skin stretched on a frame and antlers on the wood shed. It was his union with the land, this valley, these mountains, his part in its carpet of life from the smallest lichen clinging to a wind scoured mountaintop to the ancient spruce anchored in the fertile muck of the valley.

A curl of smoke drifted through the trees to hang over the river. Could Hannah accept that? To her it would sound like superstition, or worse, justification for killing. Still, he wished she could understand. He liked her, wanted her to like him. Not much chance of that now. This dead moose cinched it. And only ten minutes before he killed it he'd been thinking about sex with her.

Raz was still circling the moose, sniffing cautiously from a safe distance. "I guess I blew it, Raz. Too much to hope for, anyway...perfect weather, a moose and sex. But two outta three ain't bad. Come on, boy. Let's go get a coffee and something to eat. We've got a big job ahead of us." The dog happily joined him, looking up and wagging his tail. Dan reached down to pat his head as he walked towards the trees. "Hey, we're gonna eat well now. I'm proud of you." He ruffled behind the dog's ears. "Staying put while that moose stared you down. Good dog."

The fire had burned down to coals. Dan was out in the meadow working on the moose. He hadn't said much when he came to get his tools—axe, saw, rope, sharpening stone—and lingered at the fire only long enough to pour a cup of coffee and put on his hip waders. When she asked him *Why hipwaders?* he had said, *To keep my pants from getting covered in…dirt.* meaning blood. Was it for her sake or his? Did she make him feel guilty? The dead moose had affected her deeply, but it was strange, not as she would have expected nine days ago. She understood he had to kill for food, but was it easy for him? Was the moose an individual with a life of its own and a consciousness of self, or just meat on the hoof?

The hoof: the image of that moose foot poised in mid air before it slid out of sight into the willows came to her so clearly she knew she would never forget it. If all other memories of this trip faded, that foot would remain etched in her mind.

She picked up the coffee pot from where it nestled in the coals and poured the last of it in her cup. They would be camping here another night. What was she going to do all day, sit around and wait for him to finish? There were lots of blueberries along the edge of the meadow. The thought made her saliva begin. She was ferociously hungry. She had finished the last of the oatmeal this morning and could have eaten three times as much. What would she eat the rest of the trip? Bannock, fish, Dan's pepperonis? Moose meat?

"What can I do?"

Hannah's voice startled him. "Huh? Oh, I didn't hear you there." Dan had been concentrating, humming to himself while he finished skinning off one side of the moose. "What can you do?"

"To help."

This was baffling. "Oh. Okay. I'm gonna spread the skin out and we'll turn him over onto it, so I can do the other side. I'll position his head and we'll each take a leg." He pointed with his knife. "Just above the knee." He watched her take in the scene—the moose on its side, skin peeled back from halfway up each leg to the top of the back, exposing the tissue beneath, white where a layer of fat lay over the rump, purple-red where muscle showed through, curving ridges of rib. Beautiful in its way until his eye was drawn to the hole where the bullet entered—a splintered rib, a circle of red-black haemorrhage a hand span across. What was going through her mind? Her expression was impassive. He went to the head and grabbed an antler. "If it's all right...I mean if you don't mind...'Cause if..."

"I've seen this kind of thing before. My uncle Nathan was a kosher butcher. Dad used to take me to his shop...the back of the shop where all this went on. Where do I hold on? Here?" She took hold of the front leg

"Yeah. Just above the knee."

"This isn't the knee. It's the wrist."

"Me." It was a joyous call, full of exuberant relish at the food awaiting them.

Her mate answered from across the meadow. "Me. Me."

The young female responded from across the river. "Me."

"Big food. Fat. Good." She tucked in her breast feather and watched the two bobbleheads work on the dead moose. "Watch out. Sneaky littlewolf."

"I'll hold it while you tie. Tighter, pull it tighter. The rope's gonna give a bit when I let off." The moose was skinned except for the lower legs and the head. Dan held one front leg up, keeping the carcass balanced on the crest of vertebrae over the shoulder. The carcass lay on its skin, hind legs open, antlers stuck into the mat of sedge roots to brace the head.

Hannah quickly tied a clove hitch and secured it with a slip knot. He was impressed. "You were a Girl Guide."

"Boy Scout."

He let the weight onto the rope and the carcass sagged just off the balance point. "Perfect." He pointed to the rope. "You see how it works better above the knee?"

"Wrist."

She wasn't being squeamish at all, not what he had expected. She was interested now, watching him closely as the body of the moose was revealed. She was even beginning to joke. By now the wrist thing had become a running gag.

He smiled. "Hey, you've got a spot of blood on your elbow." He pointed to her shoulder.

"Man, you would make a fine orthopaedic surgeon." She puffed out a breath and looked at the carcass. "My God."

He searched her face. "My God?"

"It's so big."

Was that all she meant? "Imagine what it'd be like to do this to that big fellow we saw this morning. He's twice the size."

"No, I mean...everything. You know what I mean?" She looked at him intently for a moment then gestured at the sky and all around. "The whole fucking thing. I'm helping you butcher a moose. Do you know what Paul Williams and Andrea and Martin and all the ARN people would say? Do you know what the press is gonna say? Grizzly Watch was mine. I was the guiding light. Look at me, for Christ's sake, I've got blood on my hands."

He wanted to say *wrists*. "Um...There's one other thing." As soon as he said it he had second thoughts.

"What? What other thing?"

"It's nothing...really."

"What other thing?"

"He was going to run. I wouldn't have got a shot at him, but..."

"But what? Something I did?"

"Yeah. Your sound—coming through the bush—you groaned. That got his attention. He turned broadside."

"So it's my fault this moose is dead."

"No. You didn't kill him. But you must have sounded convincing."

"So if it wasn't for me...It's too weird. What am I doing here? What kind of giant plan am I being forced into here?" Dan stood gaping as she shouted up at the sky. "God, is this some kind of sick joke? Cause if it is you've succeeded. I'm laughing: ha ha ha. I get it. Enough." She tossed her head at the sky and gave God the finger. *Enough* echoed back to them from across the meadow. A raven call burbled. They both burst out laughing, reached out and touched, she on his elbow, he on her shoulder.

Dan said, "You sure told him."

"I feel much better. What's next, Doc?"

He turned to the moose. "Now it gets messy."

"Now that is gross." Hannah made a face at the mass of entrails spilling to one side of the moose carcass.

Dan had cut away the belly tissue and was completing the removal of the brisket by cutting through the cartilage that joined it to the ribs, exposing the chest cavity awash in blood. "You don't have to do this if you..."

"No, I keep telling you, it's okay. It drives away my hunger. Just tell me what to do."

He lifted the V-shaped chunk of bone and meat away, carried it to a pile of cut willow brush and laid it on top. "There. Now we can take all the insides out in one piece." He went to the throat and cut through the windpipe, pulling it up and back as he freed it from its connective tissue. "Would you like a pepperoni before we go on?"

She rolled her eyes.

He said, "Okay then, tie that piece of rope to this."

"What fun. Is that his windpipe?"

"No, it's his wrist."

"Enough with the wrist. This thing looks like a vacuum cleaner hose, except a little bloodier." She tied the rope.

"I admire your guts."

The intestines lay piled near her feet. "I'm not sure I can say the same for yours." She could feel the heat from them through her jeans. "I think my appetite is permanently suppressed."

"Soon this will all be gone. We can drag it out into the meadow away from the meat."

"Don't you keep any of it?"

"The heart. Not this one, though. It's wrecked. My mother likes me to bring home the belly fat, too. Then there's the bumguts. She loves bumguts."

"Bumguts? Hell, you might as well tell me."

"It's the rectum. The last part of the intestine. Downstream from the colon, upstream of the anus."

"Congratulations. You have given me a chronic eating disorder."

"No, it's good. You wash it out, cut it thin across the grain and fry it like bacon."

"Sweet. Bumguts. Can't you come up with a better name? If McDonalds ever served it I'm sure they wouldn't call it McBumguts."

Dan laughed. "How about back-bacon? No, way-back-bacon."

"Rectalines."

"Indian doughnuts."

"Anusettes—gives it a French cache." Dan put on a French accent. "Good evening. My name is Daniel. I will be your waiter." He extended a gore stained hand. "May I suggest our specialty of the house—anussettes in cream with a hint of brandy from the Derriere region?"

They were both laughing. She said, "Are there any more delicacies in there?"

"The liver. This one looks really good. Big bulls in the rut, like the one we saw this morning with the cow, their livers go all pale and granular. But this moose is young, not ready to rut, just interested." He reached into the glistening mass and lifted a slippery dark red lobe to the surface.

"Liver. Now you're talking." She gazed off. "I remember the chopped liver from uncle Nathan's shop. His recipe went back generations, back to Poland. It was the real thing, made with schmaltz."

"Schmaltz? Corny, sentimental stuff?"

"Not schmultz, schmaltz—rendered chicken fat. And when you pour off the fat you're left with grivenitz—little crackly bits. I ate them like candy. Nathan always gave me grivenitz and my father always bought chopped liver. Nathan set it aside especially for his best customers. My mother would make liver and potato knishes. Oh." She rolled her eyes. "Everyone loved Nathan's chopped liver. It was so rich. Even when you ate it cold, it felt warm. It was the thing I missed most when I became a vegetarian."

"Ah, memories, sweet, meaty memories. Okay. Pull on the rope while I cut. And watch out when the blood drains out of the chest. Stand back a bit. When I cut away the diaphragm it's gonna pour."

She braced against the rope. "There goes my appetite again."

"Is that the last piece? We're done?"

They had dropped the second hindquarter onto the brush pile. Dan shifted it once more so it wasn't touching any other piece. "Yup. All done." There was more—piling brush on top and stretching a tarp over the whole thing, but Hannah was dirty and exhausted, her arms covered with scaly bits of dried blood and black fly bites. She must want to wash off. "Those hind pieces are heavy. I normally cut them in two, but he's small, we're close to the river, and I have you to help. Thanks."

"Don't mention it. And now I'm going to wash off in the river and make a cup of tea. You want some?"

"Yes I'll be right there, but I'm not finished. I'm gonna flesh this skin and take the hair off if there's time. It'll reduce the weight by about a hundred pounds. And I'll make big time brownie points with Mom."

She looked down at the hide of the moose, bright red flesh side up, the fur, where it showed around the edges, soaked in boggy seepage and blood. "Have fun." She turned to walk back to the camp.

"Hannah, there's one more thing you could do here. Help me drag the skin over to that fallen tree."

"Okay."

"And could you pee beside the meat?"

"That's a joke, right?"

"It's not. Animals use urine to communicate. It's a statement of ownership, a mark, a *no trespassing* sign. Ask Raz. He'll tell you." At the sound of his name the dog wagged his tail. "And if you don't believe us, believe the Yukon government. It's right in the pamphlet under *Tips to Protect Your Meat from Bears*."

She laughed. "You're too much."

"Never mind then. Raz and I will do the peeing. You don't have to."

"Damn right I don't." She started to unhitch her jeans. "Beside the meat."

"Yes. Beside. Close, but not too close, trying to avoid splash."

"Turn around."

He faced away from her. "And it helps if you think aggressive thoughts while you do it. It comes out in the urine. Right Raz?" The dog's tail wagged again.

He heard her snort behind him. "Aggressive thoughts. No problem."

The new mate took down her overskin then her underskin and squatted beside the meat. Marking it with her urine. A good sign. She was really a part of the pack now. She was protecting their kill. He was glad. He liked her. She liked him. She was a good mate. She made his Dan happy. Maybe there would be new little dans. The pack was bigger, stronger. They had a moose. It was thrilling. He wanted her to finish marking and get out of the way so he could pee there, too.

Jessica wiped the sweat and black flies from her forehead. It wasn't easy walking in the deep moss, lifting legs high and sinking to mid calf at each step, like walking through deep snow. She almost regretted the decision to leave the horses, but she realized it would have been difficult riding through all the deadfall. She looked back at Jim and David, sweating along fifty meters behind. David was red faced and breathing hard.

She had been trying to follow a set of imprints. Not tracks, just holes in the moss. There was little chance Hannah had made them, but Jessica thought she might as well follow something, even if they were moose prints. She stepped up onto a fallen tree and surveyed the route ahead. Something blue caught her eye through the brush then something white. It seemed out of place, but it could be mushrooms. As she got closer she saw it was not mushrooms. The white object was a soggy roll of toilet paper, partly shredded. Over the next deadfall was the blue object, a backpack, ripped open, surrounded by odds and ends of gear: a pair of sunglasses, an empty water bottle, food wrappers scattered about.

She called to the others. "Over here." When they struggled over the nearest fallen tree they both stopped and stared. There was no need to say anything.

David knelt and picked up the blue pack, slowly, carefully, as if it was an injured baby. "This is hers."

Jim peered over David's shoulder. "Looks like it's been torn up by a... some animal." There was a silence. "Are you sure it's hers? I mean, it could be..."

David's voice was weak. "I bought it for her."

Jim said, "There are lots of blue packs around."

"It's an Altai—obscure brand, Swiss."

"Okay, but that doesn't prove anything. Some European hunter..."

"I had this sewn into the shoulder strap." He held up the pack.

Jim read. "Happy Birthday, Hannah. All My Love. David." He sucked in a breath and stared helplessly at Jessica.

She said, "It could have been brought here."

David's face changed to a look of dread. "Brought here? By who...or what?"

"By whatever...brought it here."

"And that would be a..."

It was up to her. "Yes, it could be a bear, but not necessarily. It could just as easily be a wolf or a wolverine, or a marten, or..." She stopped as David turned the pack over. The zip-up cover flap on top was shredded: four parallel tears each an inch apart. The zipper was sheared as if by a pair of tin snips. "Or...a bear."

Jim took over. "But that doesn't mean anything. Most likely it found the pack. Look around. There's no sign of a struggle, no blood, no hair, no bits of...uh...clothing. Besides, the bear would only be interested in the pack, the food. Look at the wrappers and empty bags. Most likely the bear never saw Hannah. It found the pack after she discarded it."

"Why would she discard it?"

Jim couldn't come up with an answer. Neither could she. Still holding the backpack tenderly, David stood and looked around at the scattered debris then scanned the tangle of deadfall and underbrush surrounding them. "We'd better go back to the horses." He began walking off.

Jim went after him. "David. Over this way. This is the way back. Just follow me." David, zombie-like, fell in behind him.

Jessica imagined what he must be going through—all the horrid fantasies of Hannah's death, alone, terrified, mad with exhaustion and pain. But there was nothing to say to help the poor guy. She started after them, but something in the moss caught her eye: a glint of plastic wrap over a white package. She bent to pick it up. Before her hand touched it she saw what it was, a small box of twelve tampons. Her period had been coming on after they left Ross River, too late to buy tampons. She called ahead. "I'll catch up to you." As she ducked behind a tree she said quietly to the surrounding forest, "No more pieces of dishtowel. Thanks Hannah."

"Good." she gulped. Warmth spread into her crop. "Goooood."

Her mate's crop was already distended, full of liver. "Heavy. Good darkred. Warm." he croaked.

She tore off a piece of liver and tilted her head up to take it down in three satisfying gulps. The gutpile rippled to her motion. The young female waited her turn perched on a dead spruce snag. She tucked in her breast feather. "Littlewolf? Where?"

The young one called back. "Down. With big bobblehead."

"Where him?"

"Him?"

"Where?"

"Big dead leaner. Eating skin. Hair. Stupid."

"She?"

"What?"

"She. Other bobblehead."

"She?"

"Shut up. Where?"

"Firenest. Bobbling…Want food."

She ducked her beak to her chest. "Stay…Soon."

"Want. Me."

She gurgled to her mate. "You."

He called to the young female. "Stay."

His head and neck were covered in blood. She clucked back in her throat. "You. Red head. Red neck. Look good."

He glugged in return. "You. Ha."

"Ha. Ha."

"Good food."

A few flies buzzed, awakened by the warmth of the sun and the presence of food.

"Mmmm. Love." She swallowed more liver.

"Mmmmmm. Love."

The young female's call rang out, urgent. "Littlewolf."

Her mate sprang into the air and beat to a perch below the young female. The flies buzzed up at the disturbance, zoomed in crazy circles then back down onto the gut pile.

Stretched to her full height she was barely able to see over the top of the grass. The she bobblehead was coming across the meadow. The littlewolf's black tail bobbed above the marsh grass ahead of her. Sneaky shit littlewolf. She flew up and across the open meadow to pass above the two. The littlewolf paid no attention, its nose buried in the grass, hunting voles. The she bobblehead stopped. Its eyes touched her all over. She tucked in her breast feather and called. "Me."

"Me," the bobblehead answered.

She made a wide circle above the meadow and landed on the perch nearest to the gut pile, a dead willow that stuck above the living mass of yellow green leaves. "Me," she called.

"Me." From the bobblehead.

Maybe they could learn. Or maybe they were merely good mimics. The bobblehead extended one of its long forelegs toward the other one, who was still at the fallen tree, busily eating the moose skin. Then she called to the littlewolf.

"Go back, Raz. Go."

The littlewolf trotted away, back toward the firenest, but when it got to the edge of the willows it stopped.

"Go," called the she bobblehead.

The littlewolf slunk away and the she bobblehead walked across the meadow to the gutpile. Did she intend to feed? It regarded the gutpile for a while then crouched beside it. One bony paw reached down into the mass and pulled at the darkred. The round hairy head twisted on its flimsy neck and the eyes fixed on her.

It called. "I see you like liver, too."

She called back in clicks and warbles ending with a shallow caw. "Good darkred. Fat. Mine. Me."

The voice of the she bobblehead was all soft murmurs. "Come down here and get some. I won't hurt you."

The round head rolled down again, eyes on the gutpile. Something shiny in one paw glinted bright in the sun. Both paws dug deeper and most of the darkred emerged from the rest of the glistening mass. She checked on the littlewolf. It still lay near the male bobblehead, waiting for scraps. She launched from the dead willow and glided, angling down toward the gutpile and the bobblehead.

Her mate and the young female raven called in unison. "Watch out. Bobblehead. Danger."

She landed on the trail of flattened wet grass left when the bobbleheads dragged the gutpile into the middle of the meadow. The bobblehead eyes glanced briefly in her direction then went back to the darkred. She walked to the gutpile and climbed onto it, digging in her claws and partially spreading her wings for balance on the yielding rippling surface.

Her mate and the young female called frantic warnings. "Too close. Too close. Danger."

The bobblehead cooed, its mouth barely moving. "Hi there, you. Don't fret, I'm not gonna take it all. Here, I'll give you some."

Soothing sounds as its strange paws moved. Bobblehead front paws— always busy. Seen this close they were like many beaks working together, and the shiny object held in one was like a single long strong sharp beak. It pierced the darkred easily, no tearing. One paw now held a piece of darkred, extended toward her, offered like the burnstick of the day before. All her instincts told her this was crazy—trusting a bobblehead like this, vulnerable to the swipe of a bony paw. And those grasping eyes were on her, exploring her feathers, her beak, her bones, her insides. She looked into them, terrified yet fascinated. It was like looking into a deep abyss that held a huge, frightening secret. She looked away and ducked her head to her breast.

The bobblehead made more comforting sounds. "It's that breast feather again, isn't it? I know how it is. I have a cowlick."

Funny. That last sound with the clicks. She tried it. Funny.

"Very good. Cowlick."

"Cowlick. Ha ha."

The bobblehead croaked a response. "Ha ha."

Was the bobblehead really laughing, or was it just imitating again?

Her mate called from the dead spruce snag. "Fly. Crazy, you die."

"No. Watch." She walked closer to the bobblehead, boldly took the piece of darkred from the paw and gulped it down. "Mmmm. Love."

Her mate called. "Crazy. Scary. Me go."

"Go," she called. "With ugly stupid."

"Come," her mate said to the young female. They both flew from their tree and soared out over the meadow. When they reached the river they turned upstream.

"Have some more," murmured the bobblehead and the paw held out another piece of darkred, which she took in her beak and swallowed. The she bobblehead dug a paw into the darkred and pulled. Its paw with the sharpbeak moved in as it spat and gurgled and moaned, "I don't need all this liver. Let's split it—half for you, half for me."

"Thank you." Dan stood behind her, his drawknife held by one handle. He couldn't see what she was doing crouched at the fire, but he heard something sizzling in the frying pan.

She didn't turn around. "Thank you for what?"

"For all your help, of course."

"How's it going with the skin?"

"Good. I finished the flesh side. Now I'm working on the hair. I need a break, a cup of coffee. Is there any hot water?"

"Coffee's made."

"Great." He moved around to stand beside her at the fire.

"What are you cooking?" He could see it was liver.

"I've made a decision. I'm going to suspend my vegetarianism for the duration."

"Good idea." She didn't respond. "It makes sense. The oats are gone, even the flour is getting low. You gotta eat something. You must be so hungry. I think you..."

"Go ahead. Say it."

"Say it? What?"

"I told you so."

"I told you so?"

"Yeah."

He poured himself a cup of coffee. "I wouldn't say that. *I told you so* is petty and childish. I'm not the kind of person who says *I told you so. I told you so* is not in my vocabulary. If I was to say to you, *Hannah, I told you so...*"

"Enough. I realize I misjudged you. You're not small minded and immature. You're vicious and cruel. You want some liver?"

"Sure, but I don't want to take yours."

She took the frying pan off the fire and reached behind her for his bowl. "I've had some already. It's marvelous."

He sat down beside her. "I gotta hand it to you. When you decide to do something you jump right in."

"Well, it was either eat meat or gnaw trees."

"Yeah, but you start with liver. Anyone else would try a little piece of filet or sirloin or something. Or pepperoni. You want one?"

Hannah placed a slice of liver into a bowl. "I told you, I have fond memories. My dreams are filled with chopped liver."

"So you went back to the gut pile and fished out the liver?"

"Yeah."

"You're a weird one"

"This from a guy who takes tampons moose hunting."

He tasted a piece of liver and could almost feel its vitality flowing into him. "This is excellent."

They said nothing for a while as he ate.

She leaned back with a thoughtful expression. "She likes liver, too."

"She? Who are you talking about?"

"The raven."

"Huh?" Another piece disappeared into his mouth.

"The one from yesterday. She was eating the liver when I went out to the meadow."

"You think it's the same one?"

"I know she is."

"She?"

"Okay, I can't be sure of that. That's just a feeling." She lifted a pot of boiling water off the fire. "But she has a feather that sticks out from her breast plumage. She always tucks it in."

"Is that so?"

"Yes. She came right down to feed from my hand. And she talks to me."

Dan stopped chewing to stare at her.

"So don't believe me. I don't care." She placed a few sticks on the fire and leaned back again.

Dan regarded her awhile. "So…what does she say?"

Hannah sat up and turned toward the meadow. She gave out a short sharp caw that dipped down to a rounder tone at the end.

Dan smiled. "Well, that's…"

Hannah held up her hand to silence him, her attention focused through the trees. An identical raven call came from the meadow. She gave him a look and leaned back again, her hands behind her head.

"I stand corrected. So what did you say to…her?"

"I'm not sure. I think it's *hello*. Maybe *I'm here*, or just *me*."

"Wow. That's…impressive."

"Don't be patronizing. I told you I don't care if you don't believe it."

"I believe it, but just to be on the safe side I think I'll hide the rifle."

"It gets worse. I've figured out something, but I'm not sure I should tell you."

"What? You gotta tell me now."

"When I was wandering in a daze down Mount Riddell, I had this vision—like a dream or maybe a hallucination—I was lying on a pile of warm poker chips and—"

"Poker chips?"

"I think it must have been stones, that black shale we saw so much of upriver. Anyway, I was lying there…I think I would have died there, but…an angel appeared. She was dressed in a shiny black cloak. She woke me up and led me to the river. That was just before you came along."

"You think it was the raven? That particular one?"

"I'm sure of it. I know it sounds insane."

"No it doesn't. It makes perfect sense. She was gonna eat you."

"I suppose so. Nevertheless…"

"She saved your life. Amazing."

Hannah laughed. "Don't gimme that tone. Scoff all you want. If I care to think of her as my angel, I'll do it and you can't stop me."

Dan finished his liver and put the bowl down. "I have no intention of stopping you." He stood. "But I think I'll hide the knives, too. Thanks. That was good liver."

"Yeah. I wasn't expecting it to be so good. Moose liver. Who would guess?"

"Caribou is even better." He picked up his drawknife. "I gotta finish the skin."

Hannah stood, too. "You know, if I had the right ingredients… Remember you said something about wild onions?"

"Yeah."

"Where do you find them?"

"On the sand bars, out where most things can't grow, usually on the downstream end. They look like grass, but they've got hollow leaves. You ever seen chives?"

Her laugh startled him. "Have I seen chives? That's the name of my husband's restaurant chain. There's a picture of chives on the logo. I'll recognize them. What about mushrooms? Can we eat any of the ones around here?"

"Yeah, the orange ones with greenish rings on the cap. Milk mushrooms. The Latin name is Lactarius deliciosus."

Little Atlin Lake shimmered blue and silver in the afternoon light. A clump of aspen blazed brilliant orange against dark green alder on the near shore. Across the lake, a wide swath of sedge, bright green tinged with gold, spread back to dark spruce that clothed the lower slopes of a red-topped line of mountains.

Susan stared blankly out the passenger window of Owen's truck, barely noticing the colors. What would she do, simply drive up to Tara's place and pretend it was by chance? What then? What did she plan to say to them? Should she tell Tara what she thought of Gary? Mostly she wanted to talk to Starla alone.

She felt the truck slow and heard the turn signal begin to click. "Owen, why are you turning off? We have to get to the campground and set up."

"What's to set up? We have a camper on the back."

"Oh. Right."

There's a gravel pit just up the hill here."

"I don't want to stay in a gravel pit, camper or no camper."

He steered the truck around a bend and accelerated up a short steep hill. "Don't worry Suzy. Neither do I. I have to sight in my .22."

"You brought a gun? Why?"

"Thought I might do a little grouse hunting while I'm here. You won't believe my grouse breasts with mushrooms and white wine sauce and real butter. It's been known to give women—"

"Owen, it's a dumb idea."

"What? Giving women, you know?"

"Bringing a gun. Anyway, we're not here to hunt grouse."

"It's not clear to me exactly what we're here for." The truck bumped over the top of the hill to a flat gravel amphitheater where the hillside had been excavated. Owen stopped the truck and turned off the engine. "This'll only take a minute."

He struggled out of his seat and straightened slowly, both hands on top of the open door, his effort punctuated by small grunts and groans. He arched his back painfully and Susan saw his belly bulge over his belt. He tugged at the back of his pants and began massaging the back of his left thigh, causing undulations to ripple across the crater leading down to his navel. She watched with a strange detachment. She looked up to his face. He was looking back at her, a brief moment of embarrassment then a self-conscious smile.

He let go of his leg. "Gone are the days when I was mistaken for Patrick Swayze." He shook out his t-shirt, looked around the back wall of the pit and patted his belly. "I and my companion will be as quick as we can." He went behind the truck and opened the rear camper door.

Susan was furious with herself. How stupid to be caught staring at his gut. How embarrassing for him. How embarrassing for her. He walked out to the back wall of the pit, his gun in one hand, a small paper target fluttering in the other. Owen was a nice guy, but he wasn't Jim. She knew she shouldn't compare them, but she didn't know how not to. Maybe she never would.

Now he was walking back toward the truck in even paces. As he got closer she saw his mouth moving, counting. How many times had she seen Jim do this in gravel pits just like this one? Owen was puffing, his face a little red. Jim's face was always that even brown from being in the sun and wind. Owen had stopped and was taking his rifle from its case. It was a simple, unadorned bolt action with a scope. She knew what Jim would say about that. *You don't need a scope on a .22, it just gets in the way. A .22 is for short range.* She could predict Jim's moods, knew what he would say before he said it. She guessed that's what 25 years with someone did. Now every conversation she had, every situation, was accompanied by thoughts of Jim: what would he say, what would he do? She was an addict in withdrawal.

Of course it had all been his fault. She had been right to leave. He had succumbed to his juvenile urges, tossing away their life and their family. Any woman in her place would leave. Still, she missed him. More than that, she felt a need where he had been, a need she didn't think could be filled by anyone…at least not yet.

Owen lined up his body with the target. He straightened his back and neck then rotated his shoulders. He brought the rifle to his shoulder, tucked it in, and laid his cheek on the stock. Jim would say, *You can't sight in a rifle without a solid rest. The point is to find out where the gun is shooting under ideal conditions. You can't trust a standing freehand shot.*

Crack. She flinched, not expecting such a loud report from a .22. She supposed the sound was magnified by the walls of the gravel pit. Crack. Owen wasn't taking much time between shots. Jim would scoff. *You can't hurry it.* Crack. *You gotta give yourself time to—* Crack. *—settle down. And each shot causes vibrations in the barrel.* Crack. *You gotta let them—* Crack. *—damp down before you shoot again.*

Jim knew a lot about guns and hunting and the outdoors. For the past few years most of his conversations were about those same old things. How many times had she listened to him hold forth on the stupidity of road hunters? He could go on endlessly about the destruction left by ATVs. He had embarrassed her at a party once by lecturing the Grand Chief of the Council of Yukon First Nations about aboriginal hunters taking female moose and caribou. He could be pedantic at times, even—dare she think it—boring and predictable. There were things she didn't miss about her old life: the long commute into work in the dark and cold of winter, the lonely times in summer when Jim was away with clients and she was tied down by home chores, having to turn down offers of drinks, dinner, a concert or a play because she had to get home. Now that she was living in town she could do things she'd been wanting to do for a long time. She had joined the community choir. She wanted to travel. Her friend Judy was planning a trip to Nepal and had asked her to come along. The more she thought of it, the more she was struck by how quickly she had jumped out of marriage.

She heard the camper door open then close again and Owen appeared at the driver's door.

"All done." He was puffing as he climbed into the driver's seat and flipped the paper target onto the dash.

As he started the engine, she said, "Owen I want to tell you—"

He held up a hand "Ah, ah, ah. Love is never having to say you're sorry."

"I wasn't going to say sorry, I was going to say how much I appreciate your help…your understanding."

"Shit. I've always wanted to use that line."

Susan laughed. "Well, maybe you'll get another chance."

"I hope so. Campground, here we come."

When he turned the truck around the target slid towards her off the dash, falling to join the clutter on the floor. She caught it. The bull's eye, about the size of a quarter, was completely torn out by six shots. "Wow."

Owen glanced briefly over as the truck picked up speed down the hill. "Yeah, my uncle Willard taught me. He used to say, *Don't aim for the bulls-eye. Aim for the atom at the center of it.*"

The jingle of bells came from the sunny side of the clearing. Six horses grazed, their colors stark against dark spruce forest. Her father sat on a pack box on the other side of the fire, where a pot of water boiled. Jessica hooked a spoon under its handle and lifted it off the fire. "I hope you've got an appetite. We've gotta eat up this extra food."

"Extra? We're not home yet."

She made a hole the coals. "No sense carrying dead weight back over this mountain." She reached back for a large foil wrapped package, laid it into the hole and covered it with coals.

Jim shifted his seat on the pack box. "You're good at this."

She put a few sticks on top. "I learned from the master."

He didn't smile, just looked down into his cup. "Jess, I'm thinking of getting…trying to get…back together…with Suzy."

She stared at him. "What?"

His eyes met hers for a moment then fell back down to the fire. "I've been thinking things over."

The thought of them back together was wonderful, everything back to normal. But how could it ever be normal now? "Have you talked to Mom about this?"

"No, it's…uh…"

His embarrassment was painful to watch.

"Where's David?" She stood and reached across the fire.

He handed her his cup. "He's in the tent. I think he's asleep."

"Good." She poured tea into the cup then lifted the lid from the pack box she had been sitting on. "If I have to deal with two deeply disturbed men, let it be one at a time."

"Jess, everybody has to learn their father's just a jerk like everyone else."

She reached into the box and pulled out a half bottle of rum. "How much of a jerk?"

"You tell me."

"Major jerk. But at least you know it." She unscrewed the cap and poured the rum.

"So what do you think? You think she'll come back?"

She passed him his cup and picked up hers. "I don't know, Dad. A month ago I would have said yes, but lately…" She tipped rum into her cup.

"What?" He laughed. "Has she been seeing someone else?" He took a nervous sip.

"What's so funny?"

"Huh? You know…Suzy and…" His expression changed to concern.

She wasn't going to let him off the hook. "Sure, Mom's been seeing guys. Why shouldn't she?" She took a large swig.

"What guys? Who?"

"I don't know. Guys, men, whatever."

"So it's no one in particular. It's just going out with a bunch of people after work, that kind of thing. She's not…you know…"

"Sleeping with them? Dad, you're in no position to—"

"That's not what I mean."

"Would it make any difference?"

He looked at her a long moment. "No. You're right. It was my fault, but I'm willing to admit it. I'm willing to say I'm sorry. I just don't know how Suzy will take it."

"Yeah. I don't know. She's a lot more up these days, not so depressed all the time. I hardly ever see her. She's really into her work. I guess that's not surprising, but I've noticed she's more…independent, I suppose. Less afraid of the future."

"Oh." He went silent again. A whiskeyjack landed on a nearby tree. A horse blew at the edge of the bog. The sucking sound of mud as it backed out of the soft ground made Jim turn his head. He had told her stories, hours of hard work to free a horse sunk in a bog. She saw the lines etched in the skin of his face and neck, the gray in his hair. His life was coming apart at the time it was supposed to settle down. Maybe Mom could forgive him, but would she leave her new life?

"I don't think she'll want to move back home."

"Why not? She loves it there."

"Just don't be too surprised is all I'm saying."

"I hadn't thought of that."

It was cruel, but she couldn't resist. "You haven't thought of a lotta things."

Dan stood by the fire picking moose hairs off his clothes. He was sore and tired, but satisfied. The skin was fleshed and the hair removed, a hard job that usually took him much longer. It would lighten the load considerably.

"Why do you cut the fur off?" Hannah held the frying pan over a hot flame, shaking and stirring its contents.

"Too hard to tan with the hair on. Even without the hair it's a lot of hard work. The skin has to be soaked in soapy water, drying and stretching and working it in between soakings. Can't do that with the hair on. Then it has to be stretched and softened. Then finally it's smoked over a slow, punky fire. We use moose skin for moccasins and mitts, sometimes jackets."

"If you could leave the hair on, I'll bet it would be really warm."

"And really, really heavy."

"Does your mother do all the work?"

"Yup. There aren't many left who do. It's getting hard for Mom. It's a bit of a dying art, but some of the young folks are learning." He pointed to the skin hanging over a pole. "Starla said she wants to help her gramma do this hide—one of her bargaining chips for moving to Ross.'

"This hide? But she didn't know you were going to get a moose."

"No."

"What would your mother say if she saw you now?"

"She'd be very happy. She won't have to flesh and de-hair a big, stinky bull moose skin. But she'd also point out a couple of slips I made with the knife." He looked at the skin again, the last rays of the sun coming through a few holes near the edge. "She'd tell me the sun's going down and that skin will freeze so stiff I won't be able to fold it up in the morning." He began to take it down.

"What would she think of me?"

"She'd say, *Son, I'm so happy. You finally found yourself a nice Jewish girl.*"

She rocked back on her heels and laughed.

"Then she'd say, *But she's too skinny. Give her a pepperoni.*" He folded the skin into a tight bundle and set it on the moss. She was still chuckling as he came back to the fire. She scooped a bowl of diced mushrooms into the frying pan to join the finely chopped liver simmering there. "That smells great."

"Yeah, it'll be ready soon. Have you washed your hands?"

"My hands." He looked at them. He had scrubbed them in the river but a crust of black dried gore still ringed his fingernails. "There's no hope for my hands."

"Soak them in hot water." She put a stick through the handle of the pot and slid it off the fire.

"You're getting pretty good at this."

"Pretty good?"

"Very good. Hannah the Jungle Girl. Did you find any onions?"

"Yup, but they're small. It took a long time. The flavor's good, though—garlicky." She stirred the pan. "You know, there is something I'd kill for."

"What?"

"A shower."

"Oh yeah."

"I'm thinking of going in the river."

"It's too cold."

"Aren't you the big tough Yukon man?"

"If you go in that river, the title is yours."

"This is ready. You want some?"

He got the bowls and set them beside her. She spooned the mixture into the bowls and handed one to him. He tasted it. "Mmmm. This is really good."

She tried it. "It's not quite like mother used to make, but she had a whole kitchen."

They ate in silence, listening to the swish of the river punctuated by bell-like calls from the ravens. The camp was in shadow, but the mountains blazed in sun above the valley.

Dan said, "We could make a sweat lodge. That's as good as a shower."

She looked at him. "Like a sauna. Martin talked about making one but he never got around to it. How hard is it?"

"Not too hard…a willow frame covered with a tarp. We can borrow the one from the moose meat. We'd heat rocks in the fire and put them inside, get in and throw hot water on them."

"Then jump in the river?"

"Yeah."

"That sounds great."

It did. He saw it in his mind—the two of them huddled together in the steam, naked, sweating then running into the water together, her body in the moonlight. There was a pressure in his groin. She was looking into his eyes with an odd expression. Maybe she was seeing the same thing. They both looked down at their plates and continued eating. "We could take turns if you want."

She stirred her spoon around in her bowl. "No, too much trouble. Let's finish our meal."

What did she mean by too much trouble? He guessed it meant no sweat bath.

She glanced at him and continued eating. "After we eat, I'll heat rocks while you make the thing. What are we gonna do for towels?"

"I dunno." He had a feeling of lightness. "We'll think of something."

"We can use the dishtowel."

"What's left of it."

"We can build up the fire and dry ourselves by it."

An image came to him—the orange light of the flames dancing over her bare steaming body. The pressure in his groin returned. He tried to think of something else. "Where's Raz? Come on Raz. Come here, boy." He heard the dog's tail thump the ground from where he lay behind him. Then he remembered. "Hey, I've got some scotch in the boat pack. You want some?"

"Scotch. Yes. I want some. You've been hoarding scotch all this time?"

He got up and headed for the canoe. "Not hoarding. I save it for when the hunting is over. Now's the time."

"What else are you hiding in your mysterious magical boat pack?"

"If I told you, you'd know everything." When he came back to the fire with the bottle he poured some in each cup and held his up. She did the same. "To the moose."

"To the moose."

Raz watched his Dan and the new mate with interest. They were playing, doing something with the fire. Humans were crazy for fire. There they were, huffing-yipping, putting rocks in the fire, piling on sticks until the flames got scary big.

Humans could be fearless at times when they should be terrified. Now they were fishing the rocks out of the fire, carrying them balanced on two sticks held between them. Strange. Chattering. More huffing-yipping. They were putting the rocks inside the little den his Dan had put up on the narrow gravel bar. To go over and urinate on it would be nice, but His Dan would not approve.

"The sauna's all fired up, Starla. Come on." Tara stood on the path, her towel pulled tightly around her, stepping from one foot to the other.

Starla stood in the open doorway. "I don't want to."

"Are you nuts? You love the sauna."

"I just don't wanna tonight. I'm going to bed." She didn't want to go to bed, but while Gary was with Tara she was fine.

"Starla honey, you've been so...I dunno, mopey-dopey. You disappear for hours and Gary has to traipse all over the country looking for you. What's the matter?"

She wanted to tell her mother, but what would she say? She was afraid of Gary, afraid he wanted to molest her? Tara wouldn't believe it. She'd say what she always said, *Starla, the only reason you don't like Gary is because he's not Dan.* And what if her fears were imaginary? What if it was all in her mind? She had heard of kids molested by adults, but Gary had not actually done anything. Tara once told her she could ask anything at all, whenever she was afraid or confused.

She was about to ask her mother to come back in the cabin when Tara said, "I'm freezing out here, honey. I gotta get into that sauna. I'll talk to you later. You're gonna miss all the fun." And she was gone down the path.

"There's not much room in here." Hannah crouched in the small dome, holding open the flap of the tarp to let Dan in. As he stooped to enter with the pot full of hot water, she stole a look at his naked body and noticed his foreskin. She had never seen an uncircumcised man before, at least not in the flesh. What would it be like to make love to him? No, that thought was too crazy. Just because they were crammed into a tiny sweat lodge with no clothes on, a hundred miles from the nearest person, it didn't mean they were going to do anything.

He put the pot down carefully. "Now make sure you close off the opening as well as you can, and be careful you don't knock over the water."

She pushed the loose end of the tarp over the opening and pulled the bottom end down to the ground. Her knee touched one of the hot stones. "Ow."

"What happened?"

"I touched the stones."

"Oh. Don't do that, either. It'll hurt."

"Thank you."

She could barely see him now in the darkness. She edged back from the door to sit on the spruce boughs covered with the canvas tarp.

He dipped a mug of hot water from the pot and held it over the stones. "Ready?"

"Ready." The hiss of boiling water filled the small enclosure and a blast of steam struck her face and upper body. "Ooooh. That's hot. I can hardly breath."

"That's the point. You gotta stay in here 'til you can't stand it any longer."

"That's not going to be too long."

"Just relax and let it wash over you. Breath slowly and evenly."

Sweat began to trickle down her temples, down her forehead into her eyes. Her arms and legs felt prickly. She shifted to rest her weight on the side of her hip and her arm touched his—smooth, slippery and warm.

He said, "Should I put some more on?"

"Who are you calling a moron?"

He poured another mug of water over the rocks and she heard a pop. "What was that?"

"One of the rocks splitting. How are you feeling?"

"Hot and sweaty. It's marvelous."

"This'll get all the grime off. Before we go into the river we can use what's left of the hot water to soap ourselves down. You can go first 'cause I gotta work on my hands."

She pushed back her wet hair and took a shallow breath. "I can hardly wait. It's going to feel so good to wash my hair."

"You have to wait until you're hot enough. It's the anticipation that makes it sweeter."

What other kind of anticipation was going on here? She took a deep slow breath. It was getting easier to relax. "You're very good at this."

"Making a sweat lodge? There's nothing to it."

"No, I mean the whole thing...living out here, traveling the river. It comes easily to you."

He shifted his legs away from the hot stones. "I've been doing it all my life."

"Well, it seems to me you could make a living at it."

"I already told you I've guided hunters. I suppose I could go back to it."

She swiped a hand down her arm, surprised at the volume of perspiration. "It doesn't have to be hunters. Times are changing. There are lots of people who would pay you to take them down this river."

"I know, but it takes money and connections to start up. You gotta have the right gear and equipment. I couldn't expect a paying client to sleep under a tarp. Where am I gonna get the money for tents and canoes and paddles and sleeping bags and everything?"

"Minor consideration. That's what David would say." As soon as she said it she regretted bringing up her husband's name.

"By the sound of it, he doesn't have to worry about money. It's different for me. I've got no job, no house, no business experience, nothing. Who's gonna lend me money?"

"Yes, but you have the magic ingredient. You know the wilderness, you're comfortable with it, and most of all, you're good with people."

"You think so?"

"I know about these things. It's my business to handle people. You have a talent."

"I don't know how you can tell that."

Jessica handed David the last pot to dry. David took it from her. "Easy. I should be deep in depression at this moment, but instead you have me convinced there's a good chance Hannah is still alive."

"Look, David, I said I don't want to get any false hopes up, but…let's just say I have a feeling about this. Call it woman's intuition."

He placed the pot on top of the pack box they were using as a table. "I'll go with that. You were right. I can't give up hope yet. I just wish there was something more I could do."

"There is. As soon as we get to Ross we'll ask around. Maybe somebody knows who's on the river and when they left."

It was a sliver of hope at best, but it could be true. Why not? If she had made it to the river, surely she would stay there, or follow it. Anyone going by would see her, or she would see them. There was a chance. He felt better.

Then he saw the backpack lying where he had left it outside the tent. The backpack loomed over all. How long could she survive without it? Why did she discard it? Did she discard it? Lying there torn, it looked like some pitiful, disemboweled animal. His chest tightened. The paranoid fantasies returned…the bear's teeth ripping into her flesh…

"Could you do my back?" Hannah turned away from him, her eyes tight shut to keep out the soap after washing her hair.

Could he do her back? An erection began. Keep the tone light, nonchalant. "Sure." Had his voice trembled? He took a handful of water and poured it over the nape of her neck and stroked down her back. He slid them up to her shoulders and massaged around the edges of her shoulder blades. If he concentrated only on the skin of her back and the motion of his hands his desire could be controlled. He gently worked the muscles of her neck. Another few strokes up and down her back, a moment's pause with a hand on each side of her ribcage, fighting a powerful urge to slide them around and over her breasts and it was done. "I think you're ready." He held open the tarp and felt a draft of cold air. "Okay go. Fast."

She crawled out of the tent. "I can't see."

"Keep going straight. The river's right in front of you." He watched her from behind emerge into the moonlight. His pulse began to pound. Should he go out there with an erection, hoping the soap would be in her eyes awhile? Excruciating to have to stay in the sweat lodge until it went away. He left the tent and went to the water. She was up to her waist, still rinsing her hair. Soap bubbles ran down over her breasts, parting at each nipple.

When the cold water reached his crotch, all worry of an erection was gone. He dove in and glided out into the current, immune to the gripping cold for a brief time. It felt powerful, invigorating. His head came to the surface and he let out his breath in a whoop. Hannah answered with another and their echoes chased each other downriver. Raz splashed in after him. "Go back Raz, I'm coming out." He swam back to the shallow water. The current took him to where the canoe was pulled onto the bar. Raz dodged and bounced around him in play.

Hannah floated with lazy strokes downstream towards him. "The steam is pouring off your body." She stood up a couple of meters away, her skin glittering silver drops in the dazzle of moonlight on water.

He looked at her unselfconsciously, lingering on her hips, her pubic hair, her breasts, her nipples hard from the cold water. "You too. You're beautiful...very...beautiful."

Raz gave him a playful bite on the calf.

He couldn't possibly look that good. No one could. He was bronze, lean muscle sprinkled with silver droplets of moonlight. Mist poured off his body, rose in the still air and drifted out over the water. The air seemed to sparkle and buzz with electricity. The whole scene—the mist, the moonlight, the man's body—was like some fantasy conjured from a dream. It must be the pot they had smoked before the sweat bath. She hoped the paranoia wouldn't start. She wanted him, ached for him.

His eyes roamed over her body like a caress. She could almost feel them stroke her hips, her breasts, taste the moisture in the cleft between her legs. She took a step towards him. He took a step towards her. His shadow moved behind him, sliding along the hull of the canoe, revealing the name which now shone stark white in the moonlight—Hellman.

David. No. Why must he appear now? She wanted to make love to this man who stood before her, wanted to step into his arms, feel his lips against hers, feel his muscles move beneath that golden skin, engulf him in slippery pulsing warmth. But the name blazed behind him—Hellman. This was not fair. How many times had David been unfaithful? Why couldn't she? Damn the paranoia. Damn the marijuana.

She clutched her arms around her midriff. "It's cold. I'd better get back to the fire and put some clothes on." A nervous laugh escaped her and she felt foolish. She hurried toward the camp, not daring to look back, suddenly self-conscious of her nakedness. As she crossed the gravel she heard him splash back into the water.

Moonlight gave the gravel bar a diffuse glow. The river rushed over stones at the lower end. The bear lay in a shallow depression in the moss, the pain in his gut dulled for now by exhaustion. The aroma of labrador tea and highbush cranberry surrounded him, but was overpowered by the putrid ooze from the hole in his abdomen.

A sound drifted down the valley, bouncing off the blackness of the hillside across the river. He lifted his head in alarm. Was it the gull sound again? It was distant and he hadn't the strength to move, anyway. His head went back down to rest on the moss and a fitful sleep overtook him.

When she heard them laughing and splashing she turned off her light. They would be coming back soon. It was all so unfair it made her angry. They were having a good time while she was forced to hide alone all day. She wished she had stayed with friends in Whitehorse. She wished Dan would come and get her. She wished a bolt of lightning would hit Gary and kill him. How could her mother like him? Why did she always try to get her to like him?

Suddenly she was crying, tears springing from her eyes, her breath coming in sobs. She heard the door open and the shuffle of their entry, so she pushed her face into the pillow to stifle the sound.

"Starla honey, you all right?"

She took a deep breath and raised her head, but she couldn't speak or her voice would break.

"Starla, I thought I heard you. Are you okay?"

She finally got control of the tightness in her throat. "Yeah, I guess I was asleep."

"Sorry honey. You go back to sleep. Good night." There was more shuffling and Tara's lowered voice. "Be quiet Gary. Starla's trying to sleep."

She held her breath as she heard them go down the short hallway, past her door and on into their room. She was safe at least for the night. Her breath came out in a long sigh into her pillow.

There was rustling of sheets, murmured words and then a long silence. She closed her eyes. Gary's voice came over the partition. "Good night, Starla."

This was good. Raz glanced back to see if his Dan was still coming. They had been back and forth to the big dead skin scraping tree so often the way was becoming a trail. They hadn't played the groaning, licking, wriggling game after all. No intriguing musky smell. They'd put their outerskins back on and his Dan headed for the meadow. Were they hunting again? Would there be another big dead moose? No. Too dark. And his Dan didn't carry the boomstick. But still this was good. The meadow in moonlight. Smells. Scurryings. Sharp bright sounds.

He bounded ahead and veered off the trail, over and under brittle dead spruce branches to where the willows began, their roots forming mounds above the spongy black soil, their branches interlocking above, creating tunnels of rich wet scent. Lots happening at night

Brighter ahead. Moonlight on sedge grass where the willows thinned. A flash of movement and a rustle of grass. He froze, his only motion a twitching nose. No scent yet. Another flash as something passed through a stripe of light. A vole. Maybe. It went behind a mound then came twisting through the tight packed willow branches. Maybe a vole nest on the mound. They sometimes held a bundle of juicy, squishy, squeaking tastiness. Should he leap forward and try to grab? No, it was coming to him but it was not a vole. Longer, thinner. A squirrel but not a squirrel. Skinny, long. The thing was coming over a root. He gathered his back legs under him. Wait. It had a vole in its mouth. Long mouth. Flat head wider where it met a long neck. It still hadn't seen him. It stopped and began to eat the vole. A scent wafted to him. He had smelled it before but only traces. Never fresh like this. Funny. The smell reminded him of his Dan's jacket pocket—the one where he kept his little bag of dried plant. He edged forward, extending his nose to get a stronger...the thing flew straight into his face and latched onto his lip with needle teeth. He yelped and shook. Yelped again and ran. The thing let go as he plunged through the brush back toward the trail. His nose stung with the scent. His eyes watered. He had to stop, hoping the thing was not chasing him. He sneezed.

"Hey Raz. What the fuck?"

He snorted out a breath through his nose. It helped, but the unpleasant tarry smell still stung. He lapped at some boggy water seeping up at his feet, but the bitter taste stuck to his mouth. He ran to the trail out to the meadow.

"C'mere Raz." His Dan sat on the smoothed tree trunk.

The smell of moose covered the trampled grass. Nice chewy scraps lay about. It smelled powerful, warm, good, soothing to his stinging nose. He put his head into his Dan's lap, flinched when his Dan's hand stroked over his muzzle.

"What's the matter, pal. You get bitten? Here?" His Dan's fingers gently squeezed his lip. He flinched and gave a small yip. "Poor guy. Looks like you'll survive. Now go away."

Away? How far? He went to the edge of the flattened grass and lay down close to a nice long strip of chewy bit with hairs and blades of grass stuck to it.

"Go, Raz. Go back."

Back? To the crinkly den? If they weren't hunting or scraping skin, why were they here? Would his Dan sleep here? His Dan zipped down his bottom outerskin opening. Funny. He usually peed standing up. His Dan reached in with his front paw and pulled out his pisser. It was swollen. Yes. His Dan always wanted to be alone when he made the swelling go down. Weird.

"Go on, now. Don't worry. This won't take long."

He tried to be unobtrusive as he crawled under the sleeping bag. He didn't want to have to talk. How embarrassing. How stupid he must have looked, so obviously wanting her, standing there in the river with his dick pointing straight out, telling her how beautiful she looked. He had completely misread it, so sure she wanted him, too. What a dunce. It would be awkward tomorrow, having to make conversation, talking around the edges of what they would both be thinking. Things had been going so well and he had screwed it. Maybe tomorrow he should broach the subject... face it and apologize. Or he could just ignore it and get down the river as fast as possible.

All he wanted right now was to sleep. Sleep. How could he sleep with the image in his head—her standing in the moonlit river? How could he sleep so close to the warmth of her body, seeing her in his mind, imagining himself rolling towards her, against her back, her buttocks pushing into the curve of his body, his hand reaching around her to caress her belly. He felt his erection coming on again. Shit. How could he get to sleep now?

As he eased himself under the sleeping bag she was barely breathing. She felt so foolish. She had wanted him. It must have been obvious. All the body language was there, all the signals. The moon, the air, the water, the trees had all seemed to whisper desire. The sweat bath and the cold water had set her skin tingling in anticipation. If it hadn't been for the damned canoe…No, it was her fault, her fear and guilt. If it hadn't been for the marijuana she wouldn't have…No, there was only herself to blame.

How awkward would it be tomorrow? What would they say to each other? Would they carefully skirt around the issue, pretend as if nothing had happened? Maybe she should apologize, get it out in the open and face it. Would that make it even more awkward?

Sleep. She must sleep. She could feel the heat from his body, so close that if she moved just a little bit, pushed back against him, snuggled her buttocks into the curve of his body, so he could reach around her to caress her belly…the muscles between her legs clenched with a warm slippery feeling.

So what now? Things had been going so well. She had been enjoying this trip despite the circumstances. Even helping with the moose and cooking the liver. How crazy was that? What the hell was happening to her? She couldn't remember ever being this horny. Was it something in the air, the water…Did the liver contain some kind of hormones? "Crazy", she mumbled under her breath. He rustled beside her.

"What was that?"

"What was what?"

"Crazy. You said crazy."

"Did I? Maybe I was asleep."

"Were you?"

"No."

She felt a cold draft come under the cover as he went up on one elbow beside her. "So what's crazy?"

"I don't know. Life. Me. You." She rolled to her back and looked into his face, shades of black and gray in the moonlight, save for brief orange flickers from the dying fire glinting deep in his eyes. It took a conscious effort to keep her hand from reaching out to touch him.

He lay back down and stared up at the tarp, at the sky. After a long pause he broke the silence. "Crazy. Ain't it the truth?"

His face was in profile as he closed his eyes and let out a long misty breath that drifted out from under the shelter to vanish into the starry sky.

"Dan?"

His face turned to hers. "Hmm?"

"It was the canoe."

"Huh?" He went up on his elbow again to look down at her. "The canoe? What are you—"

"The name on the canoe."

"Hellman?...Oh, right. David."

"Uh huh. I saw the name and..."

He was silent for a long while, gazing at her then, "I'll burn it."

"What?"

"The damn canoe. I'll build a big fire and throw it on top. It's the only sensible thing to do."

She laughed. "Then we'll die here."

"Yes. Happily."

"Dan...I'm sorry."

"Sorry? Why should you..."

"No. I was wrong. I shouldn't have...you know."

He lay on his back and looked up at the sky. "No, it was me. I misread the whole thing. I've always thought I knew the line between fantasy and reality." He turned his face to hers. "You were just...and I thought...well, I thought there was more to it." When he spoke she felt a hint of warm breath on her cheek.

"You didn't misread anything. I should have known sex would complicate things. I was childish and selfish and irresponsible."

"No, you weren't. You're right. Sex complicates things. You stopped before we...went too far."

"So...are we agreed that sex is...out of the question?" She felt the heat radiating from his body.

He answered in a voice just slightly above a whisper. "Of course. Completely off limits. We'd ruin everything if we were to…you know."

She hadn't noticed it before, but his knee was touching hers. Now she was acutely aware of it, an almost electric buzz. "Make love?"

"Yeah. Make love."

She felt the muscles clench again. "I just hope we can go back to being…you know."

He went up on his elbow again. "Acquaintances."

She smiled. "Friends."

"Right. Friends."

Before she knew it her hand reached to touch behind his elbow and gently moved up the back of his arm. "Pals."

His hand came to rest on her abdomen then slowly slid up the side of her ribcage. His face descended towards hers. He whispered, "Sidekicks."

She moved her hands to either side of his face, pulled him down to meet her lips, and pressed the full length of her body against his. A long, warm, moist kiss, their tongues sliding over one another then she disengaged and rolled him to his back. She lay half on top of him, looking down into his eyes. "Chums."

His hands slipped under the sides of her shirt and he lifted it up as she squirmed out of it. He raised his head to take her right nipple into his mouth. As it grew harder she felt a pull from deep in her belly. He moved to the other breast and she groaned. He said, "Bosom buddies."

"Don't, please. If I laugh I won't be able to…" She rolled onto her back again beside him.

"Okay, okay. Sssh." He moved onto his knees and ran his hands up and down her belly and chest, brushing over her breasts. He kissed her mouth, chin, neck, his lips traveled down her chest, and abdomen. When he unfastened her jeans she raised her hips to let him slip them down over her thighs along with her panties.

She kicked them off the rest of the way. "Mates."

His kisses continued down past her navel. When his breath tickled the fuzz above her pubic hair a shiver coursed through her. It had been so long since a man had…then she remembered her period. It was practically finished and she wasn't using a tampon now, but…

It took all her willpower to stop him. "Dan. My period. It's almost over. It is really, but there still might be a little...

"Sssh. It's okay." He nuzzled into her pubic hair. "Blood brothers."

She gripped the pole of the lean to and put her head back, eyes open to watch the mist gathering over the river, the moon and stars above, framed by the black jagged outline of spruce.

It had been a year since the old bull last mounted a cow. It was in a spot much like this, a meadow a night's travel upstream from here. He had driven off two smaller bulls last year. This year was easy. The little bull had been no threat, took no effort to keep away then disappeared after the big thunder and the human voices.

He rubbed his nose over the cow's rump and filled his nostrils with her breeding smell. Cold air touched his penis, now beginning to protrude from its furred casing far back on his belly. He laid his head over her back. She didn't move off this time. With a slight moan she planted her hind feet in the meadow turf. It was time. She was ready.

He rose onto his hind legs, reached his forelegs to straddle her back, pawed for a moment to get his balance then slid forward to engage her. She pushed back, taking half his weight, and he felt the tip of his penis touch the warm moist smoothness of her. As he thrust forward, his whole being was inside her. No other sensations—no wind, no sound, no smell—only exquisite, slippery warmth engulfing him. His ejaculations came in pulses of cascading pleasure.

It was over in a short time. He slid down her back to all four feet, resting his head on her rump for a moment. She moved to a nearby willow and began to feed. Cold air in his nostrils again as he puffed clouds of misty breath into the still night. There would be more mounting. Perhaps he would gather more cows. He had gathered more than one in past years, but he'd had to fight for them.

There it was at last—the groaning, wrestling, licking game, and the intriguing musky smell. Raz listened from his temporary bed in the moss, head on paws. It had been a long time in coming, but it had to happen with a new mate. This was a good thing. Good for the pack. Soon they would be finished. There would be some panting and cooing sounds then he'd be able to go back under the tarp to sleep close to them. But the intriguing musky smell would be strong. Always a powerful urge to pee on the bed.

SEPT. 21

The wolf howl faded into stillness. A faint light filtered through the tent fabric. It was early. The howl had seemed to come from right outside the tent, but perhaps his half-awake mind had amplified it. Perhaps he had dreamed it. David's first thought was to go outside, but what if the wolf was there, or more than one? Wolves never attacked people. That's what they said, but here in this dark forest far from anywhere he wasn't sure.

He rolled onto his side, shifting to find his best fit to the ground. The moss was thick and soft, but uneven. Thoughts of Hannah returned—images of tearing teeth and ripping claws. Try not to think of it. Sleep.

Better to think of something else. Jessica. The way her hips moved when…No. His restaurants. Plenty to occupy his mind there. He had abandoned the business at the very moment he was needed most. It was crucial to make the right impression or the franchise deal would go down the toilet. Aaron could handle the nuts and bolts, but he could be such a klutz when it came to public relations. The company was in Tina's hands now. As soon as he could get to a phone he'd call her. Tina. He didn't have to worry about her—committed, smart, perceptive. Nice compact body, too. The feel of those wonderful breasts. She had been managing the West Vancouver Chives, doing a superb job, and he had invited her out for a sail, contriving to get stranded up the coast because of the weather. Wow. That had been some night. He remembered the feel of his fingers in her hair as she took him in her mouth.

No. He shook his head and wiggled his shoulder off a root. No thoughts of sex until he knew for certain if Hannah was alive. And if she was, what then? Would he go back to his old ways? What were the lyrics to that Joanie Mitchell song? *You don't know what you've got 'til it's gone.* He hoped he wasn't too late. He remembered how they met. He was her cousin's date at her family's Passover Seder. They had hit it off immediately and before long they were going out. On the third date she had come to his place. He woke up the next morning, her back to him, nestled into his body, *Like spoons,* she had said. Another wolf howl floated through the bush as he drifted off to sleep with the image in his mind.

"Like spoons," she murmured. Her head rested on Dan's arm, his hand stroked her belly and she could feel his hardness resting in the groove of her buttocks. His breath was a warm wash over the back of her neck. The setting moon shot blue shafts through the camp, and glowed white on the rocks of the bar. His skin was a dark contrast to hers in this light.

The air was cold in her nose. She snuggled into his body and his hand moved up to her breasts, rubbing softly over her nipples then moved down her belly again, lingering around the navel and working down into her pubic hair. She arched her back and he straightened against her, moving his hand over her pubic bone then a finger gently exploring her, massaging. She felt him against her buttocks, push and release, push and release. She lifted her leg and reached down to guide him inside.

Dan slipped from under the sleeping bag, careful not to wake her. Cold air on bare skin sent a shiver through him. His pants and underwear lay jammed in a heap at the low end of the lean-to, pushed out from under the covers last night. He retrieved them and quickly put them on. They were frigid, which made his need to pee even more urgent. Frost covered the moss outside the shelter, cold on bare feet. Instead, he knelt and peed out the open side, checking back over his shoulder at Hannah—a tuft of hair sticking out from under the sleeping bag. When he was finished he saw his shirt, a crumpled mass half covered with frost. He should have had the sense to pull his clothes under the covers, but last night…

Last night. Wow. What prolonged celibacy could do. After days of watching her, nights of sleeping beside her, he'd been like a starving man staring at a banquet. Thinking now of her scent, her taste, her warmth, filling his mouth with her nipples, he felt another erection coming on. For a moment he considered getting back under the covers just to warm up a bit. Maybe she'd wake up and…no, let her sleep. Maybe later he could slip in beside her.

He put on his socks and cold, stiff boots, left the lean-to, picked up his axe and headed to the gravel bar. Raz popped from under the sleeping bag to follow.

"Nothing exciting, fella. Just gotta cut some sticks for the bottom of the canoe."

The dog wagged his tail and trotted ahead into the mist. Dan went to the fringe of willow and alder, which edged the high water mark and began cutting saplings. When he had a pile he carried them to the canoe and dropped them beside it. He laid a bed of sticks lengthwise into the bottom then broke some into shorter pieces to lay crosswise over them.

"What are you doing?"

He turned to see Hannah, hair rumpled, wrapped in the sleeping bag, boots laces dragging, eyes puffy from sleep. She looked gorgeous.

"Oh. Hi. Good morning." His voice sounded flat, muffled by the fog drifting slowly downstream and morning-after awkwardness.

She looked at the pile of willows beside the canoe. "The sticks. What are you doing with them?"

"Keeps the meat off the bottom of the canoe. It lets air circulate and holds it above any water and mud that might get in."

"Oh." There was a long pause. She looked away, up and down the bar, across the river at the line of trees, back towards the camp, all barely visible through the mist. "Dan?"

"Yeah?" What was coming? She didn't answer right away. She just stood there avoiding his eyes and looking sad. The longer she paused, the more the let down loomed. Last night was too good to be true.

She finally spoke. "Last night was…" Again she fell silent.

She had wakened, thought about it and decided it was a mistake. He laid more willows into the canoe. "I know. Last night was a mistake. We should try to pretend nothing happened."

"Huh?" She looked confused. "You really feel that way?"

He looked up. "Well no, but...No. Not at all. Last night was...wow."

"I was going to ask if you had any gaffer's tape."

"What? What's gaffer's tape?"

"You know, that silver tape. It's used for everything."

"You mean duct tape? Yeah, I have some. In the boat pack."

"The magical boat pack....Yeah, duct tape. I want to cover that."

He followed her eyes to the name on the canoe—Hellman.

"Cappuccino?" Owen's voice came from below in the narrow kitchen of the camper.

She had been lying there listening to him folding his bed back to become the small table across from the propane stove. She was so glad for Owen's camper, for not having to set up a tent, for the luxury of a soft warm mattress, not one of Jim's thin little sleeping pads. She had heard the whir of the grinder and smelled the rich bitter-chocolate warmth of dark roast coffee. His hand—holding a steaming cup topped with a mound of white milk froth sprinkled with cinnamon—appeared over the edge of the mattress. Then his head popped into view. He was freshly shaven, his hair combed.

"Owen, you're a caffeine addict's dream." She went up on one elbow. "But I'll have to drink it down there. The ceiling's too low here."

He stepped back down. "Okay, I'll put it on the table. Do you want me to go outside while you get dressed?"

"No, just turn the other way." She pulled on her jeans while still lying down then swung her legs over the edge. Her neck was cranked over by the low ceiling, making it difficult to pull on her sweater.

Her head was inside when she heard him say, "If a picture is worth a thousand words, a touch is worth a million." Was he watching her? She pushed her head through the neck of the sweater. No. He was at the table, his back to her, intent on the paper in front of him, a pencil in his hand.

"What brought that on?"

Without turning he held up a newspaper, *The Whitehorse Star*. "The cryptoquote. I love these things."

"I can never do them. I tried once. I don't have the patience"

"Just takes practice. Pattern recognition I think they call it."

Susan sat opposite him and took a sip of cappuccino. He reached his hand toward her face and she drew back instinctively.

His hand stopped. "It's okay. Relax. There's a little spot of foam on the end of your nose."

She smiled and reached her face forward to let him wipe the small white drop with his finger. "Thanks. So who said that?"

"Bob Hope." He sang. "Thanks for the memories…"

"No, I mean the quote—a touch is worth a million."

"Oh, that. I haven't decoded the name yet." He concentrated on the paper in front of him. "Let's see, there's an N, and another, that's E, two O's, S. Looks like *source unknown*. Who would name their kid Source?"

He looked at her and she laughed. "Owen, this is great. The camper, the cappuccino, the gourmet meal last night. It was wonderful. Thanks."

"Don't thank me. Thank Mother Nature for sending that ruffed grouse wandering into the campground."

"It was fabulous. The sauce, I'll have to get your recipe."

"Oooh. Our relationship has reached the trading recipes stage. Aren't you taking things a little fast?"

"I can't help it. I'm a slut."

He burst out laughing. It took a while for him to speak. "Oh, Suzy. Don't I wish?"

"Be careful what you wish for." She took a sip of coffee. "Owen, we have to decide what we're going to do today…about Starla."

"Ah, I forgot this is a business trip. I've been thinking. You got directions to Tara's cabin from her mother. If we drop in pretending it's all by chance she's eventually going to figure it out."

"We don't have to hide it. We can just say we were in the neighborhood and wanted to see the place."

"Still it's going to seem contrived. Much better to arrive by water. You know, we're out fishing, passing by and see them on the shore. *Hey they look familiar. Isn't that Tara and Gary and Starla?* We wave, they recognize us *Hey it's Susan. And who's the guy with her, Brad Pitt? No, it's Owen Orser.* They invite us in for a chat and by dint of some careful timing on our part they're about to have lunch. Something like that."

"Great plan, but there's one important thing missing. We don't have a boat."

"We do. Three campsites away is an old client of mine. He's got a canoe down by the lake. I talked to him last night. He was pretty drunk. I steered the conversation to fishing, about how much I love it, but damn it to hell I didn't think to bring my boat. I also managed to slip in the fact he never fully paid his bill."

"We can use his canoe?"

"Anytime."

"Owen." She gave his hand a squeeze.

"I'm feeling very good, thanks."

"Have a good sleep?"

"Yes, good. Very good."

With a slight look of surprise, Jessica handed him his breakfast. "Great. It's gonna be a long day."

He surprised himself, not the grieving husband. After his dream in the wee hours of the morning, his worries had all but disappeared. It made no sense, but he was sure Hannah was alive and well. "I had the most incredibly vivid dream."

Jessica handed him a mug of coffee. "Sleeping on the ground will do that."

The sugar and cream sat between then on a pack box. Would it sound silly? Was he deluding himself? Jim was out if earshot, tending to the horses. He wouldn't feel comfortable telling him, but Jessica might understand. He wanted to tell someone.

"Remember you said you had a feeling Hannah was okay?"

"Yeah." She looked at him, waiting.

"Well, I do too. I can't really explain it, but I think she's safe. I don't know why, except for the dream." He described waking to the wolf howl and tossing for a long time, his head filled with nightmare scenarios. Then he told her about the dream, leaving out the sex. "You must think I'm kidding myself."

She sat opposite him with her coffee in hand. "Not at all. I don't think we should ignore our intuitions. There are plenty of things we can't explain."

"I've never been superstitious. It's just that the feeling I have is so strong. I know she's all right."

"Some of my First Nation friends would tell you the wolf was a messenger." She got up and began putting food containers into a pack box.

"A messenger." He thought about the idea as he ate. "Why would a wolf give a message to an urban Jewish businessman?"

"Your wolfish grin?"

He laughed and surveyed the surrounding bush. Gone was the feeling of menace.

Jim came back to the camp leading Jasper ahead of the following horses. "Good thing we're leaving. They've eaten all the grass, what there was of it."

"How long will it take to get back to Ross River?"

He tied Jasper to a tree. "If all goes well, we might get to the truck tonight. It'll be a long day, though. We'll have to camp there tonight, so we should be in Ross by noon tomorrow. Why?"

"I want to ask around to see if anyone knows who went down the river in the past week or so."

"Good idea."

Jim was humoring him, but he didn't care. "So if someone picked her up on the river, where would they be going?"

"Pelly Crossing. It's on the Mayo Road, about an hour and a half north of Carmacks." He ducked under the tarp and took the plate of food Jessica handed him.

"How long would they take to get to Pelly Crossing?"

Jim poured himself a coffee. "I don't know. I've never done the South Macmillan, but I'd guess ten days at least."

"So she's still on the river."

"Yeah, she would be." Jim turned to Jessica with a puzzled look.

"I know what you're thinking, but I'm certain she's all right." He spooned up the last of his breakfast, smiled and said through his full mouth, "A wolf told me."

Dan stood back to look at the loaded canoe floating just off the mud. It was low in the water. "Maybe I should leave the head behind."

Hannah looked at the end of an antler protruding from under the tarp. "Is it expendable?"

"The short answer is, yes."

"What's the long answer?"

"No."

"Explain."

"There's a lot of good stuff in the head. Tongue, nose, brains for tanning the skin, antlers for carving."

"Okay, so we take it with. We've got pretty good freeboard, somewhat less when we get in. It'll be hard to move, but this river is a breeze. We only have to keep it in the channel. Should be no problem. Is there something you haven't told me?"

"Yeah." Dan stared at the waterline on the canoe, thinking of Granite Canyon—a six-mile stretch of fast water where the Pelly River zig-zagged through a dyke of bedrock. He hadn't told Hannah about Granite Canyon.

She sat to untie her boots. "We don't have to go over Victoria Falls, do we?"

"Victoria Falls? We could, but most people don't take the African route to Pelly. It's the long way around."

"Okay. So…?"

"Granite Canyon, a few hours downstream from where we join the Pelly River."

She kicked off one boot. "What—chutes, drops, boils—what?"

"No, nothing like that. Just some fast water—easy stuff—except where it goes around Needle Rock. There's a couple of standing waves."

"A couple?"

"Three…and then some choppy water."

She kicked off the other boot. "Is there a turn?"

"Not really sharp." Her questions were to the point. She knew rivers. She had experience and confidence. "It's really only a matter of taking the right line and paddling through it."

Hannah stood and studied the canoe, her eyes taking a practiced walk from bow to stern. "And if we swamp, would the canoe sink or float?"

"Sink. It's got floatation compartments but with all that meat…"

"So we'd lose everything."

"Probably."

"Hmmm…Granite Canyon, Needle Rock. I'd feel much better if they were called Gentle Canyon and Pillow Rock."

Dan looked up and down the bar. "Where's Raz?"

"He's anointing the campsite one last time. That dog is a fountain of urine."

"We've all got our talents."

She stepped up close, put her arms around him and ran her fingers up and down his back. "Yeah." They stared into each other's eyes until she broke the spell. "Hey, I saw that little metal box stuck into a crotch of the big spruce. Aren't you going to take it with you?"

"No. I'll leave it for the next fool to camp here. Who knows? Maybe it'll be me."

The sound of wings and a gurgling call made them turn their heads up to see a black shape pass above. She looked up and stepped back to watch the raven land in a tree above the camp, clicking, burbling. "There she is."

"Your raven?"

"She's her own raven."

"How do you know it's the same one? Is it a different shade of black or are you some kind of raven whisperer?"

Hannah turned back to him smiling. "Skeptic. She and I have a thing."

"A thing?"

She stepped in front of him, and they embraced and kissed. "Yeah, a thing."

"If you were to drop dead right here, do you think she wouldn't chow down on your body?"

"On the contrary. I'd expect her to."

"How would you feel about that?"

"I wouldn't feel anything. I'd be dead."

"Whoa. How did you get so hard-bitten?" They kissed again. "And what about me? If I dropped dead would you and your friend up there devour my remains?"

Hannah squeezed his buttocks. "I think I'd start with a nice, juicy, rump roast."

"I'll consider myself warned." He stepped back and looked downstream. "We might start seeing people from here on in…maybe even today."

"Oh?" She looked worried.

"Yeah, we're almost at Moose Creek. People come upriver to hunt."

"That sucks. I was hoping I wouldn't have to face anyone until much later."

"We don't have to face them, just wave and pass on by."

She rolled up her pant legs. "What if someone recognizes me?"

"So what?"

"I just don't want to have to explain how I got to be floating down the river in a boat full of dead moose."

"You gotta face them some time."

She picked up her boots. "Yeah, I guess so."

"There is another way."

"What?"

"We could sail right past Pelly, on down to the Yukon River, out to the Bering Sea and paddle to Madagascar."

As she waded into the water and got into the canoe she said, "You know what I like about you? When faced with a problem you come up with such simple, practical solutions."

She glided to a landing on the gut pile. "Bobbleheads gone."

Her mate swallowed a morsel of fat. "Mmm. Good. Littlewolf too?"

"Yes. Downriver."

"Good. Hope no shitbear come."

"Where ugly stupid is?"

"Don't know. Near. Eat." He pulled back on a loop of intestine, crinkly and dry where it had been exposed to the air, to reveal fresh white fat beneath.

A sudden call of alarm came from the young female high up the hill across the river. "Danger. Whitehead."

The eagle banked and began a circling glide down to them. They flew to perches on nearby dead willow snags and vented their hatred as the huge bird dropped to the top of the pile. "Filthy. Bad. Die."

The eagle began tearing at the moose remains.

She tucked in her breast feather and called to her mate. "I go."

He called back. "Where? Up mountain?"

"No. Follow bobbleheads. Follow she."

"She?"

"She-bobblehead."

"Crazy. Bobbleheads danger."

"She good."

"You, she got thing?"

They were on the dock, Gary sitting dangling his feet over the edge. Tara stood behind him, her hand on his shoulder. Starla wasn't with them. Susan waved.

Owen was in the stern, paddling, angling the canoe closer while she held her fishing rod, trailing a lure. "Good morning." Tara waved and turned back to Gary.

Owen's whisper came from behind her. "Susan? Is that you?"

She whispered back between her smiling teeth. "Quiet, Owen."

Tara shaded her eyes. "Susan? Is that you?"

"Tara. Well, this is a surprise."

Tara eagerly waved them in. "I can't believe it. Susan. Look, Gary, its Susan." Gary sent her a weak smile and a wave. Tara was bubbling with excitement. "This is so great. What brings you here?"

Susan reeled in her line as Owen steered to the dock. "Just out fishing. We're staying at the campground. Someone told me you had a place along here, but I had no idea..."

She was glad Tara cut her off. "Come on in and visit. You want a beer or something? Gary, sweets, could you go get the beer cooler." Susan noticed a look between Gary and Owen. Gary went to the cabin and Tara said. "Or maybe you want something else? Rum and coke? Rye and ginger?"

Owen brought the canoe to the dock and held on. "A beer sounds great."

She saw Tara's eyes go from his stomach to his balding head. "Oh. Tara McKay, this my friend, Owen Orser."

"Hi Owen."

"Nice to meet you."

"You look familiar. You a curler?"

"Yeah."

"I knew I'd seen you. I never forget a face." She laughed, clapped her hands. "Susan, I'm so glad you happened by. Come and see my place."

Owen said, "That's the best idea I've heard in a long time. My legs are gangrenous."

They got out of the canoe and Tara clamped her arm around Susan's. "Come. We'll have a little drink then I'll show you the place. I can hardly wait. It's not much right now, but as you can see, lakefront property. And there's no one on the south side." Tara chattered on while they walked up the path to a half circle of chairs in front of the cabin, obviously happy to have them drop in. Would Tara be like this if Starla wasn't okay? Where was Starla?

Tara motioned to the chairs. "Have a seat. Take in the view."

Gary came out of the cabin carrying a cooler. He set it down beside the fire pit.

Tara said, "Gary Haines, this is Susan Giller...oops, sorry, Susan Field."

She met Gary's gaze. "Gary and I have met."

He smiled. "Yup. Walmart."

Susan felt butterflies in her stomach. If she spoke now it would show.

Owen came to the rescue. "Where the elite meet. How's it goin', Gary?" He extended his hand.

Gary shook it. "Not too bad, Double O."

Tara was surprised. "You guys know each other? Where? When?"

Gary was flustered. "Uh, Yeah,..."

Owen turned to her. "Gary and I worked together on a...project. Years ago."

Tara wouldn't relent. "What project? Oh no, you aren't a drug dealer, are you?"

Owen smiled. "No. Much worse. I'm a lawyer."

Tara put her arm around Gary. Susan noticed she barely reached his shoulder. "Well, you'll be glad to know Gary's not part of that scene any more. He's been clean for three years."

Gary was smiling, impassive. "You folks want a beer?"

While Gary served the beer and they settled in their chairs, Tara continued to gush. "I can't get over this. I'm sitting here with Susan, my lawyer, at my lakeshore estate." She spread her hands palm up and gestured grandly then turned quickly to Susan. "Oh, I almost forgot. Thank you so much for buying Starla the puppet. That was so nice. She loves that silly tiger. She really likes you, you know. She might not say it, but she does, I can tell." Her joy was infectious. Susan had always found Tara intense and self absorbed. In the milieu of the custody battle she could be vicious. Nevertheless, she had to admit Tara was smart, energetic, and probably good at her job. But she hadn't liked her until now. It helped that Tara didn't have her usual hairdo and jewelry.

Tara patted Susan's knee and addressed Owen. "You've got yourself a keeper here."

Owen raised his eyebrows and shot Susan a mischievous grin then patted her other knee. "I'm the luckiest man alive. And you're pretty lucky yourself, Tara. This is a beautiful spot. How long have you had the place?"

Susan settled back in her chair as Tara told in minute detail how she had bought the land, how her boss, Shirley at Red Mountain Realty, had urged her to buy it when it came on the market. The seller was a woman who had moved back down south after her husband died and the price was a steal. Nevertheless, Tara had been terrified of that much debt, but Shirley had assured her it would appreciate rapidly in value, and it had. Similar properties were going for three times what she had paid. Obviously it was her favorite subject, and Owen—bless him—had been perceptive enough to notice.

Susan listened and nodded, making encouraging sounds at the right moments, but her mind was elsewhere. She occasionally glanced at Gary, trying to divine his feelings, but he only seemed bored and distracted, probably relieved he didn't have to engage in the conversation, nothing untoward in that. He had probably heard the story a thousand times. In fact, it all seemed so normal—a regular couple at the cabin entertaining guests. Maybe all her fears were blown out of proportion. She began to feel silly at having concocted this whole charade, and even sillier at having dragged Owen into it. She would let Tara finish and at the first opportunity make motions to leave. Too bad she hadn't seen Starla yet.

"And that's it. Now it's almost paid for, and as soon as that happens I'm gonna add on to the cabin, build a new dock, fix up the driveway, that sort of thing." Tara put her hand on Gary's arm. "I mean we are. Right Gary?"

"Yeah. Sure."

Susan saw her chance. She took a breath to speak but Owen interjected.

"So Gary, What have you been up to?"

"Working."

"Oh yeah? Where?"

"Back to Front Auto Parts. No big deal."

Tara jumped in. "Gary's working the counter now. They said he's the best they've had in ages."

Owen made an impressed face and raised his beer in salute. "Great. How long have you been there?"

"Couple of years."

It was time. Susan finished her beer. "Owen, I think we should go. We've imposed long enough and the fish are waiting. Thank you so much. It's been..." She stopped when she saw Starla appear out of the bush down by the lake.

Tara saw her too. "Hey Starla. Come and see who's here." She turned to Susan. "She's been gone most of the morning. I don't know where."

Starla took a step toward them then hesitated. "Just a minute." She went out onto the dock, lay down and splashed water on her face.

Tara laughed. "Playing with her new puppet, I guess."

Starla came up the path, brushing her hair back with one hand, holding the tiger puppet in the other, a sudden look of surprise brightening to something else when she recognized Susan. Was it hope, relief? As Starla came closer to stand beside her chair, Susan noticed red streaks around her eyes.

Tara said, "Starla honey. Isn't this great? Good thing you came back when you did. You almost missed them. They're just leaving."

A look of disappointment bordering on desperation crossed the girl's face. She grabbed Susan's arm. "No, you can't go."

Susan searched Starla's eyes. "Why not, Starla?"

"I...I have to show you something."

Susan was determined to stay, now. "I'd love that, Starla. What is it?"

Starla hesitated, thinking. "My fort."

Gary spoke up. "I don't think..."

But Tara interrupted. "I've got a great idea. Why don't you guys stay for lunch then I'll give you my official tour and Starla can give you hers."

Owen quickly agreed. "Brilliant plan. My legs are still complaining. Thank you, Tara. How could we refuse such a gracious invitation from such a refined hostess?"

Tara beamed. "Jeez Susan, maybe I was wrong. You're the lucky one."

"I don't think it's a good idea."

"Gary, you're being paranoid. There's nothing wrong with fraternizing—as you put it—with my lawyer. People socialize with their lawyers all the time. Look at Conrad Black."

Gary pulled two beers from the cooler. "Yeah, his lawyer blew the whistle on him."

"You goof." She opened a package of cold cuts. "Get the potato salad out of the cooler, will you?"

Gary put the beers on the counter and bent to open the cooler.

Starla picked up the cans. "I'll take these out to them."

Gary stopped her. "No. I'll do that. You get the potato salad." He moved between her and the door and took the beers from her. "Thanks, Starla."

When he left Tara said, "What's with him?" She opened a jar of mayonnaise. "I'll cut the bread, you spread this on."

As her mother sliced a loaf of bread, Starla watched Gary out the window. As soon as he gave them their drinks he headed back to the cabin without exchanging a word. She dipped a knife into the mayonnaise jar. "Mom, can they stay for supper, too?"

"I don't think Gary's gonna go for that."

Gary came through the door. "Go for what?"

"Starla wants them to stay for supper."

"No way."

Starla faced him. "Why not?"

He looked at her, unable to come up with a reason. After a pause he turned to Tara. "We don't have enough food. This stuff has to last two more days."

Tara laughed. "That is so lame, Gary." The bread was cut and the slices laid out. "If we get low we can always go to Jake's Corner for more."

"Yeah, chicken and fries."

Starla pressed her advantage. "I know. They could park their camper beside the cabin. We could pool our food with theirs."

A shocked look crossed his face. "That is not gonna happen."

Tara was placing turkey slices onto the bread. "I don't know what's got into you Gary. I think it might be a good idea. Now come here and cut these pickles really thin."

Starla wasn't going to let the subject go. This was her chance to be free of Gary. "I like Susan. And Owen's funny, isn't he, Mom?"

"He's very charming."

Starla was finished with the mayonnaise. "I'll get the lettuce." A great weight seemed to be lifting from her.

Gary moved to the counter and opened the pickle jar. "I don't feel comfortable around Owen. You know, it brings back all that shit from years ago."

Tara took him by the shoulders and turned him to face her. "Gary, sweetie. Everybody has a past. You've put yours behind you. I'm proud of you. You should be proud too." She kissed him and turned back to the food.

Starla began placing lettuce on the sandwiches. "So can I ask them, Mom?"

"We'll see, honey."

Gary, who seemed to be deep in thought, suddenly turned to Tara. "There's something else."

"What's that?"

"I don't think it's a good idea to tell them how much this place is worth."

"I didn't tell them. I just hinted. I don't know for sure myself." She topped each sandwich with a bread slice.

"That doesn't matter. If the government finds out what this place is worth, you could lose your legal aid."

That made her stop. "You think so? No. No way."

"Legal aid isn't for landowners, you know. You'd be disqualified."

Starla didn't like where this was going. "Yeah, but Susan wouldn't tell. She's really nice."

Gary kept his focus on Tara. "Maybe she wouldn't, but what about Owen? He's a government lawyer now."

Tara stopped and looked out the window to where Susan and Owen sat talking. "Jesus Christ. I never even thought of that."

"Do you realize how much a lawyer costs? They charge about two hundred an hour."

"Holy shit."

"And they charge you even for a phone call. As soon as they pick up you're on the clock."

"But they already know I own the place. What can I do?"

"You can play down the value for one thing. And you've got to get them to leave as soon as possible."

"I don't wanna be rude."

"You don't have to. Just cool it a bit. They'll get the message."

Starla watched her mother's worried expression and felt hope fade.

Gary looked at her with sad eyes and shrugged. "Sorry, Starla, but this is important."

It sounded like the buzz of an insect at first, except for its unchanging pitch. The bear's nose twitched as a slow air current moving upstream brought a hint of burnt sweetness mixed with a pungent salty odor, the same as he had smelled back at the dead caribou before the thunder and the pain. He raised his head and cocked his ears.

"Swing wide around the sweeper."

"I can see it, Steve. I'm not blind."

"Jeez, Rob, you sound just like Brenda. The thing is, we don't have a spare prop...anymore."

"Fuck off. That wasn't my fault. You were supposed to be looking for rocks."

They had found him. They were coming upstream, hunting him. He wanted to run, but the pain, the weakness, the dizziness. Lie motionless, hope they would not sense him. He put his head on the grass where he could see down river through an opening in the willows. His breath came in sharp gasps. Would they hear it?

The insect hum got suddenly loud, bouncing off the wall of spruce on the other side of the river. They had rounded the bend. It was not a hum anymore, but a steady, throbbing buzz.

"Check out the sandbar."

"Yeah, looks like a meadow in behind there. Be nice to see something. Two years without a moose."

"If we don't get one this year, I'm giving up. I'll take up quilting."

"Ha ha ha ha ha. Not me. I'm gonna buy a satellite dish and make my own wine."

Their sounds—like gulls but more complex. This close they were gull and raven and wolf and flies and crackling brush all at once. These creatures made a lot of noise. They must be afraid of nothing—powerful, dangerous. His heart thudded, each pulse sending a throb of pain into his head until the ache in his belly was almost forgotten.

He could see them clearly now, the giant insect-fish huge and red, growling and buzzing, swimming upstream, followed by a thin blue cloud. The tall creatures riding it were as he remembered—frail, easy to crush. Their thunder must be what made them so strong, so fearless.

"You wanna pull in here and have a look?"

"Naw, let's keep going."

Their calls stopped for a long time as the giant struggling insect-fish swung over to the deep water, made a wide arc and headed away from his spot in the willows. They had not sensed him, but still he kept his head down. Maybe they would keep going. His fear began to dissolve and the grinding ache in his gut returned. The sound of the insect-fish told him they would soon be directly downwind. How could they miss the odor oozing from the wound on his belly?

"Holy shit, Rob, did you fart?"

"No."

"You did so, you bastard. I told you not to eat those hot dogs."

"I thought that green stuff on them was some kinda guacamole dip."

"Ha ha ha ha ha."

Did the huffing yipping sound mean they had caught his scent? Would they turn and come back to kill him? Could he fight them in his weakened state? But the growling buzz kept retreating, growing fainter until it was a mere hum once more. And once more the world was filled with only pain and thirst.

The river looped in lazy arcs, the outside of each bend carved steep, sweepers angling out over the water, their roots undermined. The inside of the bends were wide sandbars with an edge of dense willow and alder at the high water line. Some clumps of willow out on the exposed bar trailed debris— dried grass and bark—from their bases. The mountains—clothed in reds, yellows and gray blues—sat back, serenely indifferent, slowly going by as the day passed. The air was crystal, sounds and scents sharply defined. The whole valley seemed to pulse with life.

The sun beat on the side of her face and her bare arms. "I like this." Hannah wished this could go on forever, but she knew she had to get back to the real world, whatever that would mean now. She glanced back at Dan, he smiled and she felt a surge of...what? Euphoria, infatuation, love? "Mind if I stop paddling?"

"No problem. We're just keeping it in the current, anyway."

She reached behind her and took the sleeping bag in its sack and propped it against the bow then turned around and sat down with her back against it. She regarded him, his deep-brown, wide-set eyes, prominent nose, wide-mouth with full lips.

He returned her gaze, a slight smile playing across his face. "When you said you wanted to stop paddling, you weren't kidding. Looks like you're ensconced for the long term."

"Tell me a story."

"What? Now I'm supposed to do all the paddling and entertain you?"

"Yup. You're the guide, I'm the client." She wriggled her shoulders deeper into the pack. "This is a test run for your new business."

"Ha. My new business. Me—CEO, chairman, cook, paddler, and showman." He switched sides, pulled a long smooth stroke and switched back. "Okay, what kinda story?"

She sat forward. "Anything...how about your father."

"Lotsa stories about Dad. Let me think. Funny or sad?"

"Funny."

He thought for a while. "I could tell you about the time he ran for the Communist Party in a federal election."

"Okay."

"Hmmm. Trouble is that's pretty much the whole story. Except for the big argument he had with the party. They refused to endorse him, but he ran anyway."

"He lost?"

"How did you guess? Oh, I know. I'll tell you how he got his nickname."

She settled back into the bag. "What was it?"

"His name was John McKay, but everyone in Ross called him Morris. Dad was always going on about how Ross River needed community spirit. He said all the petty feuds and the drinking and the aimlessness could be cured. The town needed a common purpose. Get the young people involved, get people interested, passionate about something."

"Sounds reasonable."

"Sure. Aklavik...on the McKenzie Delta. Uh oh." He pulled hard and followed with a strong J-stroke. The end of a log slid by inches from the gunwale. "The priest there, Father Mouchet, started a cross country skiing program for the young folks. It did a lot for the town, didn't solve all their problems, but they sent skiers to the Olympics."

"Wow."

"Yeah. The Firth sisters caused a lot of people to look up Aklavik on the map."

"Amazing."

"I guess my Dad thought he could be another Father Mouchet. It started in November when I was about...I dunno...thirteen. Dad would come home every day and ask if there was something in the mail, a package. He wouldn't tell us what he was expecting, said it would be a surprise for everyone. Mom and I thought it was some kind of Christmas present. We secretly hoped it was a satellite dish, but Dad was against TV so we knew it couldn't be. Finally a notice arrives in the mail. We gotta go pick it up at the post office 'cause it's so big they can't deliver it. We went along to help. It's two skinny boxes about four feet long and another box maybe two feet square, heavy, home wrapping job, no company logo. I tried to imagine a satellite dish in those boxes, but in those days dishes were eight feet across. I got a quick look at the insurance slip before Dad covered it up. It said *sticks, bells, hats, tapes, instruction booklets.*" He was laughing as he finished. "Any idea what it was?"

"Sounds like some kind of game."

"Kind of. So for two weeks Dad was in the garage with the door closed every spare moment he had. Mom and I could hear him in there, stomping around, jingling bells, grunting and chanting. My friends used to come over and we'd listen at the door. Dad kept the music turned way down, so it was hard to make out, but it sounded weird...accordions, flutes, drums, that kinda thing. He'd come out of there sweating with a big smile on his face. I had never seen him so excited about anything. We begged him to tell us, but all he would say was *It's something for the whole town.* Any guesses now?"

Hannah was laughing. "I don't wanna guess."

"Okay. Every year there's a big Christmas party at the Rec Center. Dad brought his boxes along, plus a bunch of bags Mom and I carried that felt like clothing. Everybody was waiting for the big moment, so after dinner Dad gets up and announces he has a gift for the town. He opens the boxes and pulls out all the stuff—bells on straps that you tie on your legs, decorated sticks, weird little green hats with strips of cloth hanging off them, and jackets covered with the same kind of cloth strips. He'd made those himself."

Hannah sat forward. "I've got it. Morris Dancing."

"Right. You know about Morris Dancing?"

"A school friend of mine told me about it. Her uncle was into it. Some sort of Celtic ritual dance, I think."

"Yeah. Apparently it started in Britain, but it spread all over the world—Australia, the States, South Africa—Morris Dancing societies. They have meets and competitions. So anyway, after he explained all this, Dad put on the costume with the bells on his legs. Some people started to laugh, but Dad kept his cool. He popped the tape into the sound system and started jumping around and shouting like a lunatic. By now everybody was laughing their guts out. I could see he was getting angry, but he kept on and got a few people to come up on the stage to learn it. Well, you can imagine this made them laugh even more. Poor Dad. His face was beet red. He finally lost it. He said they weren't trying. Told them he was shocked and disappointed, that they were all small-minded fools who couldn't see past their own insignificant little lives. He took off his costume and threw it on the floor and stormed out. When the door slammed behind him the whole room broke out into a huge laugh. Mom gave me a look and we followed him out. We could hear the laughter all the way home. Mom tried to talk to him, but he wouldn't say a word, so a half hour later she and I went back to the party, and as we got close we could hear a fiddle and a couple of guitars cranking it out. But amidst the music we could hear bells jingling and sticks thumping the floor. When we walked in, everybody was dancing and shouting and trying to be the next one to put on the bells and the hats and grab a stick. It was the best Christmas party anyone could remember."

"Did you tell your dad?"

"Sure, but he said it was a mockery, they weren't taking it seriously, they were a bunch of ungrateful slobs. The next morning when I went outside, I saw that somebody had thrown the green hats on the roofs of houses. When Dad saw that he was livid. He went to all the houses and demanded his stuff back. They were happy to give him the hats and the jackets and the tape, but nobody seemed to know where the bells and sticks had got to. For a few years, whenever there was a dance in Ross, out came the bells and sticks."

"Did he take them back then?"

"No. He never went to another town gathering, never got involved again. He was bitter, I guess, and what made it worse were the constant reminders he had to suffer because the bells and sticks became collector's items. You can still see them around town. My friend Arty has one of the bells on his skidoo." He laughed. "But it didn't turn out all bad. Not long after that he bought a TV and a satellite dish."

"So, his nickname was Morris."

"Yup, but never to his face. He knew it though."

"Did he ever forgive them?"

"It took years. I remember one time, just after Starla was born, Dad and I went out fishing. He was retired by then. He talked about the whole episode, and by the time he was through I thought he was gonna fall outta the boat he was laughing so hard."

"To be able to laugh at yourself is a great thing. For some people it's a hard lesson to learn."

"It was for him. How about you?"

"I'm learning. By the end of this, after I've been eviscerated by the press, I expect I'll have my PhD." They glided along in silence for a while. She heard a faint hum in the distance. "What's that...a plane?"

"Sounds like an outboard motor."

She got up and turned to sit on the seat, looking downriver. "Shit."

When the boat rounded the bend Dan put his binoculars up. "Two guys in a red freighter canoe. Moose hunters I guess."

He handed the binoculars to Hannah. The one in the bow was looking back at them through his binoculars.

His voice came clearly across the water. "A white chick and a guy. Looks like he's Indian."

"I guess she likes red meat." Their laughter came ringing over the water, the river channel funneling their sound like a giant megaphone. She realized they were talking over their motor, unaware they could be heard.

Hannah looked back at Dan. He was smiling. "Bozos."

As the boat approached, the man in the bow waved. Hannah waved back half-heartedly. When they were abreast of the canoe, the man driving cut the engine.

"Hi, how's it goin'?"

Dan put his paddle across the gunwales. "Fine. Beautiful day."

The two men paddled over to them and held onto the canoe. The one in the bow looked at the antler sticking out of the load and smiled at Dan. "See you've got a moose."

"Yup, we were lucky."

"Little guy."

"Yup."

"My name's Steve. This is Rob."

Rob waved a hand, looking back and forth between Dan and Hannah.

Dan said, "I'm Dan McKay and this is…"

Hannah cut him off. "Sarah…" She struggled to remember the name she had used before. "…Hoffmann."

Steve said to Dan, "Where you from?"

"Ross"

"Did you come all the way down from Mac Pass?"

"Yeah."

"Must be some good moose country up there. Did you see lots?"

Dan laid his paddle on top of the load. "A few."

Hannah was close to the man in the stern. He was studying her unabashedly, a puzzled look on his face. "You look familiar. You from Whitehorse?"

"No, I'm from…Switzerland."

"Funny. I'm sure I've seen you before."

"You must be mistaking me for someone else. I'm in the film business. Dan is taking me down the river. I'm scouting locations."

"And hunting moose?"

"That's what the movie's about." This was beginning to get out of hand. Pretending to be a deaf mute would have been better.

Rob gave her a probing look. "A movie about moose hunting? When is it coming out?"

Hannah smiled back. "In the film business it's always hard to know. We can't start until next summer."

Steve, who was beside Dan, turned back. "Hey. Maybe my nephew can get a job with you guys. He got a part in the last one they shot up here. Had a scene with Robin Williams."

She turned to Rob. "That's probably where you saw me. I worked on that shoot." She looked at Dan with a plea.

Dan pointed downstream. "There's a submerged log coming up."

Rob turned and scanned the current nervously. "I don't see it."

"It's under water. There's the riffle. See that churning? It's a big one."

"I still don't…"

Steve interjected. "Start the motor, Rob. We're losing ground drifting back, anyway."

To Hannah's relief, Rob reached for the starter cord. Dan shoved off and made a long powerful stroke, sending the canoe away and downstream. "Good luck." Then under his breath, "I hope you sink."

Steve called over his shoulder. "The mighty moose awaits us."

Dan called back. "Yup. Be nice to have all that red meat."

As the motor roared to life Steve's voice came clearly over the water. "Did you see that little moose he got? I'm gonna kill his grandaddy."

Rob said, "Where have I seen her before?"

"There she is again."

It was Starla. That was clear even from this distance out in the lake. The red jacket crossed an opening in the trees then disappeared, moving in the direction of the next clearing along the shore where another cabin nestled against a hill of brilliant yellow aspen.

Owen stopped paddling. "Quite the switcheroo."

"What do you mean?"

"Tara, after lunch."

"You noticed it too?"

"Noticed? I was expecting the grand tour accompanied by a marching band. Instead it was down the path to the dock. *And there's your canoe.*" He started to paddle again.

"You see? There is something going on. Gary got to her. Maybe he threatened her."

"You can't jump to conclusions. She might have had other reasons."

"Like what?"

"Who knows? I don't think Tara is the kind to take threats, or abuse."

"It's not Tara I'm worried about." She turned around to look at him. "What do you think?"

"Of Starla? I see a beautiful, intelligent, shy kid. There's lots of them."

"Starla isn't shy. Remember, she's the kid who stood up in court to confront the judge. No, it's not shyness. She looked scared to me. She'd been crying. I think she wanted to tell me something but was afraid. I'm sure of it."

"Keep saying it and you'll convince yourself. She just wanted to show you her fort."

"She didn't want us to leave. You saw her pleading with Tara."

"She was just disappointed there was no time."

"Owen, she wanted us to take her out for a ride in the canoe. It was obvious she was trying to keep us there."

"I'll grant you that."

"She was desperate to have us stay."

"No, she was bored. She's a kid hanging out with her parents."

"One parent."

"Okay, but all the more reason to want fresh faces, even if they are old and not so fresh—like ours...I mean mine."

She turned forward again and watched the reflection of the far shore dance on the water. "I don't know...I just...don't know."

"You've done all you can possibly do."

"Maybe."

"For sure. There's no way we can turn up again by accident like we did today. You want a beer? I'm gonna have one."

"Sure."

Owen reached into the bag at his feet. His hand closed on something soft and fuzzy. "What's this?" He pulled out the tiger puppet. "How did this get here?"

Susan turned around. "What? Oh, that's Starla's—the one I bought for her."

"Did you put it here? In this bag?"

"Of course not. Why would I?"

"To give us an excuse to go back."

"Owen, I'm not that devious." She held out her paddle, blade up, and Owen put the puppet on it. She pulled back the paddle and took the puppet in her hands. "Starla put it there. She's the one giving us an excuse to go back."

"Well, we can't go back now. We'll have to do it tomorrow."

"I'm worried. Tomorrow might be too late."

"You worry too much." He put an extra push in his stroke—a signal he wasn't going to change his mind—and after a time she put down the puppet and took up her paddle. He said, "We'll go back tomorrow. We can pick up my sunglasses while we're at it."

She turned to look at him again. "What?"

"I left them on the window ledge."

The smell was there again, wafted by a steady gentle flow of air and the boat's motion downstream. He raised his nose off the canvas tarp where he lay on top of the load and opened his nostrils wide. It was stronger this time, the stench of decay. But now there was bear smell, plus a new layer of scent with a prickly feel—a disturbing hint of fear and pain. His Dan could not smell it. Humans could be numb to the most obvious things.

His Dan's voice came from behind. "Whaddaya smell, Raz?"

He wagged his tail, reassured when His Dan spoke his name, put his head back down and dozed, listening to the two humans chatter.

The bear lifted his head and trained his ears upstream. The thundermakers were coming back. He could hear their calls getting closer.

"Let's stop up ahead on that sandbar."

"Sure. I could use a cup of tea and something to eat."

"How about a pepperoni?"

"No. I will not give in. It's the principle of the thing. I draw the line at pepperoni."

He peered through the branches and watched through mucous encrusted eyes as a large green object floated towards him. The giant insect-fish again, silent this time.

"We'll pull in on the downstream end. The bottom's softer there."

"Okay."

The thundermakers weren't trying to keep silent. Did they know he lay there, helpless? They glided around the curve of the bar. Then the big insect-fish turned and sidled up to the shore. A black and white animal stood up and jumped onto the sand. A wolf. It was small, but wolves could be treacherous. The little wolf trotted across his field of view, nose to the ground, along the edge of the bar, away from him, but downwind. If it kept going in that direction it would get his scent. His limbs trembled as he gathered his feet under him.

Raz trotted along the water's edge, following the curve of the bar upstream. Where the stones met the trees there was a strong, musky scent. He sniffed at the well-used trail, a tunnel through the underbrush where the beavers had dragged willow and aspen into the river. His Dan and the new mate were at the canoe, pushing back the tarps and pulling out the food box. That meant they would be here for a while. There would be time to explore. Maybe he would surprise a beaver away from the safety of the water. He hopped up the short bank, stopped to inhale the aroma of damp sand and trampled grass, listened for movement in the brush ahead then lifted his leg to mark the spot.

Dan put the food box on the stones near the edge of the trees. "I'll make some bannock and we can heat up the leftovers from last night. How's that sound?"

"Great." She put the pot of water beside the box and stood up to face him. His arms went around her and they embraced, each caressing the other's back. She looked into his eyes. "Back in Vancouver if anyone had told me..." She shook her head.

"What?"

"You know." She almost said, *that I would fall in love* but she stopped herself. "That I would get it on with a hunter."

He broke away and began to gather some driftwood sticks from the bar. "You didn't count on one thing."

"What's that?"

"It's rutting season."

She walked to the edge of the bar where a small spruce yielded a handful of dry twigs for kindling. "Is it that simple?"

"Yup. We're all helpless pawns in the great carnival of love."

He had said love. Of course he was just kidding around, wasn't he? What would happen when they reached Pelly Crossing? Would they go their separate ways as if nothing had happened? Did it matter so much if they did? Dan didn't seem worried about it.

She crunched her twigs into a tight bundle and chose a spot for the fire. "What's to become of us, Dan?"

"We'll get old and then we'll die...if we're lucky."

"Stop it. You know what I mean."

"Oh, you mean *us*-us." He knelt beside her and dropped his armload of driftwood. "Let's play it by ear." He handed her his lighter.

"I wish I could, but I don't think I'm made that way" She put lighter to kindling. The bundle of twigs caught.

"I know. And I'm made too much that way. I should try to be more responsible." He looked up and down the bar. "I've got it. We'll stay right here, build a cabin, raise a litter of kids, and live on chopped liver and pepperoni. I can see by your expression you're excited."

She began putting small sticks on the fire. "First let's have a cup of tea."

Jessica ducked to the left as she pushed willow branches aside, grateful the weather was holding fine and clear. The nights were cold, but if these bushes were wet it would be a miserable trip back over Mount Riddell.

Ahead, her father was edging Jasper over to the side of the game trail to let David pass. He let the following packhorse by as well and waved her ahead when she came up then nudged his horse in behind. Jasper switched his tail, pinned his ears back and snaked out his neck at Sax, the next packhorse in line. Jessica was somewhat surprised. Jim liked to be up front. "You think David's okay in the lead?"

"Oh yeah, he's getting good at this. I think he enjoys it. Anyhow, Killer knows the way back."

She watched David lean into the hill, helping the horse by shifting his weight. He let go of the horn and pushed back willows with both hands. "He's getting the hang of it, for sure."

"I can't understand what happened to him. He's convinced she's alive. I think he must be in denial. Isn't that one of those stages of grief?"

She thought of mentioning David's dream, but guessed he wouldn't want her to talk about it with Jim. "I don't know."

"Jess?"

"Yeah?" Her father didn't speak for some time. She turned to look back at him.

"I've made a decision. As soon as we get home I'm gonna tell Helga it's over, whether Suzy wants me back or not."

She wanted to whoop for joy. "That's...good."

"Is that all you have to say?"

"What do you want me to say—I told you so?"

"Don't I deserve it?"

She ducked under a branch and looked back. "No, Dad." She almost said, *You're only human. We all make mistakes.* but decided it would sound trite. "What about Helga? How's she gonna take it?"

"I didn't think you'd care."

"You know how I feel about her, Dad, but I can't help imagining what it would be like for her."

"It's not gonna be easy. But she's sensible. I'm sure she'll see it can't work in the long run."

"Yeah, I guess so. You know her better than I do." She wondered if that was true.

He heard a rustle in the moss and stopped to listen, searching the ground ahead for movement. A small gray-brown shape appeared at the edge of the trail, hesitated a moment then darted across the opening. He launched himself forward and pounced, punching both paws down where the vole had disappeared, but felt no struggling body beneath him. He looked ahead and to both sides but saw no movement. He had missed. The vole would be safely into a burrow by now. He sniffed again at the spot then walked further along the beaver trail, alert to any movement.

Suddenly he stopped as if he had run into a wall. It was the putrid smell again, very strong, very near. His nose went up and he filled his nostrils— the powerful fetid stench, bear smell, and that other frightening trace of fear and anger.

He tried to pinpoint the source, trotting back and forth, nose high. It was close and near to the edge of the bar, near to His Dan and the new mate. He spun and raced back along the beaver trail to the river.

The little black and white wolf was out of sight, but one of the thundermakers was coming closer, stopping, turning to make its strange calls to the other one, perhaps its mate.

"I think we'll build the cabin right over there. The tennis courts can go behind it and the meadow looks like it'll make a super polo field."

The other one made more of the high pitched yipping sounds. They had not sensed him yet, but if this one came much closer…A wave of nausea rolled through his gut, as much from fear as sickness. It was too late to run away. He had only one chance. He must take them by surprise. He waited, legs tensing beneath him, training all his senses on the approaching thundermaker.

"Jesus, what's that smell?"

Now. He launched himself out of the brush.

A deep huff of breath and the sound of snapping bushes made him turn in time to see the bear, head down, ears back, charging.

"Dan. Look out!" Hannah's voice came from down the bar. There was no time to run, barely time to plant his feet and grasp the axe in both hands before the mass of brown and blonde fur was upon him.

Everything seemed to move in slow motion as a giant paw smashed into his shoulder, knocking him down. He felt the back of his head strike the ground and saw the axe spin through the air and fall clattering onto the stones. The bear's head was above him. He stared into its maw and felt its breath on his face, the smell of decay washing over him. From the corner of his vision he saw a flash of black and white. As the mouth closed over his face and the teeth began to press into the sides of his head he lost consciousness.

Frail and weak, easy to crush even in his weakened condition, but he must kill this one quickly then deal with the other one before it could make the thunder. One bite and a shake and it would be dead. As his mouth surrounded its head he felt a stab of pain in his heel. He turned to see the little wolf, felt its teeth sink deeper into the tendon above the back of his foot. He let out a roar of pain and anger and spun to send a paw crashing down onto its back, but it was quick. He stood over the fallen thundermaker and watched the black and white wolf dodge and feint. He lunged at it again, but it moved out of range.

When he turned back to finish off the thundermaker, the little wolf moved in again. He spun, swatted and missed.

He must keep the bear off his Dan. He must draw it away, must make it chase him. He watched its head as he dodged. The turn of an ear, the glance of an eye toward his Dan sent him in to challenge the bear, ready to dash back out of range of the deadly paws. It was sick, slowed by illness. Why didn't his Dan get up from the ground? Together they could kill this bear or drive it away. Where was the new mate?

The dog worked the bear, dodging, moving in when the bear tried to turn back to Dan, jumping back when it spun to attack. Dan lay immobile on the stones. Was he dead? Hannah waved her arms and ran toward the bear. It saw her and made a bound in her direction, but Raz closed in to nip its backside and it turned to swing its paw at the dog.

What could she do? She looked to the canoe. The rifle lay on top of the load. She ran to it and pulled it from its case, darting glances at the battle on the gravel bar. What was it Dan had done with the gun? The bolt. She grabbed the rounded knob of the bolt and pulled up and back, the topmost bullet moving up into position with a click. She pushed the bolt forward. The bullet slid into the chamber.

Now what? She raised the gun. It was so heavy she could not hold it straight. She tried to look through the scope but could see nothing. "Oh, God." The bear was after Raz now, swatting like some giant cat trying to trap a darting mouse, moving toward the water's edge, away from Dan.

She ran across the bar and crouched by his head. "Dan, Dan?" There was no response. A trickle of blood oozed from a puncture above his temple.

Raz felt the water on his paws as he backed, darting side to side to avoid the bear's blows. Each time the bear lunged he moved out of the way, drawing it farther from his Dan. It wasn't difficult. The bear's reactions were slowed by sickness, the smell of it all over him.

The bear stopped and looked back, panting, tired. He moved in again and once more the bear pounced, but he easily jumped out of the way. The water was up to his hocks now. He must stay out of the deep water. He bounded, splashing through the shallows to get around it, but the bear cut him off, forcing him deeper. He tried to go the other way but the current was against him.

He had only one choice. He leapt out into the river and began to swim away from the bear, rolling his eyes back to see the bear make a lunge towards him. A huge paw crashed down on his back, forcing him under. The water closed over his nose. Everything was dim fuzzy light and swirling, bubbling chaos. Then the great head plunged into the water above him. He felt massive jaws clamp over his back and heard the crunch of his rib cage being crushed.

The bear's head came up out of the water with the dog clenched in its teeth. Raz twisted around to bite at the bear's nose. Two mighty shakes sent water flying in silver arcs off the dog's fur then the bear tossed the limp form out into the current. She could hear the bear panting as it stood in the water up to its belly, gazing at the half submerged body of the dog gliding downstream in lazy circles.

"Dan." She whispered, putting her ear to his face while keeping her eyes riveted on the bear. She could not tell if Dan was breathing. The bear turned to look at her and with a deep huff it turned and strode slowly out of the water, head down, blonde fur over its shoulders rippling with each pigeon toed step. It seemed not to notice her or Dan, confused, as if it had forgotten what it was doing. It sat, flopped onto its left haunch and half raised its head, panting in painful gasps. It seemed exhausted.

Maybe if she stayed absolutely still it would go off and leave them alone. It seemed to go on for hours—the bear with its head up, gulping air, she crouching by Dan's head, trying not to shake. Finally the bear's head came down and its gaze leveled on her. It heaved itself to its feet and came slowly towards her.

She heard her voice squeaking, as if from far away, singing, "Don't throw bouquets at me. Don't please my folks too much." That was all the words she could remember. "Laa, la, la, la , la ,la ,la. People will say were in…"

The bears ears went down, its head snaked out, and it broke into a trot. "Oh, God."

She stood on trembling legs and raised the gun, managing to position her eye to the scope. The image jumped and waved around. Between flashes of gravel, water and trees, only fleeting glimpses of fur. She got down on one knee, propping her elbow to steady her aim. It helped a little. When the bear's image flashed past it was only a dark mass of fur. Next time it passed through the scope she pressed the trigger. Nothing. She pressed harder—nothing.

"Oh God. What…?" She looked at the rifle, trying to see what was wrong. She tried to picture in her mind what Dan had done and suddenly remembered—the safety catch. But where was it? She tried a lever on the top behind the bolt. It clicked forward to reveal a small red spot.

She looked up. The bear was bounding now, coming directly at her. There was no time to find it in the scope. She pointed the rifle and pulled the trigger.

It sounded like a hundred voices shouting amidst the rush of a waterfall. For a moment he didn't know where he was, or even who he was. It seemed to last a split second and an eternity.

His eyes opened and the sound was replaced by the gentle soughing of wind and the swish of the river. Hannah's tear-streaked face was above him—an arc of spruce trees and an expanse of blue framing her head.

"What the hell?" He tried to rise but a wave of dizziness and nausea made him lie back down.

Hannah put her hand on his forehead. "Don't try to move. I gotta find out if you're all right. Can you feel anything?"

"I feel like I've been hit by a train."

"Try to move your legs. Easy now."

He bent his knees to bring his heels in closer to his body. "Yeah, they're okay."

"Good. Now your arms."

He lifted his hands and a stab of pain went through his left shoulder. "Ow. Ow." He slowly moved his right hand to massage the ache.

"Your left shoulder?"

"Yeah." Slowly the memory came back. "The bear." He tried to move his head to look around, but the ache in his jaw stopped him. "Ow. Shit. What happened? Where's the bear."

"Never mind that. Take some deep breaths."

He inhaled, filling his lungs and letting the air out several times. It cleared his head. "Help me sit up."

"No. Stay down for a bit. Keep breathing. Follow my finger." She passed her hand back and forth in front of his face." Her face was wet with tears, her eyes red.

"Ow. My jaw hurts."

"Just move your eyes."

"Okay."

"You might have a concussion."

"What's that smell?"

"It doesn't matter. Breath."

"I think I can get up." He rolled onto his right side and pushed himself slowly up until he rested on his hip.

She moved to support him. "Go easy, take it slowly."

"Yeah." He tried to rotate his left shoulder. "Oooh, man, that's sore. Nothing bro..." As he turned his head to look at her his eye's stopped at a heap of brown and blonde fur behind her. "...Holy shit." He tried to stand, but fell back down to a sitting position. "Wow. You shot him?"

She began to sob. "I had to. He was going to kill you...and me. He killed..." Her voice broke and she stopped.

"He had my whole head in his mouth. The smell of his breath was... Why didn't he kill me?"

"Raz..." she stopped again, wracked by sobs. "Raz bit him...made him chase...then they were in the water and...it was awful....Dan, Raz is dead."

He stared at her, not believing. "He killed Raz?"

She nodded, putting her arms around him and burying her face against his shoulder.

He tried to return her embrace but the pain in his left shoulder stopped him. He sat, staring past her at the dead bear, a huge mound of fur, nose buried in the sand, legs splayed out on each side, long curved claws glinting in the sun. A breeze ruffled the blonde fur over its shoulder hump. It looked peaceful. "Where's Raz?"

She was looking at him as if she didn't understand the question. "He's dead, Dan."

"I know. I mean where is he?"

"In the river. He floated away."

"Oh." It was all too confusing. "Poor Raz. Such a good dog."

"If not for him you'd be..."

"Help me up." He got his legs under him and with Hannah helping he rose unsteadily to his feet. A few deep breaths cleared the dizziness and with his right arm around her he walked toward the bear. "Holy shit. Look at the size of him." A powerful stench reached his nose. "And the smell."

"Do they all smell like that?"

"No." He noticed the wound on the bear's side, oozing reddish pus. "Look at that. He's been wounded."

"Is that where I shot him?"

"No, that's been there for awhile. There's where you hit him." He pointed to a small, bright red hole between the bear's eyes. "Nice shot."

"I just pointed the gun and pulled the trigger." She began crying again. "I had to. He would have killed you...and me. I had no choice." She let go of him and went down to her knees, reaching out to put a hand in the bear's fur. "I'm so sorry."

Dan put his hand on her shoulder. "Hannah, you did the right thing."

She looked up, her eyes red and streaming. "But I've killed a grizzly bear. Don't you see?"

"I see, but look at that hole in his side. Someone else did that. No wonder he attacked us. He was wounded, in pain, scared. This bear was suffering. You ended that for him. You put him out of his misery."

"But I killed him."

"You did him a favor." He knelt beside the bear's head and ran his hand over the thick, rich neck fur. "Biggest bear I've ever seen." His thumb brushed over the small red hole in the bear's skull. "Wow. Right between the eyes."

The old bull raised his head quickly, nostrils flared, ears trained on the hillside above the meadow. It was the grunt of another bull, deep. This was not the small bull who had followed them these past few days, gone now, disappeared after the thunderclap and the human voices. This was a big one, a rival for his cow.

He grunted in reply. "Wuh, wuh, wuh." He was answered by crashing brush and breaking trees. The rival was coming quickly, confidently, down the hill. It broke through the willows a hundred meters away and stopped. They faced each other and stood for a long time, each sizing up his opponent. The cow was interested. She gave a moan of appreciation for the new bull and he grunted in response. "Wuh, wuh, wuh, wuh." He turned broadside to show his full size, tipping his head to display his antlers, easily a match for the old bull's.

The old bull took three stiff-legged steps toward his rival. "Wuh, wuh, wuh."

The dead bear looked huge—out of place against the open expanse of sandbar—like a volcano erupting from a flat plain. "I should skin him now." Dan was sitting, still woozy, leaning back against the food box. He made no move to rise, putting it off a little longer. When he moved his shoulder the pain was fierce. It wouldn't be an easy job, and he didn't know if he had the stamina.

Hannah knelt on the stones opposite him over the fire. "What?"

"Before rigor mortis sets in—the bear and my shoulder."

"Why do you have to skin him?"

"What else can I do?"

"I don't know. I hadn't thought of it." She stared into the fire. "I guess I thought we'd just...leave it...him."

"Can't do that—let a skin like that go to waste. Plus, it's worth a lot of money."

Her face was a mask of tension. He could imagine the thoughts racing through her head. "Come and sit over here. Those stones must be hard on your knees."

"I don't want to have to look at him." She massaged her temples and squeezed her eyes shut. "Can't we just bury him and pretend it didn't happen?" Before he could respond she said, "No, no. I know we can't."

"You don't have to hide anything. Yes, Hannah Weinberg killed a grizzly. But she had no choice. It was survival. And she wouldn't have had to do it if some idiot hunter hadn't screwed up. The bear was suffering. It was an act of mercy."

"I know all that. You've said it a dozen times, but the media…Can you imagine what they'll do with this?"

"Oh yeah. Of course. It'll be a huge story, but you'll be the center of attention. Wasn't that why you came up here? You'll get to tell your story. And I gather you're good at it." She still had her head in her hands. He didn't think he had made a dent in her mood.

Suddenly she raised her head, sniffed, wiped the tears from her red-rimmed eyes and gave him a crooked smile. "Okay, you wanna do it now?"

The question took him aback. "Oh? Now? Okay…Sure…we could spread the sleeping bag—"

"Dan." She rose to her feet. "I meant skin the bear. I'll help you."

"Oh."

She was standing over him shaking her head like a chiding schoolteacher. "You're insatiable."

"Help me up." He struggled to his feet with her help and stood for a while holding onto her while looking out over the sandbar to the dead bear. "God, it looks like Ayer's Rock."

For the first time she looked out over the bar. "Can't we do it tomorrow? It's getting late. How much harder is it with rigor mortis?"

"It's harder, but there's two of us…and it'll be cold again tonight…Tell you what. We'll skin him tomorrow, but we'll roll him onto his back now. Then we should set up the camp."

She pulled him a little closer. "Do we have time to spread out the sleeping bag first?"

The two bulls were a few meters apart, heads down, deep grunts pulsing from their chests. It had taken two hours of posing, tilting their heads to display their antlers, the massive necks, two walls of muscle, bone and sinew. The old bull had been in this situation before, facing an equal opponent who was unwilling to back down. He took another step forward, bringing him close enough to feel the other bull's breath on his nose. If this one didn't back off now, he must fight for the right to his cow. The other bull lowered his head and their antlers touched. The vibration traveled down through his skull and his muscles clenched. He thrust forward violently, shaking his head, sending the clash of antler against antler echoing off the hillside.

The other moose responded, pushing and twisting to gain an advantage, but the old bull planted his feet. He knew if he lost his grip in the soft marsh ground, he would be in trouble. He held firm, waiting for any tiny release of pressure from the interloper. When it came he lunged again, pressing his advantage.

The other bull lost his purchase. Forced sideways, thick clumps of turf flying around him, he backed and twisted his head away, disengaging. They both stood panting, head-to-head. The old bull had won the first skirmish, but the game was not over yet. This opponent was younger and stronger with more endurance.

More grunting, more threats, and the two moose stepped closer again. Suddenly a strange noise interrupted them—a buzzing, growling sound. They each raised their heads, turning their ears to the river. The old bull glanced back at the cow. Her attention was focused there, too. Another sound—human voices—drifted over the meadow.

"Hey, Steve, looks like a meadow up ahead. Wanna check it out?"

"Sure. Be careful of those rocks there."

The buzzing sound reduced in pitch then finally stopped. The old bull noticed his cow's ears were now angled back. She was nervous, about to retreat into the spruce at the base of the hill. The voices came clearly to them now.

"Don't forget your gun this time, Rob."

"I won't. Help me pull the boat up."

The cow trotted off down the meadow, leaving the two bulls standing together. He looked after her a moment then followed. The other bull's footsteps drummed the ground behind him. The sound of voices came again.

"Holy shit, there's three of 'em."

Thunder boomed over the meadow and echoed off the hills as the old bull plunged into the trees.

The sun was going down. Starla had spent most of the afternoon in Brian and Anne's cabin. There were magazines to pass the time, but now the print was difficult to see. Supper would be ready and Tara would be worried if she stayed away after dark.

How her mood had lifted when Susan and Owen showed up. Tara had been ready to invite them to stay before Gary came up with all that bull crap about legal aid. He was probably just making it up, the jerk. So now it was back to avoiding him. It was easy to disappear, but no fun at all, and now even her puppet was gone. Maybe hiding it in Susan's canoe was a stupid idea.

She got up off the old couch near the window, went into the kitchen to the trap door, climbed down into the crawlspace and reached back up to slide the trap door into place. Out from under the deck, a few steps down the path to the trail home, and something made her stop. It wasn't a sound or a movement, just a feeling. Her senses strained to discern shape from dark lumps in a dark forest, small scratchings and rustlings, smells. Nothing. She spun and ran to the lake, to the trail home.

"You can have a shower if you want. The towels are in the cupboard." Steam poured out of the wok Owen was stirring over the camper's propane stove. "There's just enough time before this will be ready."

Susan sat on the bench seat at the table across the narrow aisle. The aroma of his cooking was delicious. Each time Owen lifted the mixture in the wok she caught glimpses of color—red, green and yellow. "A shower while camping—how decadent."

"I suppose by your standards this is play-camping."

"That's what Jim calls it."

"I've done my share of the real thing. I once went down the Big Salmon, you know."

"Hey, you don't have to justify it to me. He's the purist, not me. I'm all for showering. He didn't shower enough at home." She felt strange telling Owen something negative about Jim. It was something she was more likely to tell a woman friend, not a man, especially one who was interested in her. "A shower would be heaven."

"This shower is considerably smaller than heaven. But there should be lots of hot water. Do you want me to go outside?"

"Of course not. You're cooking. Just be a gentleman." She squeezed by him into the tiny space between the stove and the upper bunk. How strange was this, taking off her clothes with Owen a few feet away? He was studiously ignoring her. She took a towel from the cupboard to her right then turned and hung it on the outside of the shower door. As she stepped into the small compartment she glanced at Owen and caught him sneaking a peek.

The shower felt wonderful, but her thoughts were on Starla's tear-reddened face, the look of confusion and what, desperation? When she got out he was gone and the wok simmered gently over a low flame. That was nice of him to give her privacy to towel off. What about Owen? He was more intelligent, more perceptive than Jim. He had been smart enough to leave his sunglasses at Tara's cabin. He could read people—probably what made him such a good litigator. He was generous and funny, easy to talk to. But sex with Owen? Sex with anyone other than Jim?

She was dressed in clean clothes before Owen jiggled the door handle. "You all done?"

"All done."

"Good. Can I get you another gin and tonic?"

"I'd love it, but let me make the drinks and you serve up this fabulous meal." She grabbed the bottle from the shelf and opened the fridge.

"Deal."

When they sat down to eat he raised his glass. She did the same.

He said, "To us."

"To us."

"Starla, I was worried. So was Gary. Where the hell have you been?" Tara put glasses in front of each place setting on the table.

"Nowhere."

"What's that supposed to mean? You must have been somewhere."

"No. Just…in the bush."

"Jesus. You and your father, disappearing off into the bush without telling anybody where you're going." She went to the stove and lifted the lid on the dutch oven. "This is gonna be overcooked."

"Sorry, Mom." She opened the cooler, got out the juice jug and put it on the table. "What do you want to drink?"

"Beer. Get one out for Gary, too. He should be back soon. I hope so, anyways."

Starla got the beers. "Where did he go?"

"He went looking for you. Not many guys would go to all that trouble for a kid who's not theirs, you know. He's a sweet man and he likes you. I don't know why you can't warm up to him."

What was there to say, that she was afraid of Gary? Tara would get angry and tell her she was ungrateful, or laugh and say she was childish, or snort and tell her to get over it.

Tara sat at the table, opened her beer and poured half of it into her glass. "I think you owe Gary an apology."

There were footsteps on the deck, someone whistling a tune. The door opened. "Hi, girls." Gary was carrying a .22, which he unloaded and propped behind the door.

Tara stood and went to the stove. "Finally we can eat. I'm starved. Sit, you two." She brought the dutch oven to the table.

Gary sat. "Beautiful out there. Gonna be another clear night. It's so still you can hear the mice scuffling around in the moss. Hey, maybe we can sit out and look at the stars. Wow, that food smells incredible."

Tara was spooning stew onto the plates. "Man, you're in a good mood for someone who's been traipsing all over hell's half acre looking for Starla."

"I had a great time. Almost got a grouse. Had him all lined up, dead to rights, but when I pulled the trigger it went *click*." He laughed. "Forgot to load it." He laughed harder and patted Starla's shoulder. "I shoulda had you with me."

Tara finished dishing the stew and sat across from them. "Okay, dig in."

After one bite Gary said, "Tara, honey, this is the best stew I've ever eaten. Brilliant job, Hon."

Starla glanced at her mother and back to Gary. Why was he so happy?

Tara dipped her head. "Thanks, Sweetie. Starla, do you have something to say?"

Gary put down his spoon and looked at Starla. "What, Starls?"

Starls. Was he going to start calling her that, too? "Mom, do I...?"

"Yes."

She muttered into her bowl, "Sorry."

Gary put an arm around her. "For what?"

"For you having to go looking for me." She wanted to squirm away from his touch.

He removed his arm. "No problem. Really. I had a terrific walk. Went up the driveway to the road, down to the campground and back. Beautiful. We should drive down there some time and steal some government firewood." He laughed. "Just kidding." He gave Starla a nudge with his elbow. "Don't wanna corrupt a young mind."

"Good night, Owen. Thanks. You were wonderful today."

"I know. You don't have to say it so much."

"I do. I need to. You've done more than I could ever have expected. You've made this whole hare-brained scheme possible."

"Aw, shucks."

"You're a nice guy, Owen."

Owen lifted an eyebrow. "But not the guy for you?"

"I didn't say that." She slid into the narrow aisle and stood.

"Is it too soon, or..."

"I haven't slept with a man but Jim for 25 years. I don't know. It's all so confusing. You'd think sex would be simple at our age."

"It's never simple. It's always fraught with meaning. If it wasn't, I wonder if we'd have the wits to appreciate it."

"You're a constant surprise, Owen." She stepped to his side of the table and bent over to give him a hug. He reached his arms behind her and hugged back. They stayed that way for a while then she patted his neck. "Time for bed." As she drew back to stand up his hand slid down her arm and a gentle squeeze stopped her. He was looking into her eyes. She knew he wanted her to kiss him. She returned his gaze, torn between giving in and pulling back. Just as it started to become awkward, she felt his grip relax and release her.

"Owen, I..."

"It's okay. Goodnight.'

"Goodnight."

SEPT. 22

"Hello?" The side door stood open, no sound from inside. Susan hadn't thought of the possibility they wouldn't be there. Should she leave the puppet and a note? No, she had to talk to Starla. She turned to Owen who sat in the truck, shrugged, and raised her hands, palms up.

There were footsteps on the front deck and Tara's head appeared around the side of the building.

"Oh. Hi, Susan."

"Tara. Hi. I came to return Starla's puppet."

Tara craned her neck to look at the truck. Owen waved and she gave him a weak smile. "How did you get it?"

Susan walked along the wall to stand below her. "She must have dropped it in our canoe yesterday."

"That kid. She can be so out of it sometimes. Okay, I'll give it to her." She held out her hand to take the puppet.

Susan looked past her—no one else on the deck or down by the lake. "I was hoping I could give it to her myself. I'd like to talk to her."

"Why?"

She scrambled to think of a convincing reason. "Uh, I don't know. I like Starla. I had puppets when I was a kid...loved them...played with them constantly...call it a kindred spirit thing." If Owen would get out of the truck he could think of something more convincing.

Tara said, "I don't know where she is. She left this morning before we got up. But Gary's gone to look for her, so I'm not worried."

A spurt of adrenaline fluttered her stomach. "Oh?"

"Yeah. I don't know how long they'll be, so why don't you leave the puppet with me and I'll make sure she gets it. Thanks." She held out her hand again and waited.

Susan stood clutching the puppet as if it was a lifeline and looked down the path to the lake then back to the truck. Owen couldn't be seen behind reflections on the windshield. There was no choice but to hand over the puppet.

Tara took it from her. "Thanks, Susan. I guess I'll see you back in town. Safe trip." She walked to the front door and went inside.

Could she tell Tara about Gary? What if she was wrong? She walked back towards the truck. As she passed the open side door she stopped briefly and caught a glimpse of Tara sitting on the couch reading. What if Starla was in danger right now? At the truck she said, "Sorry, Owen. A few minutes more." and turned back to the open cabin door. If she was wrong, she could live with it. If she was right, could she live with it?

She walked to the door and strode inside. "Tara, I need to talk to you."

Tara looked up in surprise. "What about? The court case?"

"No, it's about Starla…and Gary."

Starla put the novel down and sighed. She couldn't concentrate on the story. It was a spy novel. Brian called them his weekend escape reading. The book had helped her pass most of the morning, but by the second time Jonah Slate was left for dead in the catacombs, she had lost interest.

The cabin was warm now, sun streaming through the window over the couch where she lay. It was probably close to lunchtime. Her mother would expect her back. She felt like getting up and doing something, but knew there was no more of the cabin to explore except for the bedrooms. Brian and Anne were good friends and she didn't want to invade their privacy. She stood up and walked over to their bedroom door. No, it wouldn't be right to go in. Besides, their room was probably just as boring as the living room. Natalie's room was down the hall. Natalie wouldn't mind. They were friends. And she'd be careful with her stuff. There would surely be something better to read.

She turned the knob and swung the door open. A poster over the bed showed a leering death's head, empty eye sockets and grinning teeth all in black and white, *Nemesis,* a Whitehorse band, spelled in stark gothic lettering. It made her slightly uneasy. Natalie's aroma filled the room—fresh, energetic.

A haphazard pile of magazines caught her eye. She sat on the bed and thumbed through the top few titles—*Thrasher, Vice, Bust, Nuvo.* The next one down was *National Geographic,* the cover an azure blue background of open ocean, shafts of sunlight striping an open mouth of saw-edged teeth, bottomless black eyes, *Great White Shark* emblazoned in red below.

When she slid the magazine from the pile she noticed a set of earphones protruding from under the bed. She pulled and out slid a portable CD player. On the other side of the bed was a stack of discs—metal, hip-hop, rock, soul, blues, and a '40s swing compilation. She found a Ben Harper album and opened the case—empty. It must be the one in the player. She pushed the play button and lay back on the bed.

"Why is everyone so down on Gary? You don't even know him. You have no right to come in here and accuse him of...of...Oh my god, you people are so...You...you're supposed to be my lawyer."

"Tara, listen. I know I've overstepped my bounds here, but it's Starla I'm concerned about."

"Do you think for a moment I wouldn't know if my own daughter was being...I...Get out. Get out of my house right now."

"In these cases often the parents are the last to find out."

"Shut up and leave."

"Tara, please, before I go let me tell you about one little girl, just one of the girls Gary abused in the past."

"No. I won't listen. Get out."

Susan ignored her and pressed on. She told her the story of Amanda Morris, the girl's tragic life, Gary's part in it and how her mother had been unaware. By the time she got to her phone call to Leslie Morris her voice was beginning to break and tears were stinging her eyes. "I'm sure you wouldn't want something like that to happen to Starla."

Tara stared back at her, eyes wide. "That doesn't prove anything. Gary isn't like that. I'm sure of it."

Susan took a deep breath, one final plea to make. She was glad Owen was still in the truck, unable to stop her. "Tara, I feel very strongly that Starla is in jeopardy. I promise you if I'm wrong about this I will report myself to the Law Society. Do you know what that means?"

"No."

"I will be disbarred. I won't be able to practice law again. I could even face criminal charges."

Tara was silent for a long time. Finally she said, "Okay, but what the hell can we do? I don't know where Starla went."

"I think I know. There's a cabin to the north of this one."

"Brian and Anne's."

"When we were going back to the campground yesterday I saw her heading in that direction. Remember she said something about a fort?"

"All right, we'll check it out. But if all this turns out to be a wild goose chase I don't want Gary or Starla to know anything about it. This is between you and me. And if it is true…Come on, let's go."

They went out the front door to the deck and Susan suddenly remembered Owen waiting in the truck. Tara was walking quickly down the path. There was no time to tell him where they were going.

This was more like it. Why hadn't she found the music sooner? The disc playing now was great. Impossible not to dance to the beat, and what this guy could do with his voice was amazing. He must be someone new. She'd have to remember his name—Al Green. Dancing, feeling free, she sang along. "Love and happiness. It'll make you do right and make you do wrong."

She half closed her eyes and spun around, "Love and hap…" She stopped. There, leaning against the doorjamb was Gary, a smile playing across his face. Where had he come from? How had he found her? Panic rose in her throat like a hand closing over her windpipe. She tore off the headphones.

He stepped into the room, a strange wild gleam in his eyes she had never seen before. "Looks like you're having fun."

"Umm." She was trembling so hard she could barely speak. "I…should go back home." She took a step toward the bedroom door but he moved to block her, filling the opening. She backed up until her legs hit the bed. She looked at the window and thought for an instant of jumping through, but knew that kind of thing only happened in the movies.

"What are you listening to?"

"I...don't know."

"Your Mom's pretty mad at you."

"Sorry. I lost track of the time. I'll go and..."

He didn't move from the door. "No rush. I won't tell her you broke in here. Your secret is safe with me."

"I didn't break in."

"That's debatable."

"Brian and Anne wouldn't mind."

"You don't know that."

"I do."

"Poking through their stuff? You sure? I know Tara would be furious." He laughed. What was so funny? Her heart began to pound. He looked her up and down and pushed himself off the doorjamb. "Sit down."

She could feel the heat in her face and the tears welling in her eyes. "I don't want to. I wanna go."

"Don't be afraid. I'm not gonna hurt you. I just want you to do something for me."

"What?"

"Sit down. I'll show you. It'll be fun. I promise."

Her legs felt weak. She sat on the bed and he came towards her, his hands moving to undo his belt. "It's easy. All you have to do is..."

She leapt up to run around him to the door, but he was quicker. His hands clamped around her upper arms, lifted her and plunked her back down on the edge of the bed. His strength was huge and terrifying, but his voice remained calm. "It's okay. I told you I won't hurt you. Relax."

"Let...me go.... Please." She was sobbing now, each breath a convulsion.

He stood in front of her and unzipped his pants. She had heard of erections, but had never seen one before. It was hideous, the bulbous end an angry purple-red. She closed her eyes and turned her head away. "No."

"It's all right. Touch it."

"No."

"If you do, I'll let you go."

"No. Gary, please." She looked up at his face but his eyes stared back with a glazed intensity she couldn't penetrate.

She tried to calm herself by taking three large breaths and blowing them out. It helped to steady her and her head began to clear. Fighting her revulsion, she reached out and placed her fingers on it then snatched her hand back. "There. Can I go now?"

"No way. That was nothing."

"But you said…"

"Give me your hand." He grabbed her wrist and pulled it towards him. She struggled against his grip but he was too strong. "Relax. It's not so bad. Just accept it and I won't tell your Mom anything."

As her hand was drawn closer she remembered something her mother had told her about men. She calmed her breathing as well as she could. "Okay. I'll do it. Let go of my hand."

"Promise?"

"Yes."

Her hand free, she steeled herself and reached under his crotch to his scrotum. His testicles felt like two slippery eggs in a wrinkled, hairy, sweaty bag.

He moaned, closed his eyes and put his head back. "Oh yeah. Start there. That's good. Good girl."

She clenched her teeth, took one of his testicles in her hand and squeezed as hard as she could. He flew back and curled up on the floor, both hands clutching his groin, writhing like a salted leech. She stood to run out the door but he rolled across the opening. She had to get out now. She had no idea how long it would take him to recover.

She ran towards him and the open door and jumped. As she sailed over him, his arm came up and knocked her shins. She tried to keep her feet under her but she fell out into the hall and landed hard on her side. Dazed, the wind knocked out of her, she tried to get up, but his hand closed on her ankle and she fell again, scrabbling at the carpet, feeling her fingernails tearing as she dragged herself down the hall.

He pulled her back. "You…little…bitch."

She rolled onto her back, and with her free foot drove her heel into his face. She felt a crunch. He howled and let go, blood gushing from his nose. She ran to the kitchen and jumped down through the trap door. As she crawled to the light she could hear him coming across the floor above then heard him grunting and cursing as he came down after her.

He was still well back under the house when she emerged from under the deck. She ran down the path and glanced over her shoulder. His .22 leaned against the deck. She ran back, but before she could reach the gun his head appeared.

She turned again and ran down the path to the trail home, heard his breathing and his feet pounding, gaining on her. Big slow Gary, suddenly so fast. She didn't dare look back. When she reached the trail home he was almost on top of her. She made as if to turn onto the trail then dodged the other way and plunged through the fireweed and roses into the thick trees.

She heard him curse.

"Fuck. You little fuckin' bitch."

Dodging branches and leaping deadfall, her small size now an advantage, she ran.

"Can you see anything?" Susan stood behind Tara, who had her face pressed to the front window, hands cupped beside her face to block the reflections.

"The trap door is open in the kitchen." She ran to the corner of the deck and reached around the side of the cabin wall under the eaves. She came back to the front door and inserted a key into the lock.

Susan followed her inside to stand over the trap door. She pointed down at a smear of red on the lip of the opening. "It's blood."

"Oh my God." She followed the trail of red splotches to the hall. "Oh shit. Oh shit." She ran down the hall to the open bedroom door and called. "Starla." She looked around helplessly. "She's not here."

"We have to stay calm. We have to think." Susan heard a sound—muted music. It was coming from the Discman on the floor. She picked it up and put the headphones to one ear. "It's still playing. They can't have left here too long ago."

Tara pushed past her, ran to the front door and called at the top of her lungs. "Starla, Starla!" She turned back to Susan. "Where is she, Susan?"

Susan could feel her own panic rising. She went out onto the deck and down the steps, searching the ground. A drop of blood glistened dark red on a dandelion leaf. "There's blood here." She walked down the path toward the lake, stooping to peer at the ground. "Another drop here. Looks like it heads down the path."

Tara came down the steps and reached to pick something off the ground. "Oh my God, no."

"What is it?"

Tara walked down the path and held open her hand. In it was a small piece of paper. "That son of a bitch."

"It's just a piece of paper."

"It's a flap. It's a fuckin' flap. Cocaine. See the way it's folded? That lying asshole." She threw the paper away. When she spoke her voice was high pitched and breaking. "But the only place they could go would be back along the trail to our place. We would have seen them." She looked in every direction, her hand to her forehead.

Susan walked down the path scanning the ground. No more blood. At the side trail she stopped. So many footprints made it impossible to tell if Starla or Gary had gone that way. Time was passing. On the other side of the path, freshly broken stalks of fireweed lead into the thick forest. "They went this way."

The slope up the ridge was steep. Each step sank deep into the moss. It was like one of those dreams—trying to run, but her feet didn't want to move. His breaths huffed behind her. She shot a look over her shoulder, a red splash of blood down his shirtfront. He was gaining on her. Her legs ached, her lungs burned, her pulse pounded in her ears. If she could get to the top of the ridge the moss would be thinner, the footing more secure. She might be able to dodge into the thick trees on the other side, change her direction, hide in some thicket, gain some time to catch her breath.

She grabbed a branch to pull herself up, heard it snap, and felt herself losing her balance, falling back. When she stopped herself, she could hear him right behind her. She dug her feet into the hill and pushed herself up. His hand landed in the middle of her back, forced her to the ground, pinned her face down deep into the moss. With his weight pressing on her back, she could only manage short sharp breaths. Her muscles ached, her head swam and her vision began to go white around the edges. The smell of his sweat filled her nose.

"Fuckin' little bitch. Now I'm gonna teach you a lesson."

He flipped her over onto her back. She was unable to fight, no strength left in her limbs. He was on top of her, his hand over her mouth and nose, pushing her down into the moss and tearing at her pants. She was suffocating, feeling consciousness slipping away, powerless to stop him as he forced her legs apart. When he rose on his knees to undo his pants she gulped air desperately, trying to fight off the dizziness. Her eyes opened and she saw the .22 lying beside her. Slowly she reached out her hand and slid the gun closer. He grabbed her above the hips and forced her body down toward his, clamping a hand over her mouth and nose again. Unable to breathe, her vision dimming, she wrapped her hand around the grip of the gun and raised it until it stood on its butt in the moss, muzzle up. All her muscles were limp except for her right hand. Her thoughts were strangely detached—a vague sensation of pain in her groin, a song playing in her head, *Love and happiness. It'll make you do right and make you do wrong...*

Concentrating all her remaining strength to her right arm she let the gun fall, able only to guide it down. When the muzzle passed his head she pressed her thumb to the trigger.

Crack.

The sound of the shot was like a smack across her face. She stopped short and looked back at Tara. Nothing needed to be said. They both took off at a dead run, ignoring the scratching branches. They jumped deadfall, smashed through thickets, Tara's frantic whimpers punctuating the crash of breaking brush. Ahead was a small creek bed, thick with alders. Susan pushed through the dense tangle of woven branches to the other side and stopped to catch her breath.

Tara came up beside her, a wild desperate look in her eyes. "I think it came from up there." She forged ahead up the ridge.

Susan could not muster the energy to keep up with her. She bent at the waist, hands on her knees, gulping air. When she straightened she scanned the side of the hill and saw a small patch of red. Could it be Starla's red jacket? Moving around some trees for a better view, she saw them, Gary on top, Starla's arm protruding from beneath him, neither of them moving. She called up to Tara who was almost at the top. "I see them. Over there. To your right."

She hurried along the bottom of the hill until she was directly beneath them and started struggling up through the deep moss, the sting of sweat in her eyes.

Tara was running across the hillside in enormous bounds pushing herself off trees. "You bastard. You fucking, filthy bastard! Get off her! Get off!" She reached them while Susan was well below, fighting her way up. "I'll kill you, you fucking asshole!" She grabbed Gary and with a strength that amazed Susan, heaved him off Starla. His body rolled and slid like a jelly filled bag to stop against a large pine trunk. Tara went down to her knees beside her daughter. "Starla. Oh God, Starla, are you all right, honey? Starla, please tell me you're all right."

As Susan passed Gary's inert form she knew he was dead—blank, staring eyes, a smear of red across his face, a small trickle of blood coming from his ear. His pants were around his knees. She turned away and climbed to where Tara was trying to revive Starla.

Tara was hugging her and crying. "No. No. No. Oh Susan, I don't think she's breathing. Oh Starla. Oh my darling."

Susan put a hand on Tara's shoulder and tried to pull her away, but the woman would not let go. "Tara, let me see. We have to check her breathing and pulse." Tara let her daughter back down onto the moss and Susan checked her pulse, it was there. "She's got a pulse."

She heard a branch snap, footsteps and heavy breathing. Owen was coming down the hill. Tara jumped up defensively.

"She needs air." Pushing Tara out of the way, Owen knelt beside the girl and put his ear to her nose. "She's breathing." He rolled her onto her side.

Susan was surprised to see him. "Owen...where...?"

He ignored her. "Starla. Starla? Can you hear me? Come on, Starla."

Finally the girl's body stirred and she took a gulp of air.

"Starla, Starla, can you hear me? It's Owen. Tara and Susan are here."

Her eyes flickered open and she groaned then coughed and began to take in big breaths.

Owen moved out of the way to let Tara in beside Starla. "Keep her on her side."

Susan looked at Owen. "Where were you?"

He was still trying to catch his breath. His dripping face almost glowed red. "Down by the lake…I thought…that's where you were…Then I heard the shot and…" He stopped speaking, face dirty, red, streaming sweat.

Starla was regaining consciousness. "Mom? What happened? I thought…"

Tara was weeping, trying to cover Starla, stopping for a brief horrified look and a tiny panicked yelp at the smear of blood between her daughter's legs. "Everything's okay, darling. You're gonna be fine. I'm here. Nobody can hurt you."

Susan stood back to let Tara attend to her daughter.

Owen sat on the hill, regarding Gary's dead body below them. He raised his eyes to meet hers. "So…You were right."

Starla's voice came from behind her. "I wanna go home now."

"Careful. Take your time." Susan turned and bent to take Starla's arm with one hand and support her with the other. Owen got up and came to her other side. Together they maneuvered her, still groggy, down the hill. Susan was relieved to see Owen block Starla's view of Gary's body as they passed, glad too that he partly blocked her view. But the grotesque lolling tongue and the pants still down around the ankles would haunt her for a long time. She focused on Starla. "We'll get you home and into bed. Don't worry. We're here. Your mother is here, too. Everything is all right now. I brought your tiger puppet back." How silly she sounded. Would everything really be all right for Starla after this? But she had to say something to fill the void, even if it was meaningless chatter.

Tara was behind them. Her voice was a low hiss. "You fucking creep."

Susan looked over her shoulder to see Tara, the .22 in her hands, standing over Gary's body. She thrust the barrel into his lower abdomen. There was a muffled thud and a sickening wave rippled over the dead man's flaccid belly. Tara tossed the gun aside and strode down the hill, fierce determination in her eyes. Her voice, in stark contrast, was controlled, almost calm as she gently took her daughter's arm from Susan. "I'll do that. Thank you, Susan."

"Pull straight back…That's it." Dan worked the knife in smooth arcs, cutting through the layer of connective tissue under the skin. He would leave some of the flesh and fat on the skin, to make the job go quicker, and easier to flesh later on. Anything to make it go quicker. The stench from the bear's stomach wound was beyond foul. He glanced at Hannah, who was grimacing and taking short sharp breaths. He wished he could use both hands. "Change your grip as I move along."

"Whooo. How long is it gonna take? The smell…"

"Hang in there. You're doing great."

He worked as far as he could down the side of the bear's body. "Okay, take a rest. We'll roll him onto his side now." They both stepped back upwind of the carcass.

Hannah wiped the hair from her forehead with the back of her hand. "What happens to the body after we skin him?"

"We'll leave it here. The scavengers will eat it. Lots of fat on him."

"Seems like a waste."

"Yeah, I know, but grizzly meat is pretty strong and tough. It takes a great chef to make it edible. Anyhow, we can't possibly take any meat. It'd sink us. Even the skin is gonna put us way down in the water." He looked downriver. "Could be dodgy in Granite Canyon."

"Oh yeah. Granite Canyon."

He could see she was concerned. "No sense worrying about that now. One thing at a time. Let's finish this."

They stared in silence at the bear for a while until she said, "Somebody must eat bear meat. I've heard of it."

"Some people eat black bear. I went to a wedding a few years ago and they served wild meat at the reception. Each dish was labeled—moose curry, sheep croquettes, roast of caribou, and so on. There was one dish labeled spruce forest ham, so anybody who was squeamish about eating wild meat went right for it, some of them raved about it. One guy said it reminded him of traditional Spanish jamon. Later on they found out it was black bear."

She was staring at the bear's partly skinned body again. "I can't believe there's anybody in the Yukon who's squeamish about eating wild animals."

"They're a small percentage. We keep them in fenced off areas behind razor wire."

She laughed. "What about you? Have you eaten grizzly bear?"

"Once. A guy gave me some. I stewed it a long time. I only ate a bit. Even Raz wouldn't eat the leftovers." His laugh stopped, his face fell, his mood sank instantly. Her face was filled with pity. "Oh...yeah." He turned from her to look out over the river.

She moved closer to put a hand on his shoulder. "You must feel terrible. I'm sorry. I don't know what to say."

"Nothing to say. Best dog I ever knew." He tried to stare hard at a stone, hold his breath so the tears wouldn't come. It was impossible. He wiped his eyes on his sleeve and sniffed. "C'mon, let's get busy." He went to the bear. "You take his back leg and pull. I'll do the front. On three."

With Dan able to use only one hand it was a struggle to roll the bear onto its side. A sickening gurgle came from the wound in its abdomen. He was glad it was on the underside for now. As soon as he let off on the leg the body started slumping back. "We're gonna need something to hold it."

"Want me to get some rope?"

"Nothing to tie it to."

"I could drive in a stake."

"Too much trouble. It's not gonna take long to do that side. We just have to hold the front leg here. Trouble is, I need two hands to skin. You do it."

"I can't."

"Sure you can. You saw me. Pull back on it 'til you see where the skin starts. It looks like a whole lot of fine threads, like silk. Cut through that. This is an easy part of the skin to do. Don't worry."

She took a breath in resignation, putting on a Yiddish accent. "All right already. Go on and on, you don't have to."

He handed her the knife, mimicking her accent. "Here knife is the."

She laughed as she took it and went to the opposite side. She took a wad of the pelt in her left hand and pulled. The muscles stood out on her arm. She was not a soft woman. He liked that. Distracted for a moment he suddenly became aware of the knife in her hand, about to cut a long slice through the skin. "Hold on. Stop. Careful."

"What? That's the way you did it."

"Angle the knife away from the skin, and watch where you're going with the blade. The angles are always changing. Can't have any cuts in the skin."

"Jesus, you said this was easy."

They talked and laughed as Hannah skinned off the side downwards to the back.

They didn't hear footsteps on the sand. The first thing they heard was the click of a camera just as Hannah was holding up the knife, laughing in mock threat to Dan. Her head snapped up and she jumped back in surprise. He let go of the leg and turned. The two men they had seen yesterday, Rob and Steve, stood there. Steve, mouth agape, couldn't take his eyes off the bear.

Rob, with a look of suppressed glee, studied the display on his camera. "Ha. Got it." He looked at Hannah then burst out laughing. "I got you. I got you. I finally figured out who you are. How's it goin', Hannah Weinberg?"

Hannah glared angrily back. "I don't know what you're talking about."

"What a picture. You gotta see this." Rob moved beside Dan and reached across the bear to Hannah. She held out her hand to take the camera but he snatched it back a few inches. "I'll hold it."

When she looked at the picture, Dan watched her face flush, saw the skin around her mouth tighten, a look of embarrassment and defeat on her face. Beaming, Rob shoved the camera in front of Dan, but didn't look away from Hannah.

The picture showed Hannah's gleeful expression, animated, full of joy, full of life. He couldn't help thinking it was a flattering picture of her, except one hand was full of bear skin while the other held the knife in blood smeared fingers.

He couldn't think what to say except, "Nice. Look good blown up."

Steve had said nothing. While Rob had been crowing, he had walked slowly around the bear and was now kneeling at its head. Steve whispered in awe. "Holy fuck." His hand touched the fur of the bear's neck reverently. "Look at that fur, how it shines." His eyes traveled down the carcass. "I didn't know they got this big."

Rob didn't seem to notice. He was too wrapped up in his joy at humiliating Hannah. He looked at the camera screen again then sharply up. "Hey, I just thought of something. The media. They'll go crazy for this. This baby's worth money." His mocking laughter, echoing off the riverbank, seemed to fill the valley.

Steve was inspecting the bullet hole in the bear's skull. "This where you hit him? Fuck me. Nice shot, man."

"Well, actually it wasn't me who…" He caught himself just before Hannah shot him a warning glance, but not before Rob noticed. The man's eyes grew large. "What's this? What's this? You mean you…" He pointed at Hannah. "Oh, man, this is too rich." He danced around holding the camera up to the sky. "Thank you, God. Thank you very much. This picture just quadrupled in value."

Dan wasn't sure what to say. He only wanted to shut the guy up. Instead he turned to Hannah and shrugged in apology, mouthing silently *I'm sorry.*

She didn't see it. Her rage exploded at Rob. "I killed it because some cretin like you wounded it. Otherwise it wouldn't have attacked us."

Steve's voice came from below them. "It attacked you?"

Hannah swung on him. "Yes it attacked us, numbskull. It injured Dan, it killed his dog, and it was going to kill me. It was in pain, suffering and terrified, you brainless fucking twit."

Steve shrank back from the onslaught. "Hey, take it easy." He went back to examining the head. "Fuck. Right between the eyes. You're one cool customer." Hannah snorted with derision. Steve rose to his feet and spoke to her. "Mind if I get my tape measure?"

She didn't answer, turning her withering glare back to Rob. Steve turned to Dan, the question still in the air.

Dan had no objection. He was curious himself. "Sure. Go ahead."

Rob, still dancing about, said, "Pardon me while I gloat." Again his laughter filled the valley.

Dan said, "If you don't believe us we can show you the stomach wound. It's on the other side. Hell, you can smell it."

"I believe you, but it doesn't matter, man. Once people see this picture they're not gonna care."

Hannah and Dan exchanged looks. They both knew he was right.

"I thought you went to call Helga." Jessica sat at the table in the small café in Ross River.

Jim sat across from her, his forearms on the table. "No answer. I left a message. I'll try after lunch."

"Can't have a conversation like that on an empty stomach."

"What? Oh, I see what you mean. No, I wouldn't attempt it over the phone. I just wanted to check in. I left a message for Suzy, too, so you don't have to call."

"Good." She noticed he was fiddling with the saltshaker. "You nervous, Dad?"

"Of course I'm nervous. You enjoying it?"

"No…well, maybe a little."

"You wait. You'll find out. My advice to you is celibacy." He surveyed the café. "Where's David?"

"He was talking to the guy behind the counter then he left. He's trying to find out if anyone knows who's on the Macmillan."

"Pretty thin rope to hold onto."

"Yeah, but…"

"What's he gonna do if he finds out someone is on the river?"

"Hire a chopper."

"He's nuts. If she did get rescued, all he has to do is wait in Pelly."

"He can't wait. Could you? What if it was Helga out there? Or should I say Mom? I don't know. Or what if Mom rescued Helga, or Helga rescued Mom, or what if…"

Jim shook his head. "You can't resist, can you?"

"Lighten up, Dad. I wish you luck. I really do. I wish I could help."

"You can help by ordering me a burger and fries."

A voice came from across the room. It was the man behind the counter. "S'cuse me, is your name Jim Giller?"

"That's me."

"I got a message for you to call Ron Hewitt."

"What? Is he here in Ross?"

"No, in Whitehorse. He called yesterday."

"Okay, thanks. Could we get two burgers over here?" He turned briefly to Jessica. "The works, Jess?" He called back. "Everything on it…with fries. Better make that three orders. Thanks." The man nodded and disappeared into the kitchen.

"Do you think David eats burgers and fries?"

"No, but after a trip in the bush, it's what everyone wants."

The old bull stood at the edge of the willows, panting hard to regain his breath. Torn up turf and broken trees surrounded him. Blood dripped off the bridge of his nose from a gash that stopped just short of his eye. There was an open wound on his flank. Bruising in the deeper tissue sent a stab of pain shooting down his side with each breath. Three deep grunts from his younger, stronger rival barely registered on his consciousness.

The battle was over.

"This guy, Artie, says he dropped off his friend Dan McKay at the South Macmillan on the thirteenth, the day before Hannah was reported missing. He says he thinks the timing works in Hannah's favor." David was turned in his seat, animated.

Jessica listened with feigned enthusiasm. "That's good news. What about others? Did he know if anyone else is on the river?"

"No, just his friend. He seemed quite sure of that. He drives up there a lot, works for Lyle Kessler trucking hunters and supplies back and forth. He says he'd know if anyone had gone up there to run the river. I also checked with the ferry operator. As far as he could remember there was nobody else."

Jessica tried to muster some optimism. "So are you still planning to rent a chopper?"

"You bet I am. I'd do it right now, but there aren't any here at the moment. Where's your dad? Are we leaving soon? I'm thinking if there's time I could get into the air today."

She didn't want to dampen his enthusiasm, but she had to be realistic. "I don't think we can be back to Whitehorse before dark. It'll have to wait until tomorrow. Sorry."

David looked out the window towards the café. "There's Jim."

Her father stepped into the sunlight. He approached slowly, aimlessly, ashen faced. He opened the truck door, climbed in and flopped down on the seat, heaved a big sigh and stared blankly through the windshield.

"What's wrong, Dad?"

"Helga had an accident. Thrown from her horse. She's in the hospital."

"Oh no. Is she badly hurt?"

"Spinal cord injury. They don't think she'll walk again. Too early to tell, but she might lose the use of her arms as well."

"Oh my god." Jessica suddenly felt guilty for all the nasty thoughts she'd had of Helga.

The surface of the river, always in motion—an upwelling here, a small whirlpool there, constantly shifting colors from silver black through gold yellow. Floating leaves of aspen were tiny, bright yellow sailboats curled to catch a swirl of breeze. Occasionally one would skid upstream on a gust, only to be trapped again by the inexorable flow. Time and water would give them to the river. Hannah looked up and down the valley then up to the mountains. They made her feel small, not the same kind of small as when she was struggling exhausted through the bush. Then it was terrifying—the immense uncaring mountains watching her pain, her fear, her despair—watching her die. But now, sitting here by the river, there was a strange comfort in the sensation. She had felt it before on trips into the BC interior and while out sailing. What did her problems matter? She was only a tiny speck in this huge valley in this immense wilderness on this planet in this infinite universe. It reminded her of what her mother used to say when Hannah came home from school full of indignation from some slight by a schoolmate or a teacher's unfair treatment. *A thousand years from now, will anyone remember it?*

But it was impossible to rid her mind of the photograph. She saw it in her mind on the front page of a newspaper. The caption read, *Hannah the Barbarian.* Even if people could accept her killing the bear in self-defense, they could never understand the image of her laughing over its dead body while she skinned it. Her friends in ARN could never forgive her, the larger animal rights movement would revile her, the hunters would make her a laughingstock, and the general public would be disgusted or contemptuous. Her paranoid fantasies even saw Jay Leno cracking jokes about her in his opening monologues. This was the end. If Grizzly Watch had been crippled by her disappearance, the picture of her with the bear would crush it flat along with her reputation.

She wished Dan would stop yakking with Steve over where the skin hung on a pole. All Steve could think about was the bear. He had helped finish skinning it. He had pestered her endlessly about the attack, down to the tiniest detail. She had finally escaped to come and sit by the river, but Dan had stayed with Steve. He had even helped him take his endless measurements, had listened while the man chattered about the Boone and Crockett record book, guns, calibers, bullet weights. She couldn't help feeling betrayed. Dan didn't even object when they announced they would be setting up camp fifty meters down the bar. She couldn't understand it. Maybe it was some kind of hunters' code. Maybe Dan didn't care that these assholes were going to destroy her. Maybe she had been wrong about him.

Finally, Steve was walking to his camp and Dan had started back to theirs. She stood and walked over the smooth cobbles. The spruce trees cast long stripes across the bar in the late afternoon sun. When she passed the skinned carcass of the bear she stopped. It lay belly up, legs spread, thick yellow fat layered over muscle and bone. Without its fur it looked vaguely human. Was it chance they had stopped at this particular sandbar, or was fate conspiring to bring all this upon her? With a twinge of guilt she realized she was still stewing over her own problems. She turned away to walk to their camp, but stopped when a familiar sound rang out—a short sharp rasping call. A raven circled down to land on the carcass. It looked up at her, its beak went down to its chest to tuck in a wayward feather.

"Hi there. So we meet again." As usual, the bobblehead's calls were soft and round, coming from inside its head.

She tried to imitate the last sound, forcing it back into her throat. "Awk – eh." She was happy. Once again this bobblehead had provided food. Delicious food. The biggest, fattest shitbear carcass she had ever seen. Succulent, energy-rich fat to fill her crop. Fat to last. Fat to store for the long cold season ahead. Fat for her and her mate and the young female and all the others who would come to feast. She gurgled a call to the bobblehead. "Fat. Good? Yes." She ripped off a chunk and swallowed it.

The bobblehead muttered back. "Well, I suppose you're happy. That's some consolation."

"Mmmm. Love."

"I envy you. Not a care in the world, flying around looking for carrion to eat. Well, maybe the carrion part wouldn't be so great. Anyhow, enjoy it. See you later." The bobblehead stopped chattering and walked away toward its firenest at the edge of the trees.

She tried to make the sound. "Glater."

The bobblehead stopped, turned back and called. "Did you say, *glater?*"

"I can't believe you let those two assholes camp here."

Dan settled gingerly onto the rolled up canvas, favoring his left shoulder. She suspected he was in more pain than he let on. He leaned back against the food box and sighed then flipped a stick into the fire. "We can't keep them from camping here…that is until we get title to our homestead. Of course, we'll have to start small. First we'll grow oats – lots and lots of oats. Then we'll work our way up to a mango plantation."

Why was he in such a good mood? How could he joke at a time like this? She sat beside him. "I thought you hated those guys. Think of what they're about to do to me. It's malicious."

"Rob's a prick. Steve's not so bad. He sure is impressed with the bear."

"You're telling me? I think he wants to make love to that skin." As if on cue, Steve came out of the spruce trees where his tent was pitched, hopped down the short bank onto the cobbled bar, strode past his fire and headed towards them. "Oh crap, he's coming over. Isn't it enough they have to…"

"Now, now, we gotta learn to be neighborly. We won't have any neighbors at first, but once the oat harvests improve, there'll be road and rail links, eventually hydro-projects. You know what would be nice? A movie theater and a Tim Horton's, right across the river over there."

"You're nuts."

"Nuts. That's a good idea. We'll plant a grove of brazil nuts."

Steve stopped to look at the bearskin once more. The camera hung from around his neck. He raised it and took another photo then with a short shake of his head he turned and walked to their fire. "I compiled all the measurements and scored the bear. He beats the Yukon record by a mile. And there's a very good chance he's the record interior grizzly, Alaska included. Either way, he'll be in Boone and Crocket for sure."

Dan said, "Great."

Hannah scoffed, "Boone and Crocket. The record book. The holy grail of trophy hunters. Who's got the biggest dick? It makes me want to vomit." Then a horrible realization struck her. "Wait a minute. No. You can't do it. Nobody can force me to have my name in that…I don't believe you guys. Haven't you done enough to hurt me? Why don't you just kill me and put my skin on the fucking wall?" Dan's hand touched her arm and she snatched it away. "And you, Dan. You seem to be amused by all this."

Dan said gently, "Not your name. His."

"What?"

"I offered the skin to Steve. Only if you agree. We can't take it in our boat. It'll sink us in Granite Canyon. He's gonna put his tag on it and say he shot it."

She stared at Steve while she tried to absorb it, her eyes narrowed in concentration.

Steve's expression changed from happiness to concern. "Listen, I had no idea Dan hasn't discussed this with you. After all, technically it is your bear. If you don't wanna give it up...that's unfortunate, but..." He looked at Dan. "If she doesn't the deal is off."

Hannah said, "What deal?"

Steve popped the memory cube out of the camera and offered it to her. She reached slowly towards it and he passed it into her hand.

She looked at it awhile. "Whoa. Hold on. This all a bit sudden. I don't understand." She turned to Steve. "You would claim you killed him?"

"Yes."

"Why? Doesn't it kind of miss the point of..."

He cut her off. "I know. If it was any other bear...but this one's record book."

"Right. Boone and Crocket trumps all. You guys are insane."

Steve studied her face eagerly. He looked worried. "Uh...there's just one small problem."

"Your friend? Rob?"

"Rob doesn't know about it yet. He might not like it at first, but I think I can handle him. No, the problem is it's slightly illegal."

"Slightly?"

"Yeah. Putting your tag on somebody else's animal is technically against the law, but it's one of those..."

Dan broke in. "It's illegal and the conservation officers take it very seriously. If you agree to this, there's no going back...no changing the story. We could all be charged."

Hannah looked at Dan. "You think I should do it?"

He shrugged. "It was my idea."

"You don't care that we'd be breaking the law?"

"In this case, I tend to favor the spirit of the law. The greater good."

Hannah looked at the small cube in her hand. "It's all so confusing. I don't know. What if I just brazen it out—face the music? It was self defense after all. Who would blame me?"

Dan said, "Steve, let her see it again."

Steve took the card from Hannah and in a moment there she was: one hand full of bear skin, the other holding a knife, her forearms splattered with blood and bits of tissue. But the worst was the expression on her face—laughing, joyful, high-spirited, happy. In love.

She looked at Dan. "Damn your incessant joking."

Steve removed the card from the camera again and put it into her hand. "Well?"

She stared at it a moment. "Deal." She rocked forward over the fire and dropped it into the coals.

The three of them watched it smoke ever more furiously until it burst into flames, the plastic curling, twisting, writhing like a dying demon. She raised her eyes to meet Steve's.

His big broad smile was back. "Thank you, Hannah. You have no idea what this means to me. It's like getting my name in the Bible."

She stared at the burning cube, still trying to sort it all out. "Jesus Christ."

He patted her shoulder. "That's okay, you can call me Steve."

The reception area of the Whitehorse hospital was quiet. Two receptionists sat ready at the wide, curved desk. Halfway down a spacious high-ceilinged foyer of potted plants and colorful artwork, a man stood reading a poster about liver disease. At the far end a big sign said *Emergency*. A few people sat apart in rows of chairs, reading, staring, waiting.

As they approached the desk Jessica kept a close eye on her father. Jim had always admitted hospitals bothered him. It was the smell mostly, some kind of disinfectant. Right now he looked pale and scared. He leaned against the counter and took a deep breath.

A woman with a kind face looked up from her computer screen. "Yes? Can I help you?"

"Yeah, I guess...um...I think..."

"Do you need emergency? It's right down..."

"No. I'm...I'm fine. I..." He took off his hat and ran a hand over his forehead.

Jessica nudged him aside. "We're here to see someone. Helga Schaeffer."

"Oh yes. She's in the surgery ward, but it's not visiting hours." She looked up at the clock—almost midnight. "Are you a relative?"

"No…Well, yes, kind of. My dad is a friend. A close friend."

Jim said, "That's okay. I don't want to cause any problems." He looked as if he wanted to bolt for the door.

The woman said, "Tell you what, I'll call the ward and see if you can go up."

"No. Really. I don't want to…" The woman was already on the phone. "Okay." He waited nervously.

The receptionist canted the phone away from her mouth and looked up. "Your name?"

"Jim. Jim Giller."

She went back to the phone. "Jim Giller…Uh huh…" He waited, staring at his grimy hands while she listened. He turned to Jessica and whispered, "Christ, I must look like a hillbilly."

The receptionist said, "Yes, I'll tell him." She hung up. "Ms. Schaeffer is asleep—sedated. Her physician, Doctor Chandrasekar, is not here, but she left instructions to tell you she would like to speak to you before you see Ms. Schaffer."

Jim nodded. "Sure, that's fine, good."

"The doctor will be in from ten until noon tomorrow."

"Thanks. Thank you very much. I'll come back tomorrow. Ten…give me time to…okay." He walked fast for the doors, fast enough he had to break his step before they opened. Jessica, trying to keep up, watched him exit into the night, stop, and lean on a pillar to breathe the cold night air.

She caught up to him and put a hand on his shoulder. "You okay, Dad?"

"Yeah. Sure. I'm fine…now."

"You sure?"

His eyes met hers with the expression of a frightened child. "No."

"Come on, Dad. Let's go."

They walked across the drive to the parking lot. Jim headed for the driver's side of his truck.

Jessica said, "I'll drive."

"No, I'm okay to drive." He got behind the wheel and closed the door.

Jessica got into the passenger seat, relieved to be going home after a long day of travel to unload the horses and gear. A few carrots pulled from the garden had been their only dinner while driving back to town and the hospital. A bath and bed would be heavenly. But Jim sat staring out the windshield, his hands gripping the wheel.

"Dad?"

He didn't look at her, just kept staring straight ahead. After a long silence he said, "What the hell is this, Jess? Punishment?"

She shifted to face him. "Don't be silly."

He rested his elbows on the wheel and put his head in his hands. "Four months ago my life was Suzy, you and Charlie, the horses, friends. I'd signed to work on the movie job. I was set to open a whole new niche for myself. Things were looking so good." He told her how it had happened. The German company had hired him and his horses for an adventure movie to be filmed in the Kusawa lake area. Helga was the assistant director. She loved the horses and spent all her free time with them. It started with short rides up into the hills. Helga couldn't get enough of his stories about horses, wildlife, clients. Then one beautiful, cloudless day they rode up to a waterfall Jim knew of and Helga brought a lunch. Jim paused. "I thought it was just an innocent little affair. In fact, that's what I said to Suzy when she found out." He punched the steering wheel. "What an idiot."

Jessica didn't know what to say. Her father had only himself to blame, but Helga's accident wasn't his fault. How could she not feel sorry for him, so lost and forlorn. "Let's go home, Dad."

Jim started the truck and turned in his seat to face her. "Come with me tomorrow."

"I dunno, Dad."

"Not to see Helga. To talk to the doctor. Please."

"Okay."

They drove out of the parking lot, down the hospital road to Lewes Boulevard and across the bridge. At the intersection to the South Access Jim stayed in the right hand lane.

"Where are you going, Dad?"

"A little detour."

"Where to?"

"The 202. Offsales."

She knew what that meant: a bottle of rye whiskey. "Dad. No."

SEPT. 23

Susan sat at the little table in the camper, still parked in the driveway beside Tara's cabin. She was exhausted and her hair felt greasy and matted. "God, I must look like a witch. What time is it?"

Owen closed the door, turned to face her and looked at his watch. "Three eighteen a.m. You should go to sleep."

"I don't know if I can."

"You want a drink?"

"Yes…No…I don't know what I want. Don't ask me to make any decisions. I can't think anymore."

Owen took two glasses and a bottle of scotch out of the cupboard. He poured two stiff ones and put them on the table as he sat across from her. "You want a shower?"

She imagined it, the hot water streaming over her, washing away the filth, the anger, the despair. It was an inviting thought but…"I don't have the energy." She took a long gulp of scotch and let the burning liquid slowly trickle down her throat. Numbness. "I feel like I should be doing something."

"There's nothing more to do."

He was right. Tara had left with Starla in the ambulance hours ago. The police had asked endless questions. Gary's body had been taken to Whitehorse and the area taped off. Now it was over she felt helpless, empty.

Owen took a sip from his glass. "You should go to bed. You'll be asleep in no time."

"You're probably right. Oh, Owen, I'm sorry. I'm being so selfish. You must be beat. You want to go to bed."

"It's okay. Take as long as you want. You've been through a lot."

"Me? What about Starla?" The thought of Starla made her want to cry. She fought the feeling, knowing if she gave in to it she would be unable to stop. "Do you think she's going to be all right?"

"That depends on a lot of things. She's going to need support…maybe counseling and therapy. But most of all she's going to need love, tons and tons of love. But let's not think about that now. Now you need sleep."

"You're right, as usual." Susan rose wearily and headed for the bed above the cab. She kicked off her shoes, took off her shirt and pants and left them on the floor. In her bra and panties she climbed into the bed, pulled the covers over her, and stared up at the ceiling. She felt her eyes begin to burn, her throat constrict. She rolled over to look at Owen as he folded down the table to make his bed. "Owen…"

Without looking up he answered. "I know. *Thank you, Owen.* For the last time, you don't have to say it." He turned to meet her tear-filled eyes.

"That's not it." Her voice breaking, her breath coming in gulps, she said. "Would you please sleep up here? I need someone to hold me."

They had risen early, had a quick breakfast of bannock and moose, keeping their voices low. An expectant hush hung over the valley. It was cold. Mist was heavy all around. While they loaded the canoe they had heard the argument start in the other tent, mostly loud and angry from Rob. It still raged.

"I think we're ready. You?" Dan gripped the gunwale of the canoe with his good hand to heave it off the sand.

Hannah, already sitting in the bow, picked up her paddle. "Is your shoulder going to be okay to paddle?"

"We'll know soon. It's feeling a bit better this morning."

"You think there's a chance we'll get to Pelly today?"

"I dunno. It'll be a long one if we do. Do you know where…?" He stopped before he said, *where Raz went?*

The voices got louder. Rob came out of the trees, bootlaces dragging, and pulled the tarp off their gear. He gave it a savage shake and it made a sharp crackle. A cloud of frost sprang up then rained back down to engulf him. Steve appeared behind him, saw Dan and Hannah and waved.

Hannah waved back. "I'd say Steve will be looking for a new hunting buddy."

"I don't think it matters much to him."

"I don't understand it. He didn't shoot the bear. Doesn't that kind of take the bloom off the rose?"

"Sure, but as you said, Boone and Crocket trumps all."

Steve jogged over to them. "Hey, you guys are getting an early start. I'm glad I didn't miss you. I wanted to say thanks again."

Dan waved a hand. "No need."

Steve spoke to Hannah. "Hannah, I know how you feel about hunting, but for what it's worth I gotta tell you how much I admire your courage. Standing up to that bear...To be honest, I'd be...I dunno. And then you go and hit him between the eyes. That's...classic."

"I keep telling you. It was a car crash. If I'd had a phone, I'd have dialed 911. Everything went into slow motion."

Steve's eyes narrowed in thought. "Everything went into slow motion. That's good. Maybe I'll use that in my story."

"Your story?"

"Yeah. How I got the bear. I gotta have a story or nobody will believe me. I've been thinking. You know, it's a shame you can't tell it."

Hannah shook her head and put up her palm "Believe me, I..."

Steve cut her off. "Wait. Listen to this. See what you think. Rob and I are coming down the river. We hear commotion up ahead—splashing, barking, yelling. As our boat rounds the bend I see a huge bear in the water. He's got a dog in his mouth. Two shakes and he tosses it aside, dead. As we get further around, we see a guy lying up on the bar, a woman trying to revive him. I don't know if he's dead or what. The bear turns and starts towards them, slowly at first. I shout, but he ignores me. Must be something wrong with him. Maybe he's wounded. I look back at Rob. His face is white as a sheet. I tell him to beach the boat. Even before it hits the sand I'm out and running, working a cartridge into the chamber. I get to them just as the bear breaks into a full out charge. There's no time to think..."

Dan broke in. "Suddenly a feeling of calm spread over me."

"That's good, that's good. Then everything seemed to go into slow motion. I took a deep breath."

Now Hannah interrupted. "Something I learned from Jagat, my yoga master at the ashram in Kathmandu."

Steve laughed. "I'll save that for the unabridged version. Anyway, whattaya think?"

Dan was laughing. "I believe it."

Steve said to Hannah. "See, this way you get to tell the part about the wounded bear attacking you. It's all the truth except for one small detail."

"You came to save the day. Mighty Mouse. There's only one problem." She pointed behind them. "Him."

Dan and Steve turned. Rob was headed their way carrying a big plastic box. He glared at them as he walked by. At his boat he tossed in the box. Angry ripples sprang from its waterline, charging out over the surface to be damped and swallowed by the current.

He stomped back to them. "You fuckers. You're not gonna get away with this. It's bullshit, not to mention it's illegal to put your tag on someone else's animal. You're gonna lose your fuckin' license, Steve. I'm gonna tell what really happened."

Steve was unaffected. "How do you know what really happened?" He turned to Hannah and Dan. "There's one bit of the story I left out…the part where Rob faints."

Rob was livid. "Nobody will believe that shit. You're gonna regret this, Steve. You had no right to trade that picture for the bear. That was my fuckin' picture."

Steve smiled. "How could that be? You left your camera in the truck at Pelly."

"So it was your camera. That doesn't matter. I took the goddamn picture."

"What picture?"

"Fucker." Rob spat the word at him. "You're all fuckers." It seemed to Dan as if the man wanted to say more, but could come up with nothing better. He wouldn't have been surprised if steam whistled out of Rob's ears and his hat rose to hover over his head.

Steve took a conciliatory tone. "Listen Rob. Maybe you didn't faint. Maybe you were right there backing me up. You saw that the bear, in its death throes, was still coming at us, still a danger. You saw me trying to reload, but my gun was jammed. So you stepped in beside the bear, inches from its flailing claws, and pumped the final shot, the insurance shot, right into his…"

"Fuck off, asshole." Rob spun around and stormed back to his campsite, tossing over his shoulder, "You better be ready to leave in ten minutes. We're gettin' off this fuckin' river today. Son of a bitch."

Steve called after him. "You could have your name in the record book, too—a joint kill."

Without turning, Rob gave him a savage finger in the air.

Steve turned back to Dan and Hannah. "I think he'll come around." Then he called back to Rob. "Hey, I'm gonna have breakfast first, so don't pack the food yet."

"It's a Bell Jet Ranger."

David had no idea what that meant, or if it mattered, but the jet part sounded good. He sat at a desk in the utilitarian clutter of the helicopter charter office. "How far can it go up the river?"

"You want to go up the Pelly then up the Macmillan?" The man across the desk stood and consulted a map tacked to the wall behind him. "We'll fly to Pelly, refuel and start up the river. We can get up as far as…" He traced a line across the map with his finger. "…well, we can get to Mac Pass…if the weather holds. We've got a fuel cache there, so we can return to Whitehorse, or zip back to Pelly."

"Great."

"Did Karen give you an estimate of the cost?"

"No."

The man looked slightly uncomfortable. "It's not going to be cheap. We're going to need a deposit before…"

"No problem. Whatever it takes."

The man gave him a questioning look. "Do you mind me asking why you want to fly up the Macmillan?"

David knew what the man's reaction would be. He knew he must sound deluded to these people, but he didn't care. He would prove them wrong.

He almost relished the question. "Don't mind at all. I'm looking for my wife, Hannah Weinberg." He smiled at the man's attempt to hide a surprised double take.

"The grizzly woman? She's your wife?"

"Yes."

David saw his mind working.

"Oh…I was sorry to hear about her. It must be very hard for you."

"Only until I find her."

"Yes…yes of course. Closure." His expression was politely mournful. "The thing is…I have to tell you it might be hard to spot a…I mean, what with the current and the sweepers…"

"No. She's alive. She's on the river, in a canoe. She's with a guy named Dan McKay."

The man brightened. "Oh. She's been found? Jeez. That's great. I guess I should read the paper some time."

Telling him any more would be a hindrance. David stood. "So when can we get started?"

Susan locked the door to the cabin and hung the key where Tara had shown her. She walked around to the front deck and turned her face to the sun, closing her eyes and letting its warmth wash over her, feeling better than she had expected to. What a change from her desolate mood the night before. Perhaps it was the weather, still holding bright and calm, although a high bank of clouds had appeared far to the south at mid-day. Maybe it meant a change was coming, bringing wind and cold, the first taste of winter. Let it come.

She heard Owen close the camper door then open the driver's door of his truck. He was ready to go back to Whitehorse with her following in Tara's car. She had a strange desire to linger awhile, maybe even stay another day, but they both had commitments in town—work, neglected files, court dates. The let down. It would all seem a bit meaningless after the last few days. Last night Owen had called it battle fatigue.

She hadn't intended to make love to Owen last night. When she asked him to sleep with her she had meant just that. Owen had been understanding, had held her close without any sexual hints. Just as the sun was coming up—the air cold but warm under the blankets—she had wakened and reached out a hand to touch him. Without a word they had rolled together. He was like no other man she had made love with. He talked to her almost the whole time. It was surprising…and nice. When she mentioned it to him later, he called it lawyer sex.

He was in the truck's cab when she walked down off the deck and around the vehicle to the driver's window. His hand came to rest on hers. "Ready to roll?"

"Yup." She sighed. "It's going to be weird getting back to normal life."

"I know exactly how you feel—stupid clients getting into knots about the height of their neighbor's fence. Kind of pales to insignificance."

"Owen, Owen, Owen." She leaned in the window, gave him a kiss and rested her palm on his cheek. "You're a wonder." Her eyes began to brim.

"We should be going. I'm gonna have to back this thing all the way out the drive, so bear with me." He started the engine just as a car appeared and stopped behind the truck. He studied the rearview mirror. "Great. Terrific timing." He shut off the engine. "What now?"

Susan recognized the man who got out of the car—Chief Superintendent Doug Innis, RCMP, Owen's long-time friend and curling partner. "Hello Doug."

Owen stuck his head out the window and looked back as Innis approached. "Doug. What are you doing here?"

Innis smiled as he joined Susan by the truck window. "Hi Suzy…Susan. Hi Owen. I have a few details to clean up here."

Owen said, "Wow, the division commander dirtying his hands with a field investigation?"

"Yeah, it's kind of unusual, but I saw your name in the report and I called you. No answer, so I figured you'd still be here. I wanted to get out of the office, anyway—beautiful day, beautiful lake. Too bad the real reason is so—" He studied the ground and shook his head. "—horrible. Anyway, I understand if it hadn't been for you, Susan, this whole mess might have turned out a lot worse."

"Not only me. Owen deserves as much credit as I do."

"He's quite a guy, isn't he?" Innis gave Owen a couple of light punches on the arm.

Owen feigned injury. "Ow. Police brutality. I want to speak to a lawyer." They all shared a laugh. "So Doug, do you need me to move the truck so you can get in here?"

"No, I just need a few minutes of your time. I wouldn't be here if it wasn't for young Findlay."

"Findlay?"

"Yeah, Cory Findlay, a new recruit, zealous young fellow, fancies himself a reincarnated Sherlock Holmes. I hear he has every episode of CSI on DVD." Innis chuckled then continued. "He wanted to come out here early this morning, but I put him on traffic patrol. Right now he's catching speeders at the Carcross Cut-off. Anyhow, he keeps harping on one thing: the two bullet holes in Gary Haines' body. We know all about the one in the lower abdomen. It's in your statements. The other bullet, though…The entry wound was hard to find—went right in Gary's ear canal. Killed him instantly."

Owen stared out the windshield, seemed about to say something then stopped. There was a brief silence.

Susan said, "Starla did that one. She told us she remembered turning the gun towards Gary's head and pulling the trigger while he…just before she passed out."

Innis didn't look away from Owen. "Yeah, I know. It's all in the report. But Findlay keeps saying with a point blank shot there should be powder residue, possibly burns on the ear. Plus, the gun at the scene was a single shot. So who reloaded it for the second one? It couldn't be the girl. She was unconscious."

Susan was confused. "I see. Well, obviously Tara did it. Before she fired the second shot."

"She says she doesn't remember loading it. Understandable. She was distraught."

"Distraught? Distraught doesn't come close." Susan suddenly realized where Innis was headed. "Doug, what are you trying to suggest?"

"Nothing. As I said, just some loose ends. If it wasn't for Findlay… sorry, but I have to ask you this, Susan. Do you own a .22?"

She almost laughed in his face. "No, and if you think my statement is any less than—"

Innis turned to Owen. "I know you have a .22, Owen. I've been grouse hunting with you." He turned back to Susan, "This guy can nail a grouse in the head at thirty paces. Comes from shooting gophers for the bounty when he was a kid. First shot has to kill it. Otherwise it gets down the burrow. If that happens, you can't cut off the tail. No tail, no bounty. Right, Owen?"

"No tail. The story of my life, Doug."

Innis laughed then said, "So...your .22?"

Owen gazed back into the policeman's eyes. There was a long pause. "I lost it."

Susan stared open-mouthed at Owen, slow realization sinking in. She caught sight of the target from the gravel pit lying on the truck seat, red vinyl showing through the punched-out bulls eye like a spot of blood.

Owen glanced at her then smiled up at Innis. "I must have left it at the gravel pit where we stopped to sight it in. That was two days ago. Remember, Suzy?"

She could only manage a weak nod.

Innis was leaning close to the open window. "Gravel pit?"

"Yeah, just this side of the boat ramp."

"Oh yeah, I know where it is."

"I was planning to pick it up on the way home. I hope nobody's stumbled onto it. My Dad gave me that gun."

The two men locked eyes for what seemed a very long time.

Innis broke the spell by tapping the door twice. "Okay then. I'm all through here." He started back to his car then turned with an afterthought. "If you find the gun, Owen, or even if you don't, give me a call...at home. You know my number."

"Sure thing, Doug."

Before Innis got into the car he stood by the open door and called back. "You guys have a safe trip. Drive slowly...especially at the Cut-off. Findlay's quite the eager beaver. Needs experience. I'm thinking of transferring him to Old Crow."

"What are you doing?"

"Turning the canoe around. Quick. We gotta get into the eddy." Hannah paddled furiously for the downstream end of the sharp bend they had just passed.

Dan tried to dig in his paddle, but a stab of pain in his shoulder made him ease off. "I can't paddle very hard. What's the matter? You have to pee?"

"No. Head over to that big root we just passed. Over there."

When the canoe entered the eddy the current reversed. They drifted upstream toward a tangle of partly submerged trees and she reached to hold onto a root sticking up above the surface.

She looked down into the water. "There."

In among the branches was a lump of black and white fur waving in the current. "Raz." His throat closed and tears begin to sting his eyes.

Hannah's eyes were brimming, too. "He's down fairly deep. How are we going to get him out of there?"

He stared at the dog's body for a while. "We're not. It's a good place."

"I'm afraid the damage to her spinal cord is permanent, but the good news is she can grip with her left hand and raise it a little bit. That's a promising sign. It means the nerve connections are there." Doctor Chandrasekar leaned slightly forward in her seat.

They sat in padded vinyl chairs in the hospital chapel. Jessica kept half her attention on her dad, who stared blankly across the softly lit room while the doctor continued.

"With time and therapy some of the damaged nerves can grow back. There have been some amazing cases of…"

What must be going through her father's mind right now? Self blame? Self pity? A lot of *what ifs*? Maybe it was simply numbness. What would she do? What would anyone do in his place? He had two choices: end it with Helga as he had planned, or face the rest of his life caring for her. He had to decide how big a saint he could be—or how big of an asshole.

Doctor Chandrasekar glanced at her watch as she finished "…go on to live a very productive, stimulating life." Her lips came together then parted slightly to show a perfect crescent of white teeth.

Jim's head came up to meet her smile. "Yeah. Sure.…Look what Stephen Hawking has done."

An image flashed though Jessica's mind—Helga in her wheelchair at the sunny window in the kitchen, her head lolling, saying, *Good morning, Jim,* in computer voice.

Chandrasekar raised her eyebrows in assent. "Well that's not exactly spinal cord…but it's a positive thought and that's very important, especially now in the early stages. She needs lots of support right now. I've taken her off all sedatives, but we'll keep a close watch on her mood."

"Yeah." He squeezed his eyes shut. "I told her not to…shit, it's all my fault."

"I know it's difficult, Mr. Giller. But think of how difficult it is for Helga."

"Yeah, of course."

"We must concentrate on what she needs, which is support and reassurance. Love. She's strong-willed and otherwise incredibly healthy. Her prospects are good." She glanced at her watch again. "It's not easy, though. She'll have rough spells, depression. She has to know there's a future, there's hope, a life beyond the injury. You are key to that."

"I know, and I'm willing to do anything to make sure there's…I mean, I could build wheelchair ramps on all the…" He trailed off to stare at the floor.

"That's the spirit." She stood. "I'm sorry but I have to go…other patients to see."

Jessica stood and put a hand on her dad's shoulder. "Thanks, Doctor Chandrasekar."

"And you must be anxious to see her. I don't mean to rush you if you need more time. You can stay here as long as you like. There's coffee and tea outside the door. Make an appointment at my office and we'll talk more."

Jim looked up as she headed for the door. "Thanks a lot. Thanks for everything."

Before she opened it, she turned back. "I have a feeling she's going to handle this very well. The times I've talked to her she's been amazingly strong and hopeful. She talks about you all the time, you know. I think she's going to be fine, and that's because she has a lot to live for." She smiled.

Jim gave her a weak smile. "Like I said, I'll give her all the …I admit I'm kinda…you know…knocked for a loop…but, thank you for saying it."

She opened the door. Before she left she turned back again, thoughtful. "You know, in a weird but wonderful way, her pregnancy is the best thing for her. She's determined to deliver those twins."

"Here we are. Right here."

She glanced at the spot on the map where Dan was pointing then looked out over the valley. They stood on a hill high above the river that looped its way down through a wide patchwork of green and yellow. Here and there a gash of silver reflected from the surface of a small lake. Wide crescents of gold showed where old river bends, long ago cut off from the main current, were being reclaimed by sedge meadow. Older ones, thick with willow, less distinct, were a mottled rusty green. Dark green spruce dominated, making the occasional stand of birch and aspen stand out stark, bright yellow. A slight wind in the leaves was a soft rustle. The mountains, red with dwarf birch, sounded their muted roar in the background.

Dan pointed behind them. "That's the Little Kalsas River coming in from the north. It comes down from Little Kalzas Lake." He moved his hand in a wide arc. "Good moose country here—valleys converging from the mountains, lots of lakes and meadows, lots of willow, lot's of water. In the spring all those big meadows fill with water. When the cows have their calves, it's their refuge from predators."

"It's gorgeous. Beyond words."

"You can see why people lived here." He was looking down below the high knoll where they now stood, down to where the remains of some cabins huddled, their roofs collapsed, submerging slowly into the moss and willows.

She looked down to the ground at their feet where the outlines of small cabins—miniature versions of the ones below—sank in similar decay. "And these are their spirit houses. What a beautiful spot to be buried."

"Yup."

"Could any of these graves be your ancestors?"

"Could be. My great grandmother was born here. My mother has all the information. It's her passion, places like this. She's trying to piece together the history—the people, their names—before it's all lost."

"What happened to them? Why are there no people here now?"

"Smallpox, residential school, the highway, alcohol, collapse of the fur market. Take your pick."

They stood in silent thought, looking out. A band of cloud cut a line across the horizon far to the south. Dan finally spoke. "We should get back on the river if you want to get to Pelly by dark."

"Let's stay here a bit longer."

Hannah searched the riverbanks ahead. "Let's stop down there where the sandbar ends."

Dan put down his paddle. "Sure thing. I could use a break."

"How's the shoulder?"

"Sore. You've been doing the paddling. I've mostly been steering."

They nosed the canoe up beside a short, steep bank where the back eddy had carved away the sand. Hannah got out and held the canoe for him. She noticed his wince of pain when he pushed himself out of the seat. She pulled the bow up then took the rope and looked for somewhere to fasten it. The sun, just past its zenith, beat warm on their bare arms, but the line of clouds had edged closer.

Dan took one step up onto the wide tan expanse. "Nice warm sand. If I didn't know better I'd think I was in Tahiti."

"Watch out for falling coconuts." She joined him and held up the end of the rope. "No place to tie it."

"It'll be okay for a few minutes. We'll keep an eye on it. If it floats away you can swim for it. I would, but my shoulder…" He trailed off with a shrug.

"Is this the start? I didn't think you were that kind of person."

"What kind?"

"A whiner." She faced him and moved close, put her arms around his waist. "Using an injury to shirk your duties."

"Any chance I get." His eyes left hers, squinting as he studied the sky. "Clouds are moving in. It won't be so cold tonight, but it might rain."

"Let's stay here."

"The Pelly River's around the next bend. There should be enough light to make it to Pelly Crossing."

"And what do we do when we get there? You. What 's the first thing you do when we get there?"

He pursed his lips. "Hmm. I call Artie. He drives from Ross and picks me up…if he's there."

"And if he's not?"

"I leave a message and wait. Could be a few days. He's driving steady for Lyle Kessler. If it's more than a day, I'd hang the meat at Reg Albert's place in Pelly. I'd stay there, too." He looked at her. "What about you? What's the first thing you do in Pelly?"

"Slit my wrists." She surveyed the sandbar and the edge of the trees. "No, I wanna stay here. I don't want to face it all yet. And now there's Steve's story to deal with. When the press hears that…it's all too bizarre." She thought for a moment. "But I guess the first thing I do is call David."

David. What would it be like going back to him? Would things change between them? They would have to. And what about Dan? Would she ever see him again? She wanted more time. She sighed and tightened her embrace. "My life is ludicrous. Here I am in your arms, *in flagrante delicto*, talking about calling my husband."

The sound began as a far off whine, growing, deepening as it approached. Their heads turned downstream. A *whap, whap, whap* sounded as the helicopter banked into view. An image of the opening credits to *Apocalypse Now* flashed through Hannah's mind.

David's sense of anticipation grew with every bend of the river. He was going to find Hannah today. The red canoe he had spotted downstream from the canyon had been short-lived excitement, dismissed almost immediately. Artie James had said a green canoe. The pilot had passed low anyway—two men.

Now he heard the pilot's voice in his headphones. "Macmillan River coming up."

The helicopter banked left, flying over a low island at the mouth, heading between two high hills at the valley's opening. It banked again to the right around the first bend and he saw it immediately, tucked in close at the bottom end of a wide sandbar. "There it is—a green canoe. And there's a person standing on the bar. Only one. There should be two."

The aircraft slowed its forward speed. The pilot peered ahead. "No, it's two people, they're just standing close together."

Now David could see them. The two people stepped apart but remained arm in arm, looking up at the helicopter. The distance was decreasing as the helicopter gradually lost altitude. Sudden recognition. "It's her. It's Hannah. I knew she was alive. Land here."

"Looks like a good spot." The pilot brought his machine to a halt, hovering above the two people.

David waved frantically, watching Hannah through the window in front of his feet. She shielded her eyes from the swirling sand and leaves, obviously unable to see him. The helicopter moved up the sandbar, descending in a maelstrom of blowing sand, settling with a barely perceptible bump.

The pilot, busy with his controls as he powered down, noticed David's hand on the door latch. "Wait until I tell you. You don't want your wife to witness your decapitation."

It seemed like an eternity. David looked past the pilot to Hannah. He waved but she still couldn't see him. He could barely contain his excitement. She would be so surprised, so happy. He had found her, against all the odds, despite the doubters. He felt relieved and joyful and vindicated. Hannah was going to be blown away. He pulled off his helmet.

The pilot said, "Okay, but stay low."

Hannah's first thought was *media*. Steve had arrived at Pelly and immediately contacted them with his story of saving Hannah Weinberg from a charging grizzly. God, these reporters were like hyenas. When David appeared around the nose of the chopper she was dumbfounded. Eyes wide, she whispered to herself, "David?"

Dan heard her. "That's David? Your husband?"

Had David seen them embracing? He rushed towards her, arms wide, a big exuberant smile. "Hannah. It's you. I knew you were okay. I knew it!" He scooped her up in a bear hug and spun her around, laughing the whole time. He set her back on her feet and looked her over. "How are you? Are you all right?"

"Uh...David....Yes, I'm all right. How...?"

"How did I find you?" He took a deep breath. "Oh boy, that's a long story." Still holding tight to Hannah, he looked at Dan. "And you must be Dan McKay." He broke away from Hannah and extended a hand.

"Right." Dan glanced at Hannah then back to David. "And you must be David."

"To the rescue." He beamed. "No. Not true. You're the one who deserves the credit. Thank you. Thank you for saving my girl." He put an arm around Hannah and pulled her close, smiling and searching her face.

Hannah disengaged from his arm, but kept a hand on his shoulder. "This is all too much, David. I don't understand."

"All will be revealed. But right now we've gotta get you outta here."

She looked toward the helicopter. The pilot had got out and now stood, hands in pockets, a polite distance from them. She turned back to David. "Right now?"

"Yeah. Right now." David called to the pilot, "How long will it take to get back to Whitehorse?"

"Couple of hours."

A moment ago she had been so relieved to be staying here with Dan one more day…one more night. She shook her head to clear it. "Whitehorse?"

David said, "Yeah, Whitehorse. You get to stay in a hotel room instead of…here. You must be dying for a bath."

"Huh? Oh…yeah…dying."

"So what the hell. Let's go." He started to lead her to the helicopter.

She put up her hands and stepped back. "Wait. I…" She looked apologetically, pleadingly, back at Dan. "I, uh…David, this is all too weird. I need some time to think."

"What's to think about? I don't get it. Don't you want to go?"

"I'm not sure." She watched his joyful mood begin to dissolve. Would he understand? Dan stood watching, his right hand supporting his left forearm. That was it—her excuse. "I can't go."

"Why not?"

"I have to help Dan get to Pelly. He has an injured shoulder. He can't do it by himself." Dan took a step toward them, about to say something, but she stopped him. "Dan, don't be a martyr. What about Granite Canyon? You said yourself I've been doing most of the paddling. David, we've got a boat full of moose meat."

He stared at her. "Moose meat?"

"Yes, we…Dan got a moose. That doesn't matter. What matters is the canoe's loaded to the gunwales and he can't do it alone." She watched David's expression as he studied Dan. Was there suspicion, hurt feelings, jealousy? "David, he saved my life."

David thought for a while then his eyes brightened. "I know. We'll load the moose meat in the helicopter, and drop it off at—"

The pilot's voice interrupted. "Can't do that. It's illegal to carry game meat in a helicopter. I'd lose my license."

"Oh....Well, what if we fly to Whitehorse then tomorrow morning we fly you back here."

"That's a ridiculous waste of money."

"I don't care."

"I do. Here's what we'll do: you fly back to Whitehorse, rent a car in the morning and drive to Pelly. I'll meet you there. Dan, how many hours are we from Pelly?"

"Three or four."

"Perfect." She looked at David, her mind made up.

"I guess so....Okay, sounds...good."

He was putting on a brave smile, his eyes switching from her to Dan and back.

"Thank you, David." She put a hand on his cheek. "Darling, I appreciate all the trouble you've gone to. I'm astounded. You're amazing. But I have to do this. I have no choice." She kissed him. "I know you understand."

He stared at the sky out the helicopter windshield, not caring to watch the vista passing below. *I know you understand* stuck in his mind. He understood. They had slept together. Was this the end of their marriage? He had slept with other women. How could he be outraged? Jealous? But it wasn't outrage or jealousy he felt most strongly. It was loss.

The pilot's voice came through his headphones. "Pelly Crossing. It shouldn't take long. I just gotta top up the tank. Jeez, what's all that?"

David looked down dully, uninterested. Parked haphazardly around the helicopter compound were cars, vans, people standing about, all looking up to watch the chopper descend. As he got closer he noticed logos on some of the vehicles: CBC, CKRW, Yukon News. He recognized the guy with the boom mike from his arrival at the airport a week ago. Christ, had it been only a week? This was not what he wanted now.

"Did you tell anyone what I'm doing out here?"

"No. Nobody...Well, only Martin, our mechanic. Of course he's married to Janet and she's good friends with Rick and Sharon, who..."

There were no stars, no northern lights. The moon was a pale smudge casting a gray glow over the sandbar. Dan slipped under the sleeping bag next to her. "The clouds have moved in, but I don't think it's gonna rain."

"Good."

She hadn't said much since David left. He wanted to reach out and put his arms around her, but it would feel awkward after David's arrival that afternoon. He shifted to face away, a more comfortable position for his shoulder, anyway.

She was silent for a long time. Maybe she had fallen asleep. He took a deep breath and let the gentle murmur of flowing water relax him. Then he heard her turn to him.

"Dan, I want to make love to you, but I can't. I feel like David's watching."

"I understand." He heard her move some more, felt the warmth from her body get closer.

"It wouldn't be fair. You understand, don't you?"

"Yeah, I understand. I feel the same."

"You're so…"

He felt her hand brush gently down his back. It sent a tingle straight to his groin. "I know. It's hard for you."

She moved close, pressing against him, her hand caressing his chest. He felt her breasts on his back, her hips on his buttocks. She kissed his neck. He rolled onto his back and she propped herself on her elbow, her face a shadow above him. He could feel her breath on his lips as she descended to kiss him. Her hand slid down over his abdomen.

Just before her mouth met his she said, "So understanding."

SEPT. 24

The canoe dipped and made two gentle porpoise bobs as it passed over a rock shelf into a large flat pool. High rock walls rose on both sides of the river. A stone spire stood in the center of the canyon like some giant obelisk left by an ancient civilization. A jumble of black wet rock surrounded its base. The sound of rapids pouring around both sides grew in volume as they approached.

Dan's voice came from behind her. "That's Needle Rock. We'll go to the right of it. Just paddle hard and I'll steer. I'll try to hit the waves dead on, but if we start to go off…hell, you'll know what to do."

"Okay." She stood for a moment to get a better look at the rapids—two large, peaked standing waves. She had run much rougher water than this, but only in an empty canoe. She looked back at Dan, who scanned the water ahead. "You worried?"

He gave her a tight-lipped smile. "Yeah."

"Don't worry."

"We should be okay with the first wave. It's that second one…if we take on any water, we're gonna have to get to shore and bail. I'll let you know."

The canoe drifted slowly in the slack water. Needle Rock loomed menacing above them. It seemed as if the pool had been placed there to heighten the tension, make the roar of the rapids louder, make the fear flow stronger.

"Let's get some speed up." She dug in her paddle and pulled hard, feeling the loaded canoe respond sluggishly, feeling it pick up speed over the lip of the rapids, a smooth descending curve. The smell of the water changed, a swirl of something alive. She paddled hard, knowing they would need as much forward momentum as she could muster. The first wave sent the bow up to hang for a moment, giving her a good look at the second wave. This would be fun in an empty canoe. The bow came down, plunging deep into the base of the second wave. For a moment she thought it would just keep going down. A fleeting image—the wave washing over her, filling the canoe behind her. When the bow reached its lowest point, she dug in her paddle. The bow lifted slowly, the wave rose to both gunwales, twin chutes of water pouring in as they passed along the length of the boat.

She heard Dan say, *Oh fuck*, but she couldn't look back. When the bow came down, she strained into her paddle, feeling as if she was trying to move a barge. Some smaller, steeper waves licked at the gunwales, a few of them splashing in. She shouted back to Dan, "How is it?"

"Keep paddling. It's okay. When we get through this chop, head for the left shore." His laugh was a relief. "Got some bailing to do. One more wave and…good thing we got a small moose. Paddle hard."

David stood at the edge of the high bank, with the river behind and below. A crowd of people, cameras and recorders formed a half circle around him. People watched from a scatter of houses nearby. Others lined the top of the bank, talking, laughing. Still others strolled by or hung at the periphery, listening, muttering comments behind their hands. It was an event for Pelly Crossing. The whole town was out.

"Mr. Hellman, how did you know your wife was safe?"

Yesterday he might have told the news people about his wolf messenger. The publicity might even help Chives. Now he would only feel silly. "I didn't know she was safe."

"But Artie James said…" The reporter consulted her notes. "…*He told me he knew she was alive. When he heard Dan was on the river he was sure Hannah was with him.* End quote. You knew exactly where to look."

Artie James, at the back of the group, shrugged apologetically.

David spread his hands. "Look, I thought I'd explained it. It was a last desperate hope, a stab in the dark. When we found her pack we knew she was heading for the river. Her only chance was to be picked up there. I had to look for her on the river. What else could I do?" He looked upstream, straining to see past the long curve of the bend while the reporters fired more questions.

A reporter asked, "Why did Hannah decide to stay on the river yesterday instead of flying out in the helicopter?"

Another one asked, "How will this affect Grizzly Watch?"

He spread his hands. "Hannah is a woman of principle. She felt obliged to help Dan, the man who saved her life. And he's an aboriginal hunter. She's helping him bring home his moose meat." That might be laying it on a bit thick, but this was about public relations. "Dan McKay has a badly injured shoulder, which I understand was the result of a bear attack…a bear who had been wounded by some careless hunter. If it weren't for the quick action of a passing marksman I likely would not have found Hannah alive. I still have a fellow named Steve to thank for that. As for Grizzly Watch, I think this only proves Hannah's point about the senseless slaughter of grizzly bears. I'm sure she'll have more to say on that subject."

A voice from the riverbank shouted, "I see them!"

Dan hung his binoculars over the handle of his paddle and extended it forward over the load. "Take a look. They're lining the bank."

Hannah took the glasses and put them to her eyes. "Looks like the circus is in town."

"And we're it."

She put down the binoculars. "How's my clown make-up?"

"Mom, this is unbelievable." Jessica's head came up from the paper.

Susan had told Jessica what had happened then showed her the paper. The short article mentioned no names, but she was outraged that it contained a quote from the *victim*. "Unbelievable. That reporter should be fired. Who the hell let her talk to Starla?"

She lifted a jug of milk from a grocery bag and put it into the open refrigerator. The anger felt good. Any strong emotion did. It must be part of the coming down process. Everyday things like groceries seemed surreal now, as if the last few days had been her whole life. Now she was plunked back down into some new absurd reality. The news of Helga's accident only reinforced the feeling.

"Well yeah, but I mean you, Mom. You're unbelievable. That little girl would be dead if it wasn't for you."

"I only did what any—"

"No way, Mom. Anybody else would have said it wasn't their problem. You should get some kind of bravery award."

"Don't be silly. Anyway, there's a publication ban on all the names. So you can't tell anyone what I've told you."

"Mom, this is Whitehorse. Tomorrow you'll be hearing it in the grocery store checkout line."

"Yes, and it'll be twisted all out of proportion."

"Still, you're amazing."

"Starla's the amazing one. After what happened to her, you'd think she'd be catatonic. But when Owen and I went to see her at the hospital she was watching TV and playing with her puppet. Gave us a big smile when we walked in. Talked about everything: the cabin, the rape, Gary, everything. She had already phoned Ross River. Left a message: *Tell Dad to come to Whitehorse and pick me up as soon as the moose is hung.* She's...but my God, she's a little girl."

Jessica put her index finger on the open newspaper. "It says before she passed out she killed the guy. Shot him in the head with his own gun. What kinda jam does that take? Incredible."

Susan turned away, making herself busy with the groceries. "It took a very steady hand."

They heard footsteps walk across the room above then the bathroom door close, the sound of the shower being turned on.

Jessica looked up as if trying to see through the ceiling. She gave her mother a questioning look.

Susan met her gaze, trying to present a neutral expression. "Owen stayed here last night."

"Oh." Jessica raised her eyebrows. "Oh?"

"I see you remember his old nickname."

"Huh?...Oh yeah, Double O." There was an awkward pause. "That's great, Mom." She went back to her paper.

Susan could have left it at that, but something in Jessica's tone and the little smirk on her lips was irritating. "What's great, Jess?"

"Um…Well, you know…You're seeing other people."

"And by that you mean sleeping with Owen. What makes you think we were sleeping together?"

"Your bedroom is above the kitchen."

"Oh. Well, so what? Are there two sets of rules, one for me and one for…?" She stopped, remembering Jessica's news of Helga's accident.

"No Mom, I mean it's great. Except—"

"Don't say it. I know what you're thinking." She lowered her voice. "Overweight, balding, Owen Orser—quite a step down from Jim. God, you young people can be so shallow. You have no idea what kind of man Owen is." She plunked a bag of apples onto the counter.

"That's not it at all, Mom. I like Owen a lot. I always have. It's just that Dad…Shit, I shouldn't tell you this."

"What?"

"When we were out there Dad said he's decided to end it with Helga. He wants you back."

"Oh." The cruel irony of Helga's accident sunk in. "Oh no. And now she won't ever walk again."

Jessica looked at her awhile, seeming to struggle for words. "There's more."

The landing was choked with people and vehicles. Photographers jostled with radio and print journalists for the first chance to record Hannah's arrival. A TV camera pointed up, taking footage of the crowd lining the bridge. As the canoe approached, some cheered, some shouted encouragement, a few made crude jokes—a carnival atmosphere. One young guy in a red ball cap leaned over the railing and shouted, "Hey grizzly woman, get your moose yet?" A laugh sprang from the crowd.

When the canoe glided under the bridge, Dan levered his paddle, turning broadside to the flow, heading for shore as it arced into the current. Hannah paddled hard, wiry muscles etched on her shoulders and arms. She wore a baggy t-shirt, one of his. Everyone on shore wore jackets. He spotted Artie at the front of the group, waving him in to where he stood. Without waiting for the boat to reach shore, Artie stepped into the water to grab the bow as the reporters crowded closer, shouting questions at Hannah. Artie pulled the boat onto the sand and walked in alongside of it up to his knees.

Dan smiled at his friend. "Hey man, you don't have to get your feet wet."

"I gotta talk to you alone. Before these fuckin' assholes start in on you."

Dan's brow furrowed. "About?"

"Come on." He stepped out of the water and waited at the shore. Hannah was standing in the bow while her husband David fended off the throng to give her room on the beach. When Dan finally sloshed to shore in his hip waders, the microphones were thrust forward. Artie pushed back against the crowd and took Dan's arm to lead him away.

Dan flinched. "Ow. Careful, Artie."

"Sorry man. Let's go up to the truck."

"What's going on?"

The reporters closed around them. "Mr. McKay, tell us about the bear attack."

"How badly are you hurt?"

"What sort of condition was Ms. Weinberg in when you found her."

Artie shoved them away. "I gotta talk to him. It's important. Five minutes." He took Dan's arm again and began leading him up the incline to where the truck was parked. When a couple of reporters started to follow, he turned on them angrily and pointed a menacing finger. "Fuck off."

Out of the corner of his eye Dan saw Hannah break away from the group by the shore and come towards them followed by the throng.

She rested a hand on Dan's upper arm. "Where are you going?"

"I'll be back in a minute." He turned and followed Artie to the truck.

"No, I was not happy when Steve killed the bear." What a stupid question, but she knew what the reporter was angling at and she wasn't about to fall for it. "I was happy to be alive, but I grieve for that bear. His death was a horrible tragedy—a needless act of cruelty. The bear was wounded, in pain, afraid and confused. Steve put him out of his misery." She didn't know how much to say about Steve's part, but assumed if the reporters already knew, they must have heard it from him.

"If you had had a gun, would you have shot the bear?"

If they only knew. "Would you?" Dan was approaching down the incline. He looked worried. "Excuse me, I have to talk to Dan."

David, who had been standing beside her, his arm around her shoulder, stepped forward. "Please, give Hannah some time and space. I'm sure you'll have ample opportunity for more questions, but now she needs to deal with personal matters. In the meantime I'll be happy to answer anything you would like to…"

Hannah broke away from the news people and met Dan out of their earshot. "What's the matter?"

"I have to get to Whitehorse right away. It's my daughter. Starla's been…she's in the hospital."

"Oh my God. What's wrong with her?"

"Tara's boyfriend…fucking bastard raped her."

"Oh no. That's…oh God, I'm so sorry." She hugged him, clutching him close. The reporters had all turned to watch her. Cameras rolled, photos were snapped. "Come with us. David has a car. Oh wait. What about the canoe, the moose?"

"Artie's gonna take it to Ross."

"Okay. We can leave as soon as—" She looked over at the reporters. "To hell with them. We can leave right now."

"…and I'm changing to my second name. Rose."

"Okay…Rose." Dan was astonished. She was handling the whole thing better than he was—better than anyone. He wiped the tears from his cheeks and stroked her forehead.

"I've never seen you cry before." She reached her hands around his neck and pulled herself up for a hug.

He held her in a long tight embrace, a pang of guilt at coming so close to losing her. He clutched her tight until his shoulder ached.

"When can I get outta here? I'm bored." She pushed away and flopped back down on the pillow. "I wanna go to Ross. I wanna see Gramma. I wanna help you cut up the moose. I wanna see Raz. All I do is lie here and wait. Take me with you today. Please."

Dan fought to keep his voice from breaking. "Soon enough, honey. Be patient." Was this the time to tell her about Raz? The door opened and two women walked in—a nurse and Dr. Chandrasekar.

The doctor gave him a kindly smile. "Sorry to barge in. I have to examine Starla."

Starla said, "It's not Starla anymore. It's Rose."

The doctor laughed. "Rose it is then. My goodness. I wish all my patients were as feisty as you." She turned to Dan. "I wonder if you could wait outside. It won't take long."

"Sure." He walked into the hall, feeling disoriented in its gleaming sterility, boots squeaking on the hard floor as he headed for the waiting room. He was about to push open the door when Tara came around the corner and stopped. They stared at each other for a long moment. There was defiance in her eyes, with tears welling behind it.

He held the door open. "The doctor's in there with her now. It'll be a few minutes." He motioned into the waiting room and she followed. He sat in one of the chairs and looked at her.

She remained standing, sniffed, wiped her eyes and took a deep breath. "I suppose you'll be going for sole custody now." When he didn't answer she continued. "I'll fight it. I don't give a shit what you say to the judge. Nobody's gonna take—"

"Give it a rest, Tara."

She glared at him, her lips pursed in a cold narrow line then looked away and broke into sobs. "I didn't know Gary was…he seemed so…the bastard…I wish I'd killed him." She collapsed into a chair and buried her face in her hands.

"Starla beat you to it. By the way, it's Rose now."

She tossed him a sneer, "Are you trying to be funny?"

"Yeah."

"That's why you'll never get custody. You're never fuckin' serious, Dan."

"Tara, let's not do this. It's the reason we're sitting here now."

"Then cut the sarcasm."

"Okay. I'm sorry. Look, it's time we got smart for a change. It's time we stopped fighting over her. I want what's best for her. If it means sole custody then that's what I want."

"She's gonna live with you in Ross? What are you gonna live on? You can't even get E.I."

"I'm gonna do whatever I have to. If I have to guide for Lyle, if I have to work in a bush camp, if I have to work in a sweatshop in China making

Barbie dolls, that's what I'll do." He paused. "But I draw the line at us getting back together."

"Likewise."

"Good. You see, we can agree on something. Tara, drop the court case shit. No more lawyers. No more judges. No more fighting. Here's what I wanna do. For now, I'll take Starla—Rose—home with me. That's what she wants. God knows what she'll need to get over this, but…we'll take it from there. Okay? I don't want to keep her from you. I've decided if there's no work in Ross I'm gonna move to Whitehorse, get a job and save some money…and I've quit smoking weed."

Tara rolled her eyes. "I'll believe it when I see it." She was silent for a long time, eyes blankly fixed on a poster of a cartoon condom with little arms and legs, big eyes, balloons of dialogue over its head. "I guess I have no choice."

"If that's the way you see it then yes, you have no choice." Dan thought he had made an impression, but Tara wouldn't meet his eyes, wouldn't speak. Maybe there was no way she could give in completely, but maybe her bulldog grip was beginning to relax.

He reached across the empty chair between them and gave her a brief pat on the shoulder. "The kid is incredible. Shoots him in the head as she's passing out. She's like you. Never stops fighting."

She snorted. "No, she's like you. Gotta have the last laugh." With a tired halfhearted smile, she rubbed her eyes. "You need a place to stay?"

"I'm staying at a hotel."

"How can you afford to…oh yeah, the grizzly woman."

"Yes, the grizzly woman. Hannah. And David, her husband. They're paying for the room."

She searched his face. "Mmm, how cozy. She good looking?"

It was hopeless trying to force a neutral expression when Tara locked her radar on him. He shook his head and looked away. "Grow up, Tara."

"You did, didn't you, you fuckin' mink. I can tell." She laughed. "Figures. Oh, I know exactly what you did. You put on the strong silent type to start with, the wise Indian hunter. Then you tossed in some literature and some nice words and some quotes, maybe some Rogers and Hammerstein. I'll bet you even got Raz to do a few tricks. The whole song and dance. And she bought it."

"You sound cynical. Too bad. You just lost your chance to buy into my new wilderness tour business."

"Oh yeah? Same old shit like before—dreaming and talking and never doing? What are you gonna call it, Paddle and Poke Adventures?"

"I'm sorry you feel that way, Paul, but I owe a lot to Dan." Hannah switched the phone to her other ear and resumed toweling her hair. She listened to Paul Williams' *harumph* before he answered. For a guy who was only thirty-two, Paul sounded more and more like a stodgy old man.

"It's not just me, Hannah. It's the board and the members of Animal Rights Now. It's the whole community. Paul McCartney was interviewed on the BBC. He said the killing of any wild animal is a disgrace."

"A disgrace. Paul, you have no…Dan is…Oh fuck." She pulled the terrycloth robe open. The hotel room was too hot.

"Listen, Hannah. It's not so bad. We can pull this out of the fire. I'm not telling you to ditch this Dan fellow, only to…distance yourself, especially from this guy Steve Porter, the big hero. I saw him on tonight's news. His descriptions: *I popped him, the bullet made oatmeal of his brains.* The man is an abomination."

"Gee, Paul, maybe it would have been better if I'd shot the bear."

Paul *harumphed* again. "Don't even joke about that. The point is Grizzly Watch is receiving a lot of press. This ordeal of yours is a big story. I just want to keep these hunters out of it. It's a needless—"

"You know, Paul, this is all too much for me right now. I'll call you—"

"No, Hannah. Don't hang up. We'll work this out. The important thing is to get you down here as soon as possible. Have you got a flight yet?"

"No." The door rattled. David was coming back. She pulled the robe closed and held it with one hand.

Paul said, "Tomorrow. Tonight if you can. Let me know. I'll meet you at the airport. In the meantime, no pictures with hunters of any kind."

"Goodbye, Paul."

"Hannah, promise you won't—"

She hung up and looked at David, who was dropping some bulging plastic shopping bags on a chair.

He said, "You out of the jacuzzi already?"

"Yeah, it's too hot. The hotel is too hot. I guess it's from living outside for a couple of weeks. It all feels so weird."

"Too bad. I was hoping to join you. What did Paul have to say?"

"He wants me to go to Vancouver tomorrow. I guess I will."

He pulled a large box with the Merrell logo from one of the bags. "He's an idiot. Anyway, you can't go tomorrow. Well, no, you can if you want to, but you'll disappoint a whole lot of TV and film crews and magazine people."

"What?"

"You've got messages from all over the place. There's a bunch arriving from Germany tonight." He held the box out to her. "I got you some new hiking boots."

"David. Enough with the shopping. You've bought me enough clothes."

"You gotta be presentable. MacLean's wants your picture on next week's cover. The story is being picked up by news services all over the world."

"Paul's not going to like it."

"Screw Paul. Screw ARN. You don't need them. It's your story. People want to hear it from you. Nobody wants to talk to them except maybe a couple of eco-newsletters. They need you. That's why he wants you down there—before Grizzly Watch floats out of his grasp. And I'll tell you something else. Next to you, Dan is the best thing Grizzly Watch has going for it. He's worth a zillion Pauls."

"What about you? You have to get back to Van, don't you?"

"Tina and Aaron are handling things down there. I can do much more for Chives up here. I'm a sidebar on this thing, but they're going to want my story too. Remind me to tell you about my wolf messenger."

She laughed. "You're shameless."

"Completely." He reached into another bag and pulled out a box with a logo she had never seen before: Adult Warehouse. "Speaking of shameless, I got you some pajamas."

She took the thin flat box from him and hefted it. "Pajamas? Where's the rest of 'em?"

She braced herself, ready to take his weight on her back. She could hear his heavy breaths as he struggled onto his hind legs behind her, saw his antlers rise into her peripheral vision to spread above her like dark raven wings, felt the sharp sting of his rutting scent in her nostrils. The other cow stood close by, watching. The old bull still hung in the background. Now he moved slowly toward the other cow, head down, stealthy, trying for a sniff, a taste, all the while keeping a wary eye on the newcomer.

She felt him slide inside her. She gripped. He thrust several times and she felt the pulses of his ejaculation, saw his head raised above hers, felt him shiver. When it was over he slid off her back and stood, nostrils wide, glassy eyed, unaware of the old bull's advance on the other cow. Soon he would notice and the grunts and threats would resume. The old bull would be driven away again.

The clouds had moved in. The air seemed heavier, a hint of snow in the gusty wind. The smells were less intense now, the sounds of the river and trees less sharp. Leaves drifted in wistful skeins across the meadow, leaving ranks of desolate gray branches. This would be the last time she would mate this season. The ache, the itch, the need inside her was fading. It was time to feed on the stored bounty of summer—rich willow shoots. Time to find safe places to rest and chew her cud, build fat for the winter, grow a new life.

The rhythm of her breathing told him she wasn't asleep, lying beside him with a leg and arm sticking out from under the covers. *Too hot*, she had said. She was naked. She hadn't worn the flimsy nightwear. It had been a mistake to buy it. He should let her make the first move. But would she? His desire for her was almost overpowering. Just seeing her bare leg protruding from the covers was excruciating. He had an erection.

He couldn't resist. He reached a tentative hand and rested it on her stomach, a discreet distance from her breasts. She covered his hand with hers and squeezed it.

She turned her head to him. "David. You're a good man. It must have been so hard for you."

"It was. I don't think I've ever been through such a horrible time. When I thought you were dead...I don't know. I would have given up everything to have you back." His hand edged up toward her breasts.

She stopped him. "David, I don't think I can..."

He pulled his hand away. "Of course. Sorry."

"The answer to your question is yes."

"Um…what question is that?"

"Did I sleep with him?"

"Oh. I think I knew that already."

"Look, I don't mean to be cruel. I just don't want to pretend."

"Like me." He rolled onto his back and stared at the ceiling. "I suppose I deserve it. You have to go out in the wilderness and almost die before I realize what an ass I've been."

"David, it's not you. It's…Oh God, I can't believe I'm saying that." She sighed. "I guess I'm saying I need some time to think." She put a hand to her forehead. "Christ, is there no end to my trite expressions?"

"So what do we do?"

"I don't know, but right now I'm gonna turn off the thermostat. Do these windows open?"

SEPT. 25

"All at once everything went into slow motion. I took a deep breath to steady my—"

Hannah caught Dan's eye across the round table as Steve was working up to the climax. A conspiratorial smile passed between them, hidden behind the microphones at their faces. When she sat back in her chair, she noticed David watching her.

Steve had finished his account. "—I knew he was a big bear, but until I walked up to him lying there, I didn't realize how big."

Nancy, their radio host, said, "That's an incredible story. It's amazing you were able to remain so calm."

Steve's eyes flicked briefly to Hannah's. "It's a yoga concentration thing."

She saw Dan swallow a laugh, pretending to cover a yawn with his hand.

Nancy said, "And what are your views on Hannah Weinberg and Grizzly Watch?"

Steve said, "I'll admit I was one of those who laughed at her when all this Grizzly Watch thing started, but after coming to know her, I've changed my tune. She's a very courageous lady." He gave Hannah a knowing look then became expansive. "Besides, I'd be happy to see all bear hunting stopped. I've got the record interior grizzly. I don't want anybody's name above mine in Boone and Crocket."

Nancy laughed. "I see. You have ulterior motives." She turned to Hannah. "And Hannah. How about you? After all that's happened, where does this put Grizzly Watch?"

She shifted forward, put her elbows on the table. "To be honest, Nancy, I'm still trying to grapple with that one. It's been quite an experience for me. It's been exhausting and terrifying and exhilarating and wonderful. I did things I never expected to do. I had to face some difficult choices."

"What choices?"

She hadn't intended to get specific. "Uh…well, for instance I've always said I support aboriginal subsistence hunting. Dan was moose hunting, and in fact he shot one. I had to find out if I could face that—even participate in it. I learned a lot. At times I felt as if I was being tested, and…"

She was about to make a point about a change of focus for Grizzly Watch, but Nancy quickly turned to Dan, who was sitting back, looking content to listen.

"So Dan. What do you say? Does she get a passing grade?"

Dan wasn't ready for the question. He sat forward and bumped the microphone. "Sorry. Uh…yeah, she passes…She was a big help. Hell, she made Uncle Nathan's chopped liver. That deserves an A plus."

"And what about your opinions on Grizzly Watch?"

"Before I met Hannah, I didn't give it much thought. I guess I thought it was just a clever publicity stunt. That sort of thing. Now I agree with her."

"You oppose grizzly bear hunting?"

"I oppose anything that's wasteful and pointless."

"And does that include all trophy hunting?"

"Yes."

"But you've guided trophy hunters. You've made your living from it."

"Yes." He looked squarely at Nancy, who clearly expected him to go on.

A moment of dead air then Nancy said, "So…you would end all trophy hunting?"

"I don't believe it's a good enough reason to kill an animal."

"But would you end it if you could?"

"I would, but I know I can't as long as there's somebody willing to pay thousands of dollars to kill a grizzly."

"This takes the debate to a whole new level. Don't you think your opinions could be unpopular in the Yukon?"

Dan laughed. "Anyone who knew my Dad will tell you I come from a long line of unpopular opinion. To me there's a bigger issue. It's not about money. It's not about trophy hunting."

Nancy said, "What is the bigger issue?"

"Land and water and large undisturbed wilderness. We can't have that and also have roads and mines and gas wells and pipelines. We have to make sure we protect it. Grizzlies are more than just a symbol. They're the key to healthy wilderness because they need it to survive. If grizzlies can live there, everything can live there."

Hannah glanced at David, who looked back with an expression that said, *I told you so.*

Nancy said, "So you want to really take the gloves off."

"Maybe. If that's what it takes. We need to learn to appreciate what we have, respect the land and the animals we hunt. All of us—Indians, whites, outfitters, local hunters. I know there's a lot of moose and caribou and sheep meat stuffed into freezers out there. I also know where a lot of it ends up—in the dump. Less greed, more respect. It's simple. And here's another thing that might raise a few hackles. I think we should pass a law that says you can't shoot at an animal if it's more than a hundred meters away. We'd have a lot fewer wounded ones, like the grizzly we're talking about."

"But that would be impossible to enforce, wouldn't it?"

"Yeah, but if it's a law it eventually becomes part of our ethos."

Nancy turned to Hannah. "Hannah, how does that fit with your view of things?"

"I couldn't have put it better."

"What happens now? What's next for you and Grizzly Watch?"

"Well, where do I start? Calls have been coming in…"

"I can't. I gotta meet Artie and go to the hospital to pick up Starla…I mean Rose. Then we gotta get some of her stuff at Tara's place." Dan looked up as David came to the table at the coffee bar's big street-facing window and placed three foam-topped cups in front of them. "Thanks David."

Hannah said, "I understand. You don't want a whole lot of prying reporters hounding you. You've got much bigger priorities. Your daughter. I'm being selfish. I just don't want to say goodbye."

"We can keep in touch. Ross River isn't the moon. We do have phones and email. Hell, nowadays Vancouver is right next door."

Hannah gave David a brief look then back to Dan. "I'm not going back to Vancouver right away. With all the press descending on this town, Whitehorse has become the temporary headquarters of Grizzly Watch."

"Well then…maybe I'll be seeing you."

David took a sip of coffee and leaned forward. "Dan, I know you have a duty to your daughter. I know you need to get back to Ross, but do you mind a bit of advice from a businessman?"

"I could use it."

"Hannah says you're thinking of starting a tour business. Right?"

"Yeah, I'm thinking about it."

"Then jump on this thing. Right now. Anybody else in the tour business would sell their mothers into slavery for all the publicity you've got. The whole world wants to hear your story. It's got everything—conflict, danger, heroism, wild animals. The only thing missing is…" Was David really going to say *sex*? He focused on his coffee, took a sip, noticed Hannah was doing the same. With barely a hiccup David continued. "Hell, it's got everything. Believe me, you'll get bookings to last a lifetime. Why would they go with anyone else when they can have the genuine article? Christ, you'll be so fucking busy you'll be turning away the likes of Nicole Kidman."

Dan laughed. "I wouldn't do that. Only her dislikes."

David was adamant. "I'm serious, Dan. Before you leave for Ross, get a business license. Get registered with the tourism association or whatever it is you've got up here. Get onto their web site. Get your own web site. And don't give free interviews to magazines. Have you thought of a name yet?"

"Uh…" He remembered Tara's suggestion. "No, I haven't given it much thought." He spotted Artie across the street getting out of Lyle Kessler's white truck with the green *Mac Pass Outfitter's* logo on the door. He waved to get Artie's attention. Artie waved back, beckoning as he pointed to his watch. He mouthed, *I gotta go* and got back behind the wheel. Dan turned to Hannah. "Time to go."

David said, "Me too. My plane leaves in two hours."

Hannah stood up and embraced Dan. He wondered how much he should reciprocate in front of David. Hannah wasn't holding back. She lifted her head from his shoulder and looked at his face while she rubbed her hands over his upper arms. "Thanks." Her eyes glistened, brimming.

"It was good."

"The best." She kissed him and gave him a tight squeeze then abruptly stepped back, their connection severed. "I don't know what to say...except...have you got a pepperoni to spare?"

Dan reached out, held her hand lightly then let it go. He turned to David and stretched his hand across the table. David took an envelope out of his jacket pocket and held it out. He took it. "What's this?"

"Payment."

He thought this might happen, had even guiltily hoped for it. Should he refuse? He had rescued Hannah, but anyone would have done that. It wasn't a matter of choice, payment or no. But he had slept with the guy's wife. Still, it was money, and he sure as hell needed it. "Uh..."

David cut in. "Ten days at a thousand a day."

"Ten thousand dollars?"

"It's a bargain. Special introductory offer. You're gonna charge more than that. I drew up an invoice. It's in there. As soon as you get up and going, fill in your business name and send it to me. And feel free to call me if you need any help. I've already spoken to Aaron, my solicitor. He's gonna draw up a waiver for you. Oh, and one other thing. There's somebody I want you to contact. Her name is Jessica Giller. I think the two of you would make a great team. I wrote down her information in the envelope." He stuck out his hand.

They shook. Dan said, "Thanks. I don't know what to say except... thanks...very much." He felt awkward all of a sudden. "Well then...See ya." That felt inadequate, but what else was there to say? He left with a wave and one last look into Hannah's eyes.

He walked out the doors and across the sidewalk to the passenger side of the truck.

Artie started the engine. "About fuckin' time. I gotta get this truck back to Ross. If Lyle finds out I borrowed it and burned his fuckin' gas to pick you up, he'll fire me...after he fuckin' cuts off my dick."

"No great loss."

Artie laughed. "Fuck you."

"Think you could spare a couple hours more?"

"A couple?"

"A few."

"Shit, man. I need this job."

"He won't find out. Besides, the season's almost over."

"Yeah, but he's not gonna fuckin' hire me next year."

Dan patted Artie's arm. "I might have a job for you next year. How would you like to meet Nicole Kidman?"

SEPT. 26

He stopped to rest, his chest heaving. It was hard to hear above the noise of it in his head. He had been working his way up a steep brushy gully. Tired. Pain stabbing his flank with every step. A little farther up would be the gentler grade of the mountain's shoulder. Then up to the pass, just under the clouds that blanketed the higher peaks, to a wide boggy valley where the willows grew thick and tender, where the leaves held on late into the season. He would heal when he got there.

He gathered a bundle of willow shoots with his upper lip and tore off a mouthful, the first food he had taken in many days. He had never been so ragged and thin, his gut so sunken and empty. The thick layer of fat over his rump was gone. His skin felt loose over his bones. As his strength returned and his breathing came easier, he trained his ears back downhill—wind in the branches. He turned his head, opened his nostrils and took in a long slow breath, ignoring the smell of his blood trickling past one nostril from the gash over the bridge of his nose. The bear smell was still there, heavy, dark. It had been there all day, following at a distance, stopping when he did. Up on the mountain's shoulder he would outdistance it. If it persisted he would have to try to drive it off.

A fearful memory flashed through his mind: when he was a calf, a huge mass of dark brown fur crashing out of the brush behind him, bowling him over, engulfing him, pinning him, his nose filling with dark heavy scent, jaws closing over the back of his neck. Then a hollow double thud, a sharp exhalation of breath, sudden release, scrambling to his feet, dazed and star-ing. His mother's body looming beside him, her ears pinned back, the hair bristling along her spine. The sharp crack of hoof against hard bone. The bear lumbering off to disappear into the spruce trees.

He turned his head uphill again and walked. Stiffness in his legs, pain in his flank. He raised his chin to let the weight of his antlers ride over the brush.

The rutting season was over.

40788633R00203

Made in the USA
Middletown, DE
31 March 2019